Also by
Paul Sedlock

The Nightdream

HOW I GOT TO YESTERDAY

HOW I GOT TO YESTERDAY

A *fictionalized memoir*

Paul Sedlock

ISBN: 1518790933
ISBN 13: 9781518790935
Library of Congress Control Number: 2017902876
CreateSpace Independent Publishing Platform
North Charleston, South Carolina

AUTHOR'S NOTE

I have changed the names of some of the characters to protect their privacy. I have also altered certain geographical features.

For Faye

PART 1

CHAPTER ONE

A thin red needle swept past twelve for sixty heartbeats. Chin on crossed hands, elbows pointing out, I gazed at the glistening silver band, the polished transparent disc. These shiny miracles made it mine.

I imagined the rear sliding glass door ajar, my fingers scurrying across warm glass. I'd quickly snatch the treasure, pocket it, and stroll out whistling "Glow Worm." Busybody Sister Ann burst into my brain reciting strict catechisms. Father Mark also intruded. "*Sententia vadum non rapio*," he said, expecting me to translate. My larcenous hand ignored them. Father Mark bellowed in English, a language I understood, "David Crobak! You'll be condemned to Hell where a little molten silver disc will burn a watch-sized hole into your wrist for all eternity." I pushed away from the glass counter, and fled out the door. I turned toward the Bank of Carthage, where my Western Flyer leaned against a shaded wall below a bronze plaque:

AT NOON
ON APRIL 29, 1872
JESSE JAMES AND HIS GANG
ROBBED THIS BANK

The riled but obedient bankers must've muttered the Lord's name in vain when the James gang burst in at lunchtime, their guns drawn, faces twitching beneath dusty red bandannas.

The bank, a tall building with fancy windows, brass door handles, and marbled counters, anchored one block on our downtown square, but it wasn't the most impressive structure. That honor belonged to the majestic Jasper County Courthouse. It rose from the middle of the square and dominated our downtown. Above its medieval turrets and columns, the clock tower peaked at seven stories. Some said it was the highest point in Jasper County.

Before the air warmed, the courthouse looked stately, a castle befitting the Knights of the Roundtable. Then, for reasons unknown to me, every sparrow in southwest Missouri decided to make it home. Riding in on afternoon breezes, they alighted, stood wing to wing, and defecated at will.

Within days of their unwelcomed arrival it looked like a rowdy flock of modern artists had painted the sidewalks and benches around the Courthouse a crazy white and gray. Folks worried that come fall the plastered leaves of the maples dotting the grounds wouldn't change color. Quickly the sparrow invasion became *the* topic of talk, displacing front-page stories of eggs sizzling on hot sidewalks and five ways to beat heatstroke.

I gripped my handlebars, rolled my bike down the block, and glanced over my shoulder. Men carrying shotguns were surrounding the Courthouse. The *ad hoc* firing squad itched with civic revenge.

Charlie Seven, the smartest kid in my fifth grade class, said the fretting turned into action after Judge Baker and a nearsighted big shot from Jefferson City bought ice cream cones at Ramsay's, the drugstore cater-cornered from the courthouse. They licked their melting cones in the shade of maples near the front steps of our town jewel and glad-handed every passing ma'am or sir. Then a squadron of sparrows swooped over.

Spat! A wet missile hit the back of the Judge's hand and sent his cone south. The politician from up north was holding his vanilla cone waist high. Spat! Spat! So intent on finishing a salient point, he hadn't noticed the two new flavors. He paused and raised his cone, intending to give it a good licking when he heard the judge holler, "Bird shit!"

The outraged judge wasted no time seeking civic revenge. He stormed into the mayor's office and demanded an Official Emergency Meeting of Outraged Citizens. The following afternoon, twenty quick-stepping men waited until they were well inside before they cautiously peeled off their speckled hats.

"What should we do?"

"Gas 'em."

"And what, kill us too?"

"Poison 'em."

"How?"

"Have Clarence fly over in his crop duster."

Twenty men rubbed their chins, considering.

Then someone said, "Shoot the ornery sons-of-bitches."

The headline read **THE BIG SHOOT**.

Keeping a sideways eye on resolute men shoving red shells into their shotguns, I pushed my bike along the curb, weaved around clusters of noisy onlookers, and aimed for daylight at the end of the block.

Storekeepers locked their shops and rushed out to bear witness. In front of the opulent Tiger Theatre, Judge Baker and the mayor stood on a platform and addressed the multitude with a bullhorn, their civic words lost in the din. I was almost at the corner, ready to step into my stirrup and hightail it downhill when the first thundering blasts shook the air. I nearly dropped my bike. I pushed on, heart pounding, and at Ramsay's mounted my steed as The Kid, a lesser-known member of the James Gang who knew it was high time to vamoose. I glanced back.

All around the Courthouse, twelve-gauge shotguns exploded like strings of cherry bombs. A hail of spent cartridges pelted the street. A sulfurous stench hung in the square. Waves of sparrows dropped from the sky. They spiraled downward like mottled rocks, their dead wings outstretched, unmoving.

CHAPTER TWO

In the summer of '49, my pals and I played baseball in a big yard across the alley from Mom's chicken coop. A tall hedge walled two sides of our makeshift field and a lofty Victorian, its windows always tightly draped, lined the third side. A tall sycamore, its thin skin dappled as though by interior light, shaded home plate.

"That's a strike," Elmer said. He was the oldest, soon to be in third grade, and brawny like a man.

"I didn't swing," I said.

"You broke your wrists."

"No, I didn't." I swept my foot across home plate, an anvil-shaped slab of black granite Elmer lugged in from the alley.

"God, you're dumb." He punched his floppy glove. "That's a strike. Wally, tell the dummy why."

Wally, his rosy cheeks faint in the shade, tossed the lopsided hardball back to Elmer and took the scarred bat from me. "See, it's a strike if you start to swing and then try an' stop." The bat whipped forward and froze. "See, your wrists turn over like they're sorta broke." He shrugged *not my rules.*

After the game everybody scattered fast except Elmer and me. We stood in the sycamore's quiet shadows. He hitched his glove to his belt, and we sauntered toward the cinder-strewn alley. He lived a block down from me. His family had the only TV in the neighborhood. The rabbit ears sitting on top of their new RCA picked up two stations. Agitated worms disrupted the picture on channel two. On channel five Buffalo Bob and Howdy Doody came in as clear as Rocket Man at the Saturday matinee. Even though I was only seven, and Elmer a third grader, I wanted him to like me so I could watch his family's TV.

"Thanks for letting me use your glove when you was batting," I said. He sprinted across the alley to Mom's chicken coop, picked up a big stick and clacked it across the wire, stirring up a cluck ruckus.

"Shouldn't do that."

"Aw, nuts." He threw the stick against the wire. It made an angry thwack. "Your mom sure keeps lotsa chickens."

"Yup."

"Ever seen 'er kill 'em?"

"Nope."

"Here's how I'd kill 'em." He snarled, balled his hands into thick knuckled fists, and twisted them like he was wringing out a wet towel.

"She doesn't do it like that."

"Ya said ya ain't never seen."

He threw me a mean look and stomped off down the alley. I quickened my pace to match his long strides and kicked a rock. It rolled into downy brome choking the rundown garage behind the spooky Victorian. Elmer once said a pair of warty old maids, like the ones in the card game, lived in the house, and on Halloween they turned into witches.

"Now I know about breaking my wrists."

I swung an imaginary bat to illustrate how well I'd learned his lesson. He looked down at me and snorted. We neared the street. He picked up a twig, snapped it in two, stuck one piece between his teeth, and tossed the other over his shoulder. He pointed toward the garage.

"Ya gotta be careful of 'em weeds. Blue racers hide in that cheat grass. Ever laid eyes on a blue racer?"

"No."

"They're snakes."

"I know."

"Know how fast they run?"

"Run? Snakes crawl."

"Not a blue racer!" He jumped back. Puffs of dust sprayed from beneath his scuffed Buster Browns. "I just seen one pokin' its slimy head out. Ya gotta watch out."

I looked at the dirty cloud painting his shoes and then at the menacing weeds. He stepped forward. His index finger stabbed the air in front of my nose.

"Blue racers can outrun ya. Big, mean snake. Don't never let one take out after ya 'cause, bein' poison, it'll getcha."

"I have to go."

He picked up a baseball-sized rock.

"I'll keep an eye on the weeds. If one pops out, I'll nail 'im. You skeered?"

I glanced at the distant chicken coop and the snake-infested weeds.

"I'll walk down to the corner with you."

"You ain't no fraidy-cat, is you?"

"No."

"Prove it."

I stood still. He stomped his foot, spit out the twig.

"Damn you! Run!"

I bolted. Cinders flew from beneath my PF Flyers. Snake-infested weeds blurred past my bouncing eyes. I heard his horsy laugh and a loud bang. I glanced back. The rock tumbled from the garage roof and crashed in the brome. Another motion raised my eyes. One of the wizen-faced witches stood at the second-story window, her evil eyes staring a spell at me. My heart stopped still. My legs lost all thought of motion. Then the witch's bony fingers grasped the curtains and yanked them shut.

I hightailed it home.

⊷⊷ ⊶⊶

On a warm southwest Missouri day, I was tossing a red rubber ball on the tarpaper pantry roof when the door flew open and Mom burst into sunlight wearing a brown rubber apron and black rubber gloves that sheathed her arms to the elbows. Her right hand gripped a hatchet. Before I could ask, she stormed past, strode alongside the clothesline to a weathered oak stump, and drove the blade deep. She hastened to the chicken coop, disappeared inside, and came out a few minutes later, a speckled hen hanging by its legs from her left hand. The upside down bird's wings thrashed the air as mom swung it back and forth. I edged closer.

"Stand back, Davy." She slammed the bird down on the stump and her right hand took hold of the hatchet and raised it shoulder high. Sunlight flashed across its sharpened edge. The heavy blade fell like a hammer and the bird lost its head. The rest of it flew from the stump and hit the ground running. Blood gushed from its neck. It darted toward the house, veered right, and swung a crazy circle around a clothesline pole.

"It's still alive!" I yelled.

Twice more it circled the pole, each orbit tighter than the last, and then it stiffened and fell over.

10

At dinner Cathy, my big sister, said the fried chicken smelled "deevine," her new favorite word. I sculpted mashed potatoes into a volcano, filled the cone with hot buttered corn, and took a golden breast from the plate. Mom said grace and we dug in.

Later, she dialed the radio to the *Bob Hope Show*. I sat next to her on the couch. She put her arm around me.

"I hope he's funny tonight. I need a good laugh. I made a big mistake today."

"You did?"

"I never should've killed that hen. It hadn't laid an egg in weeks. I figured she'd retired from the egg-laying business, but when I opened her up, there were lots. She would've have given us plenty for trade."

"It tasted good."

She sighed and stroked my hair. "Reminds me of your father's."

"Mom, who lives in the big house across the alley?"

"Betty says two sisters."

"They kinda give me the creeps."

"Mind yourself and stay away from them, Davy. I hear they're very old and they don't need kids pestering them." She turned up the volume. "Show's starting."

⟩⟨ ⟨⟩

An oil portrait of Dad in his captain's uniform hung on the wall alongside my bed. A German POW at Camp Crowder painted it. Mom said she wanted me to remember what Dad looked like so I'd know him when he came home. His likeness may have been true, but his stern expression gave me the willies. On moonlit nights his dark uniform and hair blended into shadows on the wall. The remaining pale curves of his flesh bulged out. Framed by owlish white circles, his piercing black eyes glared into me. I never told Mom.

I had last seen Dad when I was five and my few memories of him were fading fast: his hand guiding me up the stairs to our apartment above the Walcott's house during a thunderstorm, his towering figure leaning over me as he tilted a beer bottle to my boy lips, his slender chest heaving with each persistent cough.

After a year at Camp Crowder, the army shipped Dad off to a VA hospital in Denver and then to one in Tucson, where the doctors said the desert air would dry up his TB. By then Mom had taken a job sewing overalls at the Big Smith factory, and we'd moved into a two-story house on Fulton Street. We didn't have a car, and she liked the balance of being within a few blocks of her work and the corner grocery store.

I rolled away from the painting and pulled the sheet up to my chin. I thought of how great the chicken tasted, how I could tell Elmer, and I wondered what happened to its little head.

⇥ ⇤

At the east end of town a bunch of trailers huddled beneath clusters of oaks and pines. A few primroses dotted Cozy Acres' graveled grounds. Wally and his mom lived in an Airstream Clipper that looked like a breadbox on wheels. One morning in October Wally's dad left for work toting his rocket-shaped Blackhawk Tool Kit and never came back.

I only visited Wally's home a few times, and we never played inside the cramped mobile. Rows of closely spaced trailers and gravel walkways weren't much better. Wally biked over to my house when we became best friends. We played catch, kick-the-can with kids in my neighborhood, and any game that popped into our heads. On summer evenings we punched air holes in the lids of washed pickle bottles and trapped lightning bugs. Flickering lanterns in hand, we crept around the backyard, searching for the Man in the Moon.

"Let's get some gas and burn those weeds," I said, nudging his ribs.

He rolled his eyes. "Why?"

"Aw, I was just kiddin'."

In the quiet night, rainbows from unseen rains painted the aging leaves of elms, maples, ashes, and hickories. Their flaming colors dazzled us for days. Then the leaves fell, one by one. On my way to school, I scampered through deep drifts of crisp leaves.

November winds swayed the groaning arms of naked trees and whisked the pungent smell of raked leaves burned in barrels to places unknown. Wally and I retreated indoors. We both loved reading, though unlike my *Classics Illustrated* or *Kid Colt* comics, he favored sci-fi magazines.

"We're gonna have atomic cars when we grow-up and fly from place to place," he said the day after Thanksgiving. We were sitting cross-legged on the floor. "I read all about it in Grandpa's *Mechanics Illustrated*."

"I thought *atomic* was for bombs."

"You hear the Russians got one? Grandpa said so. Find China on your map."

I skipped into the dining room and hurried back with the tin globe I kept on a corner table. I set it between us, turned the metal ball, and pointed to a large yellow patch.

"But—Grandpa said it was red. He even took the Lord's name in vain."

"Maybe he's color blind, like my cousin Johnny-With-the-Hair-on-His-Chest. He says red's green."

We spun the rattling continents until Wally said he wanted to see if chicken feet froze on cold ground. Frost-crusted grass crunched beneath our shoes as we crossed stiff blades on the way to the coop. The cold illuminated Wally's cheeks. He leaned on the honeycombed wire and studied a rooster pecking the frigid ground in search of stray kernels.

"Feet don't look frozen to me," I said.

"I bet it's got some kinda heat shield." He pushed off the wire. "I didn't tell you 'bout the other thing. We'll park our flying cars, go into our houses, and punch buttons on the wall. Zap!" He snapped his fingers. "Fried chicken'll come out."

"Who's gonna to make it?"

"Machines in the wall, I guess."

He blew steam into his cupped white hands and shoved them into his pockets. I wondered how the wall machines would kill the chickens. Would they use little chicken guillotines or mechanical Elmer hands?

A gray trail of smoke drifted skyward from the old ladies' chimney. I envied their coziness, taking in heat beside a glowing fireplace.

⇥ ⇤

Wally and I exchanged gifts on Christmas Eve Day. Sitting on the carpeted floor in the front room, I smiled as he opened Tinkertoys.

"Good, huh?" I said.

"Oh, yeah!"

He slid across the floor a shoebox-sized package wrapped in butcher paper and bound by a red ribbon. Inside was a wooden truck. There were two stainless steel milk cans with handles on a little running board. A stocky round-headed man in white stood behind the steering wheel. He was pale, like Wally. He even had little red circles on his cheeks. I wondered how he could stand and drive.

"Mom picked it out," he murmured, his eyes downcast.

"I like it," I fibbed.

"Really?"

"Sure. Maybe later you can build a garage for it."

The front door opened. Mom bustled in and set two shopping bags down on the maple dining room table. She looked at us while shedding her brown and yellow babushka.

"I bet you two'd like some oatmeal cookies and milk." She unbuttoned her brown overcoat.

Cathy slinked in, wearing a sly sisterly smile, hands behind her back.

"Betty took Mom and me shopping, and I got you something."

"Lemme see." I started to get up.

"Stay there." Her large hand outstretched like a traffic cop's.

"What is it?"

"It's a surprise. Close your eyes. You too, Wally."

I clamped my eyes tight and heard floorboards creak closer. Then, I heard a record drop and Gene Autry sang, "Rudolph, the red-nosed reindeer, had a very shiny nose . . ."

"You got it!"

"Oh, boya," Wally said. "I love this song."

Cathy laughed. Mom came in with milk and cookies. Between bites, gulps and smiles, we sang along.

I kicked an empty Jolly Green Giant can across the backyard while Mom unpinned the clothes she'd hand-washed the day before. Left out overnight, they were as rigid as boards. She'd forgotten all about them yesterday when shrill sirens and flashing lights set the air afire.

We'd stood alongside the alley with our next-door neighbors, Betty and her husband, Little Ed, and gaped at the acrid clouds of black smoke billowing from the Victorian's windows. An ambulance howled up the alley, turned into our makeshift field, and skidded to a stop near third base. Two men leapt out and jerked open the rear doors. They reached inside, pulled out a canvas, wooden-poled stretcher, and rushed toward the side porch where a fireman waved them inside.

15

"May God have mercy," Mom said, crossing herself and directing me back to our house.

Now Mom unhooked the rigid clothes. I ducked under the line and kicked the Jolly Green Giant toward the coop. Betty, who was tall and thin and angular, and who traded vegetables for eggs, must've been spying out her window because all of a sudden she was hurrying over. In summer she and Little Ed rested on three-legged wooden stools at the end of a garden row and munched red onions. She once offered me a ripe one, and I ran away.

She and Mom hauled the frosted laundry inside, laid the frozen garments across oilcloth on the dining room table, and shrugged off their coats. Mom said there was fresh coffee. I shed my coat, plopped down on a rag rug near the kitchen, and thumbed a *Superman* comic.

"Little Ed talked to Ben Garrison. Ben axed the door," Betty said.

I scooted a few inches closer and leaned an ear toward them.

"Which one?"

"Older one. Name of Catherine." Betty bent her head and lowered her voice. "Say she was dead 'fore they got there. Smoke."

"Sweet Jesus, Mary, and Joseph!" Mom crossed herself and shook her head. She poured a stream of cream into her coffee and stirred in a level teaspoon of sugar.

"If the fire trucks hadn't raced there lickety-split, well, Lord only knows—they found Marie balled up by one of the walls, chokin' for air. And you know what else?"

"What?"

Betty put her elbows on the table and clasped her hands as in prayer. "They was so poor they couldn't 'ford heat. They'd ripped the upstairs floorboards out and throwed 'em in the fireplace." She made a clucky sound with her tongue and leaned back in the chair. "Don't know how they found the strength. Ben said all they had in their cupboard was a few cans of green beans and corn and a half sack of potatoes and a few eggs and a stick of butter in the ice box. Can you believe it?"

"Didn't they have children?"

"Spinsters."

"I'm going to light a candle for Marie."

"Ed says she'll be in the hospital a right long time."

"She'll be warm."

"Yes, she will."

"I'll say a rosary for her, too."

"Bet she'd like that even if—I think—she's a Holy Roller."

Mom shook her head. "You just don't know do you, what hardship we'll see in this world. But the Good Lord always has his reasons."

"Amen to that."

➤✦◄

The diffuse light of a cold January day dimmed into darkness. Mom was sitting in a big green chair in the living room, knitting a brightly colored Afghan that was slowly inching across her lap. Cathy and I hunched over the dining room table playing Clue, one of my Christmas gifts that Santa had left under our tree, though the eighth grade cursive on its little to-and-from card had a brunt-bearing slant that looked a lot like Mom's.

"Colonel Mustard," Cathy said as the phone rang, "diditinthekitchenwithawrench. I'll get it." She dashed across the room. A little wooden phone table and a straight-backed chair stood in front of two tall windows. I slid the answer cards out of the black envelope.

"It's long distance from Tucson, Mom. There's a lot of static." Mom shoved the Afghan aside and hurried in. Cathy handed her the phone, and Mom perched on the edge of the chair. Cathy stood beside her, a hand on Mom's shoulder.

"Hello."

"Who is it?" I said.

"Oh, dear God! No!" She dropped the phone and fell forward, hit the floor hard, and squirmed like a hooked fish. It scared the bejeezus out of me, seeing Mom sprawled on her back, wild eyed, nose running. "Dear God, what have I done to deserve this?" she cried as her fists assaulted the hardwood floor, her mouth so twisted she was nearly smiling.

"Mama," Cathy said. Tears rolled down her cheeks. She sank to her knees and her skinny arms reached out. "Mother—" and then she heard a staticky voice and she reached down and retrieved the phone. "Yes," she murmured. "Okay." She pulled open the drawer in the table and withdrew a notepad and a pen, wrote something down. "Call tomorrow." She hung up and her tear laden eyes looked at me.

I fanned the cards. "You won again."

———

The ringing woke me. I tossed under twisty blankets, drifting off until the harsh sound started up again. I rolled out of bed and padded to their bedroom, the linoleum icy beneath my bare feet. Mom always turned down the heat at night. I stood at the foot of the four-poster bed. Cathy and Mom were snoring.

I tiptoed back to my room and put on slippers and a terry-cloth robe over my pajamas. I crossed the short hall. The slick oak railing guided me as I crept down the dark staircase. For just a second, standing alone on the last step, our dark and quiet house felt spooky. Then the piercing trill enlivened my nerves. I edged toward its jolting echoes and stared at the chunky blackness, illuminated by faint moonlight. The receiver looked like dog ears. It rang again and jangled my brains.

"Hello?"

"Hiya, Buddy," he said.

"Dad?"

"I don't have much time, so listen carefully. I want you to be a good boy."

"I will."

"Promise me that you'll always take good care of Mom and Cathy."

"I will. Dad?"

"What is it, David?"

"Is it warm there? In Arizona?"

"Yes."

"It's cold here." I shivered, trying to imagine warm Tucson light streaming through our frosted panes.

"Remember, Son, I love you always. Good-bye."

"Good-bye," I said as the dial tone hummed.

I kept my back to his portrait as I crawled into bed. The sheets were cold. I pulled my knees up to my stomach and the woolen army blanket over my chin.

I woke up late, dressed without bathing, wet my hands and slicked down my wild hair. I sat on the edge of the bed and pulled on my socks and slipped into my shoes, tying the laces tight. I stood and stared at Dad's portrait. He looked sad.

Mom sat at the kitchen table. Her red eyes blinked through me. The corners of her mouth curved into the weakest outline of a smile. She turned her head and stared at the cold stove. I poured Wheaties into a bowl and drowned them in milk. Cathy came in and sat in the chair next to Mom. She touched Mom's hand, looked at me, and said, "Uncle Joe's driving in from Pennsylvania."

"When's he gonna get here?"

"Tomorrow."

I finished the cereal, slipped into my red-and-white plaid jacket, pulled on my black hat with the flaps that warmed my ears, gloved my hands, and went out. The steely sky was frozen hard;

spiky grass crunched underfoot. Uncle Joe would probably sleep in the spare bed in my room.

I hiked past the silent chicken coop, cut across the alley, and stepped into the big yard. Buttonball fruits hung from the sycamore like brown bulbs on a dried-up Christmas tree. A layer of frost fuzzed home plate. I slid the tip of my shoe across it. Something mean and ugly was beating up my insides. A curtain of smoky black stain rose from the smashed downstairs windows. Firemen had fought flames. Dad would've helped. He's a soldier.

A light snow began to fall.

I hopped over wheel-scarred ground, marched to the rear of the house, and stood by the downy brome. Two dark and empty smoke-stained upstairs windows stared down at me. I felt lightheaded-yet-heavy, half-blinded by thickening snow. Icy air stole my breath's steaming vapors as I bent down and picked up baseball-size rocks, their weight hefty in my gloved hands.

CHAPTER THREE

The following summer I turned eight and Mom bought a TV when we moved into a modest stone house at the corner of Clevenger and Forest Streets, our third home in five years. Mom and Cathy shared the downstairs bedroom. I had a cozy hideout in the finished attic. Only one drawback: my bedroom roasted in summer. Had there been a thermometer on the wall, it would have exploded; Cacti would have wilted. I waited until bedtime to go up, only wore my underpants to bed, and slept on top of the sheets. Woolen army blankets kept me toasty in winter.

Our other homes were close to downtown, Mom's work, school, and St. Ann's. With the stone house we'd landed in a nicer neighborhood across town, but Mom's easy stroll to work turned into an arduous hike. For a year she depended on Bertha, a co-worker, for rides and on obliging parishioners for rides downtown and to church. Then, at Cathy's urging, Mom decided to buy a car.

⇜✦⇝

Herman Davis was a round man in an ill-fitting short sleeve white shirt. A wide red tie brightened his chest. His well-oiled, spiky crew cut glistened beneath bright lights.

"Mighty fine choice you made for a family sedan," he said. "Sure am glad you came to Herman Davis Auto instead of buyin' in Joplin."

"Are the prices cheaper there?" Mom said.

He cleared his throat. "Uh-uh. Same car, same price."

"Then why would I go to Joplin?"

"My point exactly." He rubbed his dimpled hands together. "Just a few papers for you to look at. Don't want any surprises, right? First one tells why we're the finest dealership in Southwest Missouri. No deal we can't beat. No hitch we can't fix." He passed her a sheet of paper and glanced at Cathy and me. "Fine lookin' kids you got." He rolled his chair back to the wall, twiddled his fat thumbs, and hummed "The Tennessee Waltz."

She looked over the paper, and then laid it on the desk. He pushed off the wall, rolled forward, and peeled another sheet from a pile of papers about half as thick as a skinny comic book. This one had tightly packed sentences top to bottom.

She read slowly. Every so often she frowned and asked Cathy for help with a word. Mom wasn't stupid or anything. She had crossed the Atlantic when she was a kid and could speak fluent Czech when she was around relatives. She finished eighth grade before her parents yanked her out of school so she could take a job as a maid. She read the *Press*, made the best lemon meringue pie, and knew more prayers than Father Mark.

This car buying business was taking forever. I aimed my Winchester like John Wayne in *Stagecoach* and drilled precise holes in windows. Then, I kneaded and rounded Herman the way Mom shaped Easter loaves and dribbled the squealing car salesman across the showroom floor. I wanted to tell her, but I knew she'd frown and say I shouldn't daydream mean things, so

I rounded up my joy low in my throat, lassoed a stray giggle, and fidgeted.

The fun part had been when Herman carted us outside, where a row of six identical mint green cars eyed the street. Mom picked one from the middle. I thought we'd climb in and head home, but she sealed her lips and didn't even shuffle her feet. She just stared at the lustrous Plymouth.

"Let's take a closer look," Herman said.

He squeezed behind the steering wheel, turned the ignition key, and roused the engine. Wipers smeared the dusty windshield, headlights paled in sunshine, and the horn's piercing sound set a dog sleeping in a corner of the lot to howling. Then Herman's hefty hand gripped the knobbed lever sticking out from the steering wheel, and he shifted through the gears, focusing our attention on how precisely he worked the clutch pedal.

Smiling, he eased out. Mom, always suspicious of leaks, opened and shut all four doors before we followed Herman's busy voice back inside and sat in a line in front of his desk.

"Your price is twenty dollars too high," Mom said when the paper avalanche ended.

He frowned, scooped up a brochure from the corner of his desk, and deftly displayed three glossy pages confirming the Plymouth's 1951 state-of-the-art workmanship.

"Maybe I should go to Joplin."

That cinched it. He uncapped a Parker fountain pen, altered the amount due, and passed the pen to her.

"Sooo, I s'pose you want the keys." He chuckled as if he'd just told a clever joke, then slid back to the wall and snatched a small set of keys dangling from a hook on a pegboard. "Here ya go." He laid the keys in front of her. She looked at them, inked the check, and handed it to him. He centered it near the bottom of his desk and the tips of his thick fingers smoothed the already smooth paper, the way Doc Griffin stroked my neck when I had mumps.

"You can take 'er away, Mary."

"I don't drive."

He looked mighty thunderstruck, and for some reason this was news to me too, though I'd never thought about it.

"But, you just bought a car." He glanced around. "Someone comin' to drive you?"

"I expect you to teach my daughter."

"Me!" His chair shot back and thumped the wall, jangling keys hanging like little swordfish. Cathy gasped.

Right then an urgent need hit. I crossed my legs tightly, like I did during a Charlie Chan movie when I'd prayed for a commercial. Before I could ask where to go, Mom said, "She paid for her Missouri license with a Bennie Franklin yesterday. All she needs is a few lessons. This is a small town, Mr. Davis. You don't want people saying you took advantage of a widow by selling her a car she can't drive." She smiled and patted her perm.

"There's talk of a driving test."

"I heard about that, but the man at the Courthouse—Cathy, show Mr. Davis your license."

He pushed his puffy hands toward us. "No need, no need." He cleared his throat and ran his hand down his tie. "This is all fine and good, but most folks usually, ah, sort of get it home, or out to the farm, and then learn on their own."

"I want my daughter to have proper training. The car will leave here when she can drive it or I'll have my check back."

"Mom—"

"Just a minute, Davy."

Herman surveyed my beanpole sister and forced a bitter smile. Cathy and Mom smiled, and so did I.

"When's a good time to start?" he said.

"What's wrong with right now?" She looked across the show-room. At the far end, a spindly salesman in a baggy white short-sleeved shirt and broad red tie leaned against a doorjamb, cleaning his fingernails with the blade of a pocketknife. "Besides, maybe she'll get the hang of it like she did makin' cakes."

"I gotta go," I said, tugging Mom's arm.

"Men's room's 'round the corner." Herman pointed. I stood up. "Wait!" His bulbous eyes bulged as if he'd just seen the Wolf Man or a blue racer.

The spindly man folded his knife and looked at me impishly. Then I knew Herman had seen my bouncy thoughts. They'd been mixing with the air and just now swept into his globular brain.

"Maybe you'd like to take him to the Ladies," he said, as if nothing strange had just happened and he was telling Mom where she'd find a cold Dr. Pepper.

"Davy's big enough to go by himself." Mom snapped her large patent leather purse.

I hurried to the men's room and unzipped. Standing at the urinal, greatly relieved, I looked at the wall to my right and my eyes popped. I quick-washed my hands, shook them dry, and eyeballed the picture. I could hardly wait to tell Larry and Charlie Seven about the leggy lady on the calendar, though not Mom. She'd brain Herman a good one with her purse and march me over to see Father Mark for confession.

Back in the chair, I gazed out the big showroom window and the Plymouth rolled by with Herman at the helm. I wished they'd hurry up. I counted nineteen sets of hooked swordfish twice, then tilted my head back and followed the flight of a loud bumble bee as it buzzed like a Sabre jet across the white ceiling.

A flashy green bronco bucked by with Cathy in the saddle. The spindly man's mouth sprung open and he danced a fine, short jig. The yellow tailed jet zoomed out over his head. Mom watched stone-faced and handed me a stale stick of Wrigley's.

Cathy finally burst in squawking louder than an agitated blue jay. She swooped down, wrapped her skinny arms around Mom's neck, and half strangled her. Herman teetered in, patting his forehead with a hanky, mumbling about a few more lessons. Mom freed herself, thanked him, and asked if she could use the phone to call kind Father Mark for a ride.

⇥⊹ ⊹⇤

Cathy mastered the clutch in one after-school lesson and steered our pristine steed to each of her girlfriend's houses before she found her way home.

Near the end of July Mom bought her own license and reckoned her daughter would teach her. The following Saturday we piled into the Plymouth. Cathy drove to a lonely country road and pulled onto a rocky shoulder. Off to our right, half a dozen Holsteins lazed in the shade of broad oaks by a twisty creek. I imagined a wagon train heading west. I was their trusty scout, on lookout for marauding Comanche.

A horn tooted and Mr. Graham's gleaming blue Olds whizzed by. His shoe store had a four-foot-high walnut-veneer box with an x-ray machine inside. Standing on a small, wooden platform, I once stuffed my feet into shoe-sized caves, flipped a switch, and a greenish-yellow glow exposed bony puzzles in my feet.

Cathy and Mom switched seats, stumbling on the bumpy ground, laughing as they touched the warm hood to steady themselves. Before turning the key Mom rubbed the St. Christopher medal hanging on a silver chain from the rearview mirror. The engine fired right up, quiet, just as it had for Mr. Davis. Mom depressed the clutch and shifted into first.

"Gas, then release the clutch" Cathy said.

Mom fed the engine. The car hiccupped and hopped once or twice before we gained speed.

"Shift into second and go easy on the clutch."

I was impressed. Mom was zipping right—Good God! Her go for second sounded like nails on a blackboard. I cringed and covered my ears with my hands. The car sputtered and conked out.

She started over. The cantankerous Plymouth bucked like a rodeo bronco. She started over again and again.

Cathy lost her marbles and lashed out: "Let the clutch out *slow-ly*! More gas! Less gas! Don't ride the clutch!"

Just when I thought poor Mom would give up, she murmured prayers I knew and some I didn't know and miraculously found second gear. The car coughed and stuttered as we crawled down the road, an ailing turtle pursuing Mr. Graham's robust hare.

"More gas! Don't stall!"

Mom sealed her lips and sped up. The laboring engine whined.

"Shift!"

Her bid for third gear foiled when the sun's fierce rays emerged from behind a cloud and set the shimmering green hood afire.

"Sweet Jesus, Mary and Joseph! I'm blind!"

Her white knuckled hands steered us willy-nilly across lanes. St. Christopher slapped the windshield.

"Stop the car!"

Mom's short legs punished the pedals and a small cloud of dust announced our arrival on the shoulder. Slammed against the side of the coach, I looked out the open window. Big black eyes stared at me through rusty barbed wire. Then an imperturbable Comanche disguised as a Holstein lowered its head and munched grass.

⟞⟢ ⟣⟝

They never practiced together again. Instead, Mom enlisted Father Mark, and after a handful of prayerful lessons, he taught her how to subdue the Plymouth's obstinate unsynchronized transmission. I thought she'd drive herself to work, but Bertha still picked her up every weekday morning. Cathy took us to Sunday mass, me to and from Little League practices and games, herself to school, and I don't know where else. Aside from one trip to Foster's to buy me clothes, Mom only drove to Kroger's for the week's groceries, her hands molded to the sweaty wheel, her stubborn chin jutting forward. Each time she smoothly shifted, her mouth curled into a quarter-moon smile. A few years later my life took an unexpected turn when a man from Ohio visited, and Mom pursed her license and never drove again.

CHAPTER FOUR

Only a block long, Clevenger Street ran downhill from S. Garrison Street, making it a fine sled run. We started at Larry's, near the top, and whizzed down. The hill petered out alongside my picket-fenced backyard, giving us lots of time to drag our feet and stop before we slid into Forest Street. Even so, we posted a lookout for cars. The previous year, Charlie Seven made a brazen, ill-advised run on a ribbon of fast ice. He blasted off as soon as his sled touched down and rocketed downhill at speed never before seen. Neither the gently sloping ground alongside the picket fence or his foot sliding on shiny ice slowed his lickety-split momentum. He zoomed by me yelling "Mommy! Mommy!" shot across the street, and steamrolled to a stop yards inside a weedy, snow-covered vacant lot.

In warmer weather a footpath cut through the vacant lot to a high-banked narrow creek. To our right, the creek flowed under a barbed wire fence and wandered across a long, wide cow pasture before it emptied into a small deep pond that iced over in the winter.

Larry Norwood, Leon Zubeck, and I were the usual "we." Larry and I were teammates on the Southern Auto Little League team. His arm proved too weak for the outfield or third base, his stature too slight for catching or first base, so Coach Andy put him at second base. His anemic batting average mired him at the bottom of our line-up, but his smooth play in the field opened Andy's eyes wide with surprise. Larry's glove sucked up ground balls as though the seamed, red-stitched, white orbs were windblown globs of calcified dust and his leathered hand a powerful vacuum cleaner.

Tall, licorice-haired Leon didn't play baseball. He played basketball. He worked on his parents' farm during the summer and gained biceps every boy in my class envied.

We jumped the slender creek and followed a trail into the woods, passing through thin foliage of young birch and hawthorn, giant foxtail, and scattered thistle. Before heading into deeper woods, we paused and again regarded a thigh-high drystone wall. We reckoned an ambitious, muscular pioneer had crafted it to mark his land. The fence ran alongside a mature row of dogwoods, a natural boundary for sun and wind relief.

"Can'tcha just see this bein' a battleground?" Larry said.

"Sure can," I said, picking up a small, jagged rock, imagining Union soldiers crouched behind the wall, their long rifle barrels pointing toward Johnny Rebs in the black willows by the creek.

"Could be from the big battle," Larry said, squinting.

"That happened over by the river," Leon said.

"Yeah, back in 1851," Larry said, shading his eyes. "'Bout the time old Quantrill's Raiders burned down the town."

"The Civil War wasn't until 1861," Leon said, playfully adding, "And I never heard it was Quantrill's bushwhackers that lit up the town."

They set to arguing. I threw the rock sidearm at some yellow clover woven into fence. I reckoned Leon was right since there were times when I thought he might be smarter than Charlie Seven, although Confederates of some sort had burned down most of Carthage during the Civil War, but I didn't want to take sides.

"Let's go," I said.

We marched single file past the candelabra arms of silent dogwood sentries.

"I meant 1861," Larry said.

The trail led us to a bright open area at the bottom of a hill, the hospital's rear lawn at the top without cover for our hiding games. After we discovered the exposed refuse heap of soiled and broken bed pans, stained bandages, and spent needles we never went back.

"Germs, worms, and blood," Larry shouted, running.

A narrow path, worn smooth by an army of parading rabbits, angled in from the left and joined ours. We'd traced the bunny trail weeks earlier and come upon the foundation of an old burned-out building. Further on, we stood on a high bank upstream, leaned against willows, and peered across the creek and into the backyards of three single-storied houses. After a while, Charlie Seven, who was with us, said we should go because Connie lived in one of the houses, and folks might mistake us for Peeping Toms.

I peeled off from Leon and Larry and started up the rabbit path.

"Hey, where you goin'?" Larry said.

"Down this way."

"What for?"

"Be just a minute. Wanna check out good hiding places."

We toted BB guns when we played Yanks and Rebs, and I wanted to find a new spot to spring an ambush. Summer was ending. Once school started, our visits to the woods would be infrequent. With winter, they would cease. I wanted to go out with a bang.

"Well, hurry up," he said, as if we were on a train schedule.

I bent over, pushed aside a tangle of bushes, and froze solid.

A huge orange-and-black spider lay in the middle of a gigantic web between bent arms of a bramble. I jerked upright. My stomach did a double flip. I was breathless, soundless, rooted. Stretched across a web of zigzagging X's, the spider's long black legs turned bright red near its shiny egg-shaped body. Motionless, it waited for the filament's telltale quiver to announce its next meal.

"C'mon," Larry said. "Whadya doin'?"

His words fractured my spell. I turned halfway toward him, peripherally viewing the spider. "It's gigantic!"

"What?"

"It, it's—." Amazement softened my voice. "God, it's big."

They dashed to my side.

"Wow!" Larry's eyes popped wide, the way they had the first time he saw Billy Hitchcock's curveball. His hand moved toward the web.

"Careful—could be poisonous."

He jerked his arm back. "Bet it is."

Leon looked over Larry's shoulder. "Think we can trap it?"

"No," I said. The spider was perfect: foreboding, frightening, even beautiful. "It's too big. It might bite us."

"Yeah, way too big," Larry said. "I ain't touchin' it."

We watched the spider awhile longer, leaning forward as far as we dared. Finally, I said, "Let's go."

Leon was last to turn away before we regrouped and trudged in silence along the base of the hill, away from the creek, into cooler musty air. Shifting shadows danced across narrowing trails, at first translucent with shafts of sunlight dappling honeysuckle, then much darker and still, like a cool, deep cellar.

Behind us, the spider bathed in soft forest light, waiting.

Anger pinched my eyes when I saw the Mason jar on Mrs. Martin's desk. Six holes punched through its tin lid. Limp grass scattered across the bottom; the leggy spider sideways on the curved glass.

Mrs. Martin stood on the foot high platform that held her desk and lifted the jar chin high. The padded shoulders of her white blouse bunched. "This is a fine example of a *very* large Argiope." She peered over the rim of her black rhinestone glasses, as she always did to stress a point. "Leon found it and brought it in so we could all see it."

I zeroed in on him, two rows over, the traitor's broad smile proud. I glared, but he was too busy basking to notice.

"How'd ya do it?" I asked at lunch.

"Easy. I just put the jar underneath real careful like, lifted it quick, and slapped on the lid."

He pantomimed his treachery.

"Wha'dya gonna do with it?"

He cradled his chin between his thumb and forefinger, his rascally eyes studying the tiled ceiling.

"Maybe plug up the holes and watch it die. Cut it up."

"You wouldn't."

He smiled. "I dunno." His dark eyes softened and his lips curled into a slight smile. "I might let it go."

Before leaving for the day I paused at the desk. The spider stood near the top of the jar with nowhere to go, his orange-and-black body small and pitiful.

"Wasn't it nice of Leon to bring it in?" Mrs. Martin looked up from the stack of arithmetic tests she was grading.

I shuffled away silently, recalling how proud I'd felt when I brought in my Play USA game to show her how I'd gotten an A on the state capitals test. Facing her, I lifted the game, like a priest offering an enormous rectangular host. "This is what I used to memorize them."

Rowdy classmates poured in from the hall. She pushed her glasses up with her middle finger. "Nice," she said before turning and clapping loudly to quiet them.

In the playground Leon slowly swayed on the middle swing, smiling at his expanding group of admirers, a storyteller father surrounded by adoring children.

I turned away, kicked gravel, and a cloud of dust engulfed my legs. I kicked again, imagined Leon beneath my toe. Why hadn't he left it alone? Mom always reminded me that watchful God kept a tally of hateful thoughts, even those directed toward non-believers. I looked up at the still gray sky. Maybe He was on vacation. Maybe He wasn't there, ever.

CHAPTER FIVE

One windless January morning, a quiet white veil fell over the cold landscape, and the sky vanished. Mrs. Martin shivered, cinched her cardigan a button higher, and peered out the window. Above the door, the newly installed intercom crackled, and a tinny voice said: "Hello Mark Twain school students and teachers. This is Mr. Beasley, Mark Twain Elementary school principal. Due to rapidly deteriorating weather conditions, I'm cancelling the remainder of the school day. Be safe going home. Thank you."

"Yippee!" we roared.

Mrs. Martin whacked her desk with the thick wooden ruler reserved for such occasions.

"The weather is no excuse for sixth graders to go wild. Row one, you may get your coats and be dismissed."

Some of us were already standing, in place. We squirmed and whispered, girls giggled.

"No snowballing on school grounds," she said as we scurried out.

Her orders fell on the deaf ears. Cold spheres flew across the vast, white carpeted playground. I hurled hard packed ones until a curtain of large, thick, wet flakes obscured targets and the game lost its fun. I headed home.

I hadn't worn galoshes, and snow had melted inside my shoes. I peeled off icy-wet socks, toweled my feet, and wiggled my skinny red toes. Cathy stomped in.

"It's really coming down out there," she said, stamping her big saddle oxfords on the throw rug.

"We got out early." I pulled fresh warm socks over my chilled feet.

"So did I. Darn." Clumps of snow had fallen on the hardwood. "I better clean this up before Mom sees it."

"Yeah." I didn't want to admit some of it might be mine.

I spent the afternoon staring out the living room window, drawing stick figures on steamed glass. Pretty Emily Morgan lived next door. Christmas Day she'd invited me over, and we played Scrabble with her parents. A few days later, Mr. Morgan took us to a benefit basketball game between the high school squad and older ex-varsity players who never found the road leading out of town. I spent most of the game glancing at Emily. Once I snuck into the garage and peeked out the rear window. I had a clear sideways view into Emily's bedroom. My heart beat faster when her back came into good view, naked from the waist up.

I traced her outline in window fog, my finger smoothing curves, dreaming of Emily turning to show me more than her bare back. I was the brave explorer who found her lost in an Arctic blizzard. She was smiling, reaching out to hug me, ready to bare all, when Cathy sneaked into the living room with a textbook. I wiped away Emily's shapely smudge

All along Forest Street windswept snow climbed tree trunks and fences. Our ice laden Plymouth sported a foot high white pompadour.

"See any cars go by?" Cathy peered out the window, her hand on my shoulder.

"Only a few."

"I sure hope Mom's okay."

"Bertha always gives her a ride."

"I know, but we don't always get a storm like this. Maybe a plow will come by. This is an arterial residential street."

"Uh-huh," I said. I didn't know what arterial meant, but I got the idea.

Long after the snow quit, an icy beast crawled up the street, its pale, unblinking eyes seeking shelter. Bertha's Studebaker. Even at slow speed, rear wheels chained, the car slid sideways a bit when it stopped. Mom cautiously climbed out and baby-stepped across the street. The car's bound tires spun, found traction, and the beast crept into the frigid night.

Knee deep in snow, Mom paused to admire the Plymouth's new hairdo before she trudged up the walkway, her short legs disappearing and reappearing. She opened the door, closed it, and stamped her feet on the throw rug, shaking loose chunks of snow.

"Where's your sister?"

"In the kitchen. I got out of school before lunch."

She shed her woolen scarf, slipped out of her heavy brown overcoat, and hung them in the hall closet. Rubbed her hands together briskly and sat next to me on the couch.

"Burr. Cold feet. Bertha's heater's on the blink. I've got to get out of these shoes."

"My feet got cold."

"Did they get wet walking home?" She was unlacing her shoes.

"Only a little. I put on dry socks. See."

"I was worried about you and Cathy."

"She got out early too. Want the towel I used?"

"None of us thought to wear galoshes." She took the towel, shed her shoes and socks. "Sweet Jesus, Mary and Joseph, my feet like to

37

froze. Bertha's car put out a little heat for the windshield and not much else."

"Hi, Mom," Cathy said. She was holding a jar of applesauce. Her eyes darted to the snow Mom had tracked in. "I'll clean that up in a sec. I'm fixing potato pancakes."

Mom either didn't appreciate the cleaning up business or the dinner selection, for she glared at Cathy.

"Have you seen the car?" she said in her fierce motherly tone.

"The car?" Cathy glanced at the frosted window.

"I'm very disappointed in you, young lady."

"Why? What's wrong? Did someone hit it? I didn't hear anything."

"Nobody's hit it *yet*. Why is the car's out *front*?"

"I forgot to put it in the garage this morning."

"Don't be a smart aleck!"

"Mother, what are you talking about?"

"It's buried in snow. What if Bertha had hit it?"

Cathy fidgeted, chewed the inside of her right cheek. "I was going to drive it to school, but Sandra came by as I was leaving and we went in her car. I didn't know a storm like this one was coming."

"Well, it came, didn't it?"

Cathy's teary eyes cast a quizzical 'why the major fuss' my way. I returned a mystified look and tossed in a shrug.

"I'm sorry," Cathy said.

Mom pulled on dry socks. Her fingers enlivened her toes as she charted the evening.

"After dinner it goes in the garage."

"The garage! But, there's a foot of snow out there."

"Don't raise your voice to me, young lady. It wasn't *me* who left the car out *front*."

An enclosed breezeway connected the garage to the house. The driveway was off Clevenger Street. The white carpeted landscape, three-quarter moon, and a streetlight hanging from wires over the middle of the intersection made for good light. The night stole their foggy breaths as they trudged out wearing galoshes and heavy coats and gloves and ear muffs.

I clicked on *The Range Rider*, then *You Asked for It*, and looked out the living room window during commercials.

They shoveled and shoveled and shoveled twin paths for tires, and then Cathy started the car and backed up slowly. Then they shoveled again. I yawned when a Charlie Chan movie came on, and glanced outside just as the car, its rear wheel spinning like a top, began to inch up Clevenger Street. They still had a long way to go.

I caught the end of a commercial for M & M's. Yawned again. Half asleep. I clicked off the TV and crawled upstairs, looked out my bedroom window. They were creeping up the street.

I slipped beneath warm wool blankets, certain I would dream of Emily and sledding.

⇥⊹ ⊹⇤

Orphaned clouds played peek-a-boo with the sun. The air was surprisingly warm, and big drops of water fell from ice daggers hanging from gutters, punching holes in ground snow. We towed our sleds uphill to Larry's.

"I got first dibs," said Connie, a tall, slender, brown-haired tomboy who lived in one of the houses we'd gazed from the woods.

"Sure," I said.

A Chevy Styleline Deluxe crawled down from Garrison Street. Charlie Seven hopped out and opened the station wagon's rear door, pulled out a Flexible Flyer and tucked it under his stout arm. Tall and husky, he'd never stepped foot inside a barbershop. His thrifty mom gave him bowl cuts.

We took turns as lookouts. With professional hand signs learned from *Dragnet*, Charlie warned Larry to delay his ride and waved a poky car by. When I made a run, Connie guarded the intersection. I reached bottom and parked my right foot on the top of my sled. Connie pointed to the Plymouth's hard dug tracks, now decaying beneath bright sunlight.

"I seen your mom and sister last night."

"Yeah?"

"Seemed kinda dumb, it bein' so cold and all."

"Mom wanted it in the garage."

"They was at it 'til midnight."

Larry and Charlie raced down. Charlie's sled hiccupped in slush by the driveway. Larry skidded sideways in front of Connie, kicking up a wave of snow.

"Hey, watch it." Her gloved hands shielded her face.

"It's getting too mushy," Charlie said, holding up his sled with the rails facing us. "Let's go to Leon's."

I opened the gate to our backyard, and we stacked our sleds alongside the picnic table. Wet snow squished beneath our shoes as we crossed the street and high-stepped to the creek.

"Wanna take the pasture or the woods?" I said.

"I ain't goin' where I can't see cow shit," Larry said.

"Be easier along the creek," Connie said.

"She's right," Charlie said. "May be a bit muddy, but we're wearing galoshes."

"Creek may be the best way," I said to Larry.

"Hell's bells, all right."

We marched through dissolving drifts along twisting banks, crunched thin ice along the edges, and sometimes waded into icy water that looked knee deep in the middle. The snow-light was blinding. My hand shielded my eyes. At the far northern end of the pasture, toy-sized Guernseys huddled by miniature barns.

Our journey ended when the ground sloped and the snaking creek disappeared in an iced-over pond. A snow-covered dirt road on a high embankment walled the pond on the west. Leon's farm occupied the other side.

Laughing, we glissaded to the bank.

"Think we can walk on it?" Larry said. His black galoshes tentatively tested the ice.

"Leon said cows get trapped here," I said. "It gets deep fast. They sink."

"It's not really a pond," Charlie said, "just a big hole in the ground. Pipe that runs under the road's too narrow when the creek runs deep or too many rocks and stuff get in it. You'd think the farmer would put a fence around it, but the water's usually low in summer and the cows can safely drink."

"Well, that ice ain't thick enough to walk on," Connie said to Larry. "It's thawing. You'll fall through and die."

"Yeah?" Larry stepped lightly onto the opaque surface. "Seems okay." He cautiously slid away from the edge until he was about four feet out.

"Don't jump," Charlie said.

It sounded like an explosion. The ice splintering. Larry lost his balance and almost fell backwards. He tried to steady himself as fissures raced around him. He lurched toward us. The jagged ice sank beneath him. His arms thrashed the air; his wild eyes screamed oblivion. I stepped to the edge, reached for his outstretched hand, and almost burst out laughing. He stood in a foot of cold water.

"Told you," Connie said.

⊷ ⊶

Leon threw a fat snowball at the red barn. His mother looked out the steamy kitchen window, her long, dark hair gathered atop her head.

"Larry almost drowned in the pond," Connie said, sidling to Leon.

"Did not," Larry said.

Connie pinned her hands to her waist and stuck her head out like a chicken.

"Almost."

"Didn't even get my socks wet."

"We're sure not skating on it," Charlie said.

"Lookee here." Leon pointed to a ruler sticking out of the snow. Charlie bent down. "Only six-and-a-half?"

"It measured eight on the other side of the barn."

"My sister said it snowed a foot," I said.

Charlie pointed to the ruler. "Leon's got a scientific tool."

A cloud draped its shadow over us.

"Well, it's what she said."

Leon hurled a snowball at the tall chestnut by the side of his house. Charlie threw one. Soon we were all hooting and whooping, scooping up snow, blasting the old tree. There were strange brownish orange smudges on some of the lower limbs. If Leon painted them, his design was chaotic.

"Bet you can't hit me way up there," he said pointing.

I stared up at the labyrinth of stark arms reaching for spring.

"How high can ya climb?" asked Connie.

He climbed slowly, the snow laden branches slippery, threading his way until he stood on a limb far above us, one arm holding onto the trunk. We made balls, threw, and laughed. He ducked down behind forked branches.

"Can't hit me," he laughed.

We reached down, packed our missiles tighter, and threw harder.

"Can't hit me!"

"I'll get 'im this time," Larry said. He stared at Leon, who seemed to be dancing on a branch. "Easy as a throw to first."

Like a pitcher sighting the catcher's glove, he peered and launched a fastball. The snowy pitch soared between branches. He let out a whoop. I held my breath. Just below Leon, the ball nicked a limb and exploded.

"Oh, great," Connie said. "Just like the ice."

Larry glared at her, dropped to his knees, and scooped snow. "Ha ha ha. Can't hit me!"

I knelt beside Larry and angrily shoved my bare hands deep into wet snow until I felt a rock. I pressed it into the snow and shaped a ball.

"Gotta make sure it's packed hard," Larry said, squeezing.

For a moment I feared he had seen the rock. No, I'd sunk my hands wrist deep into snow. I glanced at the others. Connie was flat on her back, the snow angel. Charlie was looking up. Larry and I stood, side-by-side, teammates now, slender arms cocked.

"Can't hit me!"

We fired, and a gust of wind swept snow from weighed limbs. I ducked.

Leon screamed.

He tumbled down like a rag doll, bouncing off branches, butt bumping down to the white ground. His eyes were horror stricken. Blood gushed from a gash above his right eye, flowed down his cheek, and colored the snow. He slapped a hand over his bloody eye and ran to the porch.

"Mama! Mama!"

She flung open the door and wrapped him in her arms, took hold of his shoulders and pushed him back to see his face. Long red strings swayed from his chin.

"Let me see," she said.

She pulled his bloody hand from his face and gasped.

"Joe. Joe!" She and Leon hobbled inside. "Get the truck!"

"What happened?" Connie said, on her feet.

"I don't know," I said.

Joe burst through the doorway, vaulted down the steps, and fired up the Ford pick-up parked alongside the barn.

"I'm scared," Connie said.

Leon and his mother came out, her arm around his shoulder. Her hand held a scarlet stained white towel to his wounded eye. Joe slipped on a snowy step as he rushed up the stairs, extending his sturdy arms.

"Can we do anything, Mrs. Zubeck," Charlie said.

She jerked toward us and pointed to town.

"Get out of here! All of you—go to hell!"

CHAPTER SIX

On a warm April day, Larry and I were digging holes in the front yard intending to bury apricot pits when a pockmarked Chevy coupe with Ohio plates pulled up to the curb.

"Who's that?"

"Dunno," I said.

"Boy, it's an ugly car."

"Yeah. Looks like someone drilled it with a BB gun."

A heavyset man with a big smoking cigar tucked in the corner of his mouth got out and started up the walkway to our house.

"Which one of you is David?" he said half-smiling and staring down at us, having uprooted the cigar from his thin lips. His eyebrows were pale and his silver-brown hair slicked down city style.

"Me," I said without thinking. Mom always told me to steer clear of strangers, especially after Billy Cook murdered a bunch of people a few years back.

"I'm Henry. Come to visit."

"Who shot up your car?" Larry asked.

"Huh." He glanced back. "Oh, that. Got caught in a hailstorm."

"I never seen so many pimples," Larry said.

Henry gave him a look but didn't say anything. Mom opened the front door.

"Well, look who's come from Cleveland," she said.

⊫ ⊨

In the evening, he and Mom sat side-by-side on the backyard patio swing, talking quietly, holding hands. At dinner he complimented her on the breaded pork chops, mashed potatoes, and butter-cooked peas.

"Eat your vegetables, Davy." He winked at Mom. "He don't 'member the Great Depression."

"I'm not crazy about 'em."

Mom flicked me a frown.

"Shameful to waste good food," he said. "Cathy's eaten hers."

I forked the peas, chewed them fast, and made a sour open-mouthed face so they could see my green teeth.

"*David*," Mom said.

"Bet you'd like to have a brother," he said.

"Huh?"

"A big brother could teach you things."

I cleaned my plate. "Can I go now?"

"Why don't you visit with Henry?"

"I've got to run," Cathy said. "Debate Club practice."

"Don't argue so much you blow your stack," Henry said.

He dabbed his lips with a cloth napkin, told Mom she was a fine cook, and got up. She cleared the table and hauled the dishes into the kitchen. He went into the living room, sank into the couch, and set the Maxwell House coffee can that served as his ashtray and spittoon alongside his feet. He lit a long, fat cigar that must've come from Mexico or Spain, an El Producto. I plopped down on the floor to his left.

"This your paper?" He leaned forward and plucked the *Press* from the coffee table.

"Uh-huh."

He set his arms on his thighs, the paper hanging between his legs, and gave the first few pages the once-over. No reason local stories would interest him. He paused when he turned to the sport section and the classifieds. The back page seemed to hold his interest, a full ad for Kroger.

He drew on his stogie and exhaled a gray cloud. "Bet you'd like to see the Indians play."

"If they're playing the Yanks. Mickey Mantle played in Joplin. He took over centerfield for the Yankees after DiMaggio left. He's real good."

"So I heard. I'm just glad the Tribe don't have to face Joltin' Joe no more." He folded the paper in half and put it on the coffee table. "About the size of the sports page where I come from."

Mom said she had known him in her life before me.

That evening they came out back just as I mounted a tire hanging from an elm. "Uheeuwick," I bellowed as Tarzan searching for Cheetah. They sat on the shaded patio swing.

"Why don't you go up to Larry's," she said, and I knew it wasn't a question.

⊨+ +⊨

Larry was firing his new Red Ryder Daisy at a tin can by a walnut tree.

Ping. Ping.

"He's still here. Mom chased me away."

"Wanna shoot? You can use my old one."

He scurried off to fetch it. I laid two tin cans sideways by some large rocks and put three upright cans between them.

"Whatcha buildin'?" he said as he handed me his old Daisy.

47

"Let's pretend he's driving rustlers around."

He looked at the cans a long time before his light came on. "Oh, I get it. The ones on their sides are the wheels."

"Uh-huh."

"I'm Red Ryder." He slapped the butt of his shiny BB rifle.

"I'm Lash LaRue."

We lay in wait on crab grass.

"Little Beaver'll send a smoke signal soon as he sees 'em, Lash."

"I see it, Red."

"Yep. Smoke says outlaws come in car."

"Soon as it gets by the tree we'll blast 'em."

Ping. Ping. Ping! Ping!

A few days later Henry unhitched his studded, cattle-rustling stage-coach from the curb and rolled away. Mom stood on the sidewalk and waved until the distance stretched too great for seeing. I knew he'd turned at a wrong corner and driven into a time machine ambush. Buck Rodgers had vaporized his coach with an x-ray gun.

"I'm going to see the Morgans," she said.

I wanted to go with her to see if Emily was home, but Mom said no. I knew then she wanted to do boring grown-up talk, and I didn't think Emily would be around for that, so I went inside and looked for my glove, intending to see if Connie and Larry wanted to play ball. We practiced in the field across Clevenger Street. Two ranch style houses were rising on the field, but there was still ample room to toss a ball around. I vaulted the stairs to my attic hideaway and picked up my glove. It still faintly smelled of bacon grease. I didn't know everyone else used saddle soap. I ran downstairs, streaked through the house, and darted out the back. Cathy sat on the glider in the breezeway, lost in thought.

"He's gone," I said. "Mom's next door." Tears trickled from her radish red eyes. "What's wrong?"

"It's you I'm thinking of."

"Me?"

"I'll be going to college, so it won't affect me as much." A hanky wiped her tears and she blew her pink nose. "I always thought that when I wanted to come home, it would be here."

"Wh-Why won't it?"

"Because you and Mom will be in *O-hi-o*."

It all added up, like the ending to a Charlie Chan movie: the soft talking, the Indian's game, the smile on his pasty face, Mom telling the Morgans. I didn't want to leave our home, but I knew there was nothing I could do.

"When?"

She dabbed tears. "He's coming back when school's out."

⚔️ ⚔️

"We want you to look good when we get there," Mom said, staring straight ahead. She never took her eyes off the road or complained when other drivers went too fast. We were on our way downtown to shop for summer clothes.

"If you're not working at the jeans factory anymore, does that mean you'll be home?"

"It'll be a change, Davy, but I think you'll like it. Henry lives in Parma. He says there's a Catholic grade school there."

"Okay." I watched her short legs work the clutch and gas as she downshifted. She seldom ground the gears.

"There's one favor I want you to do for me." I didn't say anything. "Do you like Henry?"

"I guess."

"It'll be nice for you to have a father and a brother."

The Courthouse loomed above us, a medieval castle of polished granite. Inside, Emily and I sat on thrones. There was a drawbridge out front instead of wide granite steps. Poison water the color of green grass surrounded us. The sidewalks were quicksand. His cigar would be the last thing to sink.

Mom angle-parked the car in front of Foster's and turned off the engine.

"Would you call him 'Dad'? It would make it easier for me if you did."

"I'll try." To me, Dad was a still image in photographs. I was in a few of the photos, old enough to talk, but I couldn't remember ever saying Dad.

Inside, I ran my hand over a pair of light blue cotton slacks.

"Do you like them?" she asked. They had an elastic beltline. It was easy to imagine looking spiffy in them. "They look nice." She shifted two polo shirts she had picked out for me into her left hand and ran her right hand over the fabric. "Well-made. Double-stitched."

A familiar voice behind us said, "Thinking of buying?" Andy, my Little League Manager, stepped forward wearing the very same slacks I liked. "Hi. You must be David's mother."

She smiled, welcoming his presence. "We're trying to decide."

"I think they look great on a ball player," he said.

My chest puffed out a little, and just as I was going to tell Mom to buy them, he hooked his thumbs on his waistband and something flashed on his wrist. "They're sure comfy," he said, showing us how the elastic stretched. "When I wear 'em, I don't even need a belt." Something sparkled on his wrist.

"Well, what do you think?" Mom said.

I blinked, looked away, and blinked again. My watch. *My* watch. "I don't like 'em."

Andy arched his eyebrows, and without uttering a word walked away.

"But I thought you did," Mom said, the limp pants draped over her arm.

"I dunno. I changed my mind."

⊷⊶

Mark Twain Elementary shut down for the summer, and a few days later Henry parked his indestructible Chevy in the driveway. I rode in the Plymouth with Cathy. My eyes stung looking out the side window, especially when we rolled past the city limits. I thought of Emily, and of Larry, Charlie, and Connie, and even Leon.

After that snowy day, Leon didn't have much to do with any of us. When the school year ended he still wore an eye patch. I heard he'd gone to see doctors in Joplin, Springfield, and as far away as St. Louis. As I walked away from Mark Twain for the last time I saw him on the far side of the playground, striding across home plate. From now on Leon would view the world through only one eye, and it was my fault. I wanted to run after him, tell him it was me who threw the snowball, and I was awfully sorry. But I hesitated, shuffled across deep left field, my neck craned toward him. I silently watched as he opened a gate, dropped down some steps, and disappeared.

PART 2

CHAPTER SEVEN

Mom and Henry probably mentioned it, but I must've been daydreaming, for I now had a stepbrother, Mick, *and* a stepsister. Tall, stout, and busty, Gloria had a big, easy smile that would have been pleasant had she not been missing an upper canine. Three years earlier she was sitting on a barstool in west Cleveland when Ernie, a wiry, wrinkle-faced six-footer who worked for the New York Central Railroad, bought her a drink. It might've been love at first sight, cemented by their fondness for drink. They soon married and settled into an upstairs blue collar apartment a few blocks east of the fateful bar.

Though I'd been popular in Carthage, the strangeness of Parma overwhelmed me. I had no friends, no cow pasture to roam, no woods to explore. Instead, monotonous blocks of pristine ranch style houses lined perfectly poured concrete streets. Power mowers trimmed grass weekly, skirting around saplings as skinny as my arm. Even my peers looked alien from the neck up. A menacing gang of three had swaggered up the sidewalk, the backs of their shirt collars turned up, the sides of their greased hair swept back. I didn't strut, my collars were at rest, and I had no desire to weave my hair into a duck's ass. I felt like a stranger.

In the fall, Cathy went off to school in Kansas. When she came home for Thanksgiving break, Mom told her our new stepbrother bought the Plymouth for fifty dollars. She always thought of it as "her" car. Now she had to ask Mick to borrow it.

There were three bedrooms in Henry's ranch house. Mom and Henry slept in the largest one. The second largest was for Cathy when she was home and for infrequent guests when she was away. I shared the smallest with Mick. Though he had a healthy appetite for beer, his stomach was granite hard. He wore blue jeans and snug white T-shirts, usually with a pack of Lucky Strikes embedded in the sleeve, and generously oiled his crew cut with Vitalis. He was twelve years my senior, six feet two, and he outweighed me by eighty pounds. I was nearing six feet, but decades would pass before my newly sprouted string-bean physique filled out.

One day I stole two Luckies when Mick was in the shower belting out a discordant version of "Rock Around the Clock." I hid them in the pocket of my winter jacket. A few days later everyone went out, and, wearing only underpants, I lit up in front of the bathroom mirror. I wanted to hold the butt like John Wayne or dangle it from my lips à la Humphrey Bogart. I inhaled, swaggered into a smoky cabaret. A gorgeous blonde eyed me. "Hey, doll." I gagged and coughed.

When the first butt shrank to a finger scorching stub, I tossed it into the toilet, flushed, and lit the second, swept a hand across my hair, and popped my fingers to the snappy beat in my head. I strutted down a street in the Bronx, a member of the feared Amboy Dukes. I shook my hips, flexed my slender biceps, and rubbed the steel pole rising between my legs. Each drag became easier, smoother than the last. When I finished, I winked at the

56

mirror and flashed a knowing grin. "Hey, doll, what are *you* doing tonight?"

I flushed the second butt, thinking I almost had the hang of it. With a little more practice I'd have it down. I bent my head beneath the faucet for cold water to cool my hot, dry throat. I was big city hip, a cool local legend. If I sported a turned-up collar, combed my hair so it looked like a duck's ass in the back—then my stomach churned, the room spun, and I vomited.

≕⊹ ⊹≕

Mick had taken shop classes in high school and worked as a machinist. His life had a machine-like rhythm, too: the deafening five a.m. alarm, the off-key singing in the shower, the bacon-and-eggs breakfast Mom fried for him, the metallic hum of repetitive work. At night he slipped out of his jeans and left them folded like twin concertinas on the floor by the bed. In the morning, he swiveled his legs over the edge and slipped into them, ready to go again.

The easy chair was his throne in the late afternoon. He guzzled beer and played his current favorite record, *ad infinitum*. This lasted until Henry, a foreman at Republic Steel, came home and reclaimed the *chair of honor*. After dinner, Mick sprawled on the couch, had a few more beers, and watched TV with us. By ten or eleven, he burped, got up, and tumbled into bed.

I had no idea what he did on weekends. He never talked about girls or went on dates. His only literature was *TV Guide*. I do know he came home reeking of beer on Fridays, banging into walls and furniture on his boozy journey to bed.

When Mick started playing "Sh-Boom" after work, I liked it. Who wouldn't think life a dream if you and your girl were in paradise and she did what you wanted? It had a catchy rhythm and a snappy "sh-boom" sprinkled throughout. Two weeks later, I hated it.

One afternoon, just before he came home, I placed the record on the turntable and scored the record with the needle. I watched his work weary body lumber into the living room, beer in hand, and slap the 45 onto the spindle. My heart pounded. He sank into Henry's chair and rolled the cold, moist bottle across his forehead. The record dropped, the needle fell into a vinyl groove, and suddenly static roared between beats like an alien invasion.

"What?" he said, screwing his face into a wonderful despair.

I put a hand over my mouth to quell the joy welling in my throat. "What's the matter?"

He moved the needle arm back to its cradle, lifted the record from the turntable, and held it up. "Look."

I frowned oh so sorry.

He examined the record again, running a finger over the rough grooves. He knew. And I knew he knew. And he knew I knew he knew. First, he'd punch my face. Then he'd pick me up by the ankles and swing me around and fling me crashing through the picture window. Mick could have pulverized me in a thousand different ways that afternoon, but the union of our families was still too new to risk incident.

My glee was brief. The next day a fresh "Sh-Boom" spun on the player.

"The last one got screwed up," he said, eyeing me. "Nothin' better happen to this one."

⚒ ⚒

Henry and Mom were third cousins and she had to apply for a papal dispensation to marry. It sounded so official. Being young, I couldn't see how the constricting web of her devotion to Rome clipped her wings. Her commitment was absolute; no turning back. When she married Henry, she forfeited Dad's Army's pension. Without Henry, she had no income, and good paying job opportunities for a woman in her early forties with only an eighth-grade education were not plentiful in the mid-1950s. The VA paid for most of Cathy's college expenses. To offset my tuition at St. Charles, the Catholic elementary school in Parma, Mom went to work at a factory that made corrugated boxes.

I wasn't keen on going to a Catholic school. The one and only time I served mass at St. Ann's in Carthage had fractured my faith.

My heart raced when I stood at the open sacristy door beside Ron, an older, experienced altar boy. I glanced back at Father Mark, his wrinkled hands chest-high. Our short parade advanced into the church proper and panic seized me. The cassock's hem snagged my right foot. I'd put on the wrong size. I stumbled and blushed. Father Mark's reverent steps closed in from behind. I had to walk—fast!

I quickly devised a method. I kicked the cassock out as I stepped, clearing a little path. I didn't want to lift up my robe like a sissy. Luckily, attendance was scant at the weekday morning mass and the worshipers present didn't seem to notice. My hands went clammy. Only Father Mark, Ron, and the life-sized stature of Jesus above the altar were three dimensional. Everyone and everything else seemed flat. Worry moistened my brow. What if I forgot to kick? I imagined taking an errant step and falling to my knees in impromptu prayer.

When I faced the altar, I lifted the front of the cassock discreetly and avoided any swift turns. Thank God I wasn't carrying the censer. One wrong step and Father Mark would have to explain to Mom how I set myself on fire while serving mass. He'd already glared at me during one of my quick kick-step shuffles.

I had to precede Father Mark down the communion rail and hold the golden paten beneath the mouths of kneeling parishioners. The holy sacrament adheres to the tongue like glue, but just like the American flag, it must never touch the ground. I worried about catching my foot in the hem if I put my quick kick-step routine into reverse. I imagined falling over backwards in front of kneeling closed-eyed communicants, not what their outstretched tongues anticipated. I prayed for God's intervention, but I'd lied to Mom when she asked if I peed through the window screen of my attic bedroom and I thought my entreaty would go unheard. Six communicants free of sin came forward and knelt. I shuffled into position. Perspiration flooded my forehead. A sweaty river flowed down my sides. Soon my cassock would be drenched. Then I noticed how meticulously Father Mark handled the host. When he carefully laid the host on an outstretched tongue, my left hand discreetly lifted my cassock and I took little shuffling backward steps.

My lift-step timing was perfect, the service ended and I kick-stepped back to the privacy of the sacristy. Hallelujah! I could breathe again. I hadn't tripped. I hadn't fallen. I laughed, relieved.

Father Mark swung at me from behind. His sharp fists pummeled me across the small room. Shocked and shaky, I tore off the hateful cassock, tore open the door, and vaulted down stairs two at a time and sprinted across the yard behind the church to the alley. I seethed all the way home, aching to curse him out loud, though I knew it would be a serious sin, and how could I confess anything to *him?*

Yet God watched. He'd surely give Father Mark a pit stop in purgatory, or worse. First the old priest would get hot coals. Then glowing pitchforks held by short kick-stepping imps would prod him. Just as I imagined him on his knees, begging for mercy, I saw our house and tears welled up. No use explaining. Mom would always believe Father Mark had sound reasons.

Compared to St. Ann's in Carthage, a simple country church built of stone, spacious St Charles in Parma was a golden cathedral. Instead of a small corner confessional behind modest rows of lackluster pews, four imposing chambers filled an alcove alongside countless rows of polished pews.

Though Henry balked and whined every Sunday morning, he never uttered an unkind word when he drove us to church. During mass he silently followed our lead and knelt, sat, or stood at appropriate times. After a few months he abandoned our pew, preferring the thick Sunday morning *Plain Dealer*, though he remained our grudging chauffeur. At least his indifference was overt. I went through religious motions to please Mom with the same fake smile I showed the nuns at St. Charles.

One Saturday Mom told Henry that she and I wanted to go to confession, though she made-up the part about me. She said too much time had elapsed since our last. Henry grumbled a bit but silently drove us. She told him to come back in an hour.

I knelt beside her and muttered my brief penance as she threaded her rosary through caressing fingers for the second time. Two rosaries? Had she confessed a mortal sin?   I'd stuck to the venial, admitting a small lie, two blasphemous words and the paperback I'd thought of stealing from the corner drug store. In return, I had to say five Our Fathers and five Hail Marys. It seemed a fair trade for the cleansing of my soul. I dreaded The Stations of the Cross, which is what I feared my penance would have been if the priest learned I *had* stolen the paperback western, *Bitter Sage*. What if he found out I bought innocent looking movie magazines so I could clip photos of Hollywood starlets and engage in lewd thoughts while abusing myself?

"Dear Lord, grant me the strength to bear this cross," Mom's soft words touched my ears. Her fingers rolled a rosary bead, but what prayer had she spoken? "Mary, Mother of God, I seek your help."   I leaned closer and lowered my head. Her lips moved silently as she rolled four more beads between her fingers before she spoke again, "allow him . . . vision . . . Hail Mary, full of grace. . . I pray . . . your only begotten son . . . so he may . . . dear, Father who art in heaven . . . forgive him . . ."

I crawled into bed a little after ten and was drifting off when raised voices pulled me back. I sat up and flattened my ear against the cool wall.

"Why aren't you home from work sooner?" Mom said her voice strong. "What's taking you so long?"

"I dunno what you mean," Henry said, his words so faint I mashed my ear against the wall to hear. "It's the overtime. There's a lotta orders and I gotta make sure the guys keep workin'."

"You're seeing another woman."

"Please, Mary, lower your voice. You'll wake David."

"As if you care—all the hours you said you had to work over-time. Lies! All lies."

"You're nuts, Mary."

"You're the one who's mixed up, buster. You're the liar. Why did you marry me if I'm not good enough for you?"

"You are."

"It's Irene, isn't it? You were seeing her when you came to Carthage and sweet-talked me. It's her, isn't it?"

"Mary, please—"

"What does she have that I don't have? Want me to end up like my mother? Get rid of me, is that what you want?"

"I ain't seein' her."

"It's the perfume, stupid. I don't use that perfume. Don't look at me that way. I know how your shirts smell—I wash them."

Then silence. I could imagine Mom melting him with her eyes. My heart drummed.

"What can I do," he finally said, his words a distant echo.

Their voices dissolved behind the wall, as if they'd gone into another room. I slipped under the covers, tucked my hand under the pillow, and shut my eyes.

The following evening an unused knife and fork were on the napkin beside Henry's plate. We ate in silence until Mick, who'd been out drinking the previous night with a bar buddy, said, "Still

62

not feelin' up to par, Mom?" He always called her Mom, just as she'd instructed me to call Henry "Dad."

"A little under the weather, that's all."

He sopped up the last of the gravy and said, rising and still chewing. "Gotta be goin'. A bunch of us guys from work are gettin' together. Good meal."

Mom started in on the dishes and I went into the living room and watched TV.

"I'm going to rest for a while," she said after a while.

"Are you okay?"

"I just need to lay down."

"I'll wake you for Bishop Sheen. Okay?"

"That would be nice."

Life is Worth Living came on: Bishop Sheen in cassock, cape, and zucchetto, eyes shining as he stood by a statue of the Madonna, eager to enrich my evening.

"Mom," I called. I hustled down the hall to the bedroom, the door partially open. "Mom," I softly said. I slipped inside. The bureau light was on. She lay on her side, facing the wall. The bedspread pulled up to her waist. She'd fallen asleep wearing her housedress. Her breaths were heavy sighs. "Show's on, Mom," I said, giving her shoulder a gentle shake. No response. Not even a sleeper's twitch to brush off a bug. "Wake up, Mom. Bishop Sheen's on."

She didn't stir. I shrugged, assumed fatigue had hit her and sleep would do her good. I retreated to the TV. In a persuasive voice Bishop Sheen talked of the need for morality in the modern world, how the immoral, Godless Communist leaders cruelly subjugated their people. He had me for a few minutes, though I was only half-listening. I felt uneasy. She should've woken up. My mind unscrewed a chilly memory.

A few years back, in 1952, our TWA flight from Missouri taxied onto the tarmac at the Allegheny County Airport. Uncle Joe met us. He drove us in his Studebaker to Cokeburg, a backwater borough thirty miles or so south of Pittsburgh, and parked off the alley behind the family house. The night spit graupel.

Mom and Uncle Joe stepped out and loud buckets of freezing air poured in. Cathy and I were in the backseat. I shivered and moved a little closer to her. Mom and Uncle Joe were standing behind the car. I twisted around to watch. He wrapped a strong arm around Mom's shoulder and put his mouth to her ear. She stiffened and cried out, her words shredded by an angry wind. He fastened his arm around her waist. Cathy sat stock still, her folded hands in her lap, eyes fixed on the rearview mirror. The car smelled faintly of mildew and sweet chewing gum. Sleet pummeled the fogged glass. Uncle Joe slowly guided Mom up the stone walkway to Grandfather's house.

"I'm cold," I said.

"So am I," Cathy said.

We leaned into a cold wind and made for the house. Bits of ice stung my face. A man hurried toward us.

"Uncle Johnny," Cathy said.

He wore no coat. Steam billowed from his mouth. He rubbed his hands together. "Let's get you kids inside."

Grandfather sat on a wooden chair in the toasty downstairs kitchen. I expected him to reach out and beckon us into his arms. Instead, he looked right through us and stared at the door as though expecting someone else. I briskly rubbed my forearms, toweled my moist face. Cathy embraced her shoulders.

"Your mom's upstairs with Joe," Uncle Johnny said. "How about some cocoa?"

We nodded, shrugged off our coats, and sat at the table. Unlike muscular Uncle Joe, Mom's younger brother was skinny. As he stood at the stove and warmed milk and stirred in cocoa, we had no way of knowing cancer was shrinking his stomach to the size of a lemon. The following year we would return to bury him. Two more years would pass before cancer took away Grandfather. From the ages of seven to fourteen I stood beside Mom so often when she lost loved ones—Dad and his brother Uncle John, Grandmother, Uncle Johnny, and Grandfather—that I began to think it was a yearly event, like Christmas or Easter.

In the days before Grandmother's funeral, I overheard snatches of conversations—"buried in the church . . . lenient priest . . . not in her right mind . . . so sad . . . left mass early . . . walked home . . . hung herself . . ."

Bishop Sheen's blessing filled the screen. *Like my mother.* I sprang up and bolted down the hallway.

"Mom?"

I listened, shook her shoulder, exerting a steady pressure, leaned closer. Her face looked blank and peaceful.

"Mom, wake up."

She had clutched a lace doily beneath her chin. On the bureau, a brown medicine bottle lay on its side. Empty.

I sat frozen in front of the TV. I didn't know what to do. I was scared. I don't know how much time elapsed before Henry finally came home.

"I can't get Mom to wake up."

"Mary!" He rushed down the hall.

"Help! Save me! Save me!" cried The Fair Maiden to Bucky Beaver in a loud commercial for Ipana toothpaste.

Maybe an ambulance came and rushed her to the hospital, or maybe Henry drove her. Maybe she had her stomach pumped, or maybe she filled it with hot black coffee and washed away her pain beneath a cold shower. I have blocked out the facts along with my terror. I only know I sat glued to the couch and quietly watched black-and-white skeletons flicker across the screen.

CHAPTER EIGHT

I n 1955, I was thirteen when we celebrated our second Christmas in Ohio. After we'd eaten and opened gifts, Mom, Henry, Cathy, Gloria and Mick gathered around our new Philco to watch *Miracle on 34th Street*. I'd seen the movie where the post office flooded a court room with letters addressed to the North Pole to prove that kids across the country believe Santa exists. Ernie was indifferent to the movie. Ernie wanted to drink. I followed him into the kitchen and asked if he wanted to play poker for fun. Over dinner he'd talked about having bad luck with five card draw at the yard. I wanted to see if he'd notice a trick deck I'd made. Maybe somebody was using a marked deck. About an hour later, three columns of red, white, and blue plastic chips were stacked before me.

"You're a card shark, kid," he said, his wide eyes a comical mix of disbelief and astonishment.

I smiled and pointed at the faint pencil marks on the backs of the cards.

"These are really good," he said. "You're a regular Houdini." He downed a good bit of his seven and seven and scrutinized the back of the king of diamonds.

"They're not that good."

"I could win dough off the guys with these."

"It wouldn't work." I didn't believe he couldn't see the pale dots. "You're joshin',"

"I'm serious, kid. Can I use 'em?"

"Take 'em if you like."

"Thanks." He squared the deck, slipped it into his shirt pocket, and poured himself another Seagram's 7 and 7Up.

In mid-January, Mom and Henry went to visit Ernie and Gloria, and I tagged along. Their small upstairs one bedroom apartment was clean and nicely furnished. After casual greetings our coats were stowed, and Gloria put on a pot of Folgers, and Mom and Henry eased onto the couch. It was obvious the two comfy chairs nearest the couch bore the names of our hosts, so I landed in the one with frayed arms and lumpy cushion. The coffee perking serenade ended and Gloria set steaming cups on flowery saucers and served Mom and Henry. I scored a big, twelve-ounce bottle of Coke, and turned down the offer of a glass. After Ernie made stout highballs— Canadian Club with a dash of 7UP—he and Gloria slid into their butt-friendly chairs. As the grown-ups chattered, I fought the wires stabbing my butt, and scouted Ernie's furrowed face for Band-Aids, fresh scars, recent bruises, any proof he'd been dumb enough to play the marked cards. I didn't see any battery evidence, so I peered at the three framed eight-by-ten glossies on a walnut table. In each autographed, color photo, taken from slightly different angles, Liberace was wearing a gold lamé dinner jacket and sequin-studded boots. He stood by a silver candelabrum that was on top of a big white piano, his broad, ready-to-entertain-the-world smile identical in all three pictures.

"Who likes Liberace?"

"Me," Gloria said. "We watch him every week. I sent away for those. I think he's wonderful."

"He's a fruit," Ernie said.

⭑⭑

Soon after our visit we moved into a two-story brick house in a well-established middle class neighborhood. Mature shade trees lined the street. Two vacant lots (one ours) flanked our house. A long paved driveway led to a detached double garage behind our house. A masonry barbecue pit, one we would never fire, stood to the left of the garage. The house was only a block and a half from St. Charles. I abandoned the school bus, Mom walked to church, and Henry left the car in the garage on Sunday morning. Somehow Mom was able to quit working at the box factory. I no longer went to mass with her.

Nick Palmieri and Mike O'Reilly lived nearby and we became best friends during our last year at St. Charles Borromeo Elementary. Our diplomas enabled us to apply to any Catholic high school in the Cleveland area, if our parents could afford the tuition. The esteemed Jesuits taught at Saint Ignatius Loyola. It was the closest to Parma, considered elite and intellectually demanding, and the most expensive. I envisioned dreary, desk-bound days under the watchful eyes of brainy priests, their rulers tucked behind their backs as they patrolled the aisles looking for loafers to smack. We were sure we couldn't meet their stiff academic requirements. Nick planned to go to Holy Cross because he thought it was near Little Italy. Mike and I opted for Cathedral Latin. It was on the east side of Cleveland near 105th Street and getting there would require us to ride a city bus from Parma to the Rapid Transit station by the West Side Market. From there a Rapid Transit train that would whisk us through downtown, across a large section of

East Cleveland, and finally drop us at a station a few blocks from Latin, the total journey taking about an hour. Holy Cross would tack on about another ten minutes for Nick.

I suggested we meet at my house to survey our routes and pinpoint the exact locations of our schools. Mike arrived first. He'd talked to a guy who went to Holy Cross and Nick's reason for going was bogus. Nick showed up, and I spread a map of greater Cleveland across the kitchen table. We drew red circles around the locations of our schools. Mike repeated what the guy had told him; not only would Nick have extra travel time but he would also wind up in a Slavic community nowhere near Little Italy. Nick switched to Latin so fast I suspected he'd already discovered his error. We laughed and huddled up, draped our arms over each other's shoulders, and cheered his decision. We'd be the three amigos traipsing via bus and train across the City, even making a few extracurricular stops to explore downtown Cleveland, buddies forever.

⇥ ⇤

The following June, Cathy rode the Greyhound from Pittsburgh, where she attended Mount Mercy College. She'd come for brief visits during Christmas and Thanksgiving breaks and for a week between summer and fall terms, but this would be the first time she'd spend an extended time at home since the summer we arrived from Missouri three years ago.

After we picked her up at the bus station and drove home, I dragged her hefty suitcase upstairs and enlisted my knee to hoist it onto the bed in the spare room.

"God, this weighs a ton. Whatcha got in here—gold bricks?"

She smiled, laid her garment bag alongside her suitcase, and unzipped it.

"Well, I s'pose you wanna get unpacked. See you at dinner. Good to have you here. Any plans for the summer?"

"I'm looking forward to a summer of pure laziness," she said, laying a bunch of white blouses across her forearm. "I just hope I don't dream about exams and assignments."

Mom had other ideas.

"I've got it all arranged," she told Cathy over dinner. "You'll start at the bank on Monday."

"I'd planned to catch up on my reading."

"So? You can read after you get off work."

"But mother—."

"It'll be good for you," looking at Henry, "like David's paper route."

He was gnawing on a chicken leg. His silent nod blessed Mom's handiwork.

Cathy offered to treat me to a Friday night movie when she cashed her first paycheck, about the same time her feet stopped hurting. I wanted to see *Underwater* because the Catholic Legion of Decency had placed it on their coveted condemned list. We set out in plenty of time to make the eight o'clock showing.

Maples, oaks, and elms shaded the sidewalk on our block, but not the following long block leading to Ridge Road. It was as though we'd stepped out of a forest and onto a barren plain. A repetition of modest middle class homes on closely shaved emerald lawns absent of trees walled our left flank and, after a short run of similar houses, the vast St. Charles asphalt playground, the parking garages for the parish's cars, and the rear of my school bordered our right.

She chattered incessantly as we walked, asking how things were at home for Mom and me, how I liked my paper route, how I liked high school, and what I thought of the Brown v. the Board of Education Supreme Court decision. I said things were okay, though I disliked sharing a room with Mick, the paper route was okay without mentioning the bad part, and Latin had the best basketball team in Cleveland, if not the state. I skipped the Brown decision. She'd mentioned it during a previous visit and I couldn't figure why it was such a big deal. Negroes went to Latin. I also didn't tell her of the night I couldn't wake Mom or when I'd overheard her mysterious confession, as I hadn't been able to during Cathy's briefer visits.

"How's work?" I said when the light at Ridge Road halted her persistent questions as well as our feet.

"Okay now, but I was so embarrassed the second day. Mom fibbed to the bank manager. She told him I wouldn't be going back to school."

"She's always doing stuff like that for Henry."

The light changed. We crossed the four-lane highway and turned right, the theatre not far, just this side of Snow Road.

"Are you sure this movie isn't too risqué for you?" she asked, unaware of its rating.

"I saw the *Blackboard Jungle*."

"You did?"

"Uh-huh."

"Does Mom know?"

"Nope."

She opened her clutch purse and withdrew a dollar and some change as we approached the theatre.

"You know I'm going to Western Reserve next year," she said. "I want to be closer to you."

"Where's that?"

"It's in east Cleveland, not too far from your school. I'd like to live at home. Mom said I could study in the dining room, but there's no door between it and the living room, and the TV is always on at night. I wouldn't be able to concentrate. Plus I'll have a roommate, and that's kind of neat. Maybe you can visit after I get settled."

"Cool."

While Cathy paid our admission, I ogled the movie poster of Jane Russell in a red two-piece swimsuit. I could hardly wait to see her on the big screen in Superscope.

"I'm sure I'll know someone with a car who could pick you up," Cathy said in the austere lobby. "You know I promised Daddy I'd take care of you."

"Okay," I said, though in a few weeks I'd be fourteen and figured I could take care of myself.

It was dark when we left the theatre and headed to the traffic light by St. Charles' free standing bell tower.

"Not the best of movies. I suppose you liked the scenery." I nodded, replaying the smooth skin and colorful curves of half-naked girls.

As we passed a wooden bus stop shelter she gasped, grabbed my hand, and quickened our pace.

"Gee-whiz, Sis, where's the fire?" At the corner she tap-danced in place while we waited for the light. I knew something was wrong. When her worried eyes glanced back, I spotted their target. A rough looking man eyed us from the shadowy, waist high weeds behind the bus stop shelter.

"Hurry!" She jerked my arm when the light changed.

We streaked across the four-lane highway and matched long fast strides down the barren block. She peeked back often. She didn't speak. I kept my eyes straight ahead, afraid the man was bearing down on us. In the safety of our driveway, I braved a backward glance, at nobody.

⟞✛ ✛⟝

The following day I waited in front of the church for Al to arrive with the *Cleveland Press*. Across the street a thin woman wearing a coat that looked too heavy for the weather waited at the same wooden bus stop shelter. She held a small boy's hand. I couldn't see anyone lurking in sun-lit bushes.

Three paperboys, all at least two years younger than me, rolled in on their bikes. At first I had trouble remembering their names until nicknames set them in my mind: Brian the Short, Bulky Ted, and Bespectacled Sam. They called me The Scholar because I usually had a paperback jammed into my back pocket.

An ice blue chunky van zoomed up to the curb.

"Howdy, boys," Al said, setting the brake and leaping to his feet. A beefy guy, he wore his hair slicked back like a movie gangster's. "I got the news for yous."

He disappeared into the back of the Ford and hauled out heavy bundles wrapped in plain white newspaper, bound tightly with twine. He tossed them onto the sidewalk and flopped sideways into the driver's seat.

"Big contest going on," he said, leaning forward. Small beads of sweat dotted his brow.

"What?" Brian the Short asked.

"It's easy. Sign up the most subscribers in the next two weeks and ya win a two-way radio-wristwatch, like Dick Tracy's."

"Really?" said Bespectacled Sam, pushing his glasses up on his nose with his index finger.

"Does it work?" I stood back, arms folded.

"They say it does." His dark eyes narrowed and bore into me. "And *you* better get on those collections. Time's running out." He faced forward. His broad hands grasped the steering wheel. "See y'all." The van's wheels spit dirt as Al zipped into traffic behind a sleek Thunderbird convertible.

Bulky Ted, always an eager beaver, pounced on the bundles as if they were foul balls at an Indians' game. After he pulled his aside, we found our route bundles and cut the twine with penknives. We stuffed our blue bags with fresh news, folded the flyaway wrappers and shoved them, along with the cut twine, behind the papers, then mounted our bikes and pedaled away, each in a different direction.

I liked wheeling into driveways on my black Raleigh 3-speed. Collections and record-keeping were my downfall. On Saturday mornings I rang doorbells. The sleepy-eyed, unshaven, wild-haired man of the house would greet me with coffee cup in hand. Still in pajamas and robe, he'd yawn and scratch his chin or armpit.

"I'm a little short till payday," taking me into his confidence, "so couldja see your way to making it next Saturday?"

Or, the smiling Little Lady would answer. "My husband's not here right now. I haven't a cent. You'll have to come back later. Sorry." Still smiling, she closed the door gently, before I could ask when.

I had forty-two collection cards with lines at the top of each for a subscriber's name and address. Along the sides were the weeks of the year, six months to each side, and the dates when Saturday fell. A hole punched through the date indicated the customer had paid. A very efficient method, if I'd bothered to use it. After only nine weeks, I had no idea if the Hickmans owed for three or four weeks, if the Kolochuks paid for all of last month or just the first two weeks, if I'd ever collected a cent from the Lucarelli clan.

Every Monday I put my meager collections into a small manila envelope and handed it to Al. I never mentioned the people who stalled me or just weren't home. I didn't really care. In the fall I'd be a sophomore, too old for a paper route.

When Mom "personally obtained" it for me she said it would be a great way for me to earn spending money. She didn't mention her battles with tightwad Henry for my weekly allowance. A foul mood enveloped him when she called Uncle Joe long distance unless it was her brother's birthday. When she wanted to buy a power mower for our sprawling back yard and the larger adjoining lot, he said a push mower would give her good exercise.

CHAPTER NINE

Nick was sitting cross-legged on a shag carpet in his basement, the state driver's manual spread open on the floor in
front of him. He was a year older than me, having started school
late. His parents promised him a car for his sixteenth birthday
and he dreamed of driving us to Murray Hill, an area east of
Cleveland reputed to be the center of Little Italy and a Mecca
for streetwise teenagers. I had no such interest, but agreed to tag
along.

"I think I'm gonna ace this test," he said. "With a little more
practice I think I'll be able to solo, but I can't drive to school. Dad
says Latin's too close to the Negro part of town. Doesn't want it
parked on the street while I'm in class. The rest of the time I can
go where I want. Check out Lil' It'ly. Maybe even take a spin down
Short Vincent Street."

I groaned. I could tolerate venturing into Murray Hill. People
who worked honest jobs lived in homes there. Their kids went to
school. Most were law-abiding and patriotic. They watched TV in
the evening. No one lived on Short Vincent Street, the bent, short

block in downtown Cleveland where, behind unmarked doors, Mafia chieftains reputably settled territorial disputes, doled out bribes, and sealed fates. A disappearance on Short Vincent meant a snitch or someone deemed unfit or undesirable had taken a cement-shoed dip in Lake Erie or the Cuyahoga River. Or, so we had heard.

"We wouldn't have to bike or bus everywhere. Maybe even get some girls to go out with us. We could do that with a car, y'know."

"We don't know any girls, Nick. Where we gonna meet 'em? We go to an all-boys Catholic school."

"Yeah, but with a car I bet we could."

"Maybe."

"I've been talking to Mona. She lives down the block, y'know."

"Yeah?"

"Her tits really stick out when she wears a tight sweater."

My eyebrows winked.

"I dunno, I might ask her out. I could do it easy with wheels. Only problem is I don't think she's Catholic."

"So?"

The doorbell rang.

Nick's mother said, "They're in the basement."

Short and stocky, Mike galumphed down the stairs. He subdued his unruly reddish-blond hair with gobs of Brylcreem and carried a black comb in his shirt pocket for emergency repairs whenever his right-side cowlick sprouted.

"Hey, what's new?" He flopped down on the couch. Three unframed posters adorned the wall behind him—a map of Italy, a photo of the Basilica of St. Peter, and a field of evenly spaced rows of grapes on a sunlit hillside.

"Nick's getting a car."

"Just haveta take the test."

"Cool." Mike leaned forward, his right arm bent like a bracket. His left hand gripped his right arm's wrist and pushed down. His right arm resisted, flexing his right bicep, an exercise illustrated in the Charles Atlas "dynamic tension" booklet he had recently bought through the mail. He planned to join the Marines after high school, and he wanted to appear muscular when he stripped for his physical.

Nick tapped a cigarette out of a pack of Pall Mall and lit up. He tried to blow a smoke ring. Nothing alphabetical appeared.

"Gotta practice."

"When did you start smokin' at home?" Mike said.

"Dad figures I'm man enough since I'll be getting a car. He gave me this Zippo."

"Cool," Mike said.

"Hey, I got "Young Love!" today." Nick bounded to the record player, stopped and glanced back at us. "You guys can light up if you want."

He slid the 45 from its paper sleeve. "Young love, first love . . ." We smoked our Pall Malls and listened to Tab Hunter's strained voice, stared dreamily at the white tiled ceiling, and teased each other about true love, which, to our testosterone-fueled minds, meant sex.

Months passed before we rode to Angelo's Pizza in Nick's Mercury, a black sedan only a year older than the one James Dean drove in *Rebel Without a Cause.* I'd followed Dean's first film, *East of Eden,* from theatre to theatre and I did the same with *Rebel.* I yearned for a red nylon windbreaker like the one Dean wore in the movie, but the stores only stocked blue fleece-lined imitations. Mom bought mine at Sears.

It was a warm evening. A bunch of guys crowded the sidewalk in front of Angelo's. I thought they might be the Czars, Cleveland's biggest, toughest gang. In cold weather, they wore thick gray jackets with

C Z A R S appliquéd in black letters on the back. My stomach knotted as we edged past them. I remembered the day Nick and I were playing basketball at the St. Charles playground. Six basketball rims hung on my school's rear wall. We were playing at the one closest to the church when a commotion broke out four baskets down. A gang was taunting a tall, pale, gangly kid with bushy yellowish-tan hair. He stood with his back to the school's brick wall, beneath an orange hoop.

"Fruit! Fairy!"

A skirted, mean looking shiny black Chevy Bel Air bounced over the curb and onto the fenceless blacktop playground. The driver revved his engine and aimed the car toward the trapped kid, who did the only thing he could. He leaped, grasped the hoop, pulled himself up, and wrapped his legs around the rim. The car screeched to a stop inches from the wall.

"Kill the monkey! Kill the DP!" the crowd roared.

The car backed up. A short guy with knockwurst arms stood under the rim and jumped, reaching for the kid's feet. He couldn't put enough air between his feet and the ground. The mob groaned. "Pull up," he yelled to the car's driver, waving a Popeye arm. "I'll get on the hood and pull the fuckin' queer down."

The driver sneered as he applied equal pressure to the clutch and gas petals, holding the Chevy in place, rocking, menacing, rear tires spinning and spitting rubber. Then he released the clutch and the car lunged forward.

"Oh, shit," someone groaned.

A chorus of voices yelled: "Spilt! Spilt!"

Two robust priests sprinted toward us, their wooden crosses swaying like madcap metronomes. Three nuns trailed behind, their shapeless habits discreetly lifted above their black shoes.

The mob scattered. The Chevy turned a quick U. Engines roared. Tires squealed from the curb. A few stragglers threw themselves into open car doors like spears.

The priests veered toward the street, too late to catch anyone. The gangly kid had vanished. Nick and I sprinted between church and school, darted across Wilbur Avenue, and scampered through unfenced backyards on the way to my house.

"There's a spot." Mike pointed to a booth near the back of the crowded and noisy parlor. A young, good looking waitress was toweling the table as we seated ourselves.

"What's your hurry?" she said, smiling, her red lips moist.

"Hungry," Mike said.

We ordered big twelve ounce Cokes and the biggest mushroom and pepperoni pizza on the menu, talked about how we could go to a Browns or Indians game, or drive all the way up to Cedar Point, where we'd heard it was easy to pick-up girls.

"Pizza'll be up in a sec," the waitress said as she set down Cokes, glasses, plates, forks, and straws. We stripped our straws of paper and lanced our pops.

"The only problem is gas, y'know," Nick said after a while.

"We'll take turns payin'," Mike said.

"Cool."

"Nick's got a girlfriend." I lit a Pall Mall.

"There goes our rides," Mike said, throwing up his hands.

Drops of condensation from the bottles had leaked onto the table and Nick finger spread the beads in small circles. "Well, y'know," lowering his voice, "I sort of like Mona."

"Who?" Mike said.

"She lives on Nick's block. Goes to Parma High."

"She don't wear a girdle," Nick said, raising his voice a notch. "And you should see her tits in a tight sweater. I dream about feeling her up."

"Girls like to make-out in cars, especially if they feel sorry for you," Mike said.

"Think so?"

"Oh, yeah, my sister done it. She made out with Joe Babcock. Said they talked a lot—girls like that—and she let him kiss her a few times, but I think he got to second base."

"Joe Babcock's a creep."

"Like I was saying, she felt sorry for him because his girl dumped him."

"She's lucky she didn't get the clap."

"Christ, she only kissed him."

"You said he felt her up."

"Sh, sh," I said. The waitress was coming down the aisle and I was sure she was carrying our pizza. I ground out my smoke.

"There you go, gentlemen," she said as she slid a gigantic aluminum platter holding our pie onto the table. "Can I getcha anything else?"

We shook our heads and dug in. After we each scarfed down two slices and slurped half of our Cokes, I said, "Halloween'll be safer this year."

"You mean with the car," Nick said.

"It's gotta be better'n last year," Mike said. "Holy Spirit Cemetery my ass. I coulda died when those creeps jumped up from behind tombstones and took after us."

"We made tracks," I said.

Nick and I were the first to rendezvous at Wiley's drugstore, where we'd agreed to meet if separated. We hovered by the book and magazine racks, catching our breaths and tamping down our adrenalin. Nick, who'd paused to admire jack-'o-lanterns and fallen behind us, said he bolted back up the street like a runaway thoroughbred. Chased by hooligans intent on pulverizing me, I'd tapped into unknown speed, raced to Ridge Road, and darted headlong through a spilt second gap in the stream of speeding cars.

Mike stumbled in, winded. "Hey," he gasped. He stuck his hands on the sides of his waist and bent over, sucking in air. "I liked to bust my balls . . . climbing a tree. Hid on a damn garage roof until . . . the dumb bastards took off." He paused and his breaths steadied. "I think they got Jim. He's fast, but a whole bunch of 'em took out after him."

"Maybe he outran 'em," I said.

"They were big bastards." Mike clenched his teeth and narrowed his blue eyes. "When I'm a Marine I'm gonna come back with my buddies, find those bastards, and kick their asses."

"There's Jim," Nick said.

He limped by the front window and pushed through the door, licking his swollen lower lip. An angry abrasion sullied his right cheek.

Nick pulled a piece of pepperoni from his slice of pizza and casually tossed it into his mouth. "The watch saved him, y'know," he said, chewing.

"Hey, something weird happened to my sister and me a few nights ago," I said, not keen on evoking further memories of the fear I felt Halloween night. What if I hadn't made like Moses crossing the Red Sea?

"What?" Mike said.

"It wasn't anything, really."

"C'mon, you said it was queer."

"Weird. I said weird." I looked at Nick, then Mike. "Okay. We were walking home from a movie and this creep's hiding in the weeds by the bus stop, giving Cathy the evil eye. She was really scared. I figured I'd just give him the old one-two if he crossed us."

"If I'da been there I woulda beat the shit out of 'im," Mike said.

"Let's look for him later," Nick said.

"Yeah," I said with all the false enthusiasm I could muster. Not only did the guy look big enough to rearrange our faces but what if he packed a knife or a gun?

Mike flipped the pages listing the songs on the little jukebox at our table, searching for a title. Drop in coins, punch in the letter and number next to a tune, and from somewhere someone sang.

Our oft played game was about to begin, and we didn't need vocals, only song titles.

"Hey, here's a good one," he said. "Ain't That a Shame."

"Under the sheets!" we said.

Youthful male bonding united our mischievous smiles as our eager eyes scanned the titles.

"Young Love."

"Under the sheets!" We laughed.

"How 'bout—"Don't Be Cruel."

"Under the sheets!"

We hooted as our hands slapped the table.

"Will there be anything else?" the waitress said. We shook our heads. She laid the bill on the cluttered tabletop and smiled. We watched the sensuous sway of her hips as she walked away.

"No girdle," Nick said.

"Will there be anything else?" Mike whispered, mimicking her voice.

"You," Nick said.

"Under the sheets!"

⇒ ⇐

The hoods were still milling around the front door. Looking very much out of place, a small knot of collegiate types had joined them. It wasn't a friendly meeting. Close enough to exchange breaths, a tall, slender, fair-haired collegian and a stocky, round-shouldered hood glared at each other.

"He's pissed," Mike said, referring to the hood. We stepped past them, and Mike withdrew a black comb from his shirt pocket and fiddled with his hair.

"Hold up a minute," Nick said.

"Why?" Mike said.

"Be just a sec," Nick said, sidling toward the group.

Mike and I turned the corner and ambled down the sidewalk alongside the pizza parlor. We stopped halfway, lit Pall Malls, and leaned against cool cinderblocks.

"Lot of stars," I said, gazing up.

"Yeah, but it's hard to see 'em in city lights."

"Jim sure was lucky."

"Yeah, and smart, too, the way he pulled the watch off that bastard's wrist and told him he'd smash it on a rock if they didn't let him go."

"He bought time with a wristwatch"

"Hell, fast as he is they never shoulda caught him."

"They did, though."

"Cornered him, I bet. Bunch of chickenshit cowards if you ask me."

Nick sprinted toward us. "Let's go," he said.

"Where?" I said.

"C'mon."

We dashed to the Mercury.

"I got shotgun," I said.

"What 'bout the weirdo in the weeds?" Mike said.

A light blue Plymouth with painted flames flowing from behind its front tires roared away from the curb.

"Later," Nick said, slamming into first and pealing rubber.

"I don't like the middle," Mike said. "It's where a girl should sit."

"I'll take it next time," I said. "Where we going?"

"We're following them," Nick said.

"Where are they going?"

"Yeah," Mike said.

"I'm not sure. I think there's gonna be a rumble."

"There's a couple cars behind us," Mike said.

As we turned onto Snow Road, I counted four cars ahead and at least three behind.

"We're stuck," I said.

"Yeah," said Nick. His hands kneaded the wheel. "I can't turn off. These guys might think I chickened out, y'know. Remember the car."

"What do you think, Mike?" I said.

"I think this is pretty cool."

We turned onto Pearl Road, roared into Parma Heights, and parked on a grassy area two cars down from the fiery Plymouth. Cars skidded in. Doors flew open and boisterous kids spilled out, as if they were late for kickoff at a Parma High football game. They hustled down a slope to a small parking lot faintly lit by a light over the rear door of a business.

We stayed on the knoll. Nick and I stood a car length from the Plymouth. Mike sat cross-legged on the ground in front of the Mercury, his arms supporting his frame like tent posts, his head tilted back. Unseen crickets sang and a pizza moon hung high in a salty sky. The air felt tight.

Below, the college guy and the hood said something I could not hear. The hood wore jeans and a loose fitting shirt buttoned halfway, his collar turned up in back, the sides of his hair swept back. The Ivy Leaguer wore his hair short and neatly parted and he had outfitted himself in dungarees and a button-down blue shirt.

It happened fast. The hood slapped the college guy, drove a fist into his gut. The collegian doubled over. An uppercut snapped him upright. A third blow smashed his nose and buckled his knees.

The hood towered over him, his left hand cradling his right. A beefy crony gave him a friendly slap on the back and mumbled something that brought forth a thin smile. They swaggered away, the gang falling in behind. The hood grimaced and slowly folded and unfolded his right hand as they passed us.

"Bet that bastard never asks her out again," the hefty guy said.

"Think I broke my fuckin' hand," the hood said.

A few pals of the beaten lingered: silent, hands dipped into their pockets, heads bowed, shoulders hunched. He sat dazed on blacktop, his head tilted back, his face bloody.

"Did you see 'em?" Mike said, his elbow poking my ribs. We'd turned onto a well-lighted road and headed back to Parma. "Boy, I never seen so many stars."

"Bet that guy saw stars." Nick said.

"Sure got his clock rung," Mike said. He lit a Pall Mall and blew two perfect smoke rings toward the windshield. "The Commies would have a helluva time tryin' to take over this country. All the teenagers are just itchin' for a fight."

⊷+ +⊷

The following Saturday Nick gassed up at a Marathon station. Mike rode shotgun. I sat in back with Jim.

"Little It'ly, here we come," said Nick, shifting into second.

"Ever been there?" Mike said.

"Nah. I figure head downtown, then east."

"Cool."

"So, what's new, Dave?" Jim said.

"Nothin' much. You?"

"I'm lookin' to be on Benedictine's varsity football squad," he said, expanding his barrel chest. "I had a really good freshman year. You didn't try out at Latin, didya?"

"Nope. I got there too late for tryouts. I played freshman basketball."

"Yeah, you're built more for it. Tall. You were pretty good at St. Charles."

We passed the Royal Castle where I lost an eating contest to Mike. He ate nineteen little burgers. I'd called it quits after eighteen; I never should've had mine with onions.

"Hey, Dave," Nick said, "didcha ever get your collections caught up?"

"Nope."

"How many weeks behind are you?"

"'Bout a dozen."

"Twelve weeks," Mike said, whistling

"Yeah."

"You lazy or something?" said Jim.

"Gonna catch up 'fore you move?" Nick said.

"Move?" Mike said. "Where to?"

"Wadsworth. It's about thirty miles south of here, near Akron."

"How come?"

"My folks are buying a roadside tavern down there."

"Hey, maybe, you can sneak us out some booze," Jim said.

"Maybe," I said without conviction. "I think Henry got some kind of deal from work."

"Couple'a DPs," Jim said.

Two men in their thirties were strolling down the brightly lit street. They wore plain baggy suits like Grandpa's in old family photos.

"When you movin'?" Mike asked.

"Sometime next year. I think Mom's gonna ask your mom if I can stay with you 'till school's out."

"Wow, that'll be neat. We can listen to ball games. I just got a new radio."

Jim twisted around on the seat and stared at the men through the rear window. They grew smaller and fainter, like textbook examples of one-point perspective.

"What's a DP?" I said.

He turned and faced toward the front. "You know . . . a goddamn displaced person." He smiled, fisted his right hand, and massaged the knuckles. "One of them pissant refugees from Europe comin' here 'cause they got no home. Breaks my goddamn heart."

Nick's family came from Italy, Mike's from Ireland. Mom and Uncle Joe were kids from Czechoslovakia who didn't know they were poor when their ship sailed into Upper New York Bay. Blonde-haired Jim didn't look like Geronimo.

"What's wrong with 'em?"

"They screw up the country, always walkin' 'round askin' for a handout. Gimme this, gimme that."

"This ain't Little Italy," Mike said. He leaned forward and rested his hand on the dash. "That's West Side Market."

Just down the block was where we transferred from bus to Rapid Transit in our long commute to Cathedral Latin. Gloria and Ernie lived a few miles further west.

"I know," Nick said, "and the Terminal Tower's over there, so all I gotta do is head east, y'know."

"You're lost," Mike said.

"Am not," Nick said, turning.

Their words melted into a background of fuzzy vocals. The car drifted through air. I leaned my head toward the window. A comforting breeze fanned my face.

In the distance, orange flames licked the tops of a few smokestacks; others spewed gray-black smoke that stained the night sky. Block after block flickered by in neon; little stores, big and small factories, car lots, bars, apartment buildings, and diners all bled together. The tires hummed. The engine purred. The buildings grew larger, taller.

"It's gotta be around here somewheres," Nick said.

"Little Italy's downtown?" Mike said.

"No, no, Short Vincent."

"Well fuck, you been drivin' around in circles."

"What's on Short Vincent?" Jim said.

"It's the street where the Mafia takes care of serious business," I said.

"For Chrissake," Mike said.

"Some other time, O'Reilley. *Capeesh?*" Nick said.

"Yeah, like when you got a map and I ain't with ya."

I smiled. Nick abandoned his search, turned onto Superior, and followed it for a few blocks and turned right.

"Think I know a shortcut."

"Whencha dream this up?" Mike said.

I slid down further into the seat. The grease-stained pavement rolled on. My mind drifted to the night Cathy and I sprinted home after seeing *Underwater.* Did the shadow man live in one of these dives? If I saw him again, I'd report him to the cops and see my name in the *Press.* Then I'd bike into driveways to deliver spine-tingling details of my heroics. "Yep, that's yours truly," I'd say with a humble smile, knowing no one would dare shortchange a hero. If only I hadn't made a mess of my paper route. I'd let Mom down and I didn't know why.

Around seven on Friday payday Mick always managed to park the car a few feet short of the closed garage doors. It was a miraculous achievement, for afterwards he staggered to the house's side door, stumbled inside, and banged into walls as he reeled toward our shared upstairs bedroom. Beer breath clogged our air. Once he stirred in the middle of the night, belched, and vomited on his concertina jeans. Wiped his mouth on the sheet, turned over, and snored. Mom burned the jeans in the garbage incinerator in the basement and drowned the carpet by his bed in some kind of icky, pine scented cleaner.

Not long after, she found my scrapbook hidden in my lower dresser drawer, the pages filled with scantily clad starlets in alluring poses, Kim Novak my favorite. Outraged, she twisted my wrist, hauled me into the upstairs bathroom, yanked off my T-shirt, jerked up my arm, and slapped shaving cream on the wisps of hair she'd spotted.

"You're too young for this." She wielded a Gillette razor.

I wept protests of pain and humiliation on her deaf ears. She scraped until my armpits glowed bright red. Then she rinsed the razor, tidied up the sink, and went downstairs.

The following day her rage hadn't abated. After dinner, Henry and Mick settled in the living room to watch TV while Mom washed dishes and tidied the kitchen. I went to the upstairs bathroom before heading out for the evening. When I came down she grabbed my arm and spun me around.

"Just a minute, Mr. Dirty Pictures."

"What?" I shook off her left hand and spotted the yard stick in her right hand.

"I showed Henry and Mick what you've been up to. I'm so ashamed of you."

"Why? What'd I do?"

She whacked my thigh. Even with jeans on it stung.

"Mom," I said, gritting my teeth. Tears welled in my eyes. She'd never hit me before. Why now, in front of Henry and Mick?

"I burned your dirty pictures in the incinerator."

I wheeled toward the door. The small triangular glass windows at the top of the door were darkening.

"You stay right there." I froze. She lashed my thighs again and again. The last whack broke the yardstick. I stood still and silent, determined not to cry, my head bowed in mock contrition.

"We decided Mick should talk to you."

We?

Mick smiled at me from the couch. Henry rose, walked to the TV, and changed channels. She grabbed my hand and again pulled me to the upstairs bathroom. Mick followed. Mom retreated saying, "Now you listen to what he says."

Mick stepped into the bathroom and closed the door. I sat on the edge of the bathtub. His hulking frame loomed between the door and me. I raised my eyes to the greasy craters on his cheeks without lifting my head.

"Hey, Dave," smiling, "those were pretty good pictures. Where'd you get 'em?"

"Out of movie magazines."

"I can't believe girls let people take their pictures like that? I never knew girls were so dirty." I shrugged. "Mom asked me to talk to you 'bout it." I nodded, dropping my eyes to the white tiled floor. "Don't worry. I ain't gonna tell on you. I'll just say we had a man-to-man talk. Okay?" I again nodded. He shifted his feet and moved closer. "So you think about dirty girls a lot?"

"I guess."

"It's okay. Us guys do."

I looked up.

"It gets you excited, doesn't it, seeing girls almost naked?"

"Yeah." I shrugged.

"Are you big now?"

My scalp tightened.

"Let's take a look." He pointed at my crotch. A sudden paralysis seized me. He smiled and folded his thick arms. "C'mon, what're you waitin' for? You ashamed of what you got?" I shook my head and stared at the tiles. "Let's take a look. You want help?"

"I can do it," I said in a voice not my own. I unzipped and pulled down my pants and underwear. My shrunken penis looked like I'd just stepped out of a cold shower.

"That's a real pea shooter. Does it get bigger?"

"Sometimes," I said, trying not to shake.

"Let's see."

He reached for the light switch. Aside from the pale light bathing the glazed window we were plunged into darkness. His muted silhouette turned and bent down in front of me, his breath quick and heavy. He took my soft penis in his wretched hand.

"Think of them girls with their big tits showin' and their big asses stickin' out," he said as he stroked me. "The tip is real sensitive, huh? You like that."

I did and I didn't. I liked it, only I didn't want him doing it and I didn't want to imagine who I wanted to be doing it. I couldn't stop myself. I had begun to harden and I didn't want to do anything but scream, and I couldn't.

I tensed, grew longer than his palm, and I heard him make a cooing noise and he filled the space before me as he knelt and his tongue licked as if he held a lollypop instead of me and then he slipped me into his mouth and sucked. I fought the feeling welling in me, did not want the pleasure, and then he began to hum and I knew the tune, and I thought of Dad moaning in his grave, of Mom washing dishes, of Henry watching six-shooters blazing, of baseballs launched across city blocks, of Leon falling from the orange chestnut, of snowballs, yes, snowballs, cold, cold snowballs, and Mick sucked and hummed his dream as his saliva drenched me, and I vowed to deny him his warm taste, an icy beer for him, and I must think of prayer and crazed Father Mark and the jolting fear I felt when he suddenly fell upon me, yes, the fear, and then Mick pushed away, released me.

His long tentacle reached for the light switch and the globes ignited and I quickly pulled up my underwear and pants. I glimpsed his abhorrent smile. How could it be that I was here? I focused on a bar of Ivory in a dish by the corner of the tub.

"We better be quiet about this. Okay, Davy?"

I nodded, feeling shamefaced and apprehensive, unable to watch him go. Soon enough I'd be in a bed just a few feet across the room from him.

"Jesus, I knew you didn't know how to get to Little Italy," Mike said, the urgency in his voice pulling me back.

A timeworn corrugated building walled the street on my side. Nick had driven east all right. He slowed as we entered an intersection where a cluster of young Negro men haloed in the yellow light of a corner store stood beside a polished black Cadillac convertible.

"I musta taken a wrong turn, y'know."

"No shit," Mike said. "Christ, we ain't sightseeing. Just get movin'."

Jim leaned out the window and yelled, "Goddamn jungle bunnies!"

The group stiffened, their eyes flashed.

"Oh, for Godssakes," Mike said. "Knifes will be out any second."

"Go back to Africa!" Jim shouted.

Three scary guys with arms like jackhammers stepped toward us.

"Punch it," Mike said.

Nick mashed the pedal and popped the clutch. For a frightful moment I thought we might stall, but the rear tires squealed, smoked, and we screamed up the street.

"Haul ass!" Mike said.

Two of the Negroes dashed toward the Caddy. Others flooded the street, fists raised, middle fingers spearing the air. Lights on, the Caddy's driver swung a U-turn. The street was too narrow. He hit the curb, backed up, aimed for the wider intersection. Nick spun the wheel. The car fishtailed through a sharp right-hand turn. I tried to breathe. Jim laughed.

"They're gonna fuckin' kill us," said Mike, rolling up his window as if the thin glass would hold back decades of pent-up anger.

Nick hit fifty, weaved down empty side streets. At the end of a long block on Euclid, he slammed on the brakes and skidded through a left-hand turn and into a street with cars parked bumper-to-bumper. He slowed to thirty.

"I think we lost 'em," I said, looking back.

"Christ, don't slow down now," Mike said.

Jim sneered. His raised his hand out the window as if to catch the wind. "They won't do anything. They know their place."

I stared out the window, remembering a Little League game in Carthage. I was playing right field. In the top of the fifth the opposing team's power hitter, a lefty, stepped into the batter's box and launched a skyrocket, high but not far. He'd gotten under the ball a tad. I raced forward, my eyes fastened on the white orb, certain I'd make the catch. Just as I lifted my glove my spindly legs collapsed and I hit the dirt face first. Mud and water spewed from the sides of my uniform.

I slogged in after the inning, grass stains and mud plastered across my chest. A muddied face hid my shame. I couldn't tell if Andy, the team's manager and a DeSoto car dealer by day, was smiling sympathetically or smirking.

"Have a little trouble out there," he said.

"I was gonna catch it," I said, my voice cracking in an odd high-low mix of defiance and tears.

"They water out there when it don't rain. Keeps the grass from dying out." I blinked my stinging eyes. "Don't worry about it." He softly slapped my shoulder. "Next time you'll know."

Potbellied, bowlegged Coach Tim offered a wet towel. His free hand wiped a rivulet of tobacco juice from his chin. "Clean your face, Davy. We don't want folks thinking we got coloreds on this team."

Andy looked back at him and they shared a private smile.

I toweled my face, and sat at the far end of the bench, my glove in my lap. Jackie Robinson was a Negro who played for the major league Brooklyn Dodgers. Why not here? I tried to remember if I'd ever seen colored kids in my whole life. There were none at school or church, though I'd seen a few on TV, usually tap dancers, Rochester (Jack Benny's valet), or Stymie (a Little Rascal). I rolled the knotted end of my wet mitt's lacing, and stared into the velvet sky above right field.

Nick found a wide avenue, shifted into third, ignored the posted speed limit, and aimed for the white West.

"Slow down," Mike said. His hand trembled as he lit a cigarette. "I think we're okay."

⇥ ⇤

I steered the red Ferrari like a pro. Jane Russell sat beside me, wearing a tiny white bathing suit. She emitted a husky giggle as Gilbert Roland, and Richard Eagan shucked oysters into a large fishing net. I dipped my hands into the slimy catch, and fistfuls of oysters squished between my fingers.

On a warm white-and-turquoise beach, Lori Nelson, Jane's co-star, and I held hands as we strolled into a gorgeous tropical sunset. We lay on the sand and kissed, our passion hot as the frothy tide tickled our feet. Suddenly, the world convulsed. I couldn't shake the bothersome pressure.

"Wake up."

An undertow swept Lori away and I spilt into heavy chunks.

"Wake up."

Mom stood over me, jiggling my shoulder.

Her pinched brow, quivering lips, and squinched eyes said it all. "Get dressed and come downstairs, you little rascal."

I dressed slowly, dragged myself heavily down carpeted steps, and shuffled into the yellow kitchen.

She sat waiting. The collection cards for my route on the table.

Uh-oh, I thought. "What?" I said.

"You know perfectly well *what*."

I sat down and tried to look surprised.

"What?"

"Don't play dumb—your boss called this morning."

"Al?"

She paused. I studied the cloud pattern on the yellow and white Formica tabletop.

"What'd he say?" I asked with all the false innocence I could muster.

"He said you were not doing a satisfactory job. He sounded like a nice man. You disappointed him and me." Her heavy hand slapped the clouds, riffling my neglected cards. "He fired you! How could you let this happen? What am I going to tell Henry?"

I raised my eyes.

"I don't know, Mom. It just sorta got away from me."

Gray clouds scudded above me as I dragged myself to the corner. Everything was in the delivery bag slung over my shoulder: the penknife, seldom-used hole-punch, and deficient address cards.

Brian the Short kidded me about not having a book in my pocket. Bulky Ted and Bespectacled Sam chuckled. A runty little kid with a sprinkle of freckles rolled in beside me and straddled his shiny steed. A gust of wind swept dust. Al pulled up to the curb. He didn't jump up and dart to the back. Instead he sat sideways and gave me his phony hangdog face.

"Sorry, kid." He swiped his slick hair and rubbed his oily hand on his stained pants. "You left me no choice. I told ya 'bout makin' collections."

"Yeah, I know."

"I gotta a route ta run, too."

"Yeah."

He gave my gear the two-second once-over. "Looks like everything's here."

He looked over my shoulder and switched on his cartoon smile for the new kid. "Ready to go, Billy?" The kid's head bobbled. "Okeydoke, lemme get these other fellas on the road and I'll set you up."

"See ya," I said, shuffling away.

"Don't rush, kiddo," Al said.

I flipped a backhanded wave and glanced across the street. No one was waiting to board a bus. A sudden movement in the weeds caught my eye.

I waited for a traffic break, cut across the street, and patrolled the front of the bus stop. Clouds cast a dark blanket on wind-whipped weeds. Soon rain would splatter the sidewalk. Someday I'll spot him, flag down a cop, be on the front page.

CHAPTER TEN

A NASA weather plane was missing over Turkey. A spokesman said the pilot had reported oxygen difficulties. I yawned. A lost plane didn't sound like a big deal, but Mr. Samson believed any front page governmental story in the *Akron Beacon Journal* merited discussion in his Ethics class. "What happens in 1960 could well be in next year's textbooks," he'd said on the first day.

"How many eggs?"

Employing one hand, Mom set two eggs frying on the hot grill, then scooted into the bar to serve an early morning thirst.

I'd have to scour future editions for a follow-up. Mr. Samson expected us to monitor a story until he declared it dead. Sometimes the sneaky old bird sprung a pop quiz.

Within days I didn't need to search the back pages. The story of the missing plane soared into the headlines when the Soviets announced that they had shot down an American CIA U-2 spy plane. Mr. Sampson scoffed when asked about the Soviet claim. Hadn't our State Department said they deeply regretted the malfunctioning weather plane strayed 1,200 miles into Soviet airspace before it crashed? Hadn't we spoken with compassion when we requested the remains, if any, of the plane and pilot?

A few days later a classmate asked Mr. Sampson what he thought about the latest developments. Our normally opinionated teacher merely said, "The President needs our support," and grimly directed our attention to a below the fold article wherein a Justice Department official said he had unequivocal proof rock 'n roll was undermining the moral fiber of America's youth, his solemn arguments a rehash of past criticisms: wild dancing, suggestive lyrics, and thuggish appearance. He singled out Elvis Presley as a primary purveyor: "His indecent lyrics and greased hips ignite indecent thoughts in our youth."

I suspected Mr. Sampson's reticence to discuss the U-2 incident mirrored many others. The previous day, the Soviets said their missile had not badly damaged the plane and they had captured Gary Francis Powers, the pilot. With the implication clear, I imagined we and the Soviets were engaged in a serious cat-and-mouse version of *Mad* magazine's Spy vs. Spy cartoon.

＝＋ ＋＝

Our roadside tavern, The Hub Café, sat on a steel girder platform alongside a copper colored, snake-infested creek. Cars coming up State Street aimed at the bar's recessed front door before they turned onto Ohio 94, which the town named Main Street. Unlike our modern, airy brick house in Parma, our shabby living quarters above the bar emitted a musty smell. Some of the rooms lacked solid doors. Curtains separated my pocket-sized bedroom from the larger one Mick would have slept in had he not enlisted in the Navy, and the doorway from "his" bedroom into the living room was also curtained.

Molly, the barmaid, stayed on, tending alone until eleven Tuesday through Thursday evenings and with Henry on Friday and Saturday evenings. She possessed good bar business assets: in her early thirties, long black hair, pretty face. Her figure, while surely not as shapely as when she was younger, still turned many a workingman's head.

Henry and Mom logged twelve hour shifts. She was talkative and generous pouring shots, while Henry, according to Mom (from whom I gleaned information), was stingy and slow. Twice a week he made a lengthy afternoon trip to the bank and liquor store. "That man dawdles," she complained.

Early on, Henry traded booze for a .32 revolver. He stashed the revolver in a drawer under the cash register and, to my knowledge, never did test-fire it. Why he left the gun downstairs at night mystified me. The curtained doorway from the kitchen to the stairs afforded the dumbest burglar easy access to our living quarters. What would any of us do? Our only house phone hung on the wall at the foot of the stairs.

We stocked the usual assortment of bar snacks—pretzels, potato chips, teeth-cracking corn nuts, and twisted pepperoni sticks, the latter packed in tall glass jars. Mom listed her cooked contributions on a large piece of butcher paper tacked on the wall above the pop machine. She served bacon-and-eggs, white toast, pickled eggs, and hamburgers. *Halupkis,* Slovak cabbage rolls stuffed with rice and meat, were her Saturday special, scrawled on the menu as "pigs-in-a-blanket."

There were no posted service restrictions, but nearly all of the customers were white males, roughhewn transplants from the over-mined hills of West Virginia and Southwestern Pennsylvania who'd migrated north to find work in above ground factories. They cashed Friday paychecks and filled the dozen red vinyl-topped barstools and the wooden chairs around three, small black-topped tables with their tired muscles, sweat and laughter. The Christmas-colored jukebox added Eddy Arnold's velvet voice to the din of their shouts and grumbles.

Mom fancied the bar after a relative stopped by our house in Parma and boasted about his tavern in Michigan, a real money maker. Cathy and John, her new boyfriend, visited, and she said it was like stepping into a Nelson Algren novel.

One Friday night, cruising the square in Bob's two-tone, turbo-charged '57 Chevy, the car radio tuned to a Cleveland rock 'n roll station. Up front were two of Wadsworth High's elite: Bob Walcott, the football team's powerful fullback, and Joan Williams, his steady, the school's sexiest cheerleader. Karen and I snug in the back. I was nervous.

My new school pals assumed I knew my way around girls. They'd heard stories of girls going "all the way" with Big City guys, and living above a bar in the seedier part of town only added fuel to their imaginations. I quietly listened and nodded, as though affirming I'd been one of those guys instead of admitting I'd never even been on a date. I wondered what tall tales Karen had heard.

Bob swung a neat U-turn at the tail of a median divider, crept by the Western Auto store and Citizen's Bank, and stopped at one of the town's two traffic lights. The other light was in front of the Hub. Marie waved as she and Pete pulled alongside in his sweet looking blue Olds, an early graduation gift from his indulgent parents. After school, I often walked her to the street while Pete fetched his four-wheeled darling.

"What do you think of Karen Schroeder?" I'd asked Marie the previous week.

"Hmm, she's pretty. She's a junior so I don't really know her. I hear she reads a lot." She grinned. "You like her." I shrugged. "Don't be so shy." She laughed, rolled her eyes as Pete pulled his buffed Olds up to the curb. "Take a deep breath and ask her out." Pete stretched his long arm across the vinyl upholstered bench seat and pushed the door open. Marie slid in, closed the door, and tossed me a backhanded wave as they sped away.

Afraid of rejection, it took me awhile to gather the courage. Beautiful Karen smiled, and scribbled her number on a scrap of notebook paper. "Call me," she said as she backpedaled down the hall.

We tooled the square a second time. Up ahead, a man stumbled out of the Buckeye Bar.

"Poor Doc Simpson," Karen said looking away.

"Mom says he used to be good," Joan said.

"I hear he's got the shakes bad," Bob said. "Wouldn't want him cutting on me."

"A real lush," Joan said.

"What's he gonna say after a botched operation?" Bob said. "Sorry about that, kiddo. I was aiming for your appendix." Joan giggled. "Besides," Bob said, cutting the corner and revving the engine, "I heard it was a backdoor job."

The gurgling dual glasspack mufflers growled, and we sped out of town. Karen was still staring out the open window. Swift warm air rumpled her long blonde hair.

After a few miles I said, "I hear you like books."

She rolled up the window, settled back in the seat, finger combed strands of hair from her face. "I just finished *Look Homeward, Angel.*"

"I've been reading a lot of Steinbeck and Mark Twain."

Bob clicked on the turn signal. I winced when I saw the Montrose drive-in's marquee.

"Oh, I've read this," Karen said.

"Well don't wreck the ending," Joan said as she playfully clamped her hands over her ears.

Bob eased onto a gravelly hump in the ground and parked next to a steel pole. Joan unhooked the speaker from the pole and hung it on her half-raised window. Ads for the concession stand flashed appetizing towers of candy, popcorn and colossal soft drinks as orange twilight knifed through a line of elms.

We chose our treats, and Bob and I headed for the utilitarian cinder block building housing the concession stand. We fell into a line of energized teenagers filtering toward the snack bar.

"Why'd you pick this movie?" I said as we edged forward.

"Sounded sexy." He winked and elbowed my arm. "Ava Gardner on the beach."

"Ah, as in the sexy beach scene in *From Here to Eternity.*"

"Uh-huh. Puts chicks in the mood. Know what I mean?"

"You may be a bit disappointed."

"Don't tell me you've read the book too?"

"Uh-huh."

I felt bad for Bob. He was anticipating a sexy, romantic movie, not one about thermonuclear war.

"The book was better," Karen said as Bob pulled onto the highway.

"Creepy," Joan said.

"Who's not afraid of being blown up?" I said.

"It was a little too talky, but still pretty cool," Bob said.

"It scared me," Joan said.

"I'll protect you." Bob shifted into third and wrapped his muscular arm around her inviting shoulders.

I turned my head and greeted Karen's willing lips.

⊨ ⊨

Ed Schroeder opened the door, his eyes nearly level with mine. Square-shouldered, sandy hair mowed low, he stood as straight as a plumb line, his strong jaw signaling no quarter.

"Is Karen here?" The words barely cleared my lips when I saw her near the top of the stairs, wearing black shorts and a green tee. A long-legged woman I assumed to be Karen's mother was perched on a step. Karen eased by her and bounced down the staircase.

Ed issued a curt nod and stepped aside. Karen took my hand and led me toward the backyard. We walked alongside a sturdy hedge and ducked under a tall cherry tree's low branches.

"Nice legs must run in your family."

"Dad's not too talkative at first. He's a foreman at Goodyear."

So much for lighthearted praise, I thought. We skirted the graveled driveway and sat on lush grass. A wall of flowering lilacs sweetened the air. She'd just finished *Candide* and thought I'd like it.

"In an infinite universe all things are possible." She pointed at the pale blue evening sky. "Somewhere up there our twins are glued to a planet exactly like ours. Whatever we do, they do. We should blow ourselves a kiss."

We made out on the couch after Ed went upstairs.

"Did you see *Blue Denim*?" she asked. "Do you think girls always get pregnant?"

"I don't think they *always* get pregnant."

"You'd have to be nuts to take the risk without protection."

⇒+ +⇐

I polished my shoes, tamed my hair with a little dab of Brylcreem, and slipped into my snazzy, albeit rented, prom tux. I knew Mom wanted a look-see and I wanted to collect the prize.

Henry smelled like a salesman for Old Spice and El Producto. He handed me his treasured car keys, then unhooked the ubiquitous smokestack from his thin pale lips.

"Don't do nothin' I wouldn't do," he said, emitting a muted chuckle.

"You look nice, Mom said. "Behave yourself."

Karen floated down the stairs in a décolleté pink formal, her hair spun into a silky beehive. She looked like she'd stepped from a page in *Vogue*. I carefully pinned a white corsage on her formal. Silent Ed watched from the hallway.

We followed Bob and Joan to Chippewa Lake. At the Oaks lodge we drank Hawaiian punch from paper cups and munched on brownies and cookies. I didn't dance well and Karen didn't seem to mind. I liked holding her close for slow numbers.

Around midnight I parked in front of her house and kissed her. "Careful of the corsage." We kissed, kissed, kissed. I cupped her breast opposite the orchid. She murmured a word or moan and we kissed again. "It's late. I better go in."

We held hands going up the walkway to the door.

"I had a very nice time, Dave."

We embraced and sustained another whopper of a kiss.

"Will you take me to *my* prom next year?"

"Sure."

"That'll be great, to be escorted by a college guy."

⊨⊨

The following day we made out on the living room couch after Ed climbed the stairs to join his reclusive wife. I dry-humped Karen and headed home.

⊨⊨

She passed her driving test in July and the following Saturday Ed let her use the car. At Chippewa Lake we stripped to our swimming suits and unfurled bright towels on warm sand. I squirted gobs of Coppertone on her sun-browned legs and slowly caressed her oiled skin.

"Can you come to dinner tomorrow?"

"I don't see a problem. I wondered if I'd ever meet your mom."

"You never will. Laura's my Dad's wife. *My* mom died when I was seven."

I don't know why I didn't tell her my father also died when I was seven.

⇥ ⇤

I glanced over my shoulder when I rang the doorbell. Ominous clouds were gathering in the western sky, the air hot and sticky. I flapped my shirt, fanning my chest and underarms. Across the street four grade school girls played hopscotch on the sidewalk.

Karen answered my ring, looking especially appealing in a pale crepe blouse and blue skirt. Laura darted up beside her. Blonde and slender in a flowered, low-cut sundress revealing eye-catching cleavage, her dark eyes evoked a blend of fascination and alarm. Rouge lacquered her cheeks. She kissed my cheek. I blushed.

Karen claimed my hand. The dining room was off to the right, and Ed was sitting at the dressed table. "Hi," I said, and he glanced at his wristwatch and nodded. Karen and I followed Laura into the kitchen. I felt like I'd stepped into a steam bath. I fanned myself with my shirt.

"How do you like yours?" Laura said as she plopped thick steaks into a hot frying pan. The beef sizzled.

"Medium." The thought of blood pooling on my plate turned my stomach.

Laura shifted over a few feet, picked up a wooden spoon from the counter, and stirred buttered green beans simmering in a pot. She began to softly sing a tune unknown to me.

"I saw some girls across the street playing hopscotch," I said to make conversation.

The source of the hellish heat became apparent when Karen pulled a casserole dish from the oven, put it on a counter, and sedulously undressed foil wrapped baked potatoes, slit them open with a butter knife, and squeezed the sides. She gave her heated fingers a cooling shake before she buttered the steaming white flesh.

"You, uh, better take over, Karen," Laura said, looking pale as she walked away.

Karen flipped the steaks.

"Is she all right?" My fingers swept beads of sweat from my forehead.

"They're going to a movie after dinner," she said. Her eyebrows winked at me.

She stirred the green beans and poured them into a bowl and set the potatoes on a platter, and handed the bowl and platter to me and waved me toward the dining room.

"I'll be right in."

Laura, who seemed to have made a quick recovery from whatever ailed her, and Ed were sitting across from one another. A rotating fan on a small writing desk aimed a modest but ineffectual breeze at the dining table.

"Hot stuff," I said, setting the warm bowl and platter down on trivets. They exchanged cheerless smiles. I sat next to Ed. I glanced at Laura's provocative cleavage and blushed. A couple of long, uncomfortable minutes passed before Karen appeared with the steaks.

"Looks good," I said. She smiled, served me a steaming potato, and passed the green beans.

We ate in silence, as if no one knew how to jumpstart a conversation. It felt strange. I was used to hearing bar sounds and jukebox music. Even on Sundays, the bar shuttered by Ohio Blue Law, idle conversation drifted around the table as Henry, Mom and I ate. I glanced at Laura. Ed had married an attractive, younger woman.

I tried to think of something cheerful to say without seeming flirtatious. Laura intercepted my glance and smiled. I grinned and winked. Her lips quivered and she lowered her eyes.

Ed interrupted our silence. He had spent the better part of the afternoon washing and waxing his Buick. Now he thought rain would tarnish his labor. His tone and facial expression implied he was not overly upset. I admired his acceptance of what he could not control.

"The clouds were piling up when I parked out front."

"People didn't think about garages when this house was built. An added expense few could afford."

I thought of asking if he eventually planned to attach a garage and held my tongue. A storm was brewing and his freshly waxed car sat unprotected on the graveled driveway. He seemed to take it all in stride, but I didn't want to push the issue.

"Was your steak okay?" Laura asked. Her voice had taken on a throaty tone.

"Delicious," I said and smiled.

I savored the last morsels while Laura shifted her remaining green beans into geometric patterns with a butter knife. Ed reached across the table and touched her hand, startling her. "Don't worry, dear," she said. She looked at me and her soft eyes fluttered. "You must excuse me. Sometimes I do get a bit distracted."

Karen and Laura started on the dishes. Ed insisted I see his wax job. He squeezed a red shop rag as he led me out the back door.

"That pilot should be dead," he said. "They all have poison pills."

"The U-2 pilot?"

"The Russians are going to put him on trial. For what, getting lost? We should put the Reds on trial for shooting down an unarmed plane. I have the utmost confidence in Ike. He won't let them get away with it."

I didn't know what to say. Just as well, for he stuffed the rag in a back pocket and locked his hands on his waist and focused on the shiny Buick. I imagined it to be his common work stance as a hot and humid wind teased my face. I searched roiling clouds for flashes of lightning.

"Meguiar and elbow grease made the difference." The red rag hung from his back pocket like a warning flag. "So, David, I assume you do plan to go to college."

"Oh, yessir. My dad was career military when he died. The VA will pay my way through college. I'm headed to Ohio U this fall."

"What's your major?'

"Not sure yet."

He rubbed the side of his neck. "Not thinking of being a doctor, are you?"

"The smell of ether makes me sick."

"I can't imagine why someone would want to fill his days with suffering."

The sky flashed not far from us and thunder shook the air. A serious wind stung my face.

"Maybe we should go inside."

"Here, now don't be hasty. I'll demonstrate my professional technique. Looks like I missed a spot anyway." With rag in hand, he stretched to reach an unglazed speck on the hood. "See what it takes?" He wiped thin lines of overlooked wax from around portholes. "Always sweat the details, David. Double-check the fractions. That's what I tell my men. It's why we build the best tires."

I nodded, put aside my fear that any moment a bolt of lightning could toast me, and shadowed him as he circled the car, a hardworking guy who'd landed a desk job and saved enough to buy a nice house in a small town near Akron, a house no bigger or better than the one we'd had in Parma. Just because I now lived in a dumpy apartment above a dive frequented by men with dirt under their nails didn't mean we were all that different. I wanted to tell him we'd had a two-story brick house in a spiffy suburban neighborhood and Henry had been a foreman at Republic Steel, and the Hub Café with its mini restrooms was a temporary stop, but the sky grew darker, thunder wrinkled the ground beneath our feet, and an ominous dust devil danced down the street.

"Sheeets! I picked the wrong day."

He wadded the polishing cloth, flung it on the ground, and stomped toward the house. I bent to pick up the rag as a sort of courtesy.

"Let the goddamn thing be!" he growled from the door.

⇒⊹ ⊹⇐

Karen was sitting on the couch in the living room. I plopped down beside her, feeling a bit shaky after Ed's rag outburst. Ed started to ask her something when a loud crack of thunder smashed his words. Heavy rain pelted the window. He stared out, then turned to face us.

"Where's your---"

Karen rolled her eyes and pointed up. He spun around and dashed up the stairs. I sat beside Karen, searching for words to explain my unease. Angry voices erupted upstairs. I looked at Karen. Her lips tightened, her averted eyes fastened on the opposing wall. An awkward few minutes passed before Ed and Laura descended.

Wearing an unadventurous, high-necked brown dress, Laura shuffled across the rug and stiffly sat in an overstuffed chair, her hands primly folded on her lap. Ed stood by the window, somberly staring at the downpour assaulting his day's labor.

"Maybe we shouldn't do it," he said, clenching a fist at his side.

Laura sank deeper into the chair, her face ashen.

"Oh, go ahead and go," Karen said. "You've talked about seeing *Some Like it Hot* for weeks."

"We talked back then," Laura said, turning toward Karen and me. "About what we should or shouldn't do." She lowered her eyes. "It could've been different."

Ed wheeled and faced her. "For the love of God it's over and done," he said, his pitch somewhere between anger and impatience.

"It's really coming down," I said for no apparent reason.

"It's only rain," Karen said.

"Maybe it will vanish, like summer children," Laura said.

"She's been saying that since I started first grade," Karen said.

"Please excuse my wife, David. Sometimes she gets too wrapped up in . . . things."

"We'll only do it if you say so, Eddie. We always do."

"Then let's get ready and brave the elements like good soldiers," he said, forcing a smile and patting her sloping shoulder.

The fast-moving storm raced toward drier ground, and Ed and Laura climbed into the drenched Buick and drove off into orange-yellow shafts of sunlight. Karen and I sat on the front stoop for a while, enjoying the cool air and talking. When we went back inside, she locked the doors and we necked on the couch. Within minutes I was hot to dry-hump her. She gently pushed me back, arched her blonde eyebrows, and unbuttoned her blouse. It slid off her gorgeous shoulders. She reached behind her back and unhooked her bra, leaned slightly forward and with a little shake the straps slipped down her arms. I ogled her naked breasts.

"Well," she said.

My heart raced mightily. I fondled her breasts, fingered her erect nipples. She unzipped me. My penis sprang to life. I pushed up her skirt. She wasn't wearing panties.

"Do you have—?"

I shook my head—who did I know with a rubber? She pulled me down and took my hard penis in her hand and closed her eyes, and rhythmically rubbed me against herself and I dissolved, mixed with her dissolving, in warmth, the tip of my penis dipping in for a small taste, no more than an inch, sweetly, her hand tight, in control, rubbing me against her wet warmth for a long, long time . . . until she softly moaned. Then she pushed me away, sat up, and yanked down her skirt. I sat beside her ready to burst, yet strangely contented.

"Pull your pants up," she said, rising and brushing the front of her skirt. "I forgot to close the drapes."

≕ ╪═

We ventured outside. The air smelled of ozone. We strolled down the block and back. She was reading Ibsen and thought I would like *Peer Gynt* because it was unusual. I nodded, thinking that something she had said earlier sounded odd, but I couldn't remember why I thought so or when I'd heard it. Back inside I wanted to make out again, but she had lost the fire. Still keyed up, I headed to the Little Inn, the beer and wine bar a few miles outside of town.

At best, the red cinder block building was functional and clean: undressed concrete floor, utilitarian chairs and tables, unadorned walls. The bare bones atmosphere didn't bother me and I never heard any of my pals complain about our hangout's lackluster ambience. We came to shoot the breeze, play euchre, and guzzle 3.2 beers, the only alcoholic drink an eighteen-year-old could legally buy in Ohio in 1960.

As usual, Bill, the owner, was behind his small horseshoe shaped corral. I ordered a frosty mug and carried the golden liquid into the open room to the side of the bar and settled in with friends dealing euchre. I wanted a beer or two and their company. I had no intention of telling them what had happened between Karen and me.

I'd played a few hands when Bob came in looking low in the saddle. He flicked a halfhearted wave our way, slumped down on a stool at the bar, and ordered a beer. He inhaled a deep pull and hunched over the mug. Bowling Green had given him a football scholarship. I hadn't seen him since he returned from freshman practice and it didn't look as though it had gone well. I bowed out of the next hand and eased onto the stool next to him.

"Hey, buddy." I lightly tapped his brawny shoulder. "How're ya doing?"

"Shitty," he said without looking at me. "I'm second string on the goddamn *freshman* team."

"Really?" Bob our star, record-setting running back, a bench-warmer? Four schools had offered him football scholarships.

"A goddamn hotshot from Massillon beat me out."

Ah, Massillon, the powerhouse Ohio football school.

"Bastard cuts and fakes like a goddamn fish." His thick fingers swept his disheveled hair as he turned his head and looked at me. "Hell, I never was much of a swimmer."

"You're a power runner, Bobby. Hit the line, break tackles."

"Linemen are a helluva lot bigger." He jerked a thumb at the red cinder block wall behind us. "Almost like runnin' into that."

We drank. I thought it best to drop the football talk.

"How's Joan?"

"Aw, shit." He gulped his beer, wiped his mouth with the back of his hand, and ordered another pint. "Her aunt lives in Toledo, so she came up with me. We figured to have a great time." He grunted. "Bitch fell for some varsity bastard—wide receiver."

I grimaced. Unlike Bob, I'd never tell a guy a girl broke up with me.

Bill put a cold mug in front of Bob and scooped up the charge from an assortment of coins scattered on the counter.

"Dammit, I'm all screwed up. I can't believe she did that to me. We'd only been there a week. How the hell was I gonna concentrate on football?" He sucked off the foamy head and made short

111

work of round two. "I don't think I'm gonna stick it out. I hear they're hirin' at Goodrich. Pay's good." He fingered the mug as though debating another quick round. "So much for my bullshit. How 'bout you? Still seein' Karen?"

"Yeah."

"Know what I think? Fuck her if she'll put out and date other broads. If she's for real it'll only make her want you more."

Before I could question why he thought jealousy would make the heart grow fonder he stood, retrieved a few coins from the counter, and laid a heavy hand on my shoulder.

"That's what I fuckin' shoulda done."

"Hmm, I'll keep that in mind. Hey, wanna jump in a game?" I head gestured to the guys at the tables.

"Nah, I just popped in to prime the pump. I snuck some Seagram's 7 outta the house. I'm gonna head up to the lake and get smashed." I frowned. He grunted. "Don'tcha know it don't make a goddamn bit of difference, Dave. They're gonna blow us all up anyway."

⇥ ⇤

World affairs were far from my mind at Ohio U. I missed Karen and masturbated when I read her scented letters, the upside down stamps on her sky blue envelopes a silent message of love. I sent her my longings wrapped in plain white envelopes, the stamps inverted. A few weeks into the semester she, Ed and Laura drove down to nearby Nelsonville for a weekend visit with Ed's elderly parents.

After lunch on Saturday, Karen skipped out with the car. She looked sexy in a flowing green skirt and white blouse. The warm afternoon spent kissing, talking and holding hands as we toured the campus. It felt good showing off my world, one far removed from the Hub's shabbiness.

"I just finished *Lady Chatterley's Lover*," she said. "Have you read it?"

"Parts of it."

"Probably the dirty parts, huh."

She didn't have to be back until eleven. We ate a country fried steak dinner at Blackwell's, a popular eatery on Court Street near the campus. It was dark when we stepped out. I wanted to take her someplace where we could be alone. I knew my roommate went to Zanesville for the weekend, but a sacrosanct rule enforced by instant expulsion said girls couldn't step foot inside the dorm.

I drove to a large, poorly lit parking lot along the Hocking River, set the brake, and kissed her. I soon pinned her against the seat, slipped my hand under her dress, and caressed her firm naked thighs. I wanted her to unzip my pants, take off her panties, and rub me against herself.

"Not here," she said.

"Please. I love you."

She sighed and wrapped her arms around my back. Without trying to lift her skirt again or unzipping my pants, I pressed against her, smelling her perfume and the vinyl seat as I ejaculated in my underwear.

⊨ ⊨

On the drive home with Pete and Marie for Thanksgiving break I thought of Karen's brief letters. Both arrived in plain envelopes, the stamps upright. The first complained I'd bruised her thighs; the second, a short note of weather and routine. I wondered if she had gone out with anyone. I had had a few dates. Why did I think it would be different for her? I cringed when I thought of some oversexed, zealous jerk trying to paw what was rightfully mine.

I'd been naive, more country bumpkin than city slicker, content with dry-humping. I now knew she yearned for naked passion. I should have scoured the dorm, found someone with a rubber. Surely there was a Travelodge in Athens.

As we drew closer to Wadsworth the rush of trees and fields sang warm memories of our summer rambles. I had the prized rubber tucked in my wallet and an article about The Pill. Maybe Ed and Laura would go to a movie.

⇌ ⇋

"You should've called," Ed said.

A woman was crying. It sounded like Laura.

"Is Karen home?"

"She's out."

"When will she be back?"

"She knows to be home before twelve."

"I'll call her," I said as he shut the door.

I dialed on Thanksgiving and hung up after countless annoying rings. I tried again on Friday. Ed answered. Karen had gone out with friends. He would tell her I called. Crestfallen, I didn't know what had gone wrong between Karen and me or how to fix it. I felt on edge, anxious to go somewhere or do something without knowing where or what. I found myself in the drab living room, ready to kill the evening watching TV with Henry and Mom. A traffic light hung over the intersection outside the living room window. When Henry sat in the chair with the shade up the changing light softly painted his face: green, yellow, red. Now the shade was drawn and I imagined the muted flashes to be the cries of silenced souls trapped in purgatory.

The following day I wore out my finger dialing her number. Henry finally surrendered his car keys. I turned around halfway to her house. I didn't want to look as desperate as I felt. It was early evening before she finally picked-up. Her frosty voice said she didn't write because she no longer knew what to say; "No," she wasn't involved with anyone; "No," she didn't think we should see each other right now.

"But I'm leaving tomorrow and won't be back until Christmas break. I wanted to show you my new boatneck. They're in style now."

"I'm sure they are," she sighed.

⟞⟝ ⟞⟝

It was dark when I drove my disheartened self to the Little Inn. My euchre buddies must have been home packing or out on dates with their sweethearts, for I drank alone at a table, shuffling and reshuffling a worn deck. I was draining my third pint, ready to call it a night, when Bob sauntered in and pulled up a friendly chair.

"Goin' back tomorrow?" I said after we exchanged warm greetings.

"Hell, man, I never went. I got on with Goodrich building tires. It ain't the worse thing in the world and the paychecks are fat." He pointed at my empty mug. "I'll get us a round."

Bill pulled two frosted mugs out of the cooler, filled them from a tap, and Bob carried them to the table. I drank deeply. He tasted shallow waters.

"Nothing like a cold beer," he said.

"I owe you one."

"Don't sweat it."

I took a short pull, not wanting to speed too far ahead. "Ever see Karen around?"

"Saw her with some guy a few weeks ago. I figured you must've broken up 'cause he had his arm around her waist."

He could just as well have hit me in the gut. I felt cold and empty. How cozy was an arm around her waist? My eyes met his and I set the mug on the table. What to say?

"I'm right, aren't I?" he said, his brow creased. "You did break up with her?"

"Oh, yeah," and having given the lie birth I added a life, "I suggested it before I left for Ohio U. She wrote me a few times and came down once and we made out some, but I told her it was her senior year and she should enjoy it, not feel tied down. Come summer I'll see how I feel." I drank, deeply. "Yeah, that's what I told her." In my mind's eye I imagined some mealy-mouthed creep with his tongue in Karen's mouth while he felt her up.

"You must've wanted to play the field a bit."

"Yeah."

"Did she ever, you know, put out?"

"Nah, but we came close." I drank.

Bob took a deep pull, wiped his chin with his hand, wiped his hand on his pants, and said. "I'm dating Sheila Barnes. 'Member her?"

"Cute, but standoffish."

He smiled. "That's what I thought. Turns out she was shy. I think she just developed too fast."

"She always was a looker."

"You should see her now. I'm going slow if you know what I mean, but, I dunno, she might be the one." He leaned forward, a spy with info. "Say, didcha hear about old doc Simpson?" I shook my head. "Messed up on some girl and got disbarred."

I frowned. "Disbarred? Isn't that what happens to lawyers?"

"You know, I think you're right. Anyway, scuttlebutt says it wasn't his first by any stretch, just the first that went sour." He snapped his fingers. "Hey, remember the time I said I wouldn't want that booze hound operating on me?"

"Sure. The night we double-dated and you wanted to drool over Ava Gardner."

"Hey, that's right."

"Poor Doc Simpson," I said, shaking my head.

"Way it goes. He was our doctor when I was a kid."

"And Karen's."

A couple of our friends bounced in, scouting for poker players. Bob was game. I said my sister was in town and I promised to spend some time with her before I went back to Ohio U. I drained my mug and told Bob it was my turn next time, and he nodded.

The autumn night had cooled when I pulled out of the Inn's parking lot and headed toward town. Cathy and John had married, and they were still in Cleveland. I declined the poker invite because I had to talk to Karen. I wanted her to tell me Bob had seen her on a harmless date. Say she'd temporarily yielded her waist to some pushy cretin. No big deal. The rubber rode in my wallet.

My reverie wrecked as I entered the city limits. How romantic would a face-to-face be if I reeked of beer? Even so, I held my course through town, spun a new plan, and parked down the block from her house. I was wearing jeans and a dark brown shirt, which I thought lent me a good degree of invisibility. I planned to sneak up to the living room window and, if the curtains weren't drawn, peek at her while she watched TV or read a book. I didn't know why I thought a few minutes of sight alone would mend my fractured spirit.

No sign of life downstairs. A light sketched an upstairs bedroom. The thought of ogling her as she undressed inflamed my mind. I saw no sign of wakefulness in the house next door as I crept alongside the hedge and crouched beneath the cherry tree. My heart raced as I stared up at the maze of hibernating branches. Problem: I'd never been a tree climber as a kid. The muscles in my arms protested as I hoisted myself up. The relatively smooth bark irritated my sweaty hands. I should've thought to wear gloves. But, I hadn't intended to scale a tree. I gingerly climbed higher. Some of the lower branches were as thin as my arm. They bent beneath my 160 pounds. Best not step too far out on any of them. Stick to the middle.

I settled on a sturdy limb twelve feet or so above the ground, just below a crotch that would shield me and offer a splendid view into her bedroom. Problem: I was not fond of heights.

Afraid of falling, a few edgy moments passed before a noise frightened me. Something rustling leaves. I peered down, didn't see anything. The sound quieted. I shivered. The night was quickly turning cooler. I looked down again, though I hadn't heard a sound. I felt disquieted. Other than a few stubborn leaves nothing screened my flanks. Anyone who approached from either side and looked up would spot me. And just what was I doing in the tree outside her bedroom window when cherries were out of season? If Ed discovered me he'd call the police and report a Peeping Tom, namely me, or, being short-tempered, grab the shotgun he must own. What would I tell her if she was taking a late stroll? Oh, hi, I've been looking for you.

I shivered again. What was I thinking? Climbing a tree had been a crazy idea. Retreat the only option. How to get down? Jump? Sure, invite a broken neck. I planted my right foot on the limb below, the branch not as thick as I would have liked.

A motion in her window caught my eye.

I glanced up.

"Uh-oh," I muttered, wishing I could vanish.

She was smiling at me and she was naked. For some reason she looked much older. Her lips moved behind the glass, words I could not hear. She obviously didn't know I was a poor lip reader, especially at night while freezing and clinging to an unforgiving tree.

I felt my face flush and I shifted my weight without thinking or looking down. The limb bowed. My sense of equilibrium vanished.

"Shit!"

Branches lashed my face as I fell. I hit the ground hard, feet first. Pain radiated up my legs. Stars momentarily lit my eyes. I toppled over. Being a fast thinker, I alertly rolled across slumbering grass and slammed into a sturdy obstacle, the hedge.

Too late for flimsy explanations, I scrambled up. My left ankle felt sprained, hopefully not broken. I limped to the sidewalk. Flee to the car.

I didn't look back, limped down the sidewalk. I gently touched my chafed cheek; blood dotted my fingertips. I pulled a handkerchief from my back pocket and applied a steady pressure to the wound. I felt foolish. I had never seen her bedroom.

An owl hooted. I glanced up. Something faraway flickered in the sky.

The rumble of the powerful V-8 engine imparted a sense of safety. I pulled away from the curb, U-turned, and sped toward the Inn. If there were no familiar cars parked outside I'd go in, solicit a Band-Aid, and tend to my abraded cheek in the men's room. Hot, soapy water would soothe my tortured hands. I could check for splinters. Then I'd order a mug, compose myself before going home. If any of the guys came in I'd tell them . . . what? Karen tore into my face like a wildcat when I stopped by to retrieve a book? I imagined their skeptical faces. I knew the poker players would be long gone, along with Bob. They were all workingmen filling a night, hunched over a table, staring at cards, mentally counting chips and calculating odds as they shot the manly breeze and guzzled beer that would necessitate multiple pee trips to the john. Only I wandered the lonesome highway.

My headlights shone on a few unfamiliar cars. I parked, eased out, and limped inside.

Bill, the constant observer of our comings and goings, looked up. "What the hell happened to you?"

Oh, why not. "My girlfriend broke up with me, and I fell out of a tree."

CHAPTER ELEVEN

Lightning whips drove gray-muscled clouds overhead as I rushed toward my dorm. On a parallel path Marie, my high school friend, hurried toward the Chubb Library. My eyes followed the girl matching strides with her. Tall and willowy in a tight knee-length black skirt, white blouse, and unzipped black jacket, her angular face defiant beneath the gloom. I rushed across wind shaken grass.

"Hi," I said to Marie at the library steps. Caught a breath, turned to the girl and said, "David Crobak."

"Julie Harris," she said, her lips hinting an amused smile.

"The movie star?"

Her smile widened. "In name only."

"My pleasure, Julie Harris." I executed a gentlemanly bow. I don't know why. I feel stupid when I think of it. "Where're you from?"

A gust of wind whipped her jacket. She jammed her notebook under her left arm, pulled the winged jacket ends together, and zipped up.

"Columbus." She brushed honey-colored hair from her face. A bolt of lightning crashed nearby.

"We better go," Marie said.

"See you later," I said, smiling at Julie.

I hadn't gone far when I swiveled around. She held the library door open for Marie and glanced back. Had she intended her eyes for me or the dancing leaves?

⊷ ⊶

The following week she was sitting at a round table in the Baker Center with Marie, whose romance with Pete had soured the previous summer, and two of my friends. I bought a Coke at the concession and sat between Marie and Malcolm, an edgy guy from Brooklyn who liked the quaint village look of Athens, Ohio.

"Take Sartre's short story about the prisoner who gives out a phony location to the police," said Jacob, a heavyset guy from New Rochelle who blamed his flourishing weight on his glazed donut addiction. "He tells them his comrades are hiding in such-and-such a place, which he knows isn't true, only he doesn't know they've changed their hideout to that very spot and he's unwittingly issued their death sentence."

"It's a good story with a twist at the end," Julie said, "but I think Camus is better, though he always denied being an Existentialist."

"They think he may have committed suicide when his car crashed into a tree," Malcolm said, his bouncy legs matching the pace of his rapid words. "Is that his final answer to life—that it's absurd to want to live in a world without ultimate meaning?"

"It was rainy in Paris that night. There's no proof he killed himself. He wasn't even driving. But think about Meursault in *The Stranger*. Why *did* he shoot the Arab? Was it the blinding sun? Prejudice? Was he a psychopath? And why does Meursault find meaning only in his impending death?"

I listened as her lips sang her thoughtful tunes and I fell in love. I wanted to fling aside the table and embrace her.

"Even at his trial, he's surprised to be found guilty," I said.

Julie looked at me, her smile reassuring, blue eyes warm and penetrating, and she nodded.

"I agree Camus is the better writer," said Jacob. He pushed back his chair and stood. "Sorry to duck out, but I've got to run. Got a one o'clock."

"Me, too," Julie said, rising. "She picked up her copy of *Catcher in the Rye.*"

I watched her weave around scattered tables on her way to the door chivalrous Jacob parted.

"You like her," Marie said.

I drained my Coke. "She's very pretty."

"Like a movie star," Malcolm said.

A long bar ran down one side of the dimly lit Blue Onion, a place where bartenders seldom asked to see an ID. Tables and chairs sprawled across the floor like unfitted pieces of a jig-saw puzzle. Recessed lights in the deep blue ceiling simulated a starry night. I was drinking alone, my third Manhattan. The Root brothers, Ted and Ed, beer guzzlers who chattered about contact sports they never played, fast cars they wanted to own, and loose women they yearned to bed had left in a huff after they told me the oft repeated putdown of a Nigerian exchange student's response to a snowfall. It had made the rounds the previous winter. As told: Emeka wanted to package snow and send it home. "Can you believe that dumb nigger?" the Root Brothers said in jovial unison. I knew Jacob was present when Emeka said, "I *wish* I could package snow and send it home." Though I thought the tone of my voice innocuous when I relayed the correct version and pointed out the inherent racism in the altered version, they found the truth highly offensive and called me names I chose to ignore.

They huddled with three cronies at a nearby table, and very soon I heard raucous laughter. Feeling I'd squandered another evening I figured it was time to drink up. I inhaled the smell of bourbon mixed with sweet vermouth and bitters, intending to gulp down the remains of the pricey Manhattan and leave when the door swung opened and I abandoned the thought. Julie walked in, eye-catching in a dark blue skirt and cream-colored blouse, a clutch purse pressed against her slim hips. Had my heart ever beat faster? I put the glass down. She ordered at the bar, and soon her hand held a glass of red wine, and she looked around, and I stood halfway up, expectantly, and waved. Did she smile? Yes. Her magnificent body collected eyes as she squeezed between tables and headed for the empty chair next to mine. She crossed her legs and the hem of her skirt crept a few inches above her knee. My stomach tightened. I sipped my drink.

"Hi," she said, laying her purse on the table.

I wanted to say something profound, memorable.

"We meet yet again," I said.

"Is that my cue to add 'third time's the charm'?"

I scrapped my brain for a witty comeback. Nothing came.

"Wine, huh" I said, and it sounded idiotic.

"Chianti." She sipped and waved to a guy I didn't know. For a moment I felt anxious, fearful she would desert me and join him. She stayed put.

"I liked what you said about Camus and *The Stranger*," I said.

"Thanks." She took a long drink of wine and then ran her finger around the rim of her glass. "Did you like it? The novel, I mean."

"Oh, yeah. I was riveted. The character was so unredeemable, yet I found myself caring about him."

"Exactly. Interesting how he pulled that off."

I smoked a Pall Mall and she a Gauloises, though she said she disliked the smell of cigarettes and smoke irritated her eyes. We talked. She had another glass of wine, and I, a fourth Manhattan.

It was unseasonably warm when we stepped outside.

"Look, a shooting star!"

"Make a wish," I said as the thin streak of light arced across the northeast sky.

"Did *you* make a wish?" I nodded. She put her index finger to her lips. "Sh, it won't come true if you tell."

We strolled up to Court Street. I ached to take her hand, but I felt strangely shy. Instead, I pointed at the brick street. "These are kinda neat, like Old World cobblestones."

"Have you been to Europe?"

"No, but I like to read."

"Me either." She smiled and wet her lips. "You live in the dorms?"

I sucked in my breath. I roomed with a guy and shared a bathroom a few doors down the hall with twenty.

"Gamertsfelder," I said, and hurried to add, "but I plan to move out soon. Get a place."

We paused at the corner, unsure of our direction.

"So, you're a sophomore," she said.

"Yeah. You?"

"Junior."

"Are you and Marie good friends?"

"I think so. We met last year at a concert. She came down to Columbus and spent a week with me when Pete dumped her. She'd forgotten about him when she left."

We ambled toward the Hocking River. Though only a year older, Julie's confident voice and manner conveyed a mesmerizing maturity many years beyond mine. We hadn't gone a block when she stopped, looked me up and down and said, "Let's go back. I want to show you my place." She took my hand and a jolt of pleasure zinged up my arm.

"You have calluses."

"I was a pickle-dipper for Dolly Madison last summer."

"Sounds like fun."

"It was a summer job." Standing on a platform five feet above a concrete floor I dipped a long-handled net into a huge wooden vat, hauled in my briny catch, swiveled, and dropped the sliced cucumbers onto wide stainless steel tables where hair netted women with fast-moving hands packed them into glass jars and sent them for a ride on a conveyer belt to Pickleland.

Her apartment was on the second floor of a large house. A separate entrance and wide stairway led up a landing with doors on either side.

"Not another one."

Someone had taped a note on her door.

"Note from the underground?"

"More like a creepy secret admirer." She jerked the note off the door and took out her key.

"Who's next door?"

She glanced over her shoulder. "No one. My landlady keeps it vacant for relatives, though I've been here almost a year and I don't think it's been used more than once." She opened her door, flipped on a light, wadded the unread note, and tossed the lumpy ball into a wastepaper basket by her desk. "My humble abode. Make yourself at home. I'll be right back"

The hardwood floored living room had a high ceiling. Cozy throw rugs and colorful pillows warmed the airy space. Elegant simplicity gleamed from a teak coffee table, a sleek Norwegian style couch and two tall-backed chairs. Humble, but still too expensive for my wallet.

Three framed prints hung on the walls: Van Gogh's *Starry Night* shone above the couch; Munch's *The Scream* rose from a large wooden desk covered with neatly stacked books and papers; Duchamp's *Nude Descending a Staircase* walked in lively planes of light toward the backs of different sized canvases propped against the wall. Two French doors led to a little balcony I had seen from the street. An easel leaned against the wall by the doors.

"So?" She carried two tall water glasses in one hand and a wicker-wrapped bottle of Chianti in the other.

"Nice," I said. Then, thinking she might have thought I referred to the wine, I quickly added, "Your room. Very tasteful."

"Flattery will get you everywhere." She smiled, put the glasses on the coffee table and turned the bottle's label toward me. "Vino?" I nodded, and she sat near me on the couch, and filled the glasses halfway.

"Thanks." I sipped. "This is good. Chianti usually puckers my lips."

"Most of what's sold is too astringent, like what the Onion offers. You have to shop around. Dad orders from a wine dealer in New York."

"I'm impressed."

"I'll tell my Dad next time I talk to him."

Unable to think of anything to keep the wine discussion going, I looked for a conversation piece. "I noticed your balcony. Do you ever use it?"

"I like to have morning coffee there. It's also a nice place to relax on warm evenings. The ash tree gives good shade." Her hand fanned her face. "It's a bit stuffy in here." She rose and opened the balcony doors inward, then flopped down beside me and peeled off her loafers. She stretched her breathtakingly long legs on the table and crossed her ankles. Her skirt rose to mid-thigh, a pleasurable treat for my eyes and lustful imaging for my mind.

"Wild pictures you've got," I said to calm my fantasies. "I like the guy screaming over the desk. That's how I feel at finals time."

"Me, too." She took a deep drink.

"Van Gogh's my favorite artist."

"Yeah, *Starry Night*. Sometimes I can get lost in it. Know what I mean?"

"May-be."

"You'll know when it happens. You've probably gotten lost in a book or film, but when you really let yourself go, you can wander through a painting, too. It's beyond surface color and form."

I sipped and nodded, pretended I understood, tried to not stare at her naked legs. She added a splash to my glass and refilled hers.

"So, do you paint?"

"It's what I like. My family's well-heeled by Columbus standards. They expect me to be a wife someday, if I don't trick them and run off to fight for civil rights. Think I should?"

"What, run away?"

"No, silly. Fight for civil rights."

"Well, sure, I believe in it." I didn't want to tell her I had no intentions of putting my body in harm's way.

"I don't think I'm brave enough. Not like Rosa Parks." She pulled her legs from the table and drained half of her wine. "I'll just get my cute little schooling and be an educated wife for some doctor or lawyer. Meanwhile, I'll keep a quiet, well lit corner for myself and paint." She snapped her fingers and sang: "Hernando's Hideaway, ole!" She raised her right arm, twirled her hand, and laughed. "That way, my husband can say, 'She paints' when people ask what his lovely wife does." She replenished her glass, slouched into the couch, and sighed heavily. "Fuck, it won't be that bleak, will it?"

"You could get a degree and have a career." I'd never heard a girl swear.

"Not a lot of career openings for women, you know. But it's nice you think so."

"My sister Cathy went to Western Reserve. Before that she went to Mount Mercy, in Pittsburgh. She's a speech therapist.

She got married, so I don't know if she plans to go for a PhD or something."

"And that's why you think avenues are open for women." She leaned her shoulder against mine. I felt my cock growing harder.

"Marie's in school."

"She wants to be a teacher. Ever wonder why grade school teachers are invariably women? Think extended home."

"You're very smart. Pretty too."

She smiled derisively. Had she tired of men admiring her beauty?

"Are you from Pittsburgh?"

"No, just visited relatives. I'm from Wadsworth. It's a small town about thirty miles south of Cleveland, near Akron. Before that, I lived in Parma, near Cleveland."

"So, you've lived *near* a lot of places."

"Uh-huh." I felt my face heat and was glad she wasn't looking at me.

"I've lived in one house." She slowly swirled the wine in her glass. "I suppose it's a mansion of sorts—all my life. My brother goes to Harvard. He's *nearly* a lawyer." She giggled and patted my leg. "Don't take that the wrong way. I'm teasing." The sense of her touch lingered. "My parents wanted me to attend some chic New England school, but I'm a bit of a rebel. My sister's a senior in high school. I think she's heading to Bryn Mawr next year. It was on their *very* select list of approved schools. They wanted me to pick one and they almost croaked when I said Ohio U. You have any other siblings? Besides your sister, I mean."

"Uh-uh." No need to include my stepbrother who was sailing the Seven Seas. No common blood coursed through our veins.

She drained her glass, placed it on the table, took my glass, and put it next to hers.

"You have strong legs." She curled up next to me, her breast pushing against my side, and caressed my thigh. She smelled deliciously willing, and I kissed her.

In her bedroom, naked, I lay beside her fantastic body and hoped alcohol had not dulled my sex.

"You can't sleep here," she whispered. "My landlady doesn't allow overnighters."

We kissed and I fondled her small breasts. She stroked my cock, spread her legs, and piloted my hand down.

"Hmmm, that feels great," she said.

Then I remembered. What if many months riding in my back pocket had ruined it? I reached over the side and blindly searched for my jeans.

"What are you doing?"

"I gotta get something."

She gently pulled me back. "It's called the pill, silly."

I lay on top of her, my arms supporting my weight. Her hand slid between our sweating bodies and she guided me inside.

"Look at me," she whispered. "Really see me."

＝＜┼ ┼＝

On Sunday, St. Paul's church bells announced my arrival at her apartment. We lay on apple green sheets and I trembled eagerly, anxious to slip inside her and leave myself and the world behind.

"Use your tongue first," she said.

＝＜┼ ┼＝

On Monday, I hurried to see her after my philosophy class. A night rain had eased into a morning mist that the sun soon burned off. The air smelled new. I vaulted her steps two at a time, raised my hand to knock, and paused. I peeled the note off her door, glanced at it, and stuffed it into my back pocket. She'd thrown away the other without reading. I knocked.

The silky green robe she wore slid artfully to the floor when I closed the door. We made love twice; the second time with her on top. In between we sipped Chianti. We sat on her bed with our backs propped up with pillows. She offered a fat Gauloises and I smoked it. "'They' claim cigarettes cause lung cancer," she said, then smiled and rolled onto her side. Her fingers traced circles on my chest, lightly pulling sparse dark hairs.

"I love you," I said.

"It's too soon to talk of love."

I swallowed my disappointment. Too soon to embrace endearment.

"Are you still a Catholic?"

"Why do you ask?" I assumed Marie had told her and I looked for the elusive answer within myself, weighing its honesty against whatever she might want to hear.

"Just curious. Are you?"

"I don't go to church."

"Me either." She laid her head on my chest. I stroked her hair. "I was raised Lutheran. It's very close to Catholicism, except I think Martin Luther believed in sex." Her fingers slid down to my cock. "So do Catholics. They just compartmentalize it. Luther didn't believe the Pope should be a dictator. He thought the Pope and priests were fallible. I've read stories about priests making sly night trips through the tunnels connecting monasteries with nunneries." Her hand stroked my cock. She turned her head and looked up at me. She was smiling.

"So, are you still a Catholic?"

"Not actively."

"Still a member?"

"Maybe." I winced in pleasure.

She released me and I lay down. I thought she wanted to climb on top. She faced the foot of the bed and took me into her mouth. I propped myself up on my elbows so I could look at her. I'd never tasted a girl before Julie and a girl had never taken me in her mouth.

"Lay down," she said, her soft hand applying gentle pressure on my chest. "Relax."

Late that night we embraced by the door.

"Do you have classes tomorrow?" she asked.

"Only a nine o'clock."

"I'd like to go to the country."

"Long walk from here." Neither of us had a car.

"I've a surprise. You'll see."

⇥ ⇤

On Tuesday, looking delicious in lavender short shorts and a white blouse, she jiggled keys for a borrowed blue MGA 1600 coupe.

"Who's your generous friend?"

"Bobby. We dated last year. He says he raced it a few times in California, but I think he spent most of the summer picking up girls. Ever been out West?"

"No."

"Me either. Get in."

She drove at speed into the sprawling hill country. Warm wind stung our faces, whipped our hair. I was happy.

A good ways from town, she slowed, crossed lanes and parked on the shoulder beside a grassy field fenced on two sides by hickories and oaks. When I closed my door she was already wandering into ankle-high grass. Had she been here before? I caught up with her and took her hand.

"Isn't it great," she said.

"Yes."

131

"I just love the color contrasts—Green grass, rainbow leaves, dark bark, pale blue sky, wispy clouds."

"Do you want to paint it?"

She frowned. "It's only here for now, silly."

She shook free of my hand and ran, bent low, arms loosely swinging along her tanned legs, fingers delicately sweeping across tall blades of grass. I stood still, taking a moment to admire her backlit body before I trotted after her. My hand reached for hers and she suddenly stopped and rose on tiptoes, like a ballerina.

"Look!" She urgently pointed at two enormous gopher snakes slithering away, their speed surprisingly fast. A pang of fear shot through me, though their distance grew. I'd always been afraid of snakes.

"They were sunning themselves and we disturbed them," she said, crestfallen. She swiveled and walked deliberately toward the car.

On the road again, I was relieved she drove slowly, the MGA as tame as the family sedan on a Sunday outing.

"We're the danger in nature," she said. "We're always messing with it. Those snakes were happy in that field, maybe even mating, until we came along and scared them."

"We didn't know. Besides, they were so damn big they probably scared me as much as I scared them."

Her eyes took on an absent look. "Did you see anyone?"

"Where? In the field? I didn't see anyone."

"He was there."

I didn't know if she was speaking from a metaphysical point of view, as in God, or one rooted in reality, as in the note maker. I chose silence.

She opened the French doors to air her stuffy apartment, then poured wine, and settled next to me on the couch.

"I'm sorry I got so upset about the snakes."

"That's okay. They upset me, too." I shrugged. "I understand."

"Well, I don't. My melancholy comes and goes. Maybe it's only boredom. Maybe it's what Camus meant in *The Stranger.* Out of ennui Meursault shoots the Arab and blames the sun." I remained quiet and stroked her thigh. The lavender short shorts were driving me nuts. "Is that all you think about?" She smiled and drained her glass.

I kissed her and we cuddled on the couch for a few minutes before we went into the bedroom and made love. We lay on the bed for an hour, talking and touching, slow to dress.

"It's getting late." A brush swept her hair into a ponytail. She bound her hair with an elastic band and set the brush on the top of the dresser next to the car keys. "I've got to get Bobby's car back. I'll give you a lift."

"What do you want to do tomorrow?"

She shook her head. "I need a break for a few days. Don't look that way. It's not you. I've got a couple of tough exams coming up and I'm way behind. I didn't expect them so soon. I thought I'd catch up in plenty of time. Come by Friday night. I think my landlady will be gone all weekend visiting her son." She lightly kissed my lips. "You can stay the night."

"I'd like that."

She smiled and scooped up the keys from the dresser.

"Are you behind because of me?"

"Now whatever gave you that idea?" She kissed me on the cheek. We got into the MG. She turned on the headlights.

"This guy—Bobby—do you still like him?"

"You don't need to worry about him."

※ ※

On Wednesday and Thursday I dashed up the stairs at Baker Center, heart pounding, hoping to see her sitting at our favorite table, if only for a few minutes. No Julie. I walked by her apartment at night but didn't see a light on. Had she decided to spend time with Bobby?

Friday I woke with a monumental erection. After my morning classes I grabbed a bite, then hustled over to Ellis Hall, hoping to catch Julie when her one o'clock English Lit class let out. I passed the time smoking cigarettes, pacing, staring at slow white clouds, hearing the chatter of fellow students, following the flight path of a fat robin, asking passersby for the time, waiting, waiting, and all the while imagining how surprised and happy she'd be to see me now that her tests were done. No need to wait for nightfall. The doors finally flew open, releasing a lively torrent of her classmates. I stood up and held a tight smile as my eyes roamed from one face to another. No Julie.

I began to wonder if she had had exams. Maybe she used them as a ploy to cover time with Bobby. I hadn't seen his car parked by her place. At four o'clock, after searching the campus green and paying three visits to Baker Hall, I launched a frantic search for Bobby's MG. I madly raced around residential blocks until stitches grabbed my sides. I had no idea what he looked like, where he lived, or if he parked his prize sports car in a garage.

Thirsty, tired and hungry I slogged to the cafeteria. Jacob settled his bulky frame into the chair across from me. He tried to make conversation, but soon tired of my monosyllabic replies and fell silent. After a few minutes his fork gestured at my half-eaten macaroni and cheese.

"Don't like it?"

"It's okay.

"Not feeling well?"

"I'm all right."

It was dark when I reached her apartment. A dim light shone in the curtained French doors and I hurried up the stairs, my heart bouncing. Come Friday night, she'd said. I swallowed hard, inhaled deeply and rapped "shave and a haircut, two bits." I put my ear to the silent door and stood back, knocked louder.

On the sidewalk I peered up through the white ash's branches at the closed and darkened French doors. Had I, in my eagerness, mistaken a streetlight's reflection? I crossed the street and looked up. No light reached the balcony. Had I imaged it?

I dragged my deflated spirit to the Blue Onion and flopped into a chair at a table near the front door. Ordered a stout bourbon. My heart filled with hope when the door swung open and a lithe blonde with long silky hair came in, her head turned. Julie? A big bruiser had his meaty arm around her waist. My eyes flamed, my throat tightened. I averted my eyes, took a skosh of whiskey, looked back, and lit a cigarette, my hand trembling. Bobby was too big to throttle. The door shut behind them and Bobby released his captive, a cute, freckled faced pixie. Behind black-framed glasses her eyes quickly scanned me and moved on.

The door soon banged open and a loud bunch of guys from the floor in my dorm rushed in and assumed they had an open invitation to join me. They were bemoaning a failed panty raid and seeking solace in beer. Their boisterousness a welcome distraction. I ordered the second of what would be many drinks amid spirited arguments about the world's great religions (Christianity came out on top, though one guy vilified it and another endorsed Buddhism), a loud discussion of Eisenhower's warning about the dangers of the military-industrial complex and his decision to send troops into Little Rock, Arkansas, to enforce lawful school integration which, for reasons beyond my ken, though I suspected a Root brother clone had skillfully engineered it, segued into an argument about the validity of Roger Maris breaking Babe Ruth's home run record. As we bickered and our words slurred we also branched off and blathered about girls we wanted to panty raid and bed, cars we wanted to drive, and movies we'd seen, or said we'd seen.

I left when flashing lights announced last call. I walked an impeccably steady course until I passed Court Street. There confusion set in, for some malicious bastard had bent the streets and shuffled the dorms. I pressed onward, assumed an "extra cool," *à la* Lenny Bruce, look and, sure enough, East Green Street materialized. The heavy dorm door whooshed shut behind me. I wove up the stairs to the second floor, staggered down the hall, and stumbled into the spinning bathroom, knelt in front of a toilet and puked.

⇒ ⇐

The following day, an unmerciful hangover forced me to lie in bed as still as possible. Until sunset. I showered after I mentally scraped my body off the bed, grabbed a bite to eat, and rushed to Julie's. I knocked and a thin crack of light appeared between the door and jamb.

"Who is it?" she mumbled.

"It's me." I put my hand on the knob, pushed, and felt resistance.

"Is anyone with you?" She sounded odd, as though she were simultaneously trying to talk and whistle.

"No."

"I mean behind you. Look down the stairs. Is anyone there?"

The hairs on the back of my neck prickled. Had she stood at the window and seen someone following me?

"Just me."

"I can't let you in."

"What?"

"You'll want to touch me."

"What the hell?"

"Someone watched me. He stinks."

"What are you talking about?"

"Please, go away." As she pushed the door tight I thought she said "Be careful," and I heard the lock turn.

A shiver ran down my spine. I reeled and stared at the secured door for long seconds, maybe minutes, before reluctantly leaving. My hands shook, my gut hurt. I felt adrift. Who was watching? Was she truly in danger? Her voice sounded strange, belabored. I spun around at the corner and headed back to her place, then stopped and turned back to town. She'd sent me away. I couldn't make sense of—if only she'd opened the door more than a crack. What stinky bastard was watching her? The weirdo who stuck strange anonymous notes on her door? What the hell did I do with that note? Had she seen someone in the field? Why would anyone be following *me*?

On the other hand, it was *possible*. I looked both ways and behind me. This was crazy, and the word stayed with me.

—◄╬ ╬►—

I wandered downtown, aimed for the Bobcat Den, where Malcolm usually hung out. A lively crowd filled the long, narrow bar. The smell of cigarette smoke mixed with stale beer. Music blared from the jukebox, an Elvis Presley tune. I picked up a glass of draft at the bar and walked to the rear, where Malcolm was playing eight ball. The movie *The Hustler* hooked him on pool, but unlike Paul Newman he lacked Willie Mosconi's instruction. His opponent sank the eight in a side pocket. Malcolm pulled a folded dollar from his shirt pocket, flung it on the table, and racked his cue. He waved me to a small corner table cluttered with empty longneck bottles of Stroh's and another half full.

"That guy's really good," he said.

His opponent carefully chalked his cue while a new challenger racked balls. I drained half of my beer.

"Jeez, you look beat," Malcolm said. "Go easy on the brewskies. You'll bust your gut."

"And piss more." I licked foam from my lips, stuffed a comment about his empties littering the table. "This is only my opener."

He leaned forward, his right leg restless. "Then what? You look like shit."

"You're a psychology major, right?"

"Yeah." He lifted his bottle and drained it. "I've only taken a few psych courses. Damn requirements come first. Hey, let me grab another." He stood up. "Want one?"

"Still working this."

"Just as well, the way you look. You sure this is your first?" I nodded. He touched my forearm. "You okay?"

"Not really."

"Sit tight, my friend," he said, patting my shoulder. "I shall return."

The pool shark ran the solids, banked the eight, and pocketed another buck. I finished my beer. Malcolm returned holding two longnecks in each hand.

"Gotcha one if you want, and I emptied the pisser while I was at it." He glanced at the pool shark. "That guy doesn't lose." He turned to me. "So, what's on your troubled mind?"

I filled my empty glass, then drank a good measure. Filled the glass again.

"Something odd happened to me tonight."

He leaned forward, interested. "Oh?"

I told him about Julie and what occurred outside her door. I tried to conceal my concern.

"What do you think?"

"Really weird, man." He drummed his fingers on the table, emphasizing his thumb beat.

"Any other thoughts?"

His fingers stilled. "This is movie star Julie, right?"

"Yeah."

He grinned. "Wow, you lucky guy!"

"You're not helping."

"I bet she looks great nude. Say, how is she—you know?"

"Malcolm!"

"Hey, don't get mad, man. I admire you for it. You're a good-looking guy and all, but, man, she's something else, like a blonde Audrey Hepburn." He lifted his Stroh's, took a long pull, and rolled the bottle between his palms before putting it down. His face turned thoughtful. "I saw a lot of screwed up people in Brooklyn, some on the dangerous side of the street, if you know what I mean." His fingernails tap danced on the beer bottle. "Well, assuming she doesn't have another guy on the side—and you said you'd thought about that possibility and it doesn't look likely and for your sake I hope you're right—well, notes on the door from a secret admirer and all, it sounds like paranoia, pure and simple." He leaned back, tilting his chair. "Don't sweat it, man. It's not contagious."

I pushed the chair back. "Hey, she'll get over it," he said as I fled his shallow quips.

⇌ ⇌

My aching brain blinked into consciousness. Harsh sunlight assaulted my eyes. My mouth and throat sand dry. I blinked, the fuzzed silhouette of someone big standing in front of the built-in bureau; Johnny, my roommate, a football lineman from Zanesville, cinching up a Windsor knot. I tried to swallow. My throat balked. "Time is it?"

"Almost two. You missed breakfast and lunch."

I ignored his superior tone. "Where ya headin'?"

"Date. Gotta run." He opened the door and looked back at me disdainfully. "Smells like a brewery in here."

139

I sank my throbbing skull into the soft pillow and swore I'd never drink again. I woke in time for dinner.

⚊⊹ ⊹⚊

"You look dreadful," Jacob said. "You sick?" He was coming out of the cafeteria.

"Hangover."

"That'll do it every time. Better hustle, they're almost through serving."

I carried my tray to an empty table and made quick work of a crispy chicken leg, two greasy wings, a scoop of corn, and a dollop of smooth mashed potatoes. I drank three glasses of water and a 7-Up.

It was dark when I approached Julie's. The wheels of a big U-Haul leaned against the curb. Had her landlady finally decided to rent the other unit? I took the stairs two at a time and lightly tapped a shave-and-a-haircut. The door across was closed and no sound came from within. It might just as well have been a janitor's closet. I made a fist and knocked louder, impatience stinging the side of my hand.

Silence.

I went down the stairs slowly, hoping to hear her door open, her affectionate voice. Once outside an unknown thin voice startled me.

"She may be back tomorrow, young man."

It took me a moment to find her: an older woman wrapped in a pink housecoat closed at the neck, wearing what looked like thick glasses, staring at me through a slender break in a magnolia.

"If you're looking for Julie, she's not here. I just got back a while ago and heard about it. They took her away. Makes you wonder what the world's coming to." She shook her gray head. When she looked at me again I saw the change. She didn't know me and her fear had kicked in. She quickly turned away.

I stood dazed, trying to decipher the woman's words. What did she know? Who took Julie away? Where? I silently cursed my delay and rushed after her. Her door shut tight, porch light extinguished, interior dark. I raised my fist intending to huff and puff on the door and demand answers. I quickly stayed the thought. The frightened woman wouldn't answer. There was no need to further alarm her, have the cops at my back. I lowered my arm and glanced around. The night was quiet.

Were it not Sunday, I would have headed to a bar. Instead, I went to the dorm lounge and watched a documentary about the wall the East Germans and Soviets had built to separate Berlin. I wondered what, if anything, President Kennedy would do or say. Then I went to my room, tired and depressed. What did the landlady know?

⇒‡ ‡⇐

The sun warmed my back as I climbed the stairs at Baker Hall. I had overslept and a strong wake-up shot of caffeine would perk me up before I headed to Julie's. I was nervous, uncertain what lay ahead. I even hoped she might be inside. She wasn't. I carried the steaming cup carefully and sat down at a vacant table. Jacob and Marie walked in holding hands.

"Okay if we join you?" he asked.

"Sure. You two look pleased."

"We are." They giggled as they pulled up chairs.

"Good."

"You looked pretty thrashed yesterday," he said, resting his forearms on the table.

"I was. The chicken helped. So did a solid sleep."

"Didn't commit the sin of mixing the grain with the grape, did you?"

"I camped out at the Onion and had a few bourbons with friends."

"You drink too much," Marie said.

"So did a lot of other guys. I think we closed the place."

"That's no excuse." She shook her head and squinted at me, her disapproving motherly look. I shrugged. "This girl needs caffeine," she said, rising.

"Me, too," said Jacob, his right leg jittery. "Two creams and some glazed donuts." He held up two fingers, noted her chastising eyes, and folded one. She smiled and headed to the counter.

"I'm trying," he said. "So how *are* you doing?"

"I'm feeling better today," I said, sipping coffee. "I was surprised to see you two holding hands. I didn't know."

"Why are you surprised, because a Jew's making it with a Gentile?"

"Hey, don't get defensive. It's not that. God, I don't care," rolling the warm ceramic cup between my palms and thinking of Cleveland Jim who disliked anyone with chocolate skin and all people from foreign countries, though his parents had fled Germany when Hitler unleashed his legions on the countryside. Marie returned with one glazed donut broken in half. Well, she could use some weight.

"We're all equal," I said.

"Not quite, my friend," Jacob said, frowning as he took the larger half. "There are great inequalities in the world."

She bit into her half donut and blew steam from her cup. "Did you tell him?"

He chewed and shook his head.

"Tell me what?"

"We're going to join the Peace Corp next year," she said. "What do you think?"

"Mighty noble."

They briefly debated where they wanted the Peace Corp to send them. "Mexico or someplace in Central America," Marie said, insisting on a Spanish-speaking country because she spoke the language. "Egypt," Jacob said. "I want to see the pyramids." They laughed and kissed. I finished my coffee, eyed the beginning Spanish book Jacob had laid on the table, and stood up. I admired their optimism, their confidence in their future togetherness.

"Going so soon?" he said.

"Gotta see somebody."

I walked purposefully, still trying to understand. What did the landlady mean? Where had Julie been? What did her mumble through the cracked door mean? Why hadn't she opened the door?

A black Mercedes with tinted windows had replaced the U-Haul. The dealership on the license plate's silver frame read Ed Potter Mercedes, Columbus, Ohio. Were her folks in town? I looked up, glimpsed faint movement behind the French doors, and climbed the steps, my palms sweaty.

I slipped through her partly opened door and edged into an empty room. No couch, no canvasses, no books; no Van Gogh, no proof at all that Julie had graced this white space.

I heard voices in the kitchen and tiptoed toward them. A tall, well-dressed man and a short, equally well-dressed woman filled the doorway. Their demeanor let me know I'd failed an on-the-spot status exam; my family was wrong, my clothes were from J C Penny's. Then, from between them, Julie appeared wearing a full length flowery dress. I almost passed out.

"Oh, it's you," she mumbled, a hand covering her mouth. She looked at her parents. "Give us a minute."

Their eyes questioned her. She nodded. I moved aside to give them clear passage. Her mother crept by silently, her eyes downcast, a slight tremble troubling her lips. Her father gripped my shoulder and squeezed it just short of pain. "Be quick, and if you say anything to upset her, I'll trample you."

Julie was leaning against the sink. Purple bruises ringed her swollen eyes, her left swollen shut. A sling cradled her right arm. She lowered her hand. A white bandage hid her chin, another concealed her right cheek. Stitches webbed her lower lip, more above her right eye. Her face, her once-lovely face. . . .

"I'm going home," she said. I strained to hear as her battered lips barely parted. "Uncle Fred already left in the truck. My parents got here Saturday. Mom was with me when you came by, helping me pack. Dad was haranguing the police."

"I came by last night, too."

"We stayed in a motel." She painfully repositioned her arm in the sling. "It's not broken. Bruises and messed up muscles." Her free hand covered her mouth. "Cute, huh?"

"What in God's name happened?"

"Was God here?"

Her pathetic voice drew my arms and I stepped toward her. She shook her head.

"Please, don't touch me. I hurt all over."

"I'm sorry."

She looked at the blank space on the kitchen wall where a Monet once floated. "Is sex all men think about? Is that really all you want from a girl?"

I shook my head. "Who—"

"The cops thought it might've been you."

"What!"

"They thought you wanted sex, and I said no." She paused and her left index finger gently stroked the tip of her purple nose. Her hand still covered her mouth. "Only it was him." She cringed, spun around and spit in the sink. Her free hand turned on the tap. She cupped the water in her palm and sucked it into her mouth, and then spit it into the sink. She faced me, wincing. "Just in time for Halloween, huh."

Two of her lower front teeth were missing.

"Oh, God!"

"I'm so ashamed."

"Why?"

"It was my fault."

"How? How was it your fault?"

"I left the French doors ajar when we left in the MG. He was waiting for me when I got back."

"That's not your fault."

"I feel dirty. He cut off a lock of my hair. He took my panties. He's probably fingering my hair right now, smelling my panties. How can I ever be a wife?"

"You can."

"You don't get it, do you?" Her right eye flashed.

"Get what?"

"He was here for hours!"

"Oh, Julie."

Her voice quieted.

"He choked me and said he'd crush my throat if I fought. He squeezed out dirty words." Tears trickled from her good eye. Her left index finger swept them from her cheek. She drew a deep breath. "But sex wasn't enough for that *creature*. He beat me. He despised me."

"No one could—"

"How the hell would you know? How would you like to be hog-tied, defenseless, while some bastard—" Her voice broke. She stared at the living room wall, at the faint outline where The Scream had hung and the back of her good hand wiped tears from her chin. "I thought he was going to kill me. I had nothing left to give him. He took everything."

I stepped back, ran my hand through my hair.

"He left me with nothing," she weakly said.

"No, you're alive, and we love each other."

She glared at me. "*I* never said I *loved* you."

I stumbled backwards into the living room. High heels clicked on the hardwood. Her mother stared at me with alarm.

"J-J-Julie, d-darling . . . D-d-daddy wants to go."

I regained my footing and helplessly watched, speechless, as Julie limped by. I could only wonder what wounds lay beneath her full-length dress.

"Good-bye," she said without turning.

They descended one halting step at a time. I stood in the door-jamb and watched, aching for it to be my arm she depended on. I waited until they cleared the last step before heading down.

Her father opened the rear door of the Mercedes and her moth-er stepped in. He took Julie's good arm and she said something to him. He looked displeased but nodded. She limped toward me.

Standing in front of me, her weight on her good leg, she looked into my eyes and the back of her hand grazed my cheek.

"Did your wish come true?"

I nodded, fighting back tears.

She leaned into me, hugged me with her free arm, and put her swollen lips to my ear. "I really did like you," she whispered.

I gently held her and lightly kissed the top of her head as a par-ent might a child at bedtime. She shuffled to the car and carefully slipped inside. Her father closed the door. He squinted at me for a long moment. Then he went around and opened the driver's door, sat behind the wheel, lit the cold engine, and pulled away. At the corner, the Mercedes turned right and disappeared.

I stood motionless, staring at the vacant corner. A man and a woman strolled by, leisurely swinging interlocked hands. A kid zoomed by on a bike. A smaller kid followed, pedaling hard to catch up. A lean orange cat scampered across the street and disap-peared into some bushes near the corner.

The sun beat down on me as I stared blankly at the empty space where the Mercedes had been, uncertain of what to do or where to go. I looked up at the ash tree, its low limbs a natural ladder to the balcony. I'd talk to the landlady tomorrow.

CHAPTER TWELVE

I found a rolled up copy of *The Saturday Evening Post* tucked into the narrow space alongside my seat and the window and wondered how many miles it had traveled. The Trailways bus picked up speed outside of Athens. I idly flipped pages, expecting little as my concentration was on the fritz, but an article about American military advisers in Southeast Asia intrigued me. The previous year I'd read an account of the French defeat at Dien Bien Phu in 1954. Why were we there? Apparently, JFK stepped up shipments of arms and advisors when the Communists, emboldened after vanquishing our French allies, threatened to topple the legitimate government and fan their revolutionary fervor to neighboring countries, what one official referred to as a domino effect. In the name of democracy, we had to aid the embattled government since a Communist regime in Vietnam would be bad news. At least that was the gist of what I gleaned from the article. I yawned and lay the magazine aside, certain our guys would settle the issue pronto.

I stared out the window. Snow flecked fields raced by. After Julie left, I couldn't focus, no matter how hard I tried. Disheartened, I was going to Wadsworth for Christmas break, and I had no intention of returning. I hadn't penned an official withdraw notice or spoken with anyone in administration. I simply left. Had I notified my instructors, they would have given me incompletes. Instead, noting my absence at finals, each would mark Fs next to my name. I was throwing away a VA funded education, and I felt indifferent.

—⊷ ⊶—

A change had taken place at the Hub. Molly, the barmaid, had abruptly departed, replaced by an ex-Navy guy with a tattoo of a topless girl wearing a hula skirt on his upper right arm. When he worked his triceps the dancers' hips swayed provocatively.

Mom still worked a twelve-hour day. She said Henry dawdled less on his afternoon errand runs to the bank and state liquor store. In time I would understand why.

Cathy and John were moving to Houston. Cathy planned to work as a speech therapist while John pursued his PhD at Rice.

If Mom was disappointed I'd dropped out she kept it to herself. Well enough that Cathy had graduated college. She slipped me some pocket money, and I quickly fell in with old pals who, like me, had abandoned college or never gone. For a year I burned aimless nights at the Little Inn drinking 3.2 Carling Black Label, playing marathon rounds of euchre, and shooting the manly breeze. Then one night in April Bob, who'd settled in at Goodrich, spilled in, his spirits high because he'd won thirty bucks at Thistledown, the racetrack outside of Cleveland.

"Beer's on me," Bob said. "I'm going back next week. You wanna come with?"

"I'm two months shy of twenty-one."

"Yeah, but they don't seem too strict. We'll go in as a group, be in a hurry."

—⊷ ⊶—

I bought a copy of the *Daily Racing Form* at the track. The abbreviations, numbers and symbols baffled me, so I opened the sports section of the *Akron Beacon Journal* I'd tucked into the rear pocket of my jeans and bet the local handicapper's top picks in the Daily Double. A little over an hour later, I folded the two bucks I'd wagered, along with twelve new cousins, and shoved them into the front pocket of my jeans. Bob bought me a congratulatory Coke.

Easy money, I thought. Beginner's luck I soon discovered, for *winning* the Daily Double was not a daily occurrence. For a month I accepted the challenge and wheedled funds from Mom for beer and bets. Everything changed the day I woke up around noon with a zinger of a hangover. I padded down the stairs seeking a gallon of cold water and a bucket of strong black coffee.

"I got you a job with Merle's Roofing Company," came Mom's abrupt greeting. She set a steaming cup of percolated Maxwell House in front of me and slapped another patty on the grill for the lunch crowd. "You start tomorrow."

Square-jawed, solidly built, and pushing forty, Merle could've played the friendly sheriff in a Hollywood western. Four years earlier he'd bought Steady Jim's Roofing for a bargain after Steady Jim tumbled off the roof of the three-story Norton Hotel building.

"Took the docs three days to tally all his broken bones," Merle said. "He's lucky the greenhouse roof broke his fall."

Merle renamed the company Wadsworth Roofing, proving that as sheriff he didn't need imagination, only an affable smile, a steady personality, and a fast hammer strapped to his waist. Word of his lowball prices and quality work soon spread, kick-started by his hobnobbing when he tendered his bid. Merle had one other employee, Herman, a Hub Café regular who had also worked for Steady Jim.

"I told Jimmy them back pocket pints wouldn't do 'im no good," Herman said with a throaty snicker as he gleefully recounted the day of Steady Jim's topple. "'Specially the freshun after lunch. I seen 'im go over. Docs picked a helluva lotta glass outta old Steady's ass."

Herman had a slight build, a face weathered beyond repair, tobacco-stained fingers, and, as far as I could tell, about sixteen rotting yellow teeth. He could have been a hard living forty or a naturally fading out sixty. Sometimes words whistled between the gaps in his teeth. A big fan of *The Beverly Hillbillies*, he flashed a Jethro-like smile whenever I made a mistake, which, considering his sour breath, added insult to injury.

One muggy afternoon Merle was driving us to the Medina Landmark, a retail grain store, when he said, "I dreamed I fucked my next door neighbor under the backyard trees. I really nailed her this time."

"Under the trees, huh," Herman scoffed.

"You betcha," Merle said, flicking Herman's sarcasm aside, his hips undoubtedly still in motion in his mind. He parked his pickup in the shade of an oak. Herman and I sat on the rear bumper while Merle went inside to gab and present his lowball bid for their big roofing job.

Sweat annoyed my eyes as I studied the three-story Landmark building, worried about working high. The tale of Steady Jim permeated my discomfort.

"Sonbitch," Herman said, hopping off the bumper. A slender foot-long copperhead slithered on the asphalt. Herman lifted his heavy black boot and stomped on its skull. He glared at the writhing young snake. "'At's why they call 'em copperheads." He lifted his boot again and squashed the little head. His wheezing laugh sounded like the last gurgles of dish water draining from a sink.

⇒+ +⇐

I tarred roofs and hung spouting with Merle and Herman all summer. Everything changed one night when Bill leaned on the bar and said, in a heretofore unheard avuncular tone, that he'd heard they were giving the postal civil service test in a few weeks.

"Ever think of taking it?" the barkeep asked.

"Why?"

"You're a decent kid. Post office offers steady work and decent pay. Good benefits." He shrugged. "You won't be doing many roofs come winter."

⊨+ +⊨

Sure enough, Merle laid me off late September, and I started punching the time clock at the Wadsworth Post Office in November, two weeks before the murder of President John F. Kennedy in Dallas. The intense national mourning dampened Thanksgiving, but when the calendar flipped to December citizens unscrewed their fountain pens and opened their wallets and mailed, so it seemed to me, Christmas cards and parcels to any and all of the names they'd scribbled in their address books. Up to my elbows in letters, waist deep in parcels, I worked twelve hours a day, six days a week through the holiday season. With my temporarily inflated checks, I bought some new duds and a 1956 black-and-white Pontiac with fat white sidewalls and settled into the normal flow of the job. I spent most of my free time paling around with Bob, going to the track, the Inn, or shooting abbreviated games of straight pool at Charger Lanes, the bowling alley near Barberton.

My life changed again the day Bob and I opted for a long, tournament-length game of straight to 150. Three hours and fifteen minutes after I set the first triangle of balls, Bob sank the fourteen in a corner pocket and beat me out of our table time and five bucks.

"God, I can't believe it took us three hours," Bob said. He racked his cue. "C'mon, I'll buy you a consolation beer."

151

The bar in the bowling alley was dark as a cave, crowded, and stuffy. A skinny guy wearing tight slacks and a polo shirt and a busty blonde in a strapless tank top and skintight Capri pants danced in front of a brightly lit jukebox. Chubby Checker's "Let's Twist Again" pulsed through smoke and laughter.

Our eyes adjusted to the poor light, and Bob pointed to a vacant table.

"I'll grab the brewskies, you commandeer the table."

I pulled up a chair and gazed at the dancers. They weren't bad, a little jerky. The girl was pretty, filled the tank top nicely, just not my type. I casually glanced at the next table over and an absolutely gorgeous girl's smile answered mine.

"Hi," I said.

"You dated Karen, didn't you?" Wendy said, her green eyes shining.

She and Karen were classmates and friends. I wondered if they'd talked about me. Of course they had. Tread judiciously.

"Yeah, but it didn't work out."

"Oh, sorry," she said with light irony.

"It was no big deal."

Her date, a clean-cut type sporting a crop of stilted brown hair, put on a tough guy face and stabbed the ice cubes in his tall glass with a swizzle stick.

"Nice to see you," she said. The amorous expression I thought I spied in her eyes and on her slightly curled lips delighted and surprised me. A cloud of untamed auburn hair swept her shoulders as she turned back to Swizzle Stick. She was wearing nylons, and her long legs made a swishing sound when she crossed them, the hem of her skirt rising to just above her knee.

My cock throbbed.

Bob returned with four bottles of Rolling Rock, which he stood on the table. Two of the bottles wore glass hats. We poured ice cold golden liquid into our tall glasses.

"Here's to shootin' pool instead of going to the track," he said in his subdued winner's voice, not rubbing it in. Why should he? It had taken him over three hours to beat me. I'd suggest we try nine-ball next time. Our glasses clinked.

"Wanna hit the track tomorrow?" I said.

He wiggled his hand, indicating so-so, sipped his beer, licked his lower lip, collected words, scratched his cheek. "I've been thinking." He paused for another sip, lick, and scratch, his mind chasing ethereal thoughts.

"And," I said to encourage him.

"You remember Sheila and me had some heartache a while back."

"Yeah."

"Well," he said, his thumb tracing the Rolling Rock imprint on the bottle, "I just think I've been neglecting her ever since. Don't know why or if she feels the same, but I don't want us to break-up, so I think it's time . . . ."

His slow, almost tortured sounding voice told me that after tonight he was "cooling it," taking a break from pool, the horses, and beer with buddies.

The sweaty dancers sank into chairs at a table by the jukebox.

"I Want to Hold Your Hand" played. The Beatles had arrived from England bearing different looks and sounds. Good time to steal a glance at *her*. Our ardent eyes briefly met. When Mr. Swizzle Stick finally went to take a piss I leaned over and asked for her number.

CHAPTER THIRTEEN

After demolishing a pepperoni and mushroom pizza pie at Luigi's in Akron, we dropped in at Bob and Sheila's.

They'd settled into a small apartment near downtown Wadsworth. Bob seemed truly happy. Unlike Joan, Shelia had no interest in the glories of touchdowns. She wanted to be a good wife and a chatty part-time waitress at Bill's Dinner.

"Do you guys ever think of going back to school?" she asked after Wendy and I settled in.

"Not at the moment," I said.

"I'm taking a sociology class at Kent," Wendy said.

"Maybe you could start off like that, Bobby. Take a class or two to get your feet wet."

Bob, wearing a plaid shirt and jeans paled from many washing, shrugged and smiled. I knew he had his eyes on a supervisory position at Goodrich, and I wondered if he'd told Sheila. I thought of asking as I assumed Bob wouldn't mind, but before I could get a word out she said: "You two ever think of getting married?"

154

We'd been dating for months and loved each other. I wondered why I hadn't thought of it sooner. No more lovemaking in a crowded car or on Bob and Sheila's couch when they went to a movie. That very night I popped the question when we parked in front of Wendy's house. The following day we applied for a marriage license and scouted for a place of our own while we waited for the results of the required blood test. I spread the word at work. If anyone knew of a vacancy, it would be a postal carrier. There were two places: a tiny shack near the railroad tracks with walls that emitted an eerie theremin-like sound every time a train thundered past, and the other, a tight room in a boarding house with a shared bathroom at the end of an uncarpeted hallway haunted by moaning floorboards. We shifted our focus to nearby Akron or Barberton, planned to look in Friday's *Akron Beacon Journal,* highlight the places closest to Wadsworth, and begin our search on Saturday.

The very next day a change-of-address came in for a small one-bedroom apartment directly across the street from the post office and only a few blocks from Bob and Sheila's. The two-story apartment protruded from the rear of a stately house built in the mid-1800s. The house stood well above and back from the road, and since we were at the tail end, there would be little street noise. A short entrance hall and stairs separated us from the two apartments, one up and one down, that fronted the street, as though our place had been an add-on or the servant quarters. The landlords, an old couple who were toddlers when President McKinley (1843-1901) pontificated from the house's front porch (a few months before an assassin's bullet silenced him), lived in the house next door. We had good privacy and our living room window yielded a pleasant view of our landlady's expansive, flower-studded backyard.

Since we weren't religious, Wendy and I opted for a private civil ceremony. Her parents, Martin and Jean, arrived at city hall precisely at six. Martin wore his stiff upper lip. Jean's flat face remained pasty. Mom walked right up to them, and said "Pleased to meet you," and introduced Henry. The four of them exchanged a few polite remarks concerning the pleasant weather and our sudden decision. Jean spoke of missing an engagement and a church wedding without specifying Catholic for Mom or Methodist for her and Martin.

Wendy and I had wondered who would take us to the "reception" dinner at the Tangier in Akron. We didn't want to hurt anyone's feelings. Martin solved our dilemma when we stepped outside as man and wife. After seating Jean in their car, he briefly spoke to Mom and Henry.

I had my arm around Wendy's waist when he approached us. "I'm sorry, but we're going to have to bow out," he said, casting a furtive glance at me. I felt Wendy's muscles tense beneath my hand. "Your mom's feeling lightheaded. I better get her home." He shook my hand without looking into my eyes, hugged Wendy lightly, and hurried to the car. Jean didn't turn around to wave.

"She planned to do that all along," Wendy said.

⇒+ +⇐

For a guy who counted every cent, who strolled out of Republic Steel each workday with two rolls of stolen toilet paper tucked inside his aluminum lunch pail, Henry didn't quibble with his usual force about the prices on the restaurant's menu. His overall stinginess had muted of late.

"I'll take that when you're ready," the waiter said as he set the small brown plastic tray on the table next to Henry.

"Thank you," Mom said.

Henry's eyes sparked when he looked at the tab our four dinners had rung up. He puckered his lips but resisted the urge to whistle and slowly unfolded a well-worn black wallet. He deliberately shuffled two tens, a five, and three ones onto the tray. Mom eyed him severely.

"Now what?" he said.

"Don't be so cheap. The tip."

"Bill's for twenty-seven sixty. How much? I never had call to leave a tip."

Mom asked me, and I said ten per cent.

"Ten percent," Mom said.

He laid two more dollars on the tray and sank his hand into his pocket for change.

I knew why Henry didn't balk when Mom told him to tip, just as I knew why he shortened his trips to the bank and liquor store, or why they let Molly go and hired a male bartender, ex-Navy, with a faded tattoo of a hula dancer on his upper right arm.

⟞ ⟝

We traded my old Pontiac for a used black Jaguar XK140 coupe. Thought we were cool, tooling around town in a car similar to the one that outraced a Ferrari at Le Mans, until eyebrow-raising mechanic bills told us the Jag had been hard-driven and poorly maintained. Winter brought the aggravation of a balky engine and the misery of an anemic heater. We traded it for a Jeep with a canvas roof and plastic side windows, whose dicey point of adhesion made for adventurous, two-wheeled curves. Alas, its engine and heater performed worse than the Jag's, and when snow fell, we wondered why we hadn't insisted on four-wheel drive. We traded it for a deep-throated, red 1964 Pontiac GTO convertible with a 389 V8 engine, which we drove to Houston without complaint when we visited Cathy and John.

Aside from car issues, our lives fell into a tranquil rhythm. I worked five days a week, guided our muscular GTO to the track two or three times a month, and enjoyed having friends over for a few drinks and games of Risk or talk. Wendy juggled the roles of cook, cleaner and laundress with a class at Kent State, and weekend waitressing shifts at the Oaks Lodge in Chippewa Lakes. During the height of the Cuban missile crisis, when talked of a nuclear war with the Soviet Union crowded airwaves, Wendy and I went to see the black comedy *Dr. Strangelove or: How I Learned to Stop Worrying and Love the Bomb*, thankful that when we emerged from the art theatre in Akron the world was still intact. Two years passed before she suggested we leave Ohio and head to California. I balked, kidded that a fella at work had told me the country tilted one day and all the nuts rolled to California, and I wasn't sure I wanted him to think of me in that category. But I knew Wendy was serious about leaving, and since moving across country made me anxious, I suggested someplace closer: Nova Scotia. She didn't cajole, laugh, or rant, merely laid a map on the table and a copy of the providence's average weather.

We decided on San Francisco and subscribed to the *Chronicle*. Checked prices of rentals in the City and quickly decided Berkeley might be a better fit since Wendy planned to start school at UC once we established residency. We traded in our GTO for a VW bug and bought a roof rack for our bulky belongings. The rest we'd pack into the trunk or in the backseat with Cyclops. A year earlier we were smoking on the high porch behind the Hub when a plaintive wail pierced the air. A scrawny black cat with an infected eye pulled himself onto the top step of the long, wooden staircase, looked at us with his one good eye, and let out a mournful cry. Wendy's heartstrings twanged. She set down a saucer of milk and smiled as he licked it dry. I could forget about Rin Tin Tin.

⚞ ⚟

Bob surprised me when he stopped in before his shift at Goodyear. I hadn't seen much of him. His new supervisory position and Sheila's pregnancy left little time for extracurricular activities.

He looked troubled, and after a short run of idle talk I asked.

"It's this Vietnam thing," he said. "It's not going as advertised." He rubbed his chin. "I haven't been in management long, and I'm afraid this draft business is going to screw me over."

"I don't think they plan to take married men, surely not one with a kid."

"I wouldn't count on it. There's a lot of bullshit going around about this war. Aren't you worried?"

How easily it would roll off my tongue, the truth followed by a lie. "I've got Sole Surviving Son status. My dad died in the Battle of the Bulge. They gave my mom his Silver Star."

"No kidding! A silver star!" He grimaced. "Hey, I'm sorry about your dad. I never knew Henry was your stepdad." He glanced out the window at his snow-dusted car. "My old man was a gyrene in the Pacific, says war movies are bullshit. Got his hip busted up so bad it's still goes haywire when the weather changes. I'll tell you something—don't laugh willya?" I extended my hands palms up and shrugged agreement. "I'm afraid of taking a bullet in the ass while I'm crapping."

After he left, I thought about Nick and Mike, my Parma pals. We were the three amigos, buddies forever. Time inevitably scattered us forever, the news delivered in a letter from Mom, handwritten on lined paper. She'd cultivated sentimental ropes to the past: notes scrawled on Christmas cards and infrequent but newsy letters sent to distant friends, rare phone calls. No details in her brief message, just a statement about an irrevocable occurrence that happened in a land I'd never heard of when I rode shotgun with him. I wondered if a simple remembrance of home flashed through his mind as he fell, if his beloved stars lit his dimming eyes.

I flipped open the Rand McNally. My eyes traveled east. Mom and Henry had sold the Hub and moved back to Cokeburg. They settled in the house Uncle Joe and grandfather built for Uncle Johnny, across the cinder alley from Mom's childhood home. How often would Mom gaze across the alley and remember that one Sunday grandfather came home from mass and found his wife hanging on their bedroom door.

"Inheritance laws are better in Pennsylvania than Ohio," Mom told me, convinced she'd outlive Henry.

I shifted my eyes westward and scanned our route. John had recently completed his studies and secured a position at a psychiatric clinic in Indianapolis. Cathy found a part-time opening for a speech therapist with the local school district. We planned to stay with them two nights and watch the first Super Bowl before heading west Monday morning. In Missouri, I wanted to stop at the Springfield National Cemetery. It'd been a long time since Dad's funeral, but I thought I could find his grave. He'd died because he was in the wrong place at the wrong time. All the weapons issued to soldiers wouldn't have saved him. He needed a microscope to see what would kill him. I shifted my eyes from Missouri. We'd shoot out of Oklahoma's barrel, bullet across Texas, New Mexico, and Arizona and lodge in the heart of Steinbeck's Promised Land.

Berkeley, California. I'd read something in the paper about free speech and students rioting out there. I was twenty-four, excited and anxious, Wendy twenty-three, eager and certain, and California was a long, long way from anyone we knew. I would have preferred a safety net.

⋙ ⋘

The taste of merlot lingered when we returned to our apartment after dinner at a nice restaurant to celebrate the upcoming move. I opened the door and Cyclops darted in, nearly tripping me. He was a two-eyed cat again; a vet had taken care of the infection.

"He looks hungry," I said. "I'll feed him."

"Hurry up." Wendy slinked toward the stairs and twirled around before starting up, the front of her blouse unbuttoned halfway, her skirt bound hips sexily tilted.

I locked the front door, filled Cyclops' food dish, and clicked off the kitchen light. Wendy screamed.

"What's wrong?" I yelled as I dashed upstairs.

She stood with her back to me, stripped down to her nylons, garter belt and black panties, her hands trembling.

"What?"

"There." She frantically pointed a shaky finger at the wall.

I pulled an old Kleenex from my back pocket, squashed the leggy wood spider, and flushed it.

"It's gone." I stood behind her, my hands low, caressing her firm thighs.

She still faced the wall, arms across her naked breasts.

"I don't know why I'm so scared of them," she said, leaning against me.

I slipped my hands beneath her arms and cupped her small breasts, kissed her neck, and pushed against her hips.

"I love you," I breathed into her ear.

PART 4

CHAPTER FOURTEEN

We found an upstairs apartment in a fourplex on the north side of Berkeley and furnished it with a mattress and box spring, a thin, foam-cushioned brown couch, and a circular wicker chair. Luckily, the apartment came with a round, metal-framed, glass-topped kitchen table and three accompanying chairs. We painted the dull white kitchen walls bright yellow.

On trips to the Laundromat, grocery stores, and thrift stores I saw more black people than I'd seen since Cleveland, more Hispanics and Asians than I'd ever seen, and countless hippies, which I'd never seen. When compared to small town Ohio, the cultural diversities were dramatic. California felt different. And I felt oddly out of place, at once experiencing invigorating differences and longing for the familiar.

⇥+ +⇤

A row of palms lined Hearst Avenue by the North Gate entrance to Cal. The long, umbrella-like trees fascinated me. Unlike Wendy, who'd vacationed in Florida with her parents, I'd only seen palm trees in movies. We passed a row of eucalypti. Wendy said she didn't think they were indigenous to California; they came from Australia.

Hand-in-hand, we strolled across the park-like UC campus. On the south side, by Telegraph Avenue, the seductive sound of drums drew us toward Sproul Plaza. In the shade cast by the Student Union three handsome black men beat a sensual rhythm on congas. A small crowd of joyous onlookers rocked to the throbbing tempo. Many of the males had shed their shirts. Women in loose fitting halters or tank tops delighted my eyes, their unfettered breasts bouncing and swaying. They looked so unlike the people I'd known in Ohio.

"It's like the music in *Black Orpheus*," Wendy said, her shoulders and hips swaying. I nodded, too shy to join in.

A willowy, bronze-skinned girl wearing sandals, a flowered miniskirt, and a loosely tied orange blouse that barely concealed her pert breasts danced with a tall, handsome Latin man. He was wearing Capri pants, his chest bare. Their fluid bodies and the sensual drumming mesmerized me. I had no idea how much time passed before the tempo slowed, and she glided a few feet to her left and sang in Spanish, her voice sweet.

"Nice scenery, huh," Wendy said, smiling.

"Good music."

"My eyes enjoyed it, too." She took my hand, her palm moist. "C'mon."

Walking slowly along Telegraph we ogled street vendors peddling tie-dyed clothes and blankets, handmade jewelry and thrown bowls, their wares spilling across the sidewalk. Buskers wearing guitars belted out raspy rock tunes. Students in jeans and T-shirts strode past panhandlers stretching out hands for spare change. The narrow street teeming with people brought forth celluloid images of Bombay.

Further down, the crowd thinned. Across the street from a Bank of America, cars had haphazardly parked in a rutted dirt lot behind a row of businesses on Telegraph. I hadn't seen any vacant lots in Berkeley. Odd there would be one so near the university and the busy Telegraph business sector.

"Wonder why there's nothing there," I said.

"Looks like a dump. Let's cross over and check out Cody's Books."

<hr>

When our funds ran low Wendy parlayed her good looks and experience as a waitress and scored a job working weekend banquets at the posh Claremont Hotel. She wore a knee-length black skirt and a white blouse. I kidded her about being the "hostess with the mostest." In return, she treated me to a striptease.

With our bank account momentarily stabilized, there was no need for me to hustle work. Wendy's easy acceptance of the novel world unfolding outside our apartment eluded me. A diffident spirit dogged me, and I needed time to shake it, so I lazed a few months listening to music—Dylan, the Stones, the Beatles, B.B. King—and drinking whiskey into the wee hours of the night while I read parts of books, listened to Alan Watts on the radio, and looked at airbrushed girls in *Playboy*.

Wendy broke my malaise when she put on her serious face and said she wanted to talk. I expected another lecture about drinking too much, maybe a worry over money, a push for me to find work. So I was stunned when she told me of her brief affair with Andre, the headwaiter at the Claremont. She spoke in the past tense, having been the one to end their tryst. She also assured me he no longer worked at the hotel, having returned to Martinique. She said his reason for leaving was hush-hush. She suspected he put the make on the wrong woman.

I took the shocking news of her clandestine affair reasonably well. She was wearing jeans and a white blouse, no bra, and when she inserted the last period on her nefarious tale I grabbed her breasts and mauled them, as though I wanted to squeeze out the memory of his touch. She made no move to stop me, stroked my hair, held me, caressed my back.

For a few days I tiptoed around the apartment like a burglar. Uncertain words caught in my throat—were they right or wrong? We slept together, me in my underwear and she in a blue nightgown and she offered no hint she desired lovemaking. I masturbated while showering and wondered how long. The answer came after another few days passed. We had smoked some pot and were listening to Joni Mitchell's new album, *Clouds*, when Wendy kissed me. Our warm tongues danced together and I knew we had again found each other.

A year passed. We were now officially California residents. Wendy traded her high-paying weekend banquets job for two lower paying luncheon shifts and began to attend classes at UC. I was again working at the post office, having applied for reinstatement. I wanted to find something else, but had no idea what. I became friends with Gene Hooks, a member of the Black Panther Party and President of our local postal union, the National Alliance. Using his influence, I ran unopposed and became an unlikely sergeant at arms. I was not physically intimidating, had never engaged in fisticuffs, and had no idea how I would evict a rowdy from a meeting.

The Democratic primary marked the first time we could vote in California and Wendy invited a Claremont co-worker over to share the experience. I was lounging on the couch when Wendy answered the door. I overheard greetings, and then Scarlett, slender, wearing a slinky peach colored mini-dress that flaunted her shapely legs, emerged from the hallway. The smell of alyssum filled the air as she pivoted toward me, her hair the color of pale honey, cheekbones high, lips thin, breasts unfettered, nipples staring at me. Every lustful cell in my body sizzled. I leapt up, intent on buzzing around her like a horny bee before I swooped in for nectar in the form of a warm hug. I took two steps and paused, for out of the corner of my eye I spied another stranger, a flinty-faced ape my height but a stone-solid two-twenty. Aside from the ubiquitous counterculture blue work shirt he was decked out in black—jeans, biker jacket and engineer boots. Even his hair and bristly whiskers were black. I abandoned any thought of *touching* Scarlett and welcomed her verbally and she introduced her companion. I flicked a one finger salute and a nod toward Kirk. Wendy offered them the couch and she eased into the wicker chair by our small, murmuring TV. I sank into a straight backed chair. After preliminary small talk I set a bowl of ice cubes, four glasses, and a bottle each of Jack Daniel's and Johnnie Walker on our recently acquired scarred coffee table.

"I voted for McCarthy," I said, sipping bourbon. Wendy and Scarlett chimed in with votes for Kennedy. That left Kirk to either make it a draw or a landslide.

"My uncle was a Wobbly. I don't vote, runs in the family."

There followed a bit of banter about anarchism and the labor movement before Scarlett and Wendy seized the conversation. They had much in common, working together and belonging to the same woman's group. After the usual work gossip they talked about books by feminists they were either reading or had recently finished. I hadn't turned a page in any of them, but every so often I tossed out an observation or asked a sensible question. Kirk held his conversational skills to pseudo-intellectual, acerbic one- or two-liners and I wondered if he'd ever had a carefree day in his life. On TV, the results trickled in, showing Kennedy in the lead, and I lit up a joint of Panama Red and passed it around.

"So, where are you from?" I said, casually eyeing Scarlett's mouthwatering delights. Boy, her dress was short. Kirk slipped off his jacket and rolled up his sleeves. His limbs put Charles Atlas to shame. No need to rile him.

"Newport News, Virginia," she said with only a slight accent.

"Her dad exiled her out here," Kirk said, his lips snagged between a snarl and a smile.

"I've heard this," Wendy said.

"Exiled?" I said.

"There's a big naval base a tad south of Newport News, and Daddy found out I'd been messing around. The genteel women in my family aren't supposed to associate with common sailor boys, especially when the women are only 16."

"So—what?—your dad found out you had a Navy boyfriend—"

"It was a tad more than one." She crossed her legs and I caught a tantalizing glimpse of her peach colored panties.

"He damn near put her under house arrest," Kirk said.

"McCarthy's conceded," Wendy said. "Bobby's gonna talk."

"I'll admit I thought he won the debate," I said.

"I like him," Wendy said.

"He's just gonna thank everybody," Kirk said. "The usual political bullshit."

"You're such a nihilist," Scarlett playfully chided.

"And you're my ever-loving romantic." He sucked in a toke and ditched the roach in an ashtray on the floor. "She wants to join the Venceremos Brigade," he said, releasing his smoky breath. "Go to Cuba. Cut sugar cane."

I looked at Wendy, her tight lips and arched eyebrows signaling: Touchy subject.

"Can you even get there?" I asked Scarlett as I lit another joint and passed it to her.

She inhaled deeply, exhaled and passed the joint to Kirk. "You have to go via Mexico," she said. "I know there's an element of danger. We don't want to get caught *trying* to go to Cuba."

"You're gonna sweat your ass off by day and get eaten by mosquitoes at night," Kirk said. He inhaled deeply and passed the joint to me.

"I hope to hear Castro."

I took a good hit off the diminishing joint, passed it to Wendy, and poured myself a generous helping of bourbon. I passed the bottle to Kirk, my drinking buddy.

"Do you know Spanish?"

"*Si.*"

"Bobby looks good," Wendy said.

The TV screen framed the crowded stage, people smiling and waving, the jubilant supporters pressing against one another in a large hall. Robert Kennedy waved at them and flashed his wide, toothy smile.

"I never found out why you were exiled," I said.

"Dig her background, man," Kirk said.

"Scarlett's family goes back to the Revolutionary War," Wendy said, ditching the roach in the ashtray.

It amazed me how she could have one ear tuned to the TV and the other tuning into the beat of our conversation.

"Is that true?" I said.

"So the family tale goes. John Clement, a great something grandfather on my mother's side, fought alongside Francis Marion, 'The Swamp Fox,' in the revolt against the British, and Sherwood Larkin, on my father's side, was an officer in Lee's army."

"Tell him what book your mom read to you when you were a kid," Kirk said.

"*Gone With the Wind.* Mama loved that book."

"Can you fuck'n believe it, man," Kirk said, enlivened by the conversational shift.

"It's a little different than how we grew up," Wendy said without turning from the TV.

"I was fourteen when I sneaked it up to my bedroom," Scarlett said. "The pages were dog-eared and a few were marked with red and green crayon swirls I vaguely remembered scrawling. I found the pages mama skipped. It was easy. The paper clips left faint indentations. Imagine my disappointment when I discovered what she censored wasn't anything like my dog-eared copy of *Tropic of Cancer.* I guess mama thought I was too young to read about Scarlett O'Hara flirtin' with so many young studs."

"C'mon up." Wendy patted her thigh and Cyclops leaped up. His tail rose as she scratched behind his ears and stroked his back. He curled up on her lap, content.

Kirk worked his fingers and examined his broad index finger, as though he were inspecting a small cut or searching for a splinter.

"Is that when you started seeing sailors?" I said. I gave the lonely ice cubes in my glass bourbon company. "After you read the book?"

"That wasn't until I was 15 and that book had nothing to do with it. Sheila—she was a neighbor two houses and about four hundred yards down the road—was older than me and she had a car, a silver Corvette. I went with her and flipped over tight sailor pants. Say, you sure do have a healthy appetite for bourbon. Ever think you drink too much?"

"Nah. I can handle it."

"Most of the time," Wendy said, rolling her eyes.

"C'mon, it's a special night." I cast a hurt child's look at her. She frowned and shifted her eyes to the TV. Cyclops rose, stretched, arched his back and lay back down.

"So what happened when your dad found out?"

"I don't think Kennedy can win," Kirk said. "The love-it-or-leave-it bumper sticker types won't vote for him."

"Maybe there are enough of us idealists left to pull it off," Wendy said.

"Realists rule the world," he said with a strong hint of rancor, "and those in power want to keep power."

"I could only go to necessary school functions on week nights and on weekends I had to be in by ten," Scarlett said.

"At least you could go out."

"Sorta. What dad thought was debatable. Actually, it was down-right deplorable. He hired a watcher, some warty woman from our Episcopal church. If I left the grounds, she went with me. God! That was embarrassing, going to school functions with this straight-laced hag hanging nearby. Of course I couldn't see Sheila. That pissed me off 'cause I knew she was off having fun. So I started using the phone."

"Ersatz sex," Kirk said as he studied his thumb.

"I called guys and got them off."

"Howcha do it?" I said, lighting another joint.

"Dad never found out about the phone calls, but he did throw a tizzy the summer after my senior year. He dragged me into his den, literally flung me into the oversized leather chair in front of his handcrafted desk, and slammed his dungeon door. 'How could you? You're a precocious young girl. Are you color blind?' He was screaming, his face red, the veins on his forehead throbbing. I thought he was gonna have a heart attack. He ranted about family honor as I worried about him keeling over. I gazed at the photos from his life spread across the walls, noticing all the politicians and sports figures and business leaders and clergy and not one frame devoted to me."

She paused for a toke. "So what made him almost apoplectic? Somehow he'd discovered the gardener, handsome Wade Monroe, had been fucking his pristine daughter in the gazebo tucked into a thicket of river birch by the pond, less than seventy yards from our white three-storied mansion grandpa built." She sipped scotch. I inhaled a healthy slug of bourbon. Having obviously heard all of this, Wendy's eyes didn't stray from the TV. "Local rumor said Gatsby type money is what grandpa used."

"That's one of my favorite novels," I said. "So, what happened?"

"He said he was gonna ship 'that nigger bastard' to an alligator farm in Louisiana and he told me to apply to a faraway university and to be more *discreet* with the family name until I left. As if those phonies at the polo club and the double martini for lunch crowd were angels. That's how I wound up here. The first year he paid for everything. Then I called home the summer after and told him I'd moved in with Kirk and would he like to speak to him. I made it sound all nicey nice." A twinkle lit her eyes. "Kirk got on the phone, and at first it went okay. Then he lost it."

"I did not," Kurt said. "Your idiotic dad started asking stupid questions."

"And you started talking about revolution with the zeal of a true anarchist. What was the last thing you said?"

"I called him a sick, fascist, sadistic capitalist pig who sucked the guts out of the lower classes for his own perverted pleasures. He yelled 'You goddamn Communist' and hung up."

"He cut off the money then. That's when I went to work at the Claremont and met—"

"Oh my God!" Wendy gasped.

My heart leaped. Wide-eyed, her hand shielded her mouth.

"They shot Bobby," she said.

CHAPTER FIFTEEN

No one knew what would happen when the city approved the permit. State and county officials objected, predicting more mayhem. To appease skeptics, the petitioners enlisted monitors to assure a peaceful march, though they had no way of knowing.

On the day of the march Wendy and I sat in front of the TV with steaming cups of coffee.

"Do you still think Tom's coming over?" Wendy said.

"You never know with that guy."

Wendy and I focused on the TV. KQED recapped events: the rioting on May 15, 1969, after Governor Reagan ordered in police to clear the park so a work crew could erect a nine-foot high chain link fence around it, the Alameda County Deputy Sheriff's firing "00" buckshot at demonstrators (killing one), the many days of rioting during the occupation of Berkeley by the highway patrol, Alameda County Sheriffs (street named the Blue Meanies), numerous police from outlying cities, and 2,700 National Guard troops.

"They're calling it Bloody Thursday," I said.

"I could've been there. Scarlett wanted me to go with her," Wendy said.

"Did she go?"

"I don't think so, but you know how the trip to Cuba galvanized her politics."

"Yeah. How 'bout Kirk?"

"No idea."

"To think it all happened over that lot you called a dump."

"That dump really does look like a park now. It's amazing what those people did."

"Yeah, and now the university wants to concretize it."

We heard someone coming up the stairs and expected to hear Tom's keyboarding fingers on the door. Across the hall the door creaked, our neighbor returning home.

Gene was carrying a copy of *The Autobiography of Malcolm X* when he and Tom walked out of a political philosophy class. "Good book," Tom said. "It really diffuses the Establishment's picture of Malcolm." They talked while matching strides and ended up at the Yellow House Restaurant discussing Malcolm's untimely murder, civil rights, and what the Black Panthers planned to accomplish. The following week Gene and I were discussing union business at his apartment when Tom popped in. Within a few days Tom began visiting Wendy and me sporadically.

Though we spent many thoughtful evenings with Tom, discussing the war, Ingmar Bergman films, Primal Scream Therapy, and various philosophers, we worried about him. His velocity often changed, become erratic. One evening he'd show up and pace the floor as he ran disconnected thoughts, memories and feelings by us at light speed, and a few days later he plop on the couch and say little, stare at walls. It was as though he were two different people.

"Whadya think's gonna happen?" Wendy asked as the march began.

"I dunno. Gene said he planned to go. Maybe we'll see him on the tube."

"Do you think Tom went?"

"I don't know. He said he'd swing by here. Guess he changed his mind."

She held her cup with both hands, said, "Do you plan to go to the track tomorrow?"

"Maybe. Depends what happens here," I said as I pointed at the TV.

She sipped and then licked her lower lip. "Always the horses," she murmured.

On May 30, 1969, under the wary eyes of the police and Guardsmen, a hand running line of people that stretched beyond the wide-angle lenses of elevated TV cameras slowly passed the barricaded park on Haste Street. Young women wove daisy chains into fence wire. Some slid stems into bayoneted rifle barrels. A helicopter towing a banner—Let a Thousand Parks Bloom—swirled overhead. We didn't see Gene or Tom during the hours 30,000 people shuffled past the doomed park. No one threw a rock. No nightstick cracked a skull. Tear gas remained in canisters. When the last marcher turned his back only the Guardsmen, the police, and the fence remained.

The following day I went to the track and lost eight dollars.

⇒+ +⇐

Two days after my unlucky bets, Tom dropped in to tell us he was leaving town for a while, something to do with sudden intense bouts of grief over the assassinations of Martin Luther King Jr. and Robert Kennedy. He felt it would soothe his spirit if he could see where they were murdered, a spin on the Freudian theory of overcoming your fears by confronting them. He'd bought a used car for the drive to the Lorraine Motel in Memphis and planned a separate trip to the Ambassador Hotel in L.A.

━━ ━━

Aside from a near riotous rally protesting the Vietnam War, and Neil Armstrong walking on the moon, two quiet months passed. The park remained fenced but unpaved. Gene and I were sorting mail when he asked if I had seen Tom.

"Not since he went to Memphis."

"He's back. I thought he might've stopped up."

"I didn't know he was back."

"It's weird, man. He's crashing at my pad. For some reason he thinks he needs protection from some ambiguous, evil spirit. Says he needs Panther protection and he knows I've been with them since the beginning. Guess that means an extra something to him, but, man, I got no clue what's going on in his head." He flicked a few more letters into pigeonholes and paused. He was staring at a letter and smiling. I glanced over. A shaky hand had penned the letter. "So Paula?" he said. "You s'pose they mean San Pablo?"

"Good guess."

He chucked the letter into a slot labeled 1800-2600 San Pablo Ave.

"So, I told Tom school and work claimed most of my time."

"What'd he say?"

"He just looked at me with hangdog eyes. What could I do? I didn't have the heart to tell him I didn't feel as connected to the Panthers as I once did, not as dedicated. I guess he blew his bread on the Memphis trip. He's not much trouble, comes and goes and curls up in a sleeping bag under the window at night."

I pulled a handful of letters out of a stuffed bin and bedded them in a canvas sack hanging from hooks on the rack behind us. The letters were ads from various companies, bills, business-to-business mail, and a sprinkling of personal letters.

"Maybe you and Wendy could have him up for dinner sometime soon. Thing is, that dude has a lotta new demons chasing him. See what you think. I think he needs help pronto. You know a good shrink?"

⇒╫ ╫⇐

Wendy cooked pork chops and Rice-A-Roni. She put together a lettuce and tomato salad dressed in olive oil and red wine vinegar. When Tom arrived, she leaned away from the stove to greet him, and I ushered him into the living room. For about ten minutes I tried to kick-start a conversation. He only nodded. Then, he asked to use the bathroom. After an inordinate amount of time he emerged, shortly before Wendy plated the food.

At the table, Wendy and I were silent, waiting, expecting Tom to tell us about his trip. Finally, I asked. He did not speak. Between ravenous bites his nervous eyes darted from Wendy to the avocado tree outside the window, to the stove, to me, and then back to Wendy. He gnawed on a bone, shoved rice into his mouth. Wendy and I exchanged worried shrugs and ate. He finished two pork chops before I cut into my second. He laid teeth-stripped bones in the oily salad bowl, lifted his plate, and licked it clean. "Thanks," he said as he pushed back his chair and asked if he could borrow the Heidegger book he'd seen on the coffee table. No need to interrupt our meal. He'd fetch it. And he did, letting himself out.

The following week Gene said Tom sold his car and asked for a ride to the overpass on University Avenue by I-80, where hitchhikers collected. A two-by-two cardboard sign with **L.A.** printed in bright red lay on his lap. He alternated singing "Like a Rollin' Stone" and "Gotta Travel On." Gene dropped him a little before six, late in the day to be hitching, then turned around and headed back into town. He watched Tom in his side mirror, still singing, waving the sign like a distress signal at passing motorists.

CHAPTER SIXTEEN

I t was my turn. I knew dishonesty could destroy a relationship. Wendy and I had never talked of having an open marriage, which I considered an enticing but ultimately oxymoronic idea. Marriage involved commitment. Tire of the commitment, dissolve the union. I also knew there were women I wanted to bed, and I suspected there were men Wendy wanted to lay beneath. It was human nature, given our ages.

I thought of her affair with Andre, the shifty headwaiter at the Claremont. Her forthright telling edged the explicit. The first time (how many were there?) he hid her in an unused room, returned within the hour and found her sitting on the bed wearing only her white bikini panties. She said little about the actual lovemaking, and in time I attributed her misstep to curiosity. She wanted to make love with a black man. In the end, I said, "I guess that makes me a cuckold. I've never been one." Looking back, I suppose it was my way of sharing the experience, as odd as that may sound.

So now it was my turn to confess. I wasn't going to mention Sue, whose boyfriend peddled weed, and the day I went over to score a lid, and she was alone. That had been a one-time occurrence, something that just happened. But, like Wendy, I'd had a brief affair with a co-worker, Nancy, who told me she knew young boys scaled the trees in the yard behind her bedroom window at night (Did she not pull the curtains?), and, like Wendy, I shielded the secret until guilt cooled passion.

I thought my confession was going well. Curled into the wicker chair, Wendy asked if I felt cutting way back on gambling and drinking was an act of contrition. I hadn't been to the track in weeks and only drank every few days, and then judiciously. I said I guess so. She admitted the curtailments pleased her and mentioned a child, not now, but sometime. I agreed, pleased and surprised, given the current circumstances, she projected our life together forward, and yes it would be good to wait a while.

Still feeling remorseful my affair was injurious to Wendy, I put a light spin on my fling without being too glib. She listened attentively, nodded, and referenced her own betrayal (her word).

"She didn't mean a thing to me," I finally said, nonchalantly flicking ash from my cigarette.

"Do you know what you just said?" She bristled.

"Well, yeah." I frowned, couldn't figure out her reaction. "What's wrong with what I said?"

"Are you sure that's what you mean?"

"I . . . think so." I felt sudden discomfort and shifted my weight. "I just mean—I just want *you* to know that *you're* the one I love."

She sat erect and her fierce look unnerved me. Had I not said the right thing? What happened to talk of our future?

"It would have meant more if you'd told me you loved her."

"It would?"

"You really piss me off sometimes."

I squirmed beneath her spiky tongue. She averted her eyes, slowly shook her head in what I took to be either disgust or disappointment. I was at a loss for words. Hadn't I made it clear Nancy was just a passing fancy? Why did I need to love her? What happened to infatuation? Wendy hadn't said she fell in love with the slick black headwaiter. Had I missed something back then, a subtle word slipped in? Perhaps thirst or passion, surely not love.

Someone rapped on our door.

"I better get it," I said, jumping up, and then pausing, eyes asking for her permission.

"Go ahead," she sighed.

I opened the door, thankful for the reprieve.

"Tom, you old son-of-a-gun. Come in. Hey, good to see you." I squeezed his arm and nudged him toward the living room. "It's Tom, Wendy." Her mouth curved into an ironic smile. "We've been worried 'bout you, fella. Weren't we, Wendy?" She rolled her eyes. "Yeah, we wondered what happened to you. It's been months. Gene said you were hitching to L. A. How was it down there? C'mon in, have a seat. We were just shooting the breeze. Want something to drink?"

"David's been worried about you," Wendy said. "But he's right. He and I can pick up our *breezy* conversation later."

"Glass of water," Tom said, frowning.

"How 'bout you?" I looked at Wendy, certain my face displayed the radiance of an innocent.

"Water."

I returned with three tall glasses, water for them and bourbon on the rocks to lighten the distress I was feeling. Was it possible to love two people at the same time? The physical was the rub. I wanted to fuck Nancy and not Wendy. When it was over I wanted to fuck Wendy and not Nancy. I never told Nancy I loved her, never told Wendy I didn't love her. Why would Wendy think better of me if I said I loved Nancy? Only one word fit: conundrum.

"So how have you two been?"

"Fine, just fine," I said. "We're just fine."

"It depends on your perspective," Wendy said, casting a censorious eye at my bourbon.

"I get the feeling I've come at a bad time."

I felt too discombobulated to answer, certain anything I uttered would be wrong. I knocked back a few hefty shots to settle my thoughts. What had she said about the guy who fucked her? I scratched my cheek.

"David and I were having a difference of opinion." Her eyes rolled my way. "We can pick up later." Her eyes back to Tom. "I'm sorry if I sounded sarcastic. It's good to see you. We were worried about you." She smiled. It looked genuine.

Tom sipped water. "I wanted to tell you about my Memphis trip and why I never made it to L.A." He half-smiled and watched Cyclops rise from a sun spot on the floor, stretch and yawn. He padded up to Tom and sniffed his leg, and continued on, probably heading to his bowl of food in the kitchen. He liked to eat upon waking.

"Okay, man, you've got our ears."

Tom spoke quietly, employing few hand gestures. Fourteen days to make the drive in a 1950 bullet-nosed Studebaker he bought at Honest Abel's Quality Cars in Oakland. In Reno he parked the car inside Mel's Auto Repair and slept in the backseat overnight while he waited for Mel find and fix an oil leak. In Elko three days passed at Ruby's Gas & Tow before brakes arrived from Chicago.

"Something about it being an old car needing special brakes," Tom said.

Ruby told him he could sleep in the car inside the garage. "It ain't heated after we knock off at six, but it ain't been too cold neither so you won't freeze."

A shredded tire was slapping the right rear rim like an unwieldy hula hoop when the Studebaker limped into Jefferson Tire in Kansas City.

Heading south on two new rear tires and two passable ones up front, Tom tuned the car radio to a Memphis rock station and happily sang along for miles until a screeching water pump dictated a detour to Herb Chapman's Towing & Repair in New Madrid, Missouri.

He pegged Herb to be pushing fifty, a wiry, hard-muscled guy going soft who hid his thinning, two-tone hair beneath an ancient, well-greased St. Louis Browns baseball cap. Herb's oil stained fingers rubbed his oil stained knuckles as he listened to Tom's tale of woe.

"Uh-huh. Just might have one."

Tom followed him to the sprawling junkyard. He didn't see or hear guard dogs. A nine-foot high chain link fence topped by a double run of gnarly razor wire protected the yard. Standing between two tall rows of radically redesigned cars Tom hand-shielded his eyes and squinted at the damaged coffins until his eyes alighted on a tall, angular man swinging a lug wrench along his leg while he watched a forklift rearrange dead carcasses.

"Might likely take a while," Herb said, stroking his greasy forearm. "Danny's digging out a '53 Caddy. I'll set him to fetching yours once he returns the others to order." Aiming a thumb to the left, midway down the row, he added, "Likely find yours in that bunch." He paused and carefully looked Tom over. "We got a spare bed, and you're welcome to sleep over ifin we run late. Only cost you ten bucks. Cheaper than a motel."

Tom was silently humming "Danny Boy." His eyes followed the direction Herb's thumb pointed while his mind wondered when the Irish discovered an Englishman penned the ballad.

The forklift's thick blades knifed a beat-up Caddy, wrenched the twisted wreck from its dead cousins, and swung around, dropping the kill on the ground. The tall, slender man jumped back to save his toes, bent down, and popped off the front right tire wheel cover.

Tom said he'd grab a bite, be back in an hour or so, but he wasn't sure about the invite as he was in a hurry to get to Memphis.

"I'll get Danny right on it," Herb said. His broad smile displayed two rows of glossy white Chiclets.

Tom hoofed to the golden arches he'd passed, ordered a quarter pound cheeseburger, fries and Coke, and sat across from a family of four, kids giggling, licking their slender fingers after drowning fries in ketchup. He knew a water pump was an essential part, but he had no idea what function it performed. The thought of staying the night made him apprehensive and he hoped Herb wouldn't jack him around.

As he gnawed on his burger, trouble buzzed the outskirts of his memory. He turned focus knobs back to Geology 101, the 1800's. Yikes! New Madrid, Missouri, the epicenter of the strongest earthquake *ever* recorded on the American mainland. The earth rose like a shaken sheet. The mighty Mississippi River altered its course; some said it flowed backwards. Tom sprang up. His eyes bulged as he stared down at the innocent family of four. His hands flew up from his sides, fingers pointed like six shooters. The kids laughed; the open-mouthed wide-eyed parents envisioned an escaped homicidal madman.

"Bang, bang, run, run, run for dirt's a comin'," he sang, and dashed out.

"But the ground stayed steady and old Herb patched up the car," Tom told us. "The Studebaker may have been a lemon when I left Berkeley, but it was a peach by the time I rolled into Memphis."

The following day his invigorated car crept by the Lorraine Motel. Tom was disappointed it looked so *ordinary*. He meandered around nearby blocks before he finally parked near the Mississippi River. As soon as his feet hit the sun drenched street he felt chilled. He pegged the sultry air to be pushing ninety. He didn't feel ill. He knew his wintry reaction could only mean one thing: someone was watching him. Had Herb or Danny, the mysterious forklift driver, followed him, upset he hadn't stayed the night?

He moved on foot quickly, circled blocks, dashed into large stores with multiple exits, zigzagged across streets whose names he didn't know, jumped onto buses as the doors were folding, stayed if he could find a window seat. He tried to memorize cars that pulled alongside, the faces of people boarding the bus. He hopped off, speed-walked streets. At the end of the day, tired and hungry, two scary words occupied his mind: I'm lost.

He passed Stax records and saw Lorraine, a snazzy looking woman decked out in skyscraper heels, hot pink short shorts, and a white tank top that offered generous servings of her substantial breasts. Psychedelic earrings swayed across her bronzed cheeks. He stood perfectly still and gazed at her, and he knew he was nearing Nirvana. "Is there a place to hide?" he asked. For twenty bucks she said he could hide in her room for an hour. He felt he would be safe in her warm presence and offered to throw in a rib dinner and another twenty if he could stay the night. She called him "Honey" and said the night was young, a rib dinner sounded mighty fine and for sixty he could hang around 'til morning.

"Good deal," he said, imagining a long, safe and torrid night.

In her tidy, small apartment at the Mur-Keys, the smoky barbecue taste lingered in his mouth. He watched as she stripped and ran a bath. She hadn't invited him to join her, and he didn't feel offended. Surveillance would occupy him while she bathed. She sank into sudsy water. He doused the bedroom lights and stood by the window, wrapped himself in thin curtain, slightly parted two slats, and peeped through the Venetian blind, searching for suspicious activity below. He didn't hear her when she crept up behind him. She slipped her bronze arms around his waist and pressed against his hips. He screamed, jumped back, and knocked her onto the bed. She had left the bathroom light on and the door open. In faint light he eyed her succulent naked body.

"Hey, I told you I ain't into rough-and-tumble," she said.

"You're a creeper," he said, amicably.

"Hmm, the touchy type. Well, Mr. Jumpy, are you just gonna stand there ogling or you gonna give your Mr. Johnson a ride?"

"Are you FBI?"

"Jesus, are you a dimwit or what?" Her eyes narrowed, suspicious. "You got all your hairs in place?"

"I don't plan to do anything with LBJ. I don't even know him."

"Baby, you one weird white boy. Let's get it on so I can get some sleep."

She sat on the edge of the bed, unzipped him, pulled down his jeans and underwear, and mouthed him until he quickly hardened. Then she held him in her hand and looked into his dark eyes.

"Is a little head action all you want?"

Beautiful Lorraine's mouth and hand had worked a miracle. His fear vanished. He peeled off his shirt and shoes, kicked off his downed pants and underwear. She lay back on the bed. Tom climbed on top of her.

"Easy, baby."

He entered her, and for a few moments experienced pure ecstasy. Minutes later he and Lorraine were fast asleep.

When morning rays flooded the Venetian blinds, he slipped from her sheltering arms and quietly dressed. She emitted a loud, three-part snore, and he looked at her askance. Beneath white sheet, her splayed legs tempted him. But something troubled him. It'd been too easy. It had the makings of a set-up, a way to bond him to one place. Why else would she have the same name as the motel? He zipped up, retrieved a twenty from the sixty she'd put in the bureau drawer, and exited, he proudly thought, as silently as a cat burglar.

Outside, a blast of sunlight singed his eyes, and he raised a hand and gazed around. He didn't know where he was, much less where he'd parked. He started walking, not too quickly, not too slowly, no need to attract attention. Big city strut: head up, arms swinging in what he imagined to be a self-assured natural rhythm. He noted bums lounging on bus stop benches near dirty buildings with boarded-up windows.

After a few blocks he spotted a man leaning over a metal box with a clear plastic door. He quickened his pace, intending to ask directions, but, as he neared, the name of the street where he parked went fuzzy. He knew it was by railroad tracks and a river, near downtown. He wondered why he couldn't remember. Luckily, there was only one river. If he could find the Mississippi, he'd scout the waterfront.

Tom tapped the hunched man on the shoulder.

"How do I find the Lorraine Motel?"

The man shoved newspapers under his left arm and a handful of change and a screwdriver into his right pants pocket. As he unfurled himself from the box his immense Afro rose above Tom's chin and climbed higher and higher. Tom swallowed hard, sweat beaded on his forehead. What to say to a seven-foot man wearing a tumbleweed on his head?

"Jesus Christ! How tall are you?"

The man's scowl melted him.

"I'm—I'm a reporter—for the *Berkeley Barb.*" Tom gulped. "I'm doing research for a story on Dr. King's tragic murder, only I don't know how to get to the Lorraine Motel."

The man pointed down the block, his finger as long as the barrel of Wyatt Earp's Buntline Special, as seen on TV.

Tom hastened away, not knowing how long to walk straight. It could be another trick. Cohorts lay ahead. He switched to a zigzag course and wandered unknown streets, occasionally stopping to ask strangers for directions. He paused at a corner and thought of retreating to Lorraine's, but he had lost the way. Then he remembered the twenty. He wondered if she knew the Giant. Would she send him in long-legged, screwdriver-wielding pursuit to retrieve her lifted cash?

He strode on, humming a variation of Little Bo Peep: "Little ol' Tom's lost his wheels and doesn't know where to find them," certain the dotted cameras floating disguised as eyes in the skulls of walking suits passing him recorded his every move and sent coordinates to places unknown through transmitters hidden in knotted ties and button-down lapels. The fire in the sky slowed him, roasted his shadow and gave back ashes. His sweaty lifeblood oozed from his skin. His feet hurt. He lifted them up one by one, looked at his soles as if he'd stepped in dog crap. Had Lorraine planted a tracking device in his tennies?

He sighed and leaned against a lamppost. His stomach moaned. He snuck into a hole-in-the-wall, sat at a yellow Formica counter, and ordered bacon-and-eggs, toast and coffee from a waitress wearing a blue-and-white uniform. He ate and felt better, accepted a refill.

"Where's the Lorraine Motel?" he said, keeping a wary eye on the yellow missile balanced on her ear.

"Thatta way," she pointed.

He looked out the window; a blur of passing cars and people.

"How far?"

"Baby, it's on the other side of town."

His chin sank into his palm. He'd walked in the wrong direction.

"Want me to call you a cab?"

The cabbie dropped him off in front of the Lorraine. Tom studied the second story balcony, wondering where King had stood when a gunman's bullet shattered his dream.

He glanced up and down the street. Then, to be safe, he trotted several blocks in what he imagined to be a square circle until he found his car. Birds had cleverly disguised it with polka dots. A windshield wiper had trapped what resembled a parking ticket, but he knew better. His knitting fingers tore the secret spotting code into confetti, which he flung into an imaginary brisk wind that did not magically appear. He knelt to scatter the pieces with his hand and immediately knew he'd fallen into a trap. He visualized the lead story on the ten o'clock news, or whatever time they ran the news in Memphis. "Shredded parking ticket found beneath slain California tourist." Oh, God almighty, he groaned as he flung open the car door and slinked inside his trusty Studebaker. He slouched down and sped 2,100 miles without a spot of car problems. Along the way he kept a wary eye on the rearview mirror. When he crossed the California line, he decided to seek refuge with Gene.

Wendy and I exchanged worried looks. Tom seemed okay during the telling, but the telling . . .

An uneasy silence stretched for a minute or two, broken when Tom asked for a refill. I looked at Wendy and she declined. I grabbed Tom's glass and scooted into the kitchen. I ignored Cyclops' meows for attention and filled Tom's glass with water and half-filled mine with bourbon.

"Here ya go," I said. Wendy eyed my freshened drink with obvious displeasure. I made a face that said: Hell, after a tale like that. To Tom I said, "We were concerned 'bout you, remember? We had you up for d-dinner."

"Yeah, and I appreciate it, though I'm not sure I made it plain at the time. It was very good."

He smiled at Wendy.

"Thanks." She paused and shook her head. "If we'd only known what you were going through."

"There's more."

"Have at it, man," I said.

After Gene deposited him on University Avenue a menacing police car gave him "bad vibes." He ditched the L.A. sign and headed toward the railroad tracks. Memories of Memphis crowded his mind. Someone was following him. At the train tracks he paused and glanced over his shoulder and kindled a unique travel solution. It would be a tedious way to get to L.A, but he wouldn't have to stay on highways. He could hide behind brambles or in woods if necessary. He backtracked, turned down Fourth Street, and confidently walked toward Golden Gate Fields, the racetrack in Albany. He hadn't gone far when he saw people going into Spenger's Fish Grotto. He knew from conversation with me that horse owners and trainers often dined there. He thought he might be able to lasso one, submit his idea, and rent a cheap thoroughbred.

A few well-barbered, nattily dressed diners were arriving. He had neither the time nor the means to coiffure his long hair, polish his scuffed shoes, or iron his wrinkled shirt. He blinked three times and the genie woke and whispered the solution.

Tom casually fell in behind a well-dressed middle-aged couple as they strolled in the front door. Inside, he pushed his way between them and streaked by the startled *maitre d'*. Racing into a large room he passed a sign that announced a banquet for retired mechanical engineers and their wives. He forgot about track people, ripped off his shirt, and, still running, sang, "In the valley of the jolly, ho-ho-ho, Green Giant."

The frantic *maitre d'* pursued him, yelling for waiters to join the chase. Tom hopped onto a table. His shoe caught the edge of a plate and a large serving of Jumbo Shrimp Pomodoro over Linguine catapulted onto a woman at an adjoining table. He dropped his pants and underwear and spun around, giving each of the dumbstruck ladies a full, close-up view. A thin, balding husband lunged for him. Tom leaped up like a swashbuckler in an old Errol Flynn movie, caught hold of a massive ship's wheel chandelier, and swung across the table. Scurrying diners crashed over overturned chairs. The thin, balding husband planted one foot on a chair and the other on scrambled silverware and mounted the table. He looked up just as swinging Tom's feet rammed his chest and knocked him onto abandoned entrees on an adjoining table.

A portly waiter came up from behind. Tom swung into him backwards. The big man wobbled, regained his balance and locked his beefy arms around Tom's waist. Tom wiggled and kicked. The table nearly capsized when the waiter, now hanging on to Tom's legs, crumpled to his knees. The falling weight was too great. Tom's hands abandoned the ship's wheel. Two policemen rushed in. The quickest one vaulted onto the table, punched Tom in the groin, and slammed him headfirst on the table. The portly waiter was holding on to Tom's feet. The second officer climbed onto the table.

"As you stare into the acumen of his eyes," Tom sang loudly, "and ask do ya wanna to make a deeyull."

"Wrong lyric, jackass," the second cop said as he linked Tom's wrists and snapped on handcuffs. The two officers jerked Tom up. The chubby waiter regained his footing and stood behind Tom. The cops were telling Tom to step down on a chair when the waiter emitted a maniacal laugh and shoved him. A brief trip airborne, then Tom crash landed on his shoulder. The cops jerked him up, and Tom screamed obscenities as they dragged him to the squad car, its red light swirling. A few steps behind the *maître de'* waved his fist and shouted charges: disturbing the peace, indecent exposure, destruction of property, assault. One cop shoved Tom into the backseat while the other called in a 5150. Once the cops settled in the front seat, they turned on their siren and roared toward Psych Emergency at Highland Hospital in Oakland.

Tom excused himself and made for our bathroom. Cyclops rubbed against Wendy's ankles and softly meowed.

"He must be out of food," she said.

She and Cyclops padded into the kitchen and I trailed them. I wanted another drink. She unzipped a can of chicken in gravy and spooned a lion-sized helping into Cyclops' dish. He raised his head, curled his tail, and meowed. I imagined his lips smacking as his dish descended. I suddenly felt woozy. I'd ingested a wee too much bourbon. I opened the refrigerator and rescued two bottles of Pilsner Urquell from the cold. Maybe the change would placate Wendy.

The three of us settled in the living room again.

"M-Man, you're a real whacko," I said.

"David didn't mean to insult you," Wendy said. Her eyes swept over my restrained drinking choice and lashed me. I shrugged and drank from a bottle.

"You look great," Wendy said to Tom.

"You s-sure do," I said. "What brought 'bout this trans. . .for. . .mation? You coulda been c-c-conked on the noodle in Memphis."

"Dave!" Wendy nearly screamed.

"Okay, okay, t-t-take it easy. No n-need to get hysterical. Not my fault---."

"Go ahead, Tom," Wendy said. "What did happen?"

"I got lucky. They put me on ward C-1 on a 72-hour psych evaluation hold. That gave them the right to put me on drugs. I had a court hearing three days later—the court's right there in the hospital—and the judge was convinced I was still a danger to others—I guess I was still in a manic cycle—and they put me on a 14-day hold. Thankfully I connected with a neat therapist. Beth didn't buy the schizophrenic label they'd hung on me. She thought I was manic depressive, and she put me on lithium."

"You've had a hard time," Wendy said.

"Lonely," he said.

"You're lucky they didn't throw your ass in the slammer," I said, and hiccupped.

⊨ ⊨

Wendy hung up the phone.

"That was Kirk. He and Scarlett broke up."

"I can't say I'm surprised."

"He wants to know if you can give him a lift to the overpass on University."

We had visited him once after Scarlett took off for Cuba. The smell of rotting food, soiled clothes, and stale cigarettes nearly buckled us. Dirty dishes mushroomed from the kitchen sink. Stale clothes littered the apartment. Cigarette butts overran ashtrays on a cluttered coffee table. Unkempt and undoubtedly stoned, he said he'd only be happy when she returned.

I wondered what he thought when she did return, for I was disappointed. She had shed miniskirts, tight jeans and sheer blouses. In their place: work boots, blue work shirts, and unisex overalls. I found excitement short when she told us of the great joy she'd felt cutting sugarcane beside *campesinos* and the mostly young members of the Venceremos Brigade, how her sweat soaked, aching body, fingers bent with pain, never deterred her spirit, and of the afternoon a great excitement swirled in the sweltering Cuban air. Castro was coming. After a black bean and rice meal, the brigade sat on the ground in front of the maestro as he orated for two-hours. His passion galvanized her commitment to "a true revolutionary spirit."

She rolled her eyes at the notion of returning to work at the Claremont, dismissing the elegant hotel as "an aging elitist establishment." Wendy's women's group fared no better. "Eight bourgeois white gals caught up in the cerebral."

Time passed. Hurt feelings smoldered and cooled, though our visits grew infrequent. Scarlett moved on a different stage, one populated by ersatz revolutionaries wearing scarred football helmets for clashes with the cops, their resolve juiced when they listened to the Stones belt out "Street Fighting Man." Kirk called them "Cop targets."

His garb remained constant: sturdy black boots, blue work shirt, tight black jeans, and a black motorcycle jacket, ala Marlon Brando in *The Wild One.* Encased in the strong, silent version of the rough-and-tumble American male, he rarely displayed emotion or risked talk of feelings. I assumed he was standing pat, waiting for Scarlett to exhaust her newfound arsenal in her ongoing assault on her upper class family. Sometimes I wondered what lay beneath his stoic exterior.

As I headed to their apartment I thought about how Kirk and I had never become *simpatico*. Scarlett anchored us and we could not follow when she sailed into murky waters.

He was sitting on the curb and he slowly rose and lifted a bulging backpack. I noticed he had lost weight. He opened the passenger door, tossed the backpack on the backseat, and flopped in.

"Always did think you looked like a biker." I said, hoping to lighten the mood. He grunted. I took Haste Street to Grove Street, turned right, and headed toward University Avenue. At the intersection, I turned left, toward the overpass in West Berkeley where travelers hung their thumbs.

"So where you headed?"

"Dunno. Just gotta hit the road, man."

I thought I saw something new in his face. I couldn't tell if it was anticipation, reflection, or resignation. It may have been my imagination. How little we know each other, I thought. Was it also true of everyone whose paths crossed? Were we all destined to be friendly strangers?

CHAPTER SEVENTEEN

The changes were incremental.

Wendy cut her long hair shoulder-length, "Easier to wash." She upped her workload at school, "To finish faster and get a job." The increased class load signaled the demise of her luncheon shifts, "I can pick up some weekend banquets. Don't worry. Andre's long gone." (Do not memories linger?) On banquet nights she encased her lovely breasts in a bra, sheathed her long legs in panty hose, shimmied into a tight fitting black polyester skirt, and tucked in a white blouse. A white apron tied the outfit. She painted her lips pale pink, darkened her eyebrows a shade, and tightly cinched black walking shoes. She had no interest in performing the "hostess with the mostest." Her everyday garb spoke comfort: sneakers, jeans and a blue work shirt or a simple pullover, a sweatshirt when the air cooled.

I may have felt overwhelmed or intimidated by the determined fire in her eyes, for I hid behind a scruffy beard, *à la* Bob Dylan. I also resumed my weekend trips to the track and abandoned any thought of an alcohol diet. I plugged away at the post office and discovered Gene liked puzzles, a natural horseplayer. Studious Gene wanted to research the subject. A week later he told me he'd bought a book and suggested I do likewise. We read and studied *Ainslie's Complete Guide to Thoroughbred Racing* and tested our education at the track, confident that perceptive logic and selective bets would prevail. If someone asked, we were "holding our own," akin to treading water, a cagey way of saying we were probably losing and didn't know how much.

So, one fateful day I drove home from the track wrapped in vainglorious memories of a thrilling stretch run and a pocketful of cash. I parked the car behind our apartment and vaulted up the stairs two at a time, eager to boast. Wendy was in the kitchen, tasting spaghetti sauce. All smiles, I slapped the Form on the kitchen table, pulled the wadded bills out of my jean pocket, and tossed them on the paper. Yes, yes, it was true. I'd laid ten bucks on Divorce Ahead and cleared $65.

"It was great," I said. "I wish you coulda seen it. He was last coming into the stretch. I thought I'd lost. Then, he started picking up horses until, right before the wire, he forged to the front. What a race!"

"Glad you liked it. Okay if I start the spaghetti now?"

She eased pasta into a pot of boiling water.

"It's half of next month's rent," I said.

She gave the pasta a quick stir.

"I'm happy you had a good day," she said, glancing unkindly at the *Form* and money. "I need to set the table."

I sat, put the bills in sequential order, and folded the Form in half. "I still can't believe it. He was last—"

"I heard you the first time."

I opened my wallet and put the bills inside.

"Half of next month's rent."

"I made small salads. They're in the fridge."

"That's . . . good."

I picked up the *Form*, retreated into the living room, and opened the paper to the seventh race at Golden Gate Fields. There he was again, Divorce Ahead, standing out like a beacon on a foggy night. I again folded the paper and laid it on top of the previous week's, from which no light had shone. I wondered what was bugging Wendy. I shrugged. Maybe her period had come early. The racing paper's black ink had stained my hands. I went into the bathroom to wash.

As we ate I recited a shortened version of the race, hoping to ignite her spirit, my hands demonstrative. It was like trying to light a fire with damp kindling. I thought of asking about her period and decided to wait. As soon as we finished she started on the dishes. I came up behind her, pressed against her hips, and my hands cupped her breasts. She tensed.

"You think you can get a feel anytime you want," she said, her hands still submerged in soapy water. "There are times when I don't like being groped." She lifted her wet hands, shook off suds, and pushed my hands down. "We need to talk. You don't mind if I finish, do you? I was about to do your plate."

She picked up the plate and I knew it was exit time. Not all that long ago she'd impulsively thrown a plate or two and her aim was getting better.

I slinked into the living room, slumped on the couch, and lit up. Gees, I'd only fondled her breasts while she stood at the sink, an overture I'd done dozens of times without complaint. Instead of her sensual hips teasing my groin . . . what happened?

I yearned for a good shot of bourbon, but the booze was in the kitchen and I'd only worsen her foul mood. I was still sulking when she came in and sank into the wicker chair. Her severe expression told me we weren't going to cuddle soon.

For what seemed like a very long time we sat in tense silence. Words kept running through my mind, but I hadn't a clue which ones to use. She finally inhaled a breath and slowly let it out.

"I'm sorry if I sounded harsh."

I knew I had to tread softly. Just a few placating words, the fewer the better, and we would make-up and all would be hunky-dory again.

"I know."

"There you go again. How can you know until I tell you?"

Oops. Her accusatory tone and explosive eyes told me I'd mis-fired. "I . . . I don't know."

"It's *my* body, David. There are times when I like you to touch me, just like there are times when I don't. It doesn't mean I don't love you."

"Like when you're doing the dishes," I said ready to relinquish that joy to make peace.

She folded her arms across her waist, a bad sign.

"What was the name of that horse—*Divorce Ahead?*"

The way she said it, with an emphasis on the D word . . . I swal-lowed hard. I had to backtrack fast. Only I wasn't sure what lay behind me.

"Okay. I won't do it again."

"Do what?"

"What you said."

She bit her lower lip, a signal she'd shut any back door escape. She wasn't finished.

"What?" I said. I glanced at Cyclops lying on a throw rug, chin on his crossed front legs crossed. He looked serene. Of course, he was sleeping.

"I want us to see a counselor. Sometimes it's hard to under-stand the dynamics in a relationship without outside help. How do you feel about that?"

"Well, gees, I guess it'd be okay."

"I think we need some guidance."

"Okay, if that's what you want."

"It'd be better if we both wanted it."

"I'm willing to give it a try." I wasn't keen on the idea, only out of options.

⊰⊱

As soon as I saw slim, dark-haired Nadine I knew she couldn't help. Her light colored blouses and short skirts were way too distracting. I liked looking at her loose breasts when she diverted her eyes to Wendy. And her long legs were elegant. I wanted to impress her, but nothing I said pleased her.

After Wendy gave long, tortured details of the insensitivity and distractedness of someone she loved, which I took to be me, Nadine liked to ask, "How do you feel about that, Dave?" or "Do you see this as a problem?" To which I would reply, playing the strong silent obviously misunderstood husband to the hilt, "Dunno," or "Maybe." We quit after two sessions. Nadine probably thought I was a hopeless cad. I shrugged it off. In a few weeks we'd be a skinny yellowing folder collecting dust in the back of her file cabinet.

But I knew Wendy was upset. First clue: she no longer slept in the nude. Second clue: she was sullen. Third clue: she was impatient with me. Okay, the sessions were important to her and I had dismissed them, seen them as nothing more than a mild and quickly passing irritant. I'd made a mistake. It left me feeling confused and scared. There was something in the air I intellectually understood but failed to grasp.

To get back on her good side, I minded my p's and q's and implemented changes to please her. I read excerpts from feminist books. After finishing *Esquire* and *Playboy* I picked up *Ms.* and read, preferably when Wendy was in the room, a few articles. I had never imagined myself to be a sexist. I didn't think I compartmentalized or categorized women as wife, lover, cook, mother. The examples in my life endorsed a woman's place in the world outside the home: Mom, uncomplaining, bill-paying, factory-working breadwinner in

201

Carthage, and Cathy, college graduate, working as a professional in her chosen field, and Wendy who attended classes at UC while I worked. I could talk the talk and apply the lingo to the outside world, but what of my own? I thought of Kirk, given the boot. I didn't want to follow in his footsteps.

Survival changes: I neatly trimmed my bristly goatee, occasionally brought home flowers on non-special days, and listened more attentively. I tempered my drinking and abandoned airbrushed playmates. I went to the track less. Gene wasn't disappointed. He said we chased handicapping pie-in-the-sky with just enough of a positive behavioral return to hook us. He wanted to concentrate on his studies.

Wendy liked the attention I gave her instead of the bottle or the horses. I scouted recipe books and occasionally cooked dinner. We had long heart-to-heart talks. And soon we again made love passionately. It wasn't long before Wendy told me she wanted to go off the pill.

＝┿ ┿＝

A year passed. I like to believe my sperm scored a bull's-eye in 1970, the night we passionately made love to *The Rite of Spring.* Parenthood: the pleasure of sleeping in on my days off gone, waking before Wendy left for morning classes, mountains of diapers carted to the Laundromat, taking turns reading and rereading aloud Dr. Spock's dog-eared chapter on colic as Michelle bawled. We spun Dylan's "Sad Eyed Lady of the Lowlands," hoping the soft song would quiet Michelle's incessant wail. It didn't.

At two, in 1973, Michelle discovered the delight of clanging pots and pans on the kitchen floor. Our charitable non-complaining downstairs neighbor was either a masochist or deaf. We couldn't afford many toys. Most of our spare money went toward a babysitter while I worked and Wendy resumed her classes. She arranged her schedule so she would be home by mid-afternoon. On Thursday she spent all day with Michelle. When I came home from work, a harried Wendy craved quiet time before she started dinner. So, on Thursdays and Saturdays (Wendy's study day), I usually buckled Michelle into the backseat of our VW and drove up the Berkeley hills, to the sandboxes and swings at Glendale-La Loma Park. As the car slowly climbed the steep, twisting street, I sang raucous, off-key renditions of "Zippity Doo Da" just to watch her smile brighten the rearview mirror.

Winter rains put the kibosh on park trips. We bought Michelle a yellow plastic school bus and she and I spent hours in play, rolling it on the floor, creating voices and activities for the wooden kids that rode inside it. On weekdays we watched *Sesame Street* and *Mr. Rodgers Neighborhood* while Wendy hit the books in her little alcove study before she made dinner.

On a sunny summer day I took Michelle, then four, to the playground and merry-go-round at Tilden Park, the 2,000 acre wildlife and natural preserve in the hills above Berkeley. She flew on the swings, smiled going down the kiddy slide, and insisted we teeter-totter. I straddled one end and pushed down with both hands, making a silly face. She threw her head back and laughed. Later I held her hand as we climbed stone stairs leading to the merry-go-round.

"She's shutdown," the wizened little man with curly gray hair said, his hand gripping a pair of pliers. "Busted motor."

"Is it okay if my daughter sits on a horse?"

"Okay by me, I'm almost done. You got 'bout," scratching his bristly cheek, "ten, fifteen minutes before I wrap things up. Cute kid," he said, smiling.

She chose a roan with an impossible red grin. I hoisted her up and she chortled, "Giddy up, horsey," as she rocked back and forth.

The sun was reclining behind a wall of eucalypti as we went down the steps. Parents were hastily scooping up their kids. One mother was almost dragging her bawling son to the parking lot. I wondered why they were in such a rush. Michelle scampered to the sandbox, picked up an abandoned red plastic shovel and began to dig. I sat cross-legged beside her.

"Whatcha doin'?" I drew a squiggly line in the sand with my finger. "Diggin' a hole."

I smiled, but I felt uneasy. Why were the other parents in a near frenzy, collecting their kids, shoving them into cars, and slamming doors? I scanned the empty playground. It had been bursting with energetic kids and their parents when we climbed the stairs. My heart jumped. A young black man sitting on a railroad tie stared at us without smile. I glanced at Michelle, still digging. A second young black man sat on a bench on the other side of the playground, leaning forward, his forearms resting on his thighs, a look of menace clouding his face. The Death Angels leaped into my mind, the Bay Area clandestine group far more radical and secretive than the Panthers. Membership required the indiscriminate killing of an unknown white person, man or woman, young or old. Three dozen innocent people murdered, "The "Zebra Killings."

"Time to go," I said, grabbing Michelle's hand.

She dropped the shovel without protest. The men stared at us without moving. I took her small hand in mine, the protective father masking his fear. The last three cars were backing out of parking spaces. A Ford van parked on the far side of the lot remained. To look back at the men would show fear. My heart hammering the word, *faster, faster.* I had no idea what I'd do if they made a move. The cars loaded with whining kids and frightened parents fleeing. Too late to flag them down or call out, safety in numbers. I expected to hear footfalls any moment. We were almost at the car. *Faster, faster.* Michelle giggled. I reached the VW a few steps in front of her. My hand shook as I jerked the door open and pulled the back of the passenger seat down. She climbed in and I slammed the door. I darted around the car, pulled keys from my pocket. I glanced at the playground. One of the men was standing, watching, taking a step. I got into the car and turned the key. The engine fired. The second man was also standing, his hand behind his back. Reaching for a gun? They looked at one another. I shifted, backed out, and urged the VW for speed it did not possess. The small engine whined and groaned as we struggled up an incline in first gear. I reached across the passenger seat and locked the passenger door, then mine. After the curve ahead the road leveled and we would gain speed. What were the men doing? Running up the hill to intercept us or racing to the van to pursue us? I glanced at the bushes and trees for winks of sunlit metal.

"Dad," Michelle said, "you forgot somethin'."

My mind rushed past items. We hadn't brought jackets. Had she lost a shoe?

"What?"

"You didn't buckle me in."

"Hang onto your seat."

We rounded the curve, the merry-go-round alongside us.

"Dad."

"In a min—"

A blue Chevy pulled out in front of us. I gripped the wheel. Dear God, not the van. They had run up the steps. They intended to block the road, jump out of the car, and gun us down. I drew a deep breath and held it. Crash the VW into them, take our chances, Michelle not buckled in. I released my breath. There was only one person in the car. He had curly gray hair.

I glanced in the rearview mirror. Nothing. I followed him down the winding road.

⚔ ⚔

Wendy, now a thirty-three-year-old university graduate going to job interviews instead of classes, read Michelle a bedtime Richard

Scarry story. After our sleepy-eyed daughter nodded off Wendy tucked her into bed while I made popcorn. We settled on the couch and munched as we watched *All in the Family*. During a commercial break Cyclops raised his head and meowed plaintively. "Guess he likes the show, too" I said, and we laughed. Then I noticed the leaves of a houseplant trembling as though in light wind. An instant later, the walls groaned, the floor shook like a perverse carnival ride, and a book lying flat on the edge of the bookshelf crashed on the floor. I stood as if to defend myself against unseen enemies and lost my sense of balance. The room spun. I stumbled forward, backwards, and fell on the couch.

"Wow, that was a long one," I said when the shaking finally ceased.

"That's it," Wendy said.

"It was something all right."

"I've had it with earthquakes. I want to move."

I assumed her intense reaction would fade. It didn't.

The following morning over breakfast she said, "I'm going to apply for work in Oregon."

"We've never even been there. I heard it rains all the time up there. Oregon mist they call it."

"Can you get a transfer?"

"You're serious, aren't you?"

"How long would it take?"

"I'd have to quit and apply for reinstatement."

She stared at the avocado tree alongside the window. The wayward look in her eyes troubled me.

"I'll pick-up more shifts," she said, sipping orange juice, her hands wrapped around the glass, thinking. "We'll save what I make, cut back our spending, maybe bank some from your checks. It should only take us a few months. Can you get any time off for a trip?"

"I can try."

"Try for April . . . or May, when the weather's better."

"You really are serious, aren't you?" She nodded, sipped juice, her eyes faraway. "It's hard to imagine leaving. I kind of like it here."

"I used to." She drained her glass. "But it doesn't feel like home anymore."

When I gave it thought I had to agree. Berkeley had changed. Long gone were enjoyable late evening strolls across campus. Muggers lurked in shadows. One warm evening a woman in Wendy's women's group left her bathroom window halfway open. A rapist crawled in during the night and crept into her bedroom. Armed robbers made the Park Postal Station on Sacramento, where people without checking accounts exchanged cash for money orders, a monthly stop. The carefree era of mind-expanding acid and time-altering pot had given way to burned-out hippies, minds strung out on heroin. Near the Jay Vee liquor store on University Avenue, painted hookers displayed their wares in hot pants and scant tops, their gun-toting pimps off peddling cocaine, the new "in" drug. Yes, you had to be careful.

I nabbed a few days in early May and we journeyed north, stopping for gas in a small town in the foothills of the Siskiyou Mountains. We drove around a few quiet streets and parked and walked the downtown, a three-block stretch with a three-lane one-way street down the middle. A sloping sidewalk led to a plaza where two-and-three-story buildings from the late 1800's looked down on water fountains and benches. One building housed the police department and city hall; others, various businesses.

"Pretty nice," I said.

"It's beautiful," Wendy said. "Good place to raise a child."

I looked around and breathed in slow-paced tranquility. No majestic courthouse but a seven-story hotel. A brochure we'd picked up said it was the tallest building for hundreds of miles. I thought of the coincidence.

We drove into a large adjacent park, and Michelle spotted a bunch of kids cavorting in a playground.

"I wanna swing," she said.

"Let's take a break," Wendy said. "It's been a long drive."

We stayed at a cheap, but nice, motel and early the next morning took I-5 nonstop to Corvallis, the home of Oregon State University.

"Reminds me of Ohio," Wendy said, though I couldn't see why.

We headed back to I-5 and down to Eugene, home to the University of Oregon. After a pizza lunch, we toured the streets around the university and soaked up late afternoon sunshine in a park by the Willamette River.

"Seems like Berkeley without the City or the Bay," I said as I watched Michelle roll on the grass. Behind her, three longhaired guys in sandals were tossing a Frisbee. We could have been on the UC campus.

"Maybe too much like Berkeley," Wendy said.

I plucked a few blades of grass and rolled them between my fingers. "Look, Michelle," blowing grass off my hand, "green rain." She ran up beaming and gave me a hug. Then she flopped down, pulled up little fistful of grass and flung them into the air.

"Look, Daddy!"

I smiled broadly.

"Let's check out that little town again on the way back," Wendy said. "Ashland."

⇒⊣ ⊢⇐

"Scarlett's getting married. We're invited to the reception."

"Wow, I haven't seen her in months."

"She's changed."

I frowned. "You said the reception. Not the wedding?"

"Family and close friends, I guess."

"Who's she marrying?"

"Mauro. He's from Brazil."

"Brazil! Couldn't she find someone closer?"

"I guess not. They're going to live in Rio."

"She gonna try to start a revolution down there, too?"

"I doubt it . . . his family is wealthy."

⊷⊶

Eucalypti shaded the large white stucco house. Red tiled roof so typical of the area. A long but narrow redwood deck faced the bay. Flagstone steps led us to the open front door. Casually dressed guests crowded the expansive living room. I looked in vain for Scarlett's football-helmeted rioters.

"Over here," Scarlett called. She looked dazzling in an ankle-length skirt and a pale yellow blouse, her silky blonde hair, a shade darker than I remembered, loose across her shoulders. A handsome, bronze-skinned man sporting a broad, white-toothed smile stood beside her.

Scarlett embraced us lightly, thanked us for coming, and introduced Mauro.

"So you're the lucky man," I said, extending my hand. He had a confident grip.

"It's nice to meet Scarlett's friends," Mauro said.

He hugged Wendy, kissed her cheek. She blushed.

"Is this your place?" I looked around. "It's huge. I bet our apartment would fit in your living room."

"My cousin and I rent it. My family owns a construction company in Brazil. I came to study architecture. Scarlett and I will stay a month. Then we fly to Rio."

I couldn't reconcile the thought of revolutionary Scarlett peacefully settling in with an obviously upper class family in Brazil. She came from an upper middle class family, so maybe it was an example of the upper class marrying the upper class. Perhaps the times never really change. A thought crossed my mind. Mauro seemed to be easygoing. I decided to brave the issue.

"Isn't Brazil still ruled by a military dictatorship?"

He waved to some men hauling in a large galvanized bucket filled with ice and bottles of champagne.

"Come and visit us sometime," he said, excusing himself.

"I hear you're moving to Oregon," Scarlett said.

"Looks like it," I shrugged, a bit miffed Mauro had sidestepped my query. Loud popping sounds filled the room.

"Oooh, they've opened the champagne," Wendy said.

We toasted the bride and groom with expensive bubbly that went down smooth and pleasantly warmed my stomach. A cluster of smiling guests absorbed Scarlett and Mauro. Joints were making the rounds. The stereo played Blood, Sweat and Tears' version of "Got To Get You Into My Life" too loud. Wendy spotted two women from her woman's group and joined them. I grabbed an open bottle of champagne, refilled my glass, and stepped out on the redwood deck. Two lovers entwined at one end of the railing, their lips occupied, hands caressing hips. I tiptoed to the side, still carrying the bottle.

The view was magnificent. Fog was just beginning to engulf the Golden Gate Bridge. San Francisco glowed like an emerald. A few white dots, sailboats, drifted on jeweled water. Soon the fog would creep over the City and bay and sailboats would be at anchor. A cool breeze misted my face. I refilled the glass, set the bottle on the railing, and sipped. The small town in Oregon evoked memories of Carthage. I lit a cigarette and thought of my eyes opening and catching peaceful morning light in Carthage. Would I, at the age of thirty-four, feel in place, anxious to explore the unfolding day in the small Northwest town? Would Michelle experience the same? Would Wendy, for she also came from a small town?

I blew a shaky smoke ring and with it came wistful memories. How many miles to Vietnam? How many convictions lost since Scarlett baked beneath the Cuban sun?

I refilled the champagne glass. Our lives were changing, Michelle's, Wendy's and mine. Michelle would grow-up in a relatively safe environment and attend, we hoped, good schools. Wendy would embark on her career. As for me, I'd rent a studio apartment and remain in Berkeley a few months longer. It made sense financially and emotionally. Wendy and I were nearly exhausted. Given time a new horizon offered hope. I wondered if we could regain trust, passion.

I sensed her presence beside me.

"Beautiful view," she said.

"Yes, it is." I spotted an ashtray on the railing and put out the cigarette.

We stood in relaxed silence for a few minutes, as the quiet fog spread its dewy cloak across the bay.

"She's converting to Catholicism."

"I wish her luck."

She took my hand. Our fingers laced.

"Ready to leave?"

PART 5

CHAPTER EIGHTEEN

I rolled over, opened my eyes, and winced. Harsh light blazing through thin window curtains assaulted my eyes. I blinked, turned to the side. It hurt to swallow. My teeth hurt. My head hurt. Dream lost, of warm water spraying me as I lay on a billowy cloud. I slid my hand down. I'd peed the bed again.

I dragged myself into the kitchen and fired up Mr. Coffee. While he brewed my wake-up bomb two glasses of water dampened my parched throat. The taste of last night's bourbon lingered. I felt wiped out, spent. I looked at the fifth of Jack Daniels I'd bought after work. Less than half full. I returned Jack to his place on the kitchen counter, alongside his current buddy, a nearly depleted half-gallon of Gilbey's gin. Mr. Coffee gurgled the last drops of strong blackish liquid into the carafe. I filled a large cup and thought of the innumerable mornings when Sally woke me, the smell of coffee brewing. A loving way to start the day. Then she lost it, became hysterical (the Irish side of her Russian Jewish/Irish/English heritage) and ran. If she ever settled down I hoped we could work through our differences, whatever they were.

I carried the cup into the living room and sank into the La-Z-Boy, lit a cigarette and stared at cream-colored curtains the morning sun was slowly turning yellow. Squawking scrub jays didn't do much for my headache. I blew across the cup and sank deeper into the chair. The jays quieted. I sipped, thinking that it was 1994, eighteen years since I left Berkeley, and how many more years could I endure splitting headaches and sandy mouths and queasy guts? I thought of Sally.

How many days had passed since her Irish temper swelled and she looked like she was going to explode?

"My job carries a lot of built-in stress," I said. "It's my way of relaxing."

"Fishfarts! Why don't you join a fitness club?"

"You mean a gym."

The pain in her twisted face frightened me.

"So anyway," mustering my serenest voice, "I know you think I drink too much, but I don't think it's that bad. Just because—"

"Don't you know you're an alcoholic!" she screamed. I blinked. She turned, flung aside the door, and fled.

The following day I came home and met loneliness. She had returned while I worked and stripped away almost everything bearing her imprint. Only a blue and white knickknack of two Dutch youths innocently kissing, their hands discreetly held behind their backs, found upside down in a wicker basket that collected odds and ends.

Lost days passed before I woke in the middle of the night and fetched a towel. I couldn't sleep on a wet sheet. In the morning I looked at myself in the bathroom mirror. The new twitch in my left eye was going wild. I splayed the fingers of my right hand. They trembled. Maybe I needed some guidance, not that I bought the alcoholic label Sally pinned on me. I had a steady, responsible job. I was a devoted father. I was paying off credit card debt that never seemed to diminish.

"Blame Reagan for that," Sally said. "That's when The Age of Consumerism shifted into high gear. The mantra was simple: spend, spend and spend some more, all fueled by plastic that made gospel the idea of money suddenly being easily accessible and the illusion of wealth trickling down." She sighed. "It's all a shell game, a game of make believe for us suckers to embrace." She shook her head, and a slight smile parted her thin lips. "Trickle-down economics. Do you know what 'trickle' means? Think about."

I poured another cup and slumped into the La-Z-Boy. I felt like a backseat passenger in a jalopy traversing a washboard road. My stomach rumbled and a knife sliced my head when I turned a certain way. An unpleasant taste of plastic permeated the coffee. I dumped it and heated a can of Campbell's Chicken Noodle Soup. Half an hour later I almost felt alive. My grumbling gut quieted and my head remained intact. I thought about my unfinished sentence when Sally slammed the door against the wall and ran. No wonder she thought me absurd. How could I reasonably justify drinking three double (triple?) martinis before dinner, two tall boys to wash down the food, an after dinner generous gin-on-the-rocks, and a goodnight pounder? At the time, it didn't seem like a big deal. Now I imagined the drinks lined up on a table and questioned my bullheaded certainty. Maybe she had a point. Maybe it was a tad excessive. Maybe my drinking had gone haywire. Maybe I did need a helping hand.

My fingers did the walking. There were twenty-five listings under Alcoholism in the yellow pages. The first two were for Alcoholics Anonymous, the outfit for derelicts and helpless bums, people who'd drowned their souls in the bottle. I skipped them. For Chrissakes, that wasn't me, regardless of what Sally said. She was too artistically inclined, flighty, given to fits of irrational outbursts. I'd imbibed long enough to know gin or vodka on the rocks was less likely to produce a severe hangover. That proved my sensibility. My drinking had simply gone a wee off kilter. I likened myself to the driver of a fishtailing car. All I needed was a light touch on the brakes and a steady hand on the wheel. I called Serenity Lane.

⇥ ⇤

Rosemary and evenly spaced crepe myrtles bordered the parking lot. A long, low-slung building hid behind evergreens and tall holly. I had the mental image of a shy strip mall. Not what I expected, though I wasn't sure what I'd envisioned. The air smelled pleasantly sweet. I glanced at robins confabbing over stray kernels, then followed a cracked concrete walkway that led to the front entrance. I felt the pleasant air and lively birds were a good omen.

Inside, a plump, brown-haired, well-endowed looking woman in her forties cast owl-like eyes at me. I introduced myself.

Her reddened lips parted, "I remember taking your call. Welcome. My name is Belinda." Then silence as she waited, expectantly. I felt like I'd reverted to stuttering as I hemmed and hawed my way toward telling her I thought I might . . . could . . . may . . . have a possible . . . drinking problem.

"I see." She gathered a sheet of paper, a pen, and a long clipboard. "Please take a moment to fill this out." Then she picked up the phone to her right and punched a number.

I stepped back from the counter and took in the room: beige carpeting, off-white walls, and some kind of tall plant with long, thin leaves in one corner. Four chairs across from the counter, two on either side of small table beneath a rack of magazines and pamphlets. I settled into a blue plastic molded chair and scanned the paper: a form.

"Rick will be out shortly to test you."

My head jerked up. "Test?"

"It's a requirement. We don't let just anyone who wanders in . . . in." She smiled.

218

"Good to know that," I said, wondering if I sounded insipid.

I focused on the form. Basic information: date of birth, physician, income, medical insurance, current medications, work hours and so on. It didn't take long to complete. I handed it back to genial Belinda.

She gave it a quick once over and nodded satisfaction.

I sat and eyed the pamphlets: *Is AA For You? Do You Think You're Different? Am I an Addict? Youth & Recovery. One Addict's Experience.* None of them interested me. I thumbed a creased *Newsweek* and skimmed an article about the bombing of a federal building in Oklahoma City. A door swung open to my right and a young, clear-eyed, medium-built guy aimed his Colgate smile my way.

He extended his hand and said, "Hi. My name is Rick Stone."

I stood and introduced myself and we shook hands. He asked if he could call me Dave, and I said yes.

"I understand you think you may have a problem with alcohol." I nodded. "You've taken an important first step coming here, but before we can begin any treatment we have to verify that it's necessary."

"I hear there's a test?"

"Yes. The MAST test is a simple true-or-false quiz. It gives us a good indication. Are you up for it, Dave?"

I shrugged and his friendly, guiding hand put a slight pressure on my shoulder as he pointed the way. I felt as though he was leading me into a world over which I had no control. We departed the waiting room through the same door he'd used to enter and stepped into a long, brightly lit tile-floored hallway. He opened the first door on the right and we walked inside a well-ventilated, windowless room: blank cream colored walls, overhead fluorescent lighting, a table and two chairs.

"Have a seat." He withdrew two sheets of paper from a manila folder and laid them in front of me.

"I didn't expect a test."

"It catches most people by surprise. It's for insurance purposes and for ethical reasons." I looked at the papers. "Just answer truthfully. All right?" I nodded. "Good luck." He walked out, closing the door.

I felt anxious. It was all was happening too fast. Part of me wanted to pass so I could steady my rebellious wheels and part of me wanted to fail so I could prove Sally wrong.

There were pencils in a round glass container on the table. I chose one with a good point. I resisted the urge to read through before I marked my answers; best to stick with first impressions.

Did I feel like I was a normal drinker? No. I wasn't carrying a brown bag with a bottle inside, but why else was I here? Had I experienced blackouts? No. How would I know if I couldn't remember? Does anyone ever worry or complain about my drinking? Yes. Thank God for dear Sally. They don't need to know she's prone to overreaction and excessive worrying. I decided to do my best to pass for her sake. Can I stop without a struggle after one or two drinks? Yes, discounting last night's poor effort, sometimes. Do I ever feel guilty about my drinking? Yes, when I've had a few too many.

I'd figured I'd nailed four out of five and set a quick pace out of the gate. I thought long on question six. Do friends or relatives think you are a normal drinker? Except for Sally and Marie way back in my college days and Wendy when things went bad between us and Scarlett who once made an offhand remark about me drinking too much, I couldn't dredge up a name. All four were women. I'd already used Sally's response on question three and Wendy spoke under duress and Marie's were probably because she rarely drank. I settled on Scarlett's incidental comment, marked yes, and wondered if I was cheating. Seven: Are you able to stop drinking when you want to? I always stop when it's time to hit the sack, so I checked yes, though I was tempted to mark no to maintain my strong pace. Heck, even without a no on the last question this was a snap. Then I read the next two questions and my stride shortened: I'd never attended an AA meeting or gotten into fights when drinking.

Question ten gave me a chance of hanging on—has drinking ever caused problems with your wife, family, or girlfriend? Yes, Sally and Wendy. As I read questions eleven through eighteen, my chances of crossing the wire out front wilted. No one's ever gone to anyone for help about my drinking; I've never lost friends; or gotten into trouble at work; or lost a job; or neglected obligations, my family or work for two days in a row because of drinking; and I never drink before noon; or been told I have liver trouble; or, after heavy drinking, had severe shaking (an eye twitch and a slight hand tremble were hardly severe) or heard or seen things that weren't there. Question nineteen asked if *I'd* ever gone to anyone for help. I was here. I marked yes. Was that cheating? I chuckled at the absurdity. I was cheating so I'd pass a test so I could pay to have people teach me how to drink properly again so I could tell Sally she may have been partially right. Finishing fast: have I ever been in a hospital because of drinking, or been in a psychiatric ward of a general hospital where drinking was part of the problem that resulted in hospitalization, or seen a shrink or any doctor, social worker or clergyman for help with any emotional problem where drinking was part of the problem, or been arrested for drunk driving, or been arrested because of drunken behavior? I put a big X in the no square for all of them. Good lord, did they only accept criminals or bums?

I put the pencil back into the glass container and scanned the questionnaire. I knew I didn't have enough correct answers. Only the fear of Rick noting dishonest erasure marks prevented me from changing a few to assure acceptance. Then again, if I had inadvertently marked the wrong answer, why wouldn't I erase the errant answer and mark the correct one? I drummed my fingers on the table. The door swung open before I decided and jovial Rick slid in.

He scooped up the papers. "Be back in a jiffy."

Fifteen long minutes elapsed before he returned and said he'd arranged for me to attend three evening group sessions a week. Each session ran three hours; seven to ten.

"You mean I passed?"

"Your answers indicated you *may* have a problem with alcohol. Now if the schedule is okay with you I just have some papers for you to read and sign so we can bill your insurance."

On the way home I whistled my way into a Minute Market and bought two six-packs of Coors tall boys to celebrate my good fortune. I was a winner.

═╬ ╬═

Besides myself, there were three other men in the room, all at least two decades younger than my fifty-three years. Two of them would have to show IDs when buying booze. Ken, one of the youngsters, was quick to introduce himself. A short fellow, he pranced about as he talked, hands gesturing, shoulders rocking, a Type A guy whose chemistry dictated perpetual motion. He introduced the others.

"I'm thirsty," Ken said with an impish smile, his head tilting from shoulder to shoulder as if a joint in his neck had loosened. He aimed his words at a pale-faced guy with wire-framed glasses. "Still keepin' that bottle of vodka in your bottom desk drawer, Alex?"

"I'll call the cops if you burgled my place."

Ken wagged a finger. "They'd never believe a bottom drinker."

"You rat on me and Uncle Louie will pay you a visit."

"I'm quaking."

It took me a moment to realize they were jiving. Their tomfoolery disappointed me. I was here on serious business.

"They're always clowning," Burt said. I looked up at him, literally, as a line from "Down Under," the Men at Work song, played in my head: "six foot four and full of muscles." Add shoulders an elephant could lean on. I pegged him to be a hardworking construction guy, much more mature than Ken or Alex, the snide, laugh-a-minute, life-is-but-a-dream jokesters.

The door swung open and a tall, heavyset woman whirled into the room on amazingly small feet. It was fitting her name was Anna as her dervish entrance reminded me of the way Sister Ann wheeled into the shuttered back room at St. Ann's in Carthage for Sunday school class.

"What happened to Alvin?" Ken's fingers quietly snapped a tune against his thigh.

"He graduated." Anna turned her back to us and set a stuffed briefcase onto a small table. Ken winked at Alex and lifted his hand to his mouth as if it held a glass. Alex winked. Anna faced us again and hand-motioned us to sit. We unfolded four starkly utilitarian chairs and sat.

Taking center stage, she introduced herself and me to the others and vice versa and then scribbled the dangers of alcohol poisoning on a flipchart, explaining that it was review for the others and new information for me. It seemed unnecessary. All of us looked spry. Then she handed out flyers. Being new, my stack was heavier than the others:

An eleven-page opus on Guilt that was poorly copied, the pages stapled.

A full page cartoon of a bird that looked like a cross between a stork and a dodo swallowing a frog and the frog is twisting the bird's neck. At the bottom were the words: "Don't Ever Give Up."

An italicized quote by Dag Hammarskjold, the former Secretary of the UN killed in a suspicious plane crash in 1961 in Northern Rhodesia. The quote began with the word God, followed by three thick paragraphs written by someone else. Mr. Anonymous liberally sprinkled the word God throughout, ending with, "The God of my understanding can be my anchor in stormy seas."

A full-page cartoon of a King Kong-sized hand, the middle finger holding a naked toddler's hand as the baby tries to walk. Below: "It starts with the first step."

A drawing of a wide-eyed kid, hair combed down over his forehead, a cowlick sticking up from his crown like an antenna, his hands hiding his mouth. Below: "I know I'm somebody 'cause God don't make no junk."

With all of the references to God I began to wonder if I'd hired on with religious zealots. Besides, none of it seemed to be the Bam! Wham! I sought to kick-start my way back to proper imbibing.

Near the end of the session Anna told a story of temptation, her voice soft and reverent, an indication she was about to convey to us something on a par with the Ten Commandments. Without moving my head I eyed the others. She had our attention. At her daughter's wedding reception last Saturday Anna said she lifted a glass of champagne for the congratulatory toast.

"It was a very awkward moment." She swiveled her head, looking at each of us, at me an uncomfortable second or two longer. "How could I not drink to celebrate my daughter's marriage?" She scanned our faces and loitered on mine again, like a teacher eye-drilling an answer from a taciturn student. I shrugged. What did I know? She was the vessel of Serenity Lane, wasn't she? "So what I did," she raised her hand up to her mouth as Ken had done, "I *pretended* to drink."

Oh, for Chissakes, why not toss down a toast at your daughter's wedding? I wanted to ask. Instead I was silent, half expecting Ken or Alvin to cut in with some smart-alecky remark. They just smiled and nodded.

At the end of the three hours, we stood in a circle and held hands and the four of them recited some short prayer that began with "God grant me" something. Afterwards, I told Anna I had trouble following the words. "There's a copy in the papers I gave you," she said and cheerfully added, "and as part of your treatment you're required to attend two Alcoholics Anonymous meetings every week."

"Gees," I said to Burt as we walked out, "between these sessions and AA meetings I'm not gonna have any free time."

"They wanna keep you busy so you don't drink," he said. "I like AA meetings. Besides what else you gonna do?"

The kids revved their hot rods. Alex's Charger tailgated Ken's Firebird as they squealed tires and sped out of the parking lot. I shook my head and walked to my dependable, gas-frugal sedan, a 4-door Chevy Nova. Burt's long strides carried him to the vehicle one space over, a high, off-road Ford F-150 that suited his size. I leaned against the Nova and stretched my arms on the roof.

"How long you been coming, Burt?"

"Four weeks." He opened the door to his truck, stepped onto the footboard, and squeezed behind the wheel.

"Think it's done you any good?"

It was as though he'd flipped a switch. His pleasant expression dissolved and ice cold murderous eyes knifed me. When he spoke chills ran down my spine.

"You don't wanna be around me when I been drinkin'," he said.

⇥⊹ ⊹⇤

My next session at Serenity was on Monday. I knew, thanks to Anna, that there were weekend AA meetings, but I didn't want to spend my days off in the company of losers. Instead, I decided to unwind with a few drinks and ponder exactly what I'd gotten myself into. Anna was a fanatic but okay. Ken and Alex were juvenile. And I wasn't sure I wanted to be in the same room with Burt. He might have a flashback.

I sat far from him as we gathered around a TV to watch the film *Shattered Spirits*. The guy Martin Sheen played was a real jackass. In one scene he left his kid in the car in a parking lot while he went into a bar. Hours later he staggered out soused to the gills. I felt sorry for the boy. His dad was a slob.

As the film rewound Anna said, "The way to get anywhere is to start from where you are. There is hope. The only difference between stumbling blocks and stepping stones is how we use them."

Great, I thought, another slogan.

CHAPTER NINETEEN

The following day I didn't have a session. I intended to go to the eight p.m. AA meeting at the Episcopal Church. Though I wasn't sure Serenity and I were a good fit, I wanted to tell Anna I'd chalked one up, get a gold star. It would leave her with a good impression of me if I decided to walk.

It was mid-afternoon when the unexpected altered my plans. A window clerk told me someone up front wanted to see me. I anticipated an irate customer, not the man toting a backpack, his black hair streaked with gray, eyes sallower than I remembered. I knew I looked very un-Berkeley in my creased slacks, blue oxford button-down shirt, and red tie. Grateful for small habits, I only wore a sport coat when I went to official meetings. He was passing through. Yes, I could take a break.

Outside two medium-built, dour-faced guys fell in behind us as we crossed the street and headed up the block.

"They with you?" Tom nodded. I glanced over my shoulder, smiled, and aimed a sideways wave. They returned sharp nods, no smiles, and held their distance.

We ducked into the Underground, a cozy subterranean eatery, the monotony of its redbrick walls interrupted by framed travel posters of London. Aside from two women carving pieces of cherry pie, we were the only customers. We chose a side table and ordered coffee from the short, pretty waitress I'd seen a dozen times without catching her name. She wore jeans and a white T-shirt with a black-and-white portrait of Shakespeare on the front and a lengthy quotation from one of the Bard's plays on the back. I admired her young butt as she sashayed back to her station by the kitchen. Tom's fellow travelers parked at a table by the door, looking more like bodyguards than traveling companions.

"Friends?"

He waved a dismissive hand. "I'm just catching a ride with them to Seattle."

"Got something lined up there?"

"I might connect with Greenpeace, maybe go to Canada. There's a Buddhist retreat outside Vancouver."

I smiled at the waitress as she set our coffees down. "Thanks," I said, pulling the steaming cup closer. "You ever see Gene?" I asked Tom.

"He's been gone for years."

I promised Gene I'd stay in touch, relay my read on Oregon. He was cradling the idea of following. A divorce and an impetuous, potentially dangerous affair sidetracked me. I felt bad about not picking up on my promise once my life began to settle down.

"Last I heard he was teaching at a high school in San Jose," Tom said.

"Good to know he landed on his feet."

Tom tore open two packets of sugar, spooned sweetness into his cup.

"So, are you the boss?"

"Supervisor. The Postmaster's over me."

"I've never seen you in a tie," he said, a trace of curious disappointment evident in his tone. I felt like a red weight hung from my neck.

"I guess you would think it odd. It took me a while to get used to it."

"It's no odder than the post-disco, post-Reagan world. Remember the Heidegger quote, 'Distracted from distraction by distraction?'"

"Sure, all written before he sympathized with the Nazis. I also remember what you called the American motto, 'Why settle for enough when you can have too much.'"

I sipped warm coffee. The two women licked their forks and left. Tom's eyes dropped, and he fiddled with a butter knife, sliding it off a napkin and onto the slick tabletop.

"Did you know there was another riot over the park?" he said, looking up. "In '91."

"I read something about that."

He looked down again, abandoned the knife, and fingered the cup's handle.

"You know, we were pretty idealistic back then," I said. "Sometimes the old saying of two steps forward one backward is true. A lot of lifestyle changes happened in the sixties—civil rights, women's lib, gays coming out, the questioning of authority. I think it takes society time to catch up."

He looked at me. "You always were patient."

"I just think we needed a break after Vietnam and Watergate, something more festive. Besides, people sure seem to have more freedom and choices nowadays and a lot of young people are more idealistic than you may think."

He looked as though he was going to say something and changed his mind. He stared at the British double-decker bus poster behind my right shoulder. In the silence it occurred to me that conversation had always been our glue. In Berkeley friends dropped in; we talked, smoked weed, and drank; we listened to music, talked, and drank; or we went to a film, came home, discussed the flick, and drank. Wendy and I talked for hours, for days, when things were rocky, trying to erase discontent, agreeing for the sake of agreeing. After good long talks we made love. I believed, as long as the sex was good, everything else would fall into place.

"Searching for the meaning of life," Tom said in a desultory tone for no apparent reason.

The waitress returned with a fresh pot. Neither of us wanted a refill.

"Sorry I didn't stay in touch. How'd you manage to find me?"

"I knew you moved to Oregon," he said, brightening. "I thought I remembered the town and took a chance you might still be working for Uncle Sam. I was surprised when you left. It seemed so sudden."

"It was Wendy's idea. Earthquakes scared her. And I don't think she wanted to raise Michelle in Berkeley."

"How is she?"

"Wendy? She's doing well. She put in time with a firm up here until she could start her own practice. She's got all the clients she can handle."

"She's a fine woman."

Ah, woman instead of girl; he was still politically correct. I resisted the temptation to tell him about Sally, who had shared my life for years until she went bonkers and stormed out.

"Michelle graduated from the University of Oregon. She majored in business."

"Any other kids?"

"No." I knew this pleased him. He believed we needed to husband our natural resources; overpopulation only bred waste, poverty, and discontent.

"That's good. The last thing we need is more people. A couple can adopt if they want more than two kids or start a foster home. You do know we have wars to keep the population down. We're good at that, being a warrior nation."

"Really?"

"Sure. Think about it. How many generations of Americans have grown up when we weren't at war?" Before I could wade through American history he said, "Have you heard about the Greenhouse Effect?"

"I've read a few articles about it."

"Maybe that's what the Bible meant when God said 'the fire next time.' We grew-up thinking it was the bomb." He shook his head. "Life didn't seem complicated until I turned forty."

His friends had finished their sandwiches. The larger of the two jingled his car keys. "Gettin' late," he said.

"Guess it's time to go." Tom lifted the backpack he'd parked on a chair. I didn't mind his leaving. For all the Berkeley hours we'd spent bouncing ideas around I didn't think our current exchange had long to run. I left a generous tip, got the tab, and walked him to the car, a Ford Escort parked on Lithia Way. His traveling companions hopped in and the driver started the engine.

"Whoops, I almost forgot." Tom unzipped his backpack, pulled out a paperback, and handed a book to me: Martin Heidegger's *An Introduction to Metaphysics.*

"You probably forgot I borrowed it."

"Yeah, I did."

He nodded. "Say hi to Wendy for me. Sorry I didn't have time to see her."

"Okay. Good to see you."

We shook hands, and I told him to stop in again if he came back this way or to write me in care of the post office when he settled. He nodded, climbed in the back, and the Escort pulled away. I didn't expect to hear from him again. All too often people just disappear. He belonged to a time when ideas were paramount and the task of earning a living a damn inconvenience.

⇒ ⇐

After the late collection run rolled in I retreated to my small office. Time to enter the daily data: clerk and carrier times, duty designations, lunch breaks, mail volumes, and so on. Only the changing numbers gave the repetitive process variety. I much preferred the activity on the floor, the give-and-take with the clerks and carriers, problem solving, decision-making.

The wall clock read 5:25. Soon I'd be alone in the building. I felt antsy. Whispers of longing stirred my taste buds. *Soon, soon*, the voice whispered. I swallowed. Not tonight.

I clicked send and a copy of today's numbers electronically flew north. I inserted a floppy disc and hit save. My feeble knowledge of computers consisted of entering and saving data and receiving annoying harangues from Howard Gibson, the District Manager. Hunched over a desk two hundred miles distant the overweight, unforgiving micromanager hounded subordinates in satellite offices via email and occasional unannounced persecutory visits. I often flipped an unseen finger northward after reading one of his rants.

At six-thirty I locked up the post office and walked to the car. My plan for the evening set; grab a bite and go to my first AA meeting, earn my gold star. I turned the ignition key and Tom's unexpected visit infiltrated my thoughts, the Heidegger book safely stowed in the trunk. I shifted into first and slowly pulled out of the lot. I felt I had failed him. I stopped at a traffic light. What had he expected after eighteen years? Why had he thrown me off kilter? Because I imagined he judged me harshly? The traffic light turned green. The whispering voice returned: insistent, controlling, commanding. I hadn't intended to turn instead of going straight, but without debate, as though on autopilot, I swung the wheel to the right.

Aaron, tall, slender, graying widow's peak, slipped the bottle into a brown paper bag, winked, and thanked me for my being a good customer. Over the years I'd probably bought his family a car and paid for his kid's first year at college, or so it felt. I nodded, told him to have a good night.

At home I dropped two ice cubes into a glass and floated them in good old Tennessee sour mash. It'd been a rough day. Tom had shaken me. I needed to relax. The AA meeting could wait a day or two. I pondered one of the test questions—can you stop without a struggle after one or two drinks? I decided to limit myself to one, albeit generous.

I eased into the La-Z-Boy and drank. The bourbon harsh going down but pleasantly warm as it settled in my gut. The next sip smooth from the get-go.

I wondered if Sally would come back. She'd taken sudden trips in the past to meet friends, sometimes former lovers, and always returned, but this time I felt uneasy, afraid I misread obvious warning signs.

Were they the same ones I failed to interpret with Wendy? If only I'd been more attentive. Or, made love to her every night. How many chances had I missed? And what about the conversation the night I confessed I'd had a brief fling? Why was she, Wendy, upset because I *hadn't* loved Nancy? Years after our parting she told me she had had many lovers after I fled. Did she love them all? I wondered what she thought when she heard about the Juan de Fuca plate.

I also wondered how critically Tom really viewed me. I'd lied to him, committed the sin of omission. In different garb, I pretended to be the same person he used to know. "Oh yes, I'm the great pretender, pretending that time hasn't passed." I didn't tell him I hadn't read a book in years, that I watched mindless TV late into the night. I wanted to tell him I thought he had spent his life chasing Gatsby's elusive green light. We couldn't run any faster because we were too busy staying alive. "Ah, ah, ah, ah, staying alive."

The glass was empty. I refilled it and plopped in two new cubes to give the bourbon company. I lit a cigarette and opened the door. The day was fading. The air felt fresh and cool. Crows perched like sentinels on the tops of three towering pines. During storms the giant trees fanned the wind. Twilight's pinkish-orange hue dappled the mountains. Scarlett and I never made love. With the passage of time, I wished we had. I took her to a clinic six weeks after she returned from Cuba. I didn't go inside the drab green building. I waited in the VW and smoked cigarettes. After an hour or so she came out, her face ashen, her thin lips faint lines. Had something gone wrong? "Are you all right?" She weakly nodded. Conversation on the drive back proved fruitless. She silently stared out the side window.

"Thanks," she said as I pulled up in front of her apartment.

She and Mauro flew to Rio after the wedding reception and we never heard from her again, not even a postcard.

Just one more drink. I filled the glass to the brim and flopped into the chair. "I'll set you straight, Anna," I said out loud. "God, you pissed me off the way you wouldn't drink a toast at your own daughter's wedding. What's the big deal? One lousy glass of vino won't kill you. You listen to me, like I've had to listen to your righteous babbling. I'll tell you up front that what you did was egregious, shameful!"

I laughed.

"And you, Howard Gibson, you fuckin' harassin' bag of maggots. How the fuck can you run our office from outer space? You got some newfangled telescope? Don't tell the Pope about it, Mr. Manage by The Numbers. He might condemn you as a heretic, as one of his myopic distant predecessors did to Galileo. Think about your days. You sit on your fat rump, read reports on your overheated computer, and fire off snide remarks. How can you know, asshole? I'm here, you're there. Yeah, that's my finger jabbing your flabby chest. Don'tcha feel bad belittling people? Ain'tcha got no heart? There, there, no tears. What's that? You're going to repent, send messages of encouragement. Fucking-A."

In the kitchen, I dropped fresh cubes into the glass, splashed bourbon over them, and a scene from an old movie played in my mind; *Cowboy* with Glenn Ford as a seasoned trail boss and Jack Lemmon a tinhorn. Ford's soaking in a sudsy bathtub and Lemmon's pouring him a drink. "To the brim," Ford says, "that's what it's for."

"Yeah, to the brim," I said, pouring. Was the bottle half full or half empty? What's the diff? I'd obviously picked the wrong night to take The Test. I had too much on my mind.

"Hell, a man's gotta drink when he's troubled."

CHAPTER TWENTY

About three dozen casually dressed, normal looking people, mostly men, filled the brightly lit community room behind the Episcopal Church. Some sat in silence; others stood in small clumps and chatted. Five long, slightly curved rows of ubiquitous folding metal chairs faced a table parked in front of two tall windows. Not knowing what to expect, I eased onto a chair near the end of the back row, ready to scoot.

After a few minutes, a craggy-faced man with curly red hair pulled the drapes. Standing by the door, a heavyset guy dimmed the lights. The room hushed.

"Welcome to the Thursday meeting of the Easy Does It AA group," craggy face said. "My name is Justin, and I'm an alcoholic."

"WELCOME, JUSTIN!" forty odd voices boomed. I almost fell over backwards.

"This is an open meeting. All are welcome. We ask only that you honor everyone's anonymity. Leave what you hear here between these walls. Is anyone celebrating a birthday?"

"My name is Leo and I'm an alcoholic," said a bald guy. "One year."

"WELCOME, LEO!" roared the chorus.

He sprang up from the mass of heads to my right and smiled as he trotted to the table. Justin handed him something, they shook hands, and he returned to his chair.

"Is anyone else celebrating a birthday?" There were no more takers. "Do we have any newcomers?"

A guy and a gal sitting together introduced themselves. I kept quiet. I only wanted guidance, to learn how to drink properly again. I wasn't an alcoholic. I was a guest.

Justin asked for a volunteer to read The Twelve Traditions, and an attractive older woman with nicely rounded breasts and manic gray hair stepped forward from the front row. She picked up a sheet of paper from the table, returned to her seat, and introduced herself. Between "Welcome, Miranda" loudly echoing and her quiet voice I only caught the first part, something about "our common recovery comes first." Her spiel smacked of religious zeal and my mind scrambled the words until she stumbled over "anonymity," pronouncing it "anon-mittity." I smiled, expected to hear derisive laughter, but no one corrected her, no one laughed, and she demurely returned the paper to the table.

"Being the first of the month," Justin said, "we'll have a report from our treasurer."

"My name is Wayne, and I'm an alcoholic," An older guy in the third row said. The others loudly welcomed him. I had a good sideways view as his index finger adjusted his glasses and he withdrew a torn piece of grocery bag paper from his shirt pocket, held it up to the scant light. "After paying rent this month and buying cookies and donuts for tonight's break, we have a balance of eighteen dollars and sixty-seven cents."

Justin thanked him and introduced the guest speaker, who sat with his hands crossed at the other end of the table. From where

I sat the faint light fell on him poorly. He looked to be Hispanic, around thirty, pleasant face, athletic body.

"My name is Hector," he said in a deep, clear voice, "and I'm an alcoholic."

As I craned my neck for a better view I noticed a longhaired, pretty young blonde in a long white dress slit down the side.

"I started drinking beer when I was fourteen," Hector continued, "and I drank for twelve years. I'd found ways to get the hard stuff before I was sixteen. That's when I discovered boilermakers . . ."

It figures. Only an alcoholic would drown good whiskey in beer. Ugh. Her legs were incredible. I imagined caressing her taut thighs. Hector hitting bottom six years ago at a party in San Luis Obispo, called an obnoxious drunk and given the bum's rush. I imagined French kissing her and slowly pulling down her scant bikini panties, burying my eager tongue between her legs, inhaling her musky smell, my hands fondling her naked breasts. I sighed. My auto erect had stopped working. My best sex happened in my mind.

"I did the only thing a self-respecting, resentful drunk would do. I decided to burn down his house."

I couldn't believe it: an admitted pyromaniac.

"I mercilessly cursed him as I drove home and imagined lighting the match. I'd teach that rude ass a thing or two. Just then, the inside of *my* car burst into flames. Okay," broad smile "there was no actual fire, but the lights from the cop's bar flashers really had me going. I pulled over, and an officer approached. I rolled down my window, and he freaked me out when he asked, 'Where's the fire?' Then he asked me to step out, and I thought I might've been in too much of a hurry, or maybe I was driving a little erratic. I opened the door, wobbled, and leaned against the side of my car. A light flashed behind me, cop number two illuminating the inside. The cop in front of me asked me to step away from the car. I shuffled a few feet forward, and he told me to say the alphabet backwards.

I leaned back, shaded my eyes with my hand, and said, '*Christo*, I couldn't do that if I was sober'" Laughter, mine included, exploded throughout the room, and a huge, avuncular toothy smile lit Hector's face. "It wasn't my first DUI. I was ordered into a diversion program that included three AA meetings a week."

"At first I thought all of you were loco, but I stuck around and you changed my life. I learned that something was wrong with *my* wiring. *I* was different than normal people, the ones who can have *one* glass of wine with dinner or *one* social martini. In my brain there was no such thing as one. Inside walls like these, all of you helped me learn that one drink is too many, and a thousand isn't enough."

He held up a copy of the blue book Anna had given me. I hadn't opened it.

"This book and all of you saved my life. As I came to meetings I also came to believe in a higher power as I understood it. Call it God, he or she, and if that makes you uncomfortable, call it the group or an invisible force in the universe. It's greater than the self that propels us toward trouble when we drink.

"Welcome to those of you who are newcomers. Stick around for a while and come back if you slip up. I had three months sobriety when Mr. Jim Beam beckoned me for a five-day bout. Luckily I didn't burn any houses down or kill anyone with my car. Now I'm proud to say I have five years of continuous sobriety." He tapped the big book. "Between these covers, and in rooms like this one, is a different way of living, one day at a time."

He looked at the clock on the wall above the door, flashed his infectious smile. "We have some time before break. I'm going to open up the meeting."

Justin handed a wicker collection basket to Miranda. She put something in it and passed it to the person next to her. The room quieted for a moment, and then Ralph cleared his throat and said he was an alcoholic. He thanked Hector for his story and said he owed the program a lot of gratitude for saving his marriage and changing his habit of guzzling half a case of beer every night. Scott said, "Remember de Nile is not just a river in Egypt." Derek talked about a strong resentment he felt toward a co-worker. He came to tonight's meeting because he had wanted to drown his anger in drink. Marge remembered how she felt at her first meeting and encouraged all of the newcomers to keep coming back: "Don't quit five minutes before the miracle."

I had called Belinda at Serenity and told her I was sick. Of course, I didn't say I had an unrelenting hangover. Yes, I assured her, a passing illness, be there next time. I didn't mention I'd have an AA meeting in my pocket. Now I was having second thoughts. Hector's passion impressed me, touched a chord and something about the rest of them sang a familiar chorus. I almost felt comfortable. They talked honestly about their drinking, without a lot of bravado or regret. How had they found acceptance?

The guy next to me passed the basket. It held an assortment of coins, dollar bills, and one Lincoln. I fished Washington out of my wallet and dropped him in. I felt tied to these folks in ways I did not understand. There was only one problem. I wanted a drink.

At break I went out for a smoke with a dozen others.

"First time?" Wayne, the treasurer, asked. He was tall and lanky, reminded me of Gary Cooper in *High Noon*, his thin hair graying.

"Yeah." No reason to mention Serenity Lane. Better if he thought I came on my own. "I don't know why I didn't say anything when Justin asked."

"It's okay. You can do it at tomorrow's meeting if you like."

"How long have you been coming?"

"I was three years sober when I retired, and my wife and I moved up here from San Diego. I was an officer with Bank of America, and we entertained often. Beefeater martinis are what got me. Now I have eight years."

"Is that why you're treasurer?"

"Oh, no," he smiled. "It's a volunteer position. Usually for six months, mine's a year."

"I'm surprised by how little you have in the till."

"We believe in being rich in spirit. We pass the hat and people give what they can. The church charges a minimal fee for use of the room." His cigarette speared a sand-filled bucket. "You'll hear some bullshit from time to time, but most of what people share is helpful. Listen to the message, not the messenger."

The light above the door flashed three times.

"Break's over." He stepped toward the door and looked back at me. "Coming?"

The dense smell of workingman's sweat, stale beer, and boozy smoke assaulted me as I stepped inside the Log Cabin. Droning voices, laughter and jukebox music. I picked up two bottles of Henry Weinhard and a glass at the bar and parked myself at a small table by the crowded dance floor. The table wobbled. An abandoned napkin lay near an ashtray. I folded it twice and stuffed it under the misaligned leg. I filled the glass and drank half, lit a cigarette, poured again, stretched my long legs. How could I have followed Wayne back to the meeting when all the drinking talk whetted my thirst?

A good-looking, young gal wearing tight fitting jeans and a loose-fitting white blouse leaned over the jukebox and punched in a tune, The Righteous Brothers, "You've Lost That Lovin' Feeling." She swayed her hips languorously and softly sang, off key.

My mind wandered, shedding years to 1979 when Wendy and I agreed to end our burned-out marriage, the last rites delayed until we served a 90-day waiting period. No Vegas quickies in Oregon. Independent minded Wendy asked for no alimony, only child support.

I landed in a spare one-bedroom apartment across town. Sorting mail filled my days, but I had no TV to stave off nighttime loneliness and I hadn't been in town long enough to cultivate new friends. I sought the illusion of companionship in bars.

I missed seeing Michelle every day and welcomed her every-other-weekend visits. She and I liked to play pinball and video games at Take Five, the town's new (and only) arcade, so we went there for supper on one of the two nights she slept over. We demolished juicy hamburgers and poured fistfuls of quarters into the machines. She favored maze games---Pac Man and Frogger---and soon toggled through them like a seasoned gamer.

It wasn't long before I became a sociable fixture with the teens, willing to fill in at the Foosball tables, though my skills were shaky and my wrists cursed after lengthy sessions. It was all fun and games, killing time, avoiding the expense of bars, drinks at home alone later.

While the boys mounted enthusiastic campaigns against the machines, the girls were indifferent. They popped in for soft drinks and chatter and scoped out the night's roster before deciding if they should stick around or move elsewhere. Many were attractive, their innocent faces unmarked by worry or age. A few twittered and batted their eyes at me, the way they'd seen ingénues do in movies. My avuncular smiles kindly shook off their adolescent overtures, and they glumly sank into booths crammed with giggling accomplices, flung their arms on the table, and buried their burning faces.

One evening I was munching a tasty burger when Delores sauntered up to the jukebox. I smiled, remembering two days back, when she'd eased into a chair across from me and casually slid a pack of photos across the table. "Wanna see some dirty pictures?" she said, a flirtatious twinkle lighting her eyes. My heart picked up a beat. My penis stirred. Her athletic body, her judicious use of make-up---a touch of lipstick, a hint of color on her cheeks---if only I were . . . . I reached in and pulled out the photos. There were twenty, all revealing fully dressed teens smiling, laughing, drinking what looked like orange Kool-Aid, sucking on unlit bongs. She scooped up the photos and said, her dark eyes flashing, "Gotcha thinking, huh?" A teasing smile played on her full, sensual lips. She tossed back shoulder length black hair, pushed out of the chair, and glided out the door without looking back.

Now she stood in front of the jukebox wearing faded, seam-busting jeans and a white strapless tube top. She punched in a tune, a new Rod Stewart number. Her young butt rocked to the sexy beat. I strangled my burger. Gobs of mustard fled, spot-painting spiky fries a brighter yellow. Be with her, naked in bed, forever.

She looked around, as though searching for someone, then gave me a look, her shoulders bare, her small young breasts eyeing me from beneath thin fabric. I stuffed mustard flavored fries into my gaping mouth and cast edgy eyes at diners tables away, all absorbed in their meals and conversations. I glanced back at the jukebox. She had vanished.

I finished the burger, abandoned the spattered fries, drained the Coke, and wiped my greasy hands and mouth with paper napkins. Her unsubtle choice of song and her look had been unmistakable. Erotic imaginings danced through an unhinged door in my mind. I tapped my brakes. Hold on, fella. I'd look like a fool if I came on to her, mirth for her gathered friends.

I dropped a quarter into Evel Knievel's belly, fired a silver ball into play. It clanged off bumpers, whirled the thousand-point spinner, arced across the roof of the playfield like a lazy fly ball, and then, as if shot from cannon, rocketed into a gutter. I pulled back the plunger and fired another ball into play, imagining the pleasure of kissing her, caressing her, licking her open, naked body. I leaned over the machine, my faint reflection distorted in its colorful, enticing lights.

When I came out, she was smoking a cigarette, her little yellow Honda Civic parked next to my car.

"Where ya goin'?" she said.

"Home," I said, and without hesitation added, "Wanna come up?"

We sat close on my threadbare couch, our hips nearly touching. She talked a lot about her parents, how they'd stood by her when she got sent up north to juvie, and how hard they worked, he as an electrician and she as a bookkeeper, and how they'd thrown a big bash last week when she both graduated high school and turned eighteen, and how her older brother looked out for her, and she said all the girls thought I was a stone cold fox, and instead of saying I thought "stone cold fox" referred to women, or asking why she was sent to juvie, I said I thought she was very pretty and very mature for her age, as my what-am-I-thinking brain imaged fondling her young breasts, and all the while my meager radio hummed pop music in the background.

A little before ten, she grasped my left wrist and glanced at my watch.

"I gotta go."

She paused at the door, as though waiting for me to open it. I reached for the doorknob, the image of her sensual hips swaying to Stewart's song, "Da Ya Think I'm Sexy." Yes, I wanted her youthful body. I caught her eyes, or she caught mine, and she slipped into my arms. I inhaled her freshness, kissed her full, pink lips. My hand traced the warm smooth ribbon of flesh on her back between her tank top and jeans. My penis hardened. I looked into her eyes, read the glistening promise of return.

That night I shamelessly, hopelessly tumbled for an unblemished young girl who just last week had taken a diploma walk similar to the one I'd taken twenty years ago.

But how could I sustain a relationship with a girl who could not spend the night, who, as though we were co-conspirators, said we had to be careful. Her parents couldn't know. They wouldn't approve. Neither would her protective big brother, a karate second degree black belt who would only grunt when he beat on me for third degree practice. Delores said he'd scared off some other guys. We had to be vigilant, steal time, like spies.

She liked fast cars and pop music, so I bought a used, well-maintained, red Camaro with a deep-throated V-8 under its hood and, for the apartment, a state-of-the-art stereo. I financed the car through GMC and took out a bank loan to cover the stereo and sixteen top forty albums. Her dreamy expression when she spun an album and her contented smile when she sat behind the wheel and punched the gas pedal allayed thoughts of indebtedness.

When the sun flexed its muscle, she suggested a mountain drive in search of cooler air. She scored some pot, and we passed a joint back and forth as she sped us through dense forests with stops to admire quiet lakes, frothy rapids, and lofty waterfalls, our two-lane passage often shaded by trees that hugged the road.

It wasn't long before she wanted to share. I failed to see the harm when she invited two of her friends along for a day trip to the Coast.

The following week she bounded into my apartment, her grin taking up half of her face, her charcoal eyes afire.

"What?" I said. Her brother was competing in a weeklong karate tournament in Boise, and her parents had booked reservations at a nearby resort. They'd be gone ten days in all.

"When?"

"Next week. I just found out."

"Will you stay here?"

"You bet." Her arms draped my neck and she kissed me hard.

So why did I feel uneasy? The lecherous joy of imagining our naked bodies finally woven together in sex and sleep thrilled me, but what would she do while I logged my five work days, invite girlfriends over and play lady of the house, the loud pop music shaking the walls to the tune of a 7.0 earthquake? Would she pout when the older tenants next door grumbled ear damage, flee to a more rambunctious hangout, come home in a mood? And what would happen during the remaining two days, a non-Michelle weekend? Delores had seldom chanced a visit on consecutive days, and, aside from the coast trip and our mountain drive, we'd rarely cobbled together more than a few hours. I doubted we had enough in common to endure an unbroken, un-high forty-eight. What would sustain our conversations? The touchstones of my life were more than a generation removed from hers.

A few days passed before I opened the door and she slumped inside.

"I haveta go with them."

Two weeks passed before I saw her for the last time. I'd parked the Camaro after a night of pinball and started across the lot before I spied her, rooted like a morose lawn statue in deep shadows near the bottom of the staircase leading up to my apartment. I quickened my pace. She seemed disinclined to come forward. I slowed, pulled up a few feet in front of her.

"I can't see you no more," she said.

Bereft of words, I listened to an inner dialogue. What had happened? Betrayed by someone's misplaced word? A sighting unnoticed? Her brother found out?

I stepped toward her.

She pushed out a hand but held my eyes. "I can't hurt them again."

"I'll talk to them."

Had she smiled or scoffed?

"I just wanted to tell you it ain't your fault."

A car with a loud muffler pulled into the lot, its headlights sweeping across us. I glanced over my shoulder, shielded my eyes with my hand. When I turned back, Delores was gone.

For a week or so I swilled cans of beer at home and spun jittery tales until alcohol flooded my engine and I flopped into bed. An ingenious plan hid behind our break-up, a temporary misdirection conceived by her. We'd become too bold, perhaps someone with a loose tongue *had* let a word slip, her parents interrogated her, and she resorted to subterfuge, expecting me to decipher her ruse. Soon she'd feel safe, knock on my door, and we'd laugh as she explained it all.

Like when and why had she done time in juvie? Anything to do with the guy her brother scared off?

I began to act like a spellbound jilted teenager. Frenetic after work searches took me past her house, the homes of her friends, and Take Five many times. Up and down streets, always on the lookout for her little yellow Honda.

I worked the Take Five grapevine and harvested conflicting rumors from different arbors: she ran with a fresh set of friends, older gals and guys who smoked pot and drank at new hangouts; she'd fallen for a traveling drag racer; she'd taken up with a middle-aged couple and gone to Tahoe with them.

How strange, to be left wondering. Was I no more than a whim, a tale to entertain friends, or had something frightened her so thoroughly we could not even talk? Perhaps we were ill-fated from the beginning, from the night I said, "Wanna come up?" Perhaps one night she calculated our age differences, or a friend calculated them for her.

I had seen her naked only once. Unable to get an erection, my tongue pleasured her.

Nine-year-old Michelle had met Delores three times: at the apartment, when Delores mixed up weekends, at the arcade when she hovered at our table, and at a playground when she happened to be driving by. Each time Michelle's chin sank to her chest and she murmured a lower case "hi." I assumed it was her shyness coupled with her displeasure of sharing a scant minute of her Dad time, but I also thought she might dislike my young girlfriend. Had I inadvertently neglected my daughter?

Now, I imagined her happy.

Summer quietly slipped into fall. I worked long hours and drank too much. In early November my world brightened. Tony, my supervisor, transferred to Portland, and I stepped into his job, and a pretty artist from LA moved in next door. Sally's bouncy walk, long blonde hair, and full breasts caught my eye. We went out on a few dates, our sexual connection immediate. I felt grounded being with someone who was smart and quick and a mere decade removed from my time references. When she cast disparaging eyes at my oversized gin and bourbon bottles, I told her what I believed: I enjoyed drink, and it was cheaper to buy in bulk.

Michelle and I still went to the arcade, often with Sally, and I was delighted my daughter acted as though she'd discovered a second mother. Wendy and I had remained friends, though we seldom saw each other socially. The following summer Sally and I moved into a new apartment . . . .

"Last dance, last chance . . ." Donna Summer belted the call from the Log Cabin's jukebox. Handclapping, hip-shaking, feet-shuffling dancers packed the floor. A sweat-soaked couple discoed by my table, their arms outstretched, hands locked. I finished my seventh beer. I thought of what Hector said at the AA meeting: one drink is too many and a thousand not enough. An inebriated woman sang loudly at the jukebox. A tall guy with a shaggy goatee grabbed her hand and pulled her onto the dance floor. She laughed and stumbled.

CHAPTER TWENTY-ONE

The following evening, I called Serenity, cancelled, and crept into an AA meeting at the Newman Center. Why pay big bucks to learn how to control my drinking when experts could do it for the price of a draft? Once again I hid in the back row. Scott, a short guy with cropped hair and muscular arms, was running the meeting. Justin sat in the second row with Hector. I didn't see Wayne. The lights dimmed and Scott greeted everyone as Justin had. Margo, a thin woman I hadn't seen before, read the Twelve Traditions. Scott thanked her and asked if anyone was celebrating a birthday. When no one spoke he asked for newcomers. One guy answered, his presence court ordered. Scott and the others welcomed him and then Scott introduced Carl. "The body is a machine, the organs are its working parts, and alcohol a corrosive liquid," he said, the inflection in his voice as flat as his pasty appearance, unlike Hector's passionate tones and rich aura. Yet his good intentions came through. Maybe I was at the right place. I just needed to connect with people in the know.

Once again the ending felt awkward, standing in a circle, hold-ing hands with strangers on either flank, their heads bowed, their tongues reciting: "God, grant me . . ." I'd read the prayer many times, heard it thrice, and only the first three words were imbed-ded in my memory. Aside from begging for help during times of need or peril, I'd put aside the bowed head and bent knee routine, holdovers from superstitious times.

Why then, if I felt a true connection, did I stop at the store on my way home and pick up a six-pack of tall boys?

The following day I regretted going back out for the second six-pack. The twelve beers cobwebbed my aching mind. I was ir-ritable. I snapped at employees. My sluggish brain misfired until mid-afternoon. Maybe I did need to give the alkies and their ab-stinence theory an earnest try, even if only for a while. But could I find a way to circumvent the religious nonsense?

After work I went to Take Five for a burger and fries and felt lonely. Sally had finally called but remained afar, and Michelle was studying at the University of Oregon.

The meal settled well and I felt rejuvenated. When I pulled out of the parking lot, fingers in my brain snapped belief. *I* believed I could fix my drinking problem without *any* outside help. It was a matter of applying my will. Serenity Lane's booze test question was a con to vacuum money from the wallets of gullible fools. As far as Hector's one drink routine, well, I'd never seen anyone in a bar have only *one* drink. I could manage on my own, thank you. I stopped at the OLCC liquor store and bought a pint of Gilbey's gin, setting the brown paper package on the passenger seat be-side a brown paper grocery bag that concealed two six-packs of Coors pounders. The AA'ers might call what I was doing a slip, but I wasn't one of them. I was a man in control, stepping up to the plate. I had no intentions of getting drunk.

Once home I turned on the TV. I measured and poured two ounces of gin over ice, my willful, nightly limit. A little over an hour passed before I sucked the last taste of gin from an ice cube and popped open a beer. I downed seven of the sixteen-ounce cans and fell into bed.

The six A.M. alarm jolted me. I had a splitting headache. My fingers shook, my left eye blinked like a frenzied red caution light. I sat on the side of the bed, my butt sinking into piss-drenched sheets, buried my face in my hands and moaned.

Could only the drunks help me? Would I have to force myself to accept their stark sobriety?

I turned on the shower. The spray of warm water scrubbed scum from my teeth, wet my parched throat. In my mind's eye I saw a pitiful, sodden-eyed creature nearing his end; a fifty-three year old man, successful in his profession, dedicated father, lover of the arts, who sought relief from his suffering by offering his gaping mouth to a shower head. The image saddened me. I had to change. If I went to another meeting I'd have to step forward, announce, and conjure up something to call my Higher Power. The AA'ers liked to say we "came to believe" in a power greater than ourselves, and many of them had spoken of having extraordinary conversions. Maybe it could happen to me. Maybe I could run with their program and cure myself. I wondered if I had the dogged perseverance to see it through.

⊨⊧

I sat in on three meetings a week, but, unlike the Roman solider Saul becoming Saint Paul, or drunken Bill Wilson becoming Bill W., or fire-bug Hector becoming sober Hector, I didn't experience a miraculous conversion. Sometimes all the talk of past drinking actually intensified my thirst, and, as soon as a meeting ended, I hopped in my car and sped like a reckless teenage hot-rodder to the nearest market. Once there, I strode the store's width, casing aisles for AA regulars. I didn't expect to see any from the meeting

I'd just escaped (none could have outraced me), but there were others in town who knew me, and I didn't want them to catch me buying booze. Aisle inspection negative, I grabbed a six-pack of pounders and rushed to the shortest check-out line. I sauntered out; anything could be inside a brown paper grocery bag. Safely in my car and homeward bound, I hatched a frayed plan: one, and only one, beer. Six cans later, I tamed the idea of going out and risking a DUI, cursed my lack of will, and slipped between wrinkled sheets.

The following day I came across an article in Consumer Report's *On Health*. It defined an alcoholic as someone who consumed more than twenty-seven ounces of booze in a week; less, you probably weren't a drunk. Simple enough, a straightforward test which didn't limit me to one drink a night. I envisioned skipping a night or two. At the liquor store I bought a fifth of bourbon and a fifth of gin, each about twenty-five ounces, a two-week supply. I assumed the article wasn't referring to beer or wine. I put the bottles on the kitchen counter and thought of writing week one on the gin label and week two on the bourbon label, or maybe the other way around. No, only the total ounces counted. I could have one or the other, even a taste of both on the same night. Four days later I recycled the empty bottles.

The phone rang. It was Sally. I eagerly told her I did have a drinking problem and I was going to three AA meetings a week . . . They're helpful. I realized excessive drinking is a terrible affliction. You can't believe some of the stories I've heard . . . Michelle? She's still at the U of O in Eugene . . . Yes, I'm still drinking, but think of the Beatle tune about it getting better . . . Sure, I understand . . . How are you . . . I know, but after living with you for over ten years I should know how sensitive you are . . .What's that . . .Sure, I understand . . . Okay . . . Love you.

Determined, I cut my daily ration to four or five twelve ounce beers or to three or four miniatures a day. I bought the two-ounce shooters in Medford, where I was less likely to be seen sneaking in and out of a liquor store. I kept the tiny bourbons and gins at home and hid the little vodkas under some maps in the glove box. Sometimes I'd pick up a few pounders, prepared to tell any AA'er I encountered: "They're for a friend." Right.

As I experimented I maintained my weekly diet of three meetings, listened attentively as sober drunks told tales of recovery from ruinous lives. Incremental changes began the night I bowed my head and quietly recited the Serenity Prayer. Soon I tagged along after meetings for coffee and casual talk instead of hotfooting home or hunting a safe place to buy booze. Though I still felt like an outsider my orbit had spun closer to them. Some even seemed like they could be friends. Amazingly, I also began to taper off, white-knuckling my way through entire back-to-back days of sobriety. The twitch in my left eye calmed, and my hands steadied. I discovered I didn't need an assist from alcohol to sleep well. I attained an AA birthday and picked up a thirty-day plastic chip.

Having that little plastic chip made me feel good. Fifteen days passed before I listened to an insistent whisper and opened my lips and invited Stolichnaya in. I admitted my slip at a meeting the following day, and again suffered through thirty days without drink. I accepted my new chip to good applause. Scott hooted, "Good goin', Dave."

"Anyone else celebrating a birthday," Justin asked.

"My name is Al, and I'm an alcoholic. Fifteen years."

Thunderous applause greeted his announcement. Again seated, he passed his chip to the man sitting beside him. The man soon passed it on.

"Why's he passing it around?" the man sitting next to me whispered.

I shrugged, and the woman sitting in front of us turned her head and whispered, "You rub it, hoping some of his sobriety will rub off on you."

Miranda, the night's speaker, well into her story of drunken debauchery and prostitution before Scott's medal, bronze with good weight, lay on my palm. Etched on the reverse side of XV Years were the images of Dr. Bob and Bill W. I rubbed it and passed it on.

My thirty-day chip reminded me of the mills that crowded Mom's change purse, the small colorful plastic coins equal to 1/10 of a penny the state of Missouri issued to retailers for payment of sales tax. I slipped my thin chip into the roomy side pocket of an old tweed jacket and flinched when my fingers grazed something cylindrical through the torn lining. My face reddened. I eased my hand out, dropped the chip into my shirt pocket, and guiltily looked around. Did I expect my fellow drunks to frisk me, their accusatory tongues hissing, "Whaddya hiding in there, Dave?"

Once home, I dug out the unopened miniature and tossed it into the trash. I'd begun to enjoy not drinking.

⊯ ⊭

Justin chaired the night I received my 90-day chip. I told my story, taking, I thought, far longer than necessary, and ended by sharing a method I'd read in the thin volume, *Living Sober.* "I had a hard time accepting the finality of never being able to drink again so I played a trick on myself. I delayed the fulfillment of my desire a day or two. If it was Monday I'd tell myself I could drink on Tuesday. On Tuesday I'd delay until Wednesday and so on. The intervals gradually increased, though there were a few times when I weakened. Even so, I never quit trying. I kept pushing the next drink into the future, and it made it easier for me to chalk up another sober day."

At break I went out and joined the smoking crew.

"Nice job," Justin said.

"Thanks." He limped a few feet further down the ramp and lit up.

Burt's massive shoulders nearly scraped the jambs when he stepped through the doorway. He proffered his bearish paw.

Relieved he'd returned my freshly squeezed hand unharmed, I said, thinking it best to be civil, "Nice to see you."

"I liked what you shared, the idea of pushing back the urge a day or two. It's not the same as cold turkey."

"That's how we do it, one day at a time," I said, my voice edgy, remembering the homicidal stare he cast my way in the parking lot. "After a while you can push the urge two or three days into the future. Then you just keep going." My voice gained strength. "It's progress, not perfection." I liked my new role of sober drunk handing out advice. "Who knows, you may even get to where you like *not* drinking."

"I missed you when you dropped out. Those other guys were clowns."

"What happened to them?"

"Alex was gone 'bout two weeks after you. Somehow Anna found out he was still drinkin'. Vodka. I think his old lady squealed on him. Ken was still there when I ..." His lips quivered and his eyes tightened as though to fight tears, startling fragility for a man it would take a bulldozer to topple. He wet his lips. "I . . . slipped. I never went back, but I kept comin' to meetings."

"It's good you keep hanging in."

"Got to." He paused and looked around before his moist eyes swung back to mine. "After I smashed a bowl of spaghetti on the wall, the wife said she's sick and tired of living with a drunk. She was gonna walk. That was five months ago."

"How much time do you have now?"

"Only three weeks, but I really liked your idea."

"And your wife?"

"She's hanging in. She goes to Al-Anon meetings, but I know she has limits. I just have to keep showing her I'm serious."

"I'm sure you will," I said, marveling that the man who'd once scared me now sought my help. He thanked me again, said he wanted to grab a coffee before the meeting resumed. Giant strides carried him back inside.

"You found a sponsor?" Justin edged closer. I shook my head. "'Never walk unescorted through your own mind—it can be a dangerous neighborhood.' I heard that a long time ago and it's true; you can only go so far in this program alone. We've all been loners. The foundation of AA is the group, and the program works best if you find someone you feel comfortable with as a guide."

⊷ ⊶

Though it would be a big plunge, perhaps a commitment I wasn't sure I wanted to make, finding a drunk I respected began to occupy my mind. I had talked with many at meetings, gone for coffee afterwards with some. With whom had I felt most comfortable?

I'd heard Justin's story at a meeting: four times the legal limit as he sped on a twisty snowy Washington road, tangled with a log truck and lost, lying remorseful in bed in a Spokane hospital, where a nurse, eleven years sober, told him stories of recovery. Justin hobbled out of the hospital with facial scars mirrors would always reflect, a lifelong limp, and a new way of seeing. Though I found him to be amicable outside of meetings, he transmogrified into a Dutch uncle when he sponsored someone. I'd heard him mercilessly browbeat a guy for missing a single meeting.

I thought Wayne would be a good fit, someone older who had once held a position of responsibility. He would presumably empathize when I complained of white collar work pressures. Before I gathered the courage to ask, a serious health problem wiped him from my radar.

Miranda piqued my interest since we were about the same age, give or take a few years, but I knew my underlying thoughts were sexual, cuddling in her arms as I poured out my story, which was why sponsorship, from what I'd observed, ran along gender lines.

Scott had bagged years of sobriety, but he demanded a tough-minded allegiance rivaling Justin's, though I'd never seen him bully someone he sponsored. I liked him. Then I heard his tragic story.

So, when I asked Hector I wondered why I hadn't initially thought of him.

He looked at me for what seemed like an indeterminably long minute. I feared he would decline, suggest someone else. I stared at him, my eyes steady, but not pleading, telling him it was his call.

≒ ≒

The following afternoon we met at The Java Shop, a former Mom and Pop grocery store that 7-Eleven and Albertson's muscled to the sidelines. The aging owners sold the building after staging a going out of business sale. A year later it emerged, remodeled as a cozy and aromatic beanery that stocked topnotch beans and attracted mature hippies, university students, clean-cut yuppies, and recovering drunks.

Hector ordered coffee and a small pastry filled with slices of sweetened apples. Caffeine after two p.m. would wire me. I wouldn't be able to get to sleep at a decent hour. Decaf seemed second rate. I asked for a glass of water.

There were only a few other customers. We had caught in between time; the afternoon socializers had vacated and the nighthawks hadn't yet arrived. I laid the book he'd asked me to bring on the table and pulled up a chair across from him. He blew across his steaming coffee, touched the side of the cup, and delayed a taste, picked up the pastry.

"Want half?"

"No thanks." I was too nervous to eat.

257

"I'm a sucker for these. Granny Smith apples sliced thin and seasoned with just the right amount of cinnamon and sugar." He ate half, tested his hot cup again, and let it sit.

"I saw a European film where they poured coffee into a saucer to cool it and drank from the saucer."

"I tried that once," he grinned. "Made a hellish mess." He finished the roll and braved a sip of coffee without recoiling, wiped his hands with a paper napkin, then folded the napkin and laid it beside the saucer. He looked me in the eyes and said, "Congratulations on getting your ninety-day chip last night."

"Thanks." I thought of his five years, soon to become six, a span of time that seemed unattainable.

"Are you sure you want me as a sponsor? You might be more comfortable with someone older like Wayne or Scott." He winced and offered an apologetic smile. "I forgot that Wayne's on the disabled list for a while."

"How is he?"

"As well as can be expected."

He picked up his cup and held it with both hands and sipped, glanced around. No one was sitting within earshot.

"There's a straightforward question I always ask at the beginning," he said, lowering his cup. "I know you've been coming to meetings and you just racked up ninety days and I also know you had a little slip not long ago. So the question is: Do you believe you're an alcoholic?"

"Yes," I said with all the conviction I could muster. I knew heavy drinkers like me often crossed an invisible line into the pit of addiction. Did I believe I was flawed? Now was not the time to admit uncertainty.

"I ask because I can't tell you. Recovery is an inside job. I'll work the Steps with you, but it will take time and patience. Every now and then someone pops into a meeting and says they've worked the steps in a week." He sneered and shook his head. "You don't run to the finish line; you walk or crawl toward it. Anyone who says he worked the program in a week is full of it." His eyes settled on my book, *The Twelve Steps and Traditions.* "Open it up and write the date your sobriety began inside the cover." He watched as I did.

We talked for another thirty minutes or so. Actually, he talked and I listened as he rattled off concise profundities I thought I would always remember. How could I not? He spoke clearly and slowly, words grounded in absolute sensibility. I told him about my brief visit to Serenity Lane.

He drained his second cup of coffee and said, "Remember this: if you don't buy it, you won't drink it. I know that sounds simplistic, but think about it."

"Makes sense," I said, but thought it inanely obvious.

"How are you feeling?"

"A little jittery at times."

"Do you have any candy?"

"Funny you should ask. I'm usually not into sweets, but I've been craving them."

"They replace the sugar we used to get from alcohol. It helps." He rolled his head and shoulders and cracked his neck. "Gets stiff every now and then." He gave his neck a final tweak and smiled. "We'll meet at least once on weekends, other plans permitting, and before the Tuesday and Thursday meetings and any other time you feel you need help or want to talk. Call me every day."

"What time?"

"Anytime." He handed me a 3 x 5 index card on which he had written his address and telephone number. "If I'm not home, the answering machine will pick-up. I periodically check my messages."

We walked out together. I felt good. I shook his hand. He had a firm grip. I drove to Albertson's, intent on picking up a package of frozen sweet corn, some potatoes, and a few pork chops.

I picked up a shopping basket and fell into a trance-like state. I found myself standing in front of a long floor-to-ceiling cooler, face-to-face with a stupendous array of cold brews standing upright on shelves. I opened the glass door and stepped inside the walk-in cooler. The door silently sealed off the supermarket's elevator music. Softly purring fans bathed cans and bottles with cold air. Goosebumps dotted my forearms. I drifted down an aisle. On my left bottles and cans and six packs on crowded shelves and on my right tall stacks of six packs, and cases of beer. The choices were overwhelming: ales, lagers, pilsners, stouts, foreign and domestic, micro brewed and fire brewed, thousands of bottles and cans. I picked up a bottle of beer brewed in the tripel style by Trappist monks. The alcohol content rivaled many wines. *Take it,* a silent voice whispered. *There's no booze at home. Grab a six pack. No one will know.*

I had had the beer a few times, thick and fruity and bittersweet. I put the bottle down, but I did not turn to leave. I hesitated, looked around. The voice hummed: *the Czech pilsner, the Irish stout, the German lager, the Colorado Fat Tire.* One of the doors on the front of the cooler swung open. I thought it was an AA'er here to bust me, and I let out a breath when a man's hand reached in and withdrew a six pack of Bud. I thought of Hector's initial question. Had I lied? I'd dropped anchor in AA's safe harbor, yet the Land of Responsible Drinking lay on the horizon. How to get there? I strained my memory trying to call up his lucid words. They were lost. How odd.

My eyes crawled down the length of the cooler, recalling nights with cold smooth tasting liquids. I wondered how those untried tasted. The voice cocky, taunting me to savor the unknown, a dark beer from Portland Brewing. *You'll never know if you don't.* I picked up a bottle. The beer's alcohol content packed a wallop. A six pack or two would short-circuit my synapse. I wet my lips. What had Hector said? I put the bottle down, pushed the door open, and fled to the frozen food section. On my way I picked up a bottle of ginger ale and imagined the whisperer's downturned mouth as he moaned, *Aw, Christ almighty, soda pop.*

⋺⊹ ⊹⋼

My everyday phone conversations with Hector were often brief. Even so, I found comfort in the steadiness of his avuncular steady voice asking if I'd made the bed or washed the dishes. As for turning my will and my life over to the care of God as I understood him, a program prerequisite, I reached an uneasy reconciliation by calling the group my Higher Power, particularly the Thursday night meeting where I'd first heard Hector. A strong core of regulars—Hector, Justin, Miranda, Scott, and Wayne—made it their home group and I followed suit. I frequently experienced a warm sense of belonging when I walked through the door.

A few weeks after our initial meeting Hector said, "Are you sure you feel ready to take Step Three?" We were at his house. He was sitting on the couch, the Big Book pressed against his chest. I was perched on a chair across from him and for a moment I flashed on Robert Mitchum as the crazed preacher in the old *The Night of the Hunter* film. I nodded.

"There's a Step Three prayer. It's best if we do it on our knees." We knelt on his plush Frieze carpet. He opened the Big Book and we bowed our heads. "God, I offer myself to Thee . . ." he read. I felt as though I was witnessing my own baptism.

Oh, how I wanted the glorious exhilaration to endure.

CHAPTER TWENTY-TWO

I quickly spotted Hector, surprised he was alone at a back table. Scott and Harry were supposed to join us for coffee before we all went to the Thursday night meeting. I was running a tad late and Scott's punctuality was legendary.

I abandoned sleep concerns, ordered a cup, and settled across the table from Hector.

He said: "How are things going?"

"Pretty good."

"You look chipper."

"Sally and I have been talking."

We'd had a series of lengthy phone calls. She was feeling calmer, pleased I was working the program's critical Step Nine, having made a list of people I'd harmed, those who I'd backstabbed, lied to, resented, cheated, gossiped about, unfairly judged, et cetera; essentially a list of the people who'd been present when I behaved like an ass. My commitment looked good on the surface, but lately I felt my interest waning. Sometimes I left meetings at break, times

262

when I silently wondered if my original intent had been genuine; I sought a cure, a way to steady myself, not a lifelong duty.

"She's talking about coming back."

"Ah."

"She likes that I'm in AA."

"It doesn't surprise me."

I had told Hector about the day Sally called me an alcoholic and stormed out. It fit in well with my story. It made sense, the impetus I needed to seek help.

"Did you tell her about your trip?"

"She thinks it's a good idea."

Images of my childhood home began to infiltrate my dreams and waking thoughts as I worked Step Nine. The urge for a nostalgic journey took hold. It was only a question of when. Curiously, Hector wasn't keen on the idea.

I glanced at my watch. "Boy, they're running late."

"Think we should file a missing persons report?" he grinned, standing.

He headed to the counter for a refill. A young, attractive, mid-thirties woman buying coffee sidetracked him. She spoke, and pushed her hair back from her face when he answered. He leaned forward, and smiled when she spoke. I eyed the door, checked my watch again, and thought of our two late friends and their hard stories.

Scott owned a thriving construction company, an upstanding citizen, but I'd heard his abbreviated telling at a meeting and the unedited version at Hector's house.

His journey to AA began one drunken night on a cliff overlooking the Pacific Ocean. He wanted to go out in style, take flight in his 1969 Dodge Charger off a precipice near Cape Perpetua. He imagined his car crashing hundreds of feet below, embedded like a tombstone between two large salt water washed rocks. An alternate, less satisfying but acceptable possibility occurred to him if he missed his unseen bull's-eye. He and his car would simply meet Davy Jones beneath restless waves. Not as dramatic, but neat and perhaps mysterious. One foot pressed lightly on the brake as he revved the engine. Find the moment. Soar into dark space.

A thought jumped up, of his wife, Jessica, gone with their six year old son, Eric, their exit sealed when he, Scott, stumbled home wasted and she cried her complaint. A volcanic alcoholic rage erupted in his mind, burned away all reason, called her a fuckin' bitchin' whiner, the heel of his hand smacking her hard on the chin. She fell. He opened a cabinet drawer, took out his .357, and shoved it up between her legs. She begged don't hurt Eric, don't hurt Eric. He snorted, squeezed the trigger three times. Slow, then quickly. Click. Click-Click. Grabbed her wrist and dragged her into the bedroom.

"That's all I remember," he said at Hector's. "In the morning I woke up in my own piss and vomit. Jessica and Eric had spilt. She filed for divorce. It happened faster than I could read the papers." He cleared his throat. "You see, there had been other incidents. The cops had come." He let out a painful memory breath. "The judge said I was a danger to my son and my wife and she granted Jessica full custody. Jessica and Eric moved to Colorado to be near her parents, and not long after, she and I were no longer man and wife. If I'm lucky I might be able to see my son again after he's grown and living on his own . . . if he wants to see me."

I let out a whoosh of air. I couldn't imagine never seeing Michelle again.

"So I went out and got shit-faced. Next thing you know I'm at the edge of a cliff, gunnin' the engine and croonin' "Goodbye Cruel World." I was this close." He held a sliver of air between his thumb and forefinger. "I don't know what made me take my foot off the gas, shift into neutral, and roll back down. Maybe even back then an asshole like me had a higher power looking out for him. God knows I was nuts."

A tall six-three, Harry had lost a high-paying financial advisor gig at McMahon and Associates in Portland, when one of the firm's vice presidents, a pipe-smoking scrutinizer, sniffed Harry's after-lunch cocktail breath once too often, added the martini lunches to the questionable afternoon financial advice he had dispensed to the firm's valued clients, and booted him out the door. Never a saver, Harry enjoyed meals at expensive restaurants, flashy cars, the thrill of slapping a stack of hundred dollar bills on the bar of his favorite haunt, and shouting, "Drinks on me," a practice he continued after the barkeep told him a running tab on a credit card would work just as well.

The loss of his job put the kibosh on all that. He sold his condo for a tiny profit, turned in his leased Mercedes, and bought a used Chevy in good repair and headed south, uncertain of destination or purpose, living on a thinned wallet and his last valid credit card. He landed in a cheapo motel off I-5 in Ashland, Oregon, and called his wealthy, Back East parents. Their generous monthly stipend enabled him to move into a comfortable, one-bedroom semi-furnished apartment in a nice, tree-filled neighborhood. With drink, food and lodging provided he attempted to regain a measure of respectability and his parent's good graces. He sobered up, went to AA meetings, and picked up part-time menial jobs.

But he couldn't sidestep the benders. He soon bought booze by the half gallon and holed up in his apartment, shades drawn, for weeks, sometimes months. Unable to endure the harsh blazing sun, he emerged from his intoxicated cocoon at dusk and steered his car to the liquor store to lay in another ample supply of Bombay and Absolut, and then to Safeway for a stockpile of frozen dinners and snacks. He preferred martinis with three drops of Noilly

Prat vermouth and toasted the contestants in the infamous O.J. Simpson trial while he munched peanuts and drank.

I first saw his pasty face at a meeting when he asked Scott to be his sponsor. Sallow eyed, his hands shook so severely I thought he'd dump his steaming mug of black coffee. "Good to be back," he said in a low, hesitant voice as he strangled the porcelain cup with both hands and lifted it to his cracked lips. Good to be back, I silently repeated. Yes, you can always come back.

Hector returned and set his cup down, sat, stretched his legs.

He blew across his cup and sipped. "About this trip---I gotta ask you how you figure your alcoholism played a role when you hadn't yet tasted booze."

"My dad gave me a drink of beer once. I don't remember, but there's a photo of us standing in the yard, and he was tilting the beer bottle to my lips. I couldn't've been much older than four or five."

"Is that your theory," frowning, "that an early childhood drink puts the character defect into motion?"

"It's a thought I've had. A lot of people at meetings say they had their first taste when they were very young."

"Or when they were in their teens or later, and some drank sensibly for years until alcohol took control. Sometimes too much analysis can be dangerous. My sponsor once said 'glance at the past, but don't stare at it.'" He looked me in the eyes. "You were how old when you threw the snowball?"

"Eleven."

"That was over forty years ago, Dave." His thumb and forefinger wiped the corners of his mouth, pinched tight skin beneath his chin. "I don't know. It seems strange to me. You said it was an accident."

I understood why he was having trouble understanding.

"What I told you about the snowball . . . well . . . I stuffed a rock inside."

"Oh," he leaned forward with interest, "and the reason?"

"What I said before is true. I thought he was mocking us, me, and I wanted to hurt him. It did hit his eye and he did fall down all bloody. What I also didn't tell you before was that he had to see doctors in Springfield and St. Louis. He was still wearing a patch when I left. I may have blinded him."

"It's too bad you don't know the answer to that question." He scratched his forehead, ran his fingers through his hair. "Any other abridged versions running around?" I felt my face heat and shook my head. "I gotta tell you I still have a hard time with it. Forty odd years ago you bloodied a kid with a loaded snowball. It may or may not have blinded him. He went to see out-of-town doctors and wore a patch. If he'd lost an eye, I think you would've heard. Did you?" I shook my head. "Seems to me news of a boy losing an eye would make the rounds quick in a small town, especially since you went to the same school. I dunno. I just think you would've known."

We silently sipped coffee. I felt uneasy, having admitted I lied to him, and decided to change the subject.

"It seems like a lot of people come in, stay for a while, and then just disappear, dropout."

His eyes panned the room as though he were hunting a culprit. "We often read their names in the police log or the obits. Sometimes Scott hangs out in bars and spots them."

"Does he do that often?"

"Ask him." Hector raised a hand. I turned and realized he had not been seeking a dropout. Scott and Harry strode toward us. "You're looking good," Hector said to Harry.

"Feeling good!" He sat and tucked his hands under his thighs.

"Sorry we're late," Scott said. "Business."

"Scott says tonight's speaker is an out-of-towner," Harry said.

"Justin said she's racked up twenty years," Hector said.

Scott lightly slapped Harry's shoulder. "If some lush can get to be an old timer so can you." Harry vigorously nodded and went to get coffee.

"It's always good to hear someone with that much continuous sobriety," Hector said.

"Been bar hopping lately?" I said when Harry returned with two cups of coffee.

"Hec squealed on me, huh." He and Hector exchanged conspiratorial grins. "I've done it a few times. Order a soda and talk to people. If I hear someone expressing a need, I casually mention that I used to drink, but now I go to AA meetings. Always a light touch, though. You can't browbeat a drunk into sobriety." He sipped his coffee, ran his tongue over his lips. "Once I saw a guy who *was* coming to meetings, like that guy Lloyd is always doing, pretending to be sober and picking up chips. I didn't say anything, only nodded when this guy's eyes found mine." He chuckled. "I'll never forget the expression on his face. Cheaters don't expect to find an AA in a bar."

He sipped coffee, checked his wristwatch, and jumped up. "Damn, we are running late! We better scoot."

"We just got our coffee," Harry said.

"We'll grab a cup at break. C'mon."

"Dave and me need a few minutes," Hector said.

"See ya," Harry said. He fell in a few steps behind Scott, his hands behind his back, his shoulders swaying to a lackadaisical rhythm.

After they were out of earshot, Hector fastened on his let's-get-down-to-business look, planted his forearms on the table, and leaned forward.

"I know you *want* to take one of those sentimental journeys and that's fine, but be careful."

"I will. I mean," defensively, "I think most people would like to visit as an adult the place where they grew-up, especially if they were suddenly uprooted."

"Speak for yourself. There's a Wal-Mart sitting where my childhood home used to be. My parents pocketed the corporate money not long after I left. They saw the writing on the wall. Why deplete their meager savings fighting a losing battle against corporate power? Uh-uh. They took the cash and moved into one of those over-55 parks."

He paused, and it occurred to me I had picked up his life on the night he wanted to burn down a house.

"I suppose it's different for you, coming from a small town in the middle of nowhere."

"It was pretty bucolic . . . at least everything seemed to fit, be in its place. I was happy."

An unpleasant thought whirled in my brain. It took me a moment to decipher its source.

"There was probably more anxiety then I realized. My mom must've really been worried after my dad died of TB. I had to go to the VA hospital for chest x-rays every year for two or three years afterwards. They wanted to make sure my lungs were clear. I guess Cathy must've also gone."

"To say nothing of her worries about polio."

"Yeah, what with me always going to the Saturday matinee. Hmm, I can't remember any kids in Carthage getting polio." We were quiet for a bit, lost in our remembrances. "I've learned a lot about myself in the program," I finally said, truthfully.

He sucked in air. "It's still a geographic you're doing, albeit temporary. Changes of scenery can trick the mind. Any relatives back there or friends you've stayed in contact with?"

"No. Maybe I'll just call him."

"Who, the kid you think you may have blinded?" He smiled, or it might have been a smirk. "Maybe you'll find out there wasn't any permanent damage and Leon's the mayor and happily married with a couple of well-adjusted kids."

"I'm afraid he may have died in Vietnam, like my friend Mike." Hector looked taken aback, and it took me a moment to realize why. "I mean . . . if I didn't blind him."

"What's that, wishful thinking or desperation? Jeez!" he said, shaking his head. "Maybe he isn't and maybe he didn't. We can't live our lives on maybes." He glanced at his watch. "Christo, let's go."

⇢⊹⇠

"The speaker's from Seattle." Miranda said. "Twenty years."

She winked and retreated to a jacket-draped chair. A large crowd overran the room. Extra chairs unfolded. Hector pointed to two at the end of the back row.

"Was that Lloyd sitting beside Miranda?" I said.

"Didn't see him."

We had cut it close, for, just as we sat, the lights dimmed and Justin opened the meeting. Muted light obscured the guest speaker, as it had the first night I saw Hector. She wore her hair clipped short. She reminded me of someone, but these days I see so many people who remind me of someone else.

I leaned back and surveyed the room. Scott and Harry were parked two rows in front of us, further back than Scott liked to sit, his penalty for being late. Wayne was sitting near the middle. He had recently recovered from successful open heart surgery, a medical miracle. I looked at the back of Lloyd's head and wondered if his presence next to Miranda meant he'd given up his out-of-town shenanigans in favor of working an honest sobriety.

Harry read the Twelve Traditions, enunciating every word as if he'd studied to be a Shakespearean actor. I bowed my head as he read, not so much in prayer as in gratitude; in the old days I would've been working a third or fourth drink. I was definitely making headway toward single martini land.

Justin asked if there were any newcomers. A man on my far right stood and nervously said, "The court ordered me here, my third DUI." He started to sit and someone asked his name. "My name is Dale." The thunderous chorus welcomed him. I wondered if he'd stick around. Before they skedaddled after meetings court ordered people asked the chairperson to sign official slips of paper verifying attendance. Once they learned AA doesn't record the names of those who attend and the chairpersons are unknown to the courts, they forge a signature and resume their journey into lost time.

"Is anyone celebrating a birthday?" Justin said.

"I'm Lloyd, and I'm an alcoholic. Six months."

"Think he's legit this time?" I whispered.

"Got a good bounce to his step," Hector said.

Justin stood and eyed deceitful Lloyd skeptically before he smiled, shook his hand, and handed him his chip.

"Is anyone else celebrating a birthday?" Justin asked, still standing.

"I'm Ken, and I'm an alcoholic." The live wire crackled from the maze of shadowed heads and shoulders to my far right. "Four years. I usually go to meetings in Medford or Central Point, but I heard about the speaker tonight and decided to take my chip here."

Unexpected surprise fueled my smile. I hadn't seen Ken since my pit stop at Serenity Lane. Loud clapping greeted him as he bounced forward, shoulders swaying. He shook the guest speaker's hand, then grasped his chip and shook hands with Justin. I kept smiling and clapping. Hotshot Ken had made it after all. I would've laid long odds.

"I know that guy," I said. "He was at Serenity with me."

"Were you there another time?" Hector said.

I cobbled the timeline as Ken strutted to his seat. How could I have missed it? Less than two years had passed since Ken counted his clean *weeks* on the fingers of one hand, excluding his thumb. I shook my head. I wanted to speak up, but an unwritten rule frowned on cross talk at AA meetings. Had Ken become another chip thief? I intended to speak with Scott and Hector after the meeting about Ken's tomfoolery, but I soon lost the thought.

"Now I'd like to turn the meeting over to our guest speaker," Justin said. I leaned forward and craned my neck for a better view.

"It's nice to see such a large gathering," she said.

There was no mistaking her smile, her voice.

CHAPTER TWENTY-THREE

Of course Justin, Hector, Miranda and Scott wanted to scoop her up, transport her to the Java Shop. I stood by her BMW as they talked, stealing glimpses.

"I appreciate your invitation," she said, "but let's hold it for another time. Right now there's an old friend I want to see." She thanked Justin for giving her the opportunity to speak at the meeting, shook hands with all four, and walked toward me. Hector flashed his winning smile, his right thumb pointing up.

"It's good to see you," I said. Not only had she materialized from the distant past, but she had galloped into town with twenty years of sobriety in her saddlebags.

"Good to see you, too." Julie squeezed my hand warmly. "Calm down. I won't bite."

"How long's it been? Thirty, thirty-five years." I rubbed my chin, rocked foot-to-foot like a shy youngster asking a first date.

"Do you wanna go for a drink?" I deadpanned. I waited a moment before grinning and adding, "of coffee?"

"I'd like that very much."

I gave her directions to Seymour's, a seafood and steak restaurant on the outskirts of town, not far.

"This seems like a nice town," she said.

"It is, but it's changing."

"Change is happening all over. The traffic in Seattle can be horrendous."

"So I've heard."

⊨⊧

She parked, and I led her past the restaurant entrance and opened the door that led into the compact, dimly lit bar. I didn't want an intrusion and I didn't think we'd run into prowling Scott or a copycat.

"Why are bars always dark?" she said.

My eyes slowly adjusted to the subdued light, the sole customer a short, overweight guy shuffling his feet in front of the jukebox. Rusty, the red-haired, barrel-chested, freckle-faced bartender, gave Julie an admiring up-and-down look, and said the decaf was fresh. She winked at him, and took two milkettes from a bowl next to the coffee. We carried our cups to a sizeable, higher wattage side room. Ten low-backed booths hugged the walls, five to each side. We sat by a window in the back. The glass reflected our images as we slid in across from each other and I imagined two younger, slimmer people, the promise of their youthful hopes and dreams ahead.

"I sure didn't expect to see you tonight," I said.

"You weren't in my plans either. I thought I was going to give an inspiring talk to a bunch of anonymous recovering drunks."

She peeled skin from the top of a milkette and slowly poured cream into her coffee. We lifted our cups and sipped. I frowned. The coffee tasted thin, as though brewed with previously used grounds.

"Ugh, a barista Rusty is not," I said.

She smiled, and shrugged.

She gazed at me through stylish, black framed glasses. She had gained some weight and there were faint lines alongside her mouth and eyes, streaks of gray in her hair, the veins in her hands evident. I assumed she observed similar changes in me.

The speakers above the doorway spewed a staticky version of the Doobie Brothers' oldie, "What a Fool Believes," a bittersweet song about a chance meeting between two former lovers.

"Appropriate," I said, rolling my eyes. Unlike the fool in the title, I came to believe Julie meant more to me than I did to her, and I never entertained illusions of rekindling our romance.

"They have a lot of old tunes on the box," I said.

"Do you come here often?"

"A few times, years ago."

She nodded and smiled like she had the night she walked into the Blue Onion.

"I didn't know you were in Seattle. I had no idea what happened—" I bit my tongue. How foolish to mention painful memories.

She tapped her front teeth. "Porcelain crowns. It's amazing what modern dentistry can do." She cradled her cup. "I'm sorry I was mean to you when I left."

"It wasn't you who was mean."

She patted my hand, and for a few quiet moments we sipped weak coffee and gazed at each other.

"You heard my story tonight, what about you?" she finally said.

"Your teeth look great."

"Thanks. Are you married?"

"Divorced." I paused, and she waited, as though I was sharing at a meeting. "It was very good for a while. I've a daughter." I wanted a cigarette. I'd meant to get some earlier. "My ex-wife Wendy and I probably married too soon and sorta grew up together. We both had affairs. Nothing too serious, but it's hard to come back from betrayal. I think I was too immature to work at a real marriage. Women seem to grow up faster." Fingering the side of the warm cup, I said, "And I think my drinking was a bit of a problem." She arched her blonde eyebrows. "All right, it was a *big* problem." I shrugged. "She sorta threw me out at the end. I think she wanted to date other guys and had had it with me. We married too young. The nice thing is that we're still friends. It took a while, but we're friends. My daughter Michelle probably helped."

"You're very generous in accepting blame. Surely, your wife must have had a few faults of her own."

"I s'pose so, but I honestly do feel I let her down more than the other way around." I sipped coffee, thought again about a cigarette. "Truth?"

"Truth."

"One time, when she got mad at me, she said she was tired of going to bed alone and hearing ice cubes clink in my glass."

"We never see ourselves when it's happening, do we?"

"People without the curse have no idea."

A moment of silence passed before she said, "How old is your daughter?"

"Michelle?" Some parents have their child's age on the tip of their tongue. I had to remember the year she was born and do the math. "Twenty-six. She's was working in your neck of the woods, in Federal Way, but now she's in Houston. She majored in business in college—University of Oregon—and she does some kind of financial work. She's going to a school down there for her MBA."

"She'll be able to expand her horizons when she gets it." She drank and put her cup down. "It's good you and Wendy remained friends. So many people break up under terrible circumstances. Kids can be damaged."

"Yeah, it's a shame. Look, I gotta go get some smokes. Be right back." I picked up our cups. "Here, I'll get us a refill."

I didn't see a cigarette machine. The decaf in the pot at the end of the bar, reasonably fresh when we came in, still smelled okay. I loaded our cups and waited while Rusty served two guys parked on stools.

"Pack of Winston's," I said.

The door opened as he handed me the cigarettes. I gave him a twenty. He padded off to make change, and Lloyd mounted a stool on the other side of the two guys. I caught his reflection in the back bar's mirror as he eyed the liquor bottles, his expression a curious blend of joy and confusion. My change came. Using the two men as a shield, I peeled the pack open, tapped out a cigarette, and lit up.

"What can I get you?" Rusty asked Lloyd.

"What'll this buy?" He laid his six-month chip on the bar.

"House policy says a double-shot of bar whiskey."

Rusty picked up the chip.

Lloyd tossed a bill on the counter. "Glass of draft on the side."

I wondered if Ken was in a bar doing the same. What would a four-year chip buy?

Rusty put the chip in a box by the cash register and served Lloyd. The man at the jukebox swiveled around on his heels, wobbled as he faced us, and said, "Oh, Lordy, I think I killed her."

≈÷ ÷≈

"Something wrong?" Julie asked.

"No. I haven't been in a bar in a long time." I put the cups down, remembered she said smoke bothered her, though it was odd since she smoked back then, and tamped out the cigarette. "I remembered you didn't like it."

"Still true, and in case you're wondering, I no longer indulge."

I nodded, moved the ashtray to an adjacent table, and slid back in the booth. I didn't want to tell her about Lloyd. It would only disappoint her. And I had no idea what the boozer at the jukebox was blathering about.

"So, are you married?" I said.

"I've been with Colin for almost ten years—no children, by choice." She poured cream into her fresh coffee. "You might say we're touring Oregon. We went over to see some artists' friends in Bend and then dropped south and eventually came through here on our way to the coast. Tomorrow we go to Yachats and spend a few days with friends, then Newport for another few days and then follow the Pacific to Washington. Colin's at the motel, probably happily working on something on his laptop." She paused and wet her lips. "He works for Microsoft."

"They make computers, don't they?"

She giggled and couldn't stop. I began to giggle, though I had no idea why.

"I'm sorry," she said, her hand stifling giggles. "I guess you're not into computers."

"Not really," I said, feeling my face glow. "They're kind of a glorified calculator, typewriter, and Western Union all rolled into an expensive plastic box. Besides, they're always crashing. What good is a machine that quits on you?"

"An upgrade for Windows 95 is in the works. You ever use the Internet?" I shook my head. "You will. President Clinton gets emails at the White House, not that he's the one who reads them. And Microsoft doesn't make computers. They make the operating systems for PC's."

"I use a computer at work."

"What do you do?"

"I'm a supervisor at the post office."

"Do you ever send or receive information on your computer?"

"Yeah. Daily reports go out in the afternoon, and the next morning I get harassing notes from the district manager."

"Do I detect sarcasm?" I shrugged. "Whatever you send or receive is going out or coming in over the internet."

"News to me. I just turn the sucker on and type. At least I don't have to mess with Wite-Out." I felt uncomfortable. I had no idea what Windows 95 or operating system meant. A technological revolution had swept by while I snoozed. I felt like Rip Van Winkle or an abject dolt. I'd read Arthur C. Clarke and watched *Star Trek* when Captain Kirk talked to the computer, but, when I bought Michelle a new Vic-20 for her tenth birthday in 1981, I'd looked upon it as nothing more than the newest gizmo, fad, an expensive toy. I wanted to change the subject.

"Do you still paint?"

She frowned. "Does talking about computers make you nervous?"

"I just don't know much about them."

"I'm sure you'll learn faster than you think," she said in a tone implying she expected computers to spur a monumental societal change, like TV.

So I said, "Like TV?"

She cocked her head thoughtfully. "I think you're going to be amazed if only half of what Colin envisions comes true. It may even impact your work."

She picked up her cup and drank. Her eyes momentarily slipped faraway, as though she were musing Colin's possibilities. A host of societal changes crowded my mind—the wheel, plant cultivation, string, mirrors, automobiles, the printing press, electricity, antibiotics, indoor plumbing, telephones. Then she came back, smiled and, thankfully, remembered my question. "Yes, I paint. Watercolors mainly: sunsets over the ocean, landscapes, mountains, animals, that kind of thing. I sell some and do freelance graphic work. I'm also experimenting with digital art on the computer." She shrugged. "Why not? It's a new tool and not as messy. Colin's very supportive, although I do some of my work on a Mac."

"That's another kind of computer, right?"

"Hmm. Different operating system."

I nodded as if it all made sense and shifted my weight and focus. "Were you really drinking almost half a gallon of wine every night?"

"It's a fair guess. How well do we remember how much we drank? Dates weren't much fun. The guys would pass out before they could get their drunken lay." She wrinkled her eyebrows. "Those were wretched times, and I was trying to paint through it all."

"Now you have twenty years in the program, old-timer territory."

She held up her index finger. "Correction. I've been in the program for twenty-two years, and I *have* twenty years of *continuous* sobriety." She paused and looked pensive. But her voice was clear and strong when she picked up. "As you heard, I was a wreck when I arrived. You wouldn't've recognized me. Dad even had me committed for a few months. I had a righteous resentment built up for him over that, but later I was able to work through it. He understood when I got clean and made amends. We had a good relationship after that." A wistful look filled her eyes as she looked down. "He had a stroke five years ago and died quickly. Just as well—there wasn't much left of him." She lifted her cup, held it by its handle and sipped. I had trouble reading her face. Her eyes looked reflective and her smile warm. "I spent a few days with him in his final week. He went in and out of knowing me. Two days before he died we were sitting on the porch, quietly watching people and cars pass by. It was a late fall afternoon and at dusk the air chilled. I was about to suggest we go inside for dinner when my dad sprang from his chair, threw out his arms palms up, and sang, 'See the USA in your Chevrolet, America's the greatest land of all.'" She smiled and shook her head and set down her cup. "Mom's in a nursing home in Columbus. I talked to her about coming to Seattle, but my sister's back there and my brother's in Chicago. Mom's in the early stages of dementia and she rightfully wants to stay near them and what few friends she has left, so it's up to me to travel."

"It's the pits, getting older. Somehow you don't expect it to happen. Then one day you wake up and wonder where all the years went. You can't buy time."

Her eyes shone. She looked beautiful. Only she wasn't staring at me. I glanced over my shoulder, following her trail. A jocular, heavyset couple with tall, colorful drinks squeezed into the booth nearest the bar.

"They look happy," she said.

"Maybe they're the one-drink variety." Her cup was half empty. "Want another?"

"Gosh, no. Anymore and I'll be up peeing all night. I usually don't have coffee at meetings anymore, especially if it's not decaf. Ever notice how many members do? "

"And smoke."

"Well, we do have addictive personalities."

I rubbed the side of my cup. "My mom had a stroke, too. She lasted three years and died a few weeks after she turned eighty-four."

"Every Breath You Take" by the Police crackled through the sound system. Strange a song so creepy would be so popular. Presumably a man obsessed with a woman. But then "Mack the Knife," a tune about a killer, had been popular in the 50's.

Julie's face darkened and the luster in her eyes dimmed.

"God, just what I wanted to hear, a musical treat from a lovesick stalker."

I thought of the note taped to her door in Athens, the sentence pinched from a pop tune: *You send me.* It seemed innocuous at the time, albeit annoying, a shy guy's longing.

Her thumb traced a faint scar on her chin. She let out a breath.

"It's not easy when a parent dies," she said in a low voice. "Sorry about your mom."

"I'm sorry about your dad, too," I said, going along, dispatching unsaid the ghastly event that tore us apart. "My sister was always trying to find a better nursing home, but Mom died in the one Sally and I found when we went back."

"Sally?" Curiosity lightened her.

"We were living together then. She's a great gal, very perceptive and sensitive, but it's on again, off again with her. She spilt in a huff a while back, but we've been talking, and I think she may come back."

"Sounds like you want her to."

"I do, but I think the drinking got in the way with her, too."

"She should like that you're in AA"

"I've been going for about a year and a half, and I only have eleven months. I kinda bounced in and out. I had trouble with the God thing."

"That happens. God speaks to each of us a little differently. It wasn't instant for me. The first few years I was fortunate to gain three or four days, maybe a week or two. Alcohol is insidious, especially when you have an illness like ours. For a long while, I envied people who had one drink at dinners or at parties. I finally had to stop going to parties. I also avoided old movies on TV, especially ones like *The Thin Man*, where martinis seemed to be an integral part of every scene. Then one day I woke up and everything seemed different. The thirst seemed subdued, forgotten, like a tide that's gone out. Now I'm clean and sober and, as long as I stay that way, I'm happy."

She smiled, picked up her cup. "Tell me about the God thing," she said, drinking and putting the cup down.

"I settled on the group being a higher power. Someone said it could be a doorknob, but I couldn't grasp that concept." I grinned, feeling at ease talking with her, and she nodded attentively. "I could accept drunks with years of sobriety being a power greater than myself. How did you deal with it? I don't remember either of us being religiously inclined."

"We were into Existentialism."

"The basic tenet—you are your actions—still applies."

"I suppose so. Unless you believe that character is determined. There's a lot of fascinating work being done in the field of genetics."

"So I've heard."

"But I'm glad you've made the group your higher power instead of your sponsor. People do slip. We're all only one drink away."

I heard laughter and glanced over my shoulder. Three young women, tall drinks in hands, bounced into a middle booth. They looked vibrant, sexy. The overhead lights dimmed.

"It's different than when we were their age, isn't it," she said, eyeing them before looking at me. "I believe in God. I don't go to any church or practice any particular religion, but I do believe in a higher power that I prefer to call God. It, he, she, helps me to stay sober and in return I help other people any way I can."

"What about your partner?"

"Dust in the Wind" by Kansas came on to remind us our lives were transitory.

"Colin's a very spiritual person. Not religious—he abhors organized religions—spiritual. I think he believes in the sanctity of life. He's also a normal drinker, but he seldom indulges, and never around me. He's very supportive. When I called the AA number yesterday and asked for the time and place of a meeting tonight, he said 'Go for it.' Sometimes he comes to listen, if it's open. It helps him understand me, even if he also hears a lot of bullshit. Anyway, Justin happened to be on the phone, and after we talked a bit and he found out I had twenty years, he asked if I would share my story. I guess he didn't have anyone lined up, and I'm always willing to give back to the program."

"I'm not sure I have that kind of dedication." I hesitated only a moment. I needed to tell someone. "There are times when I entertain whimsical thoughts, you know, like being able to drink again."

"That's not uncommon. Maybe a 30-30 would help."

"Do thirty meetings in thirty days? I don't think I could. Sometimes I'm bored in meetings. I spilt at break."

"Oh." She stiffened and leaned against the back of the booth, her hands flat on the table. A pensive look creased her face. "I didn't know."

How could she know I was not yet a true believer?

"I go to at least three meetings a week, and I call my sponsor once or twice a week and I'm working Step Nine, but sometimes, deep down, I still wonder if I'm a true alcoholic. Maybe I'm just a problem drinker."

I studied a spot of spilled coffee on the table. She quietly waited. I gripped my cool cup, fastened my eyes on her hands. The uneasy silence stretched too long. I looked up and offered a deprecatory smile.

She said: "I should've guessed, always the agnostic."

I pulled a napkin from the holder by the window and wiped the spill. I regretted telling her my doubts. She'd analyzed my misgivings and diagnosed backslider. I felt the sudden urge to lash back. I doubted we would ever see one another again, and knowing suddenly became very important.

"Did they ever find the guy?"

Her eyes flared, reproachfully.

I'd overstepped. I looked at the stained napkin, then at her face. "I'm just, you know, curious." The words sounded all wrong.

"They didn't have DNA back then," she said, her voice flat. "Maybe they arrested him for something else, something minor like peeping, and failed to recognize his evil nature."

She ran her finger around the top of her cup. I looked at her cheerless face, her eyes downcast, afraid anything I said would be dreadfully wrong.

"I haven't thought about it in years," she said. "Sometimes it's not good to stir the past."

Four boisterous young guys, all wearing T-shirts and jeans, tumbled in with two pitchers of beer. Three of them plopped into the booth cattycorner to us. The upright one looked at us. His face wore an exciting secret he was anxious to share, a secret his animated, jabbering friends already possessed.

"Unbelievable, man," he said, pointing a soon to be filled glass toward the bar. "Cops just came in, cuffed some dude, and hauled him out."

Julie looked at her watch. "Time for this woman to go."

"So soon?"

"We're up early tomorrow." She collected her purse from alongside her hip and fished out her car keys. "I can hardly wait to tell Colin about seeing you after all these years and going to a bar with you."

But her voice sounded icy.

"Not quite like the Blue Onion."

"No, not at all." She stood up. "Let's go. I'll drop you at your car."

I grinned at the three young women as I passed their booth. None returned my charming smile.

Lloyd was still perched on the stool, a glass of beer and a highball in front of him. Julie didn't see him.

"Cops cuffed him right after he dropped more coins in," Rusty said to the two guys parked on stools, retelling the drama they must also have witnessed.

CHAPTER TWENTY-FOUR

The jukebox man led off the six o'clock news. High on methamphetamine, he fled to Seymour's after his mother caught him rifling her purse. He vaguely recalled arguing with her and picking up the claw hammer. His sister said their elderly mother suspected a gambling habit.

A few days later I pocketed a one year chip, and when I returned home Sally was waiting. We knew we loved each other and were willing to work toward mending our relationship, but I could sense her caution. She and I talked, and we made love, and I continued to go to meetings, and I kept my alcoholic doubts to myself. I was afraid it would upset her. There would come a time, just not yet. Perhaps my doubts would dissolve.

⇒⁺ ⁺⇐

The following month Justin landed at the Medford airport, home from his whirlwind cross-country trip to attend select AA conventions and meetings. In nineteen days, he had seen the skylines of seventeen cities and shaken innumerable hands. He dropped off his luggage at home and immediately headed to the Thursday night meeting.

"I need shuteye," he yawned at break.

"Good idea," Hector said. "You look beat."

"We're going to the Sacred Heart meeting in Medford tomorrow," Scott said. "Want us to swing by?"

"If you're awake by then," Harry said.

The following evening Scott wheeled his newly found and impeccably restored '69 Dodge Charger to the curb. Hector rode shotgun, Harry and I in back.

"Bet he's still napping," Harry said.

"I'll go roust him."

Scott hustled up the short walkway to Justin's mobile, punched the doorbell with his right palm, and waited with folded arms. After half a minute he knocked, waited, banged the door with the side of his fist, faced us and shrugged and walked around the side.

"The bedroom curtains were parted," he said after he called 911 on his cell. "One leg was hanging outside the bed, the other still under the blankets, like he tried to get up."

⇒+ +⇐

A chilly drizzle fell during Justin's funeral. Some in the large crowd huddled beneath umbrellas, while others donned hats. A few brave souls arrived bareheaded. I wore an off-white Panama style hat Sally had given me.

Justin had no known relatives. He had attended a local church, which may have explained the presence of the tall, slender Lutheran minister. As she spoke, my mind drifted to the night my sister Cathy called, and a part of my life closed.

Unable to return home and resume her life after her stroke Mom, and eventually Henry, moved into Park Manor's assisted living floor in "Little" Washington, Pennsylvania. Her days of turning soil in her substantial garden, of planting seeds, of harvesting vegetables were lost. So, too, hours of housework and cooking, and greeting visitors who enlivened her, and dreams of places she would never see. Mom's world shrank to a cubicle alongside other cubicles with meals provided.

After they depleted their hard-earned savings and after Cathy sold the little house in Cokeburg, after "spending down," they were officially indigent, and Medicare kicked in.

They were two aged people who had survived the hardship of the Great Depression and the anxiety of The Second World War, who had been good, frugal citizens, who lived their lives quietly. At Park Manor, Henry, whose youthful freestyle strokes once carried him across the wide Ohio River, measured his shuffling walk in unsteady inches, his legs betrayed by Parkinson's. Mom, who'd always been ten steps ahead of him, now welded to an aluminum walker. They were leaving life as they had entered unable to trust their bodies, and poor.

On a quiet December day we followed the flight of the dead from the service at St. Joseph's in Cokeburg to the cemetery in Scenery Hill, where Mom would join Uncle Johnny, Grandfather and Grandmother.

Sally, Uncle Joe, and I sat in the backseat of the rental. John was behind the wheel and Cathy beside her husband for the short journey. None of us spoke. I stared at winter's gloom and replayed Mom's last words to me. At Park Manor, lying on her bed, she'd wrapped her arms around my neck and pulled me close. "Thank you for being a good son," she said. "Thank you for being a good mother," I said as uncontrollable tears flooded my cheeks.

Cathy, John, Uncle Joe, Sally, and I lined up to the left of Father Mike as he blessed the grave. Gloria, Henry, and Mick stood on his right. Cirrhosis had claimed Ernie, Gloria's wannabe-card-shark husband.

The night of the viewing the funeral home's door swung open and a gust of frigid air ushered in Gloria and Henry. My eyes dwelt on the person holding open the door, and my gut tightened. Mick. I hadn't seen him since leaving Parma. Still wearing a crew cut, he looked as I remember him, though heavier. Time or some treatment unknown to me had smoothed the cratered acne scars on his face. His hand knifed through the air.

Mom fed me updates, especially after his visits. Twenty low-ranking years in the Navy, an honorable discharge, worked as a custodian at a hospital in Cleveland, married and fathered a child, wife and daughter unseen by Mom, whereabouts unknown.

I reluctantly accepted his cold hand, glanced at his beady eyes, and wondered what he was thinking. I wanted to rid my hand of his touch without appearing crass. I turned toward Sally, introduced her, and brushed a nonexistent speck from my pants.

Henry's glazed and teary eyes were so similar to the ones Sally and I had seen three years ago at Park Manor. There were admission papers for him to sign before he could reside with Mom in the intermediate care facility. How patiently we explained the situation to him, assured him that he could keep his car. How painful it was to watch his sad eyes as he acquiesced and slowly took pen in hand and carefully sign the life-changing document.

"Your Mom was good for Dad," Gloria said.

"Mom was always kind," Mick said.

"I'm so sorry," Gloria said, raising a handkerchief to her tear-stained eyes.

"Dad'll be lost without her," Mick said.

I felt a crazy swirl of anger, disgust, pity and despair. Mick had spent at least a week of every year in Cokeburg. Mom had cooked for him, listened to him, washed his bedding. During the past few decades he'd spent more time with her than I.

Henry shuffled away. Mick and Gloria followed. Gloria must've thought I was out of earshot when she whispered to Mick, "He's nicer than his Mom."

Father Mike blessed Mom's grave, the first of three prayers at Catholic funerals. He surveyed us before intoning the rite of committal: "Because God has chosen to call . . ." When he finished, the copper-colored casket holding my lifeless mother began its slow descent. "Thank you for being a good son." Father Mike made the Sign of the Cross, and said, "Let us pray." "Our father who art in heaven . . ." I whispered. Her casket settled inside the earth. Tears rolled off my chin. At a respectful distance, patiently waiting, two gravediggers leaned on the handles of their long shovels, the air cold and still.

After a few minutes, we left Mom with her parents and her younger brother.

Mick shepherded Henry to the brown Chevy he'd driven down from Cleveland. He opened the passenger door, and Henry slowly maneuvered himself inside. Gloria sat in back, her hand on Henry's shoulder. Mick started the cold engine, and they rumbled away. I never saw or heard from any of them again.

⟞⟝ ⟞⟝

"It was a good turnout," Scott said.

"Justin influenced or sponsored many," Hector said.

When we reached our cars, Scott's head suddenly jerked up, as if he had heard gunshot.

"Harry didn't show."

Soon we would know. Harry was pie-eyed, in the grip of another bender, unreachable. His pals were gin, vodka, and whatever was playing on TV.

It was warm in the crowded room. I knew many of the people at the Thursday meeting Scott now chaired. Most were regulars, like Miranda and Wayne; others were infrequent attendees or new-comers or drunks who came out of the woodwork to claim suspicious years of sobriety. Some were quiet drunks, some were loud guzzlers, and some were brawlers. Some would return while others would not. There was no way of knowing. AA helped many, but it also had more turnovers than a bakery.

⥈ ⥆

The Serenity Prayer had been said, and chairs put away, and I was getting ready to leave when a short, ordinary-looking kid I'd never seen before approached me. Behind a sly smile he introduced himself as Tim and asked me to be his sponsor. His request knocked me off stride. The day had come. "Never pass up an AA request," Hector said, his mantra—but I felt inadequate. I hesitated a moment, thought of asking, "Why me?" or suggesting someone else, looked into his expectant blue eyes, the hopeful turn of his grin fixed, and I knew I couldn't decline. I arranged to meet him the following night at The Three Acts, an eatery up the road from the Java Shop that served up mediocre food and passable coffee.

Not long past his twenty-first, he hadn't left his inveigling grin in his car. We shook hands. I ordered decaf and he a Coke, and we sat at a corner table. I asked him a few preliminary questions and sat back and listened. After fifteen minutes his juvenile bragging and whining fatigued my ears. I also felt an undercurrent I couldn't identify. Finally, I asked if he could go a few days without drinking, intending to follow-up with an explanation of the delay method. I expected some willingness, as in "I could try." Wasn't that why he asked me to be his sponsor? Instead, he said he liked to go drinking with girls so he could, "You know, get 'em drunk, pull down their panties and stick it in." His lips twisted into a lecherous sneer. "So I wanna get some help 'cause there's times I go overboard and have trouble . . . you know, getting it up." It took me a moment to remember I wasn't here to pass judgment. I tossed out a stumblebum comment about the pleasures of drug-free sex. He shrugged halfheartedly, as if to indicate the other was easier. I hastily ran down the delay-a-drink technique and arranged our next meeting. He never showed.

⚒ ⚒

I added two months to my one year chip and bought a new Honda Civic before I finally got around to scheduling my trip to Missouri. I planned to drive to Portland and visit Cathy and John. They had alighted in Oregon shortly before I moved from California to re-join Wendy and Michelle. John's older brother lived in Salem. Over the years we maintained a diet of once or twice a year visits. They had two daughters, one Michelle's age and the other a few years older.

I planned an overnight visit this time. Then, though I'm afraid of flying, I'd hop on a white-knuckled flight to Kansas City, rent a car, and enjoy a leisurely drive downstate.

⚒ ⚒

The day before I left, Sally and I made love and then splurged and went out for a nice dinner. She kidded me about my sudden fondness for decaf. When we returned to our apartment, my back was bothering me a bit, and I eased into the La-Z-Boy, a brown paper bag with assorted items from the Nova on my lap. I pulled out the book Tom had returned and tossed it onto the small table by the chair.

"Heidegger?" She eyed the cover from the couch.

"I loaned it to a friend a long time ago."

"I've never read much philosophy."

"You read the Tibetan *Book of the Dead*."

292

"It wasn't very cheerful." She leaned over the couch's arm and picked up the book. Looked at the front and back covers and put the book back on the table.

I told her about Tom's unexpected visit.

"I sometimes muse about looking up old places, but you know L.A.—here today gone tomorrow. Most of my friends have scattered." She shrugged. "A small town like Carthage may be more stable." Her eyes took on a reflective look. I thought she might be recalling her childhood poverty, an absent father, a mother scrambling for pennies, a family always on the move, their next bed and meal uncertain.

"It's different when you see a child's world through an adult's eyes," she said. "Besides Leon, do you intend to look up any other friends?"

"I've no idea who may still be living there."

She ran her tongue over her lower lip. "I'm thinking of buying a computer."

"They're pretty spendy."

"Uh-huh. And they're always upgrading, but I definitely think it's something to explore. Digital art."

"I went to a meeting one night, and an old friend I hadn't seen in years was there, and she was into it. She lives in Seattle."

"What did she say about it?"

"Nothing much. Said she liked it. Thought of it as a new type of art."

"Hmmm. Maybe you'll find some use for it."

"You never know."

She rose, leaned over me, and kissed me. "Maybe you'll write about your trip."

"Maybe."

"How do you feel?"

"Nervous."

She smiled. "I'm sure you're going to find joy on your nostalgic journey."

"I hope so." No matter how dire the situation, Sally always viewed the silver lining.

She kissed me again, and we talked for a while, and then she said she was going to bed, and I settled into the time-worn recliner, picked up the Heidegger book, and took a moment to reflect on those turbulent times in Berkeley when young idealists, having inherited "the best of possible worlds," noted its flaws and set about to change it.

I remembered the words of a Kenneth Rexroth poem, something about it taking "longer than expected."

PART 6

CHAPTER TWENTY-FIVE

The air felt heavy, a breath difficult to draw. Sweat trickled into my eyes as I hauled my luggage to my room at the Spring Inn, a two-story, horseshoe-shaped motel on the outskirts of Carthage. I wiped my brow with the back of my hand, shirt-fanned my chest.

"Typical July weather 'round here," the desk clerk said. "Hot and humid."

I staggered inside, closed the door, dropped my bags, and, not being a Bikram Yoga devotee, lurched toward the air conditioner. Switched it on, punched high. Grateful streams of cool air ensured my survival. I pulled curtains to dull the sizzling sunlight, and slowly made my way to the bathroom. Wetted a hand towel with cold water, and bathed my face, unbuttoned my shirt. I peeled plastic wrapping off a plastic glass and filled the glass with cold water, and drank. Once assured that I would not melt, I set about unloading my suitcase; clothes in drawers beneath the TV (why hadn't I thought to bring shorts), toiletries alongside the sink in the bathroom. I sank into a chair, and shook off my sandals. I surveyed the room. It looked clean and well-maintained, the furnishings up-to-date. It felt cool.

I got an outside line and dialed our number in Ashland. My heart picked up a beat when I heard the timbre of Sally's voice.

"I don't remember it being this hot," I said when she asked how the visit was going.

"If it makes you feel better it was 90 here today."

"But not humid."

"So how's the trip going?"

I told her about my visit to the cemetery.

"Lots of memories," I said.

"I'm sure there were."

"I remember being led up to the coffin and looking at my Dad and thinking his face looked stony."

"You hardly knew him, and you were only seven."

I nodded, as though she could see me.

"When the funeral caravan left Carthage snow mixed with sleet was falling," I said, feeling a sudden need to retell the story she'd heard more than once. "Drivers stopped and scraped ice from windshields, and one time the funeral director stuck his head in the door and told Mom the roads were right bad and did she want to go on. There were no other cars on the road. At the Springfield National Cemetery there were soldiers with rifles, and their thunderous volleys shook the frigid air three times. A bugler played taps, and Dad's coffin descended, and a lot of people cried, and I don't know why I didn't, and someone gave Mom a flag folded into a starry triangle."

My lungs felt constricted and I sucked in air. I wondered if she heard. I reached over, and wiggled my fingers in cool air.

"How did you feel?"

"I felt sad for Dad. Not then. It was all a mystery to me then, what with him being absent for so long. Now I know he died so young. Now I feel a deep sadness for Mom. She tried her best, but things didn't quite work out the way she planned."

"She did what she thought was right, given the times."

"It just makes me sad. I keep thinking of this little Czech girl who sailed on a big ship across a great ocean, her life to unfold in a new land and in a new language. She should've had it better. She deserved better. It shouldn't've been so hard."

"Maybe it was better than you think."

"Maybe, I guess. I've had to beat down feelings that Mom betrayed me when she married Henry and we moved to Ohio. Cathy and I talked about it, and I know Mom could see the time when her children would be gone and she would be alone. Cathy didn't think there were viable choices for Mom in Carthage. You have to remember this was 1954. Mom opted for security, familiarity, what she thought would be for the best, and it didn't turn out so well. We all make bad choices."

A few silent seconds passed before she asked, "Are you going to see Michelle?"

Michelle had shed her husband, fled Seattle with a new beau in tow, and finagled a job in Houston. She liked the comfort of having someone waiting in the wings. They planned to tie the knot in the fall in Las Vegas.

"I don't think so. It's quite a hike from here. Anyway, we're gonna see her in Vegas."

"Hmmm, then when do you plan to see your friend?"

"Tomorrow, if he's around. I'll head back the day after."

We talked awhile longer, and then we each said "I love you" and "see you soon," and I stretched out on the bed. Carthage had grown a bit since my time. I'd noted a lot of interesting stores in and around the square—antiques, arts and crafts, galleries, a book store advertising new and used—the makings of a tourist economy. As my eyes grew heavy, random memories visited: fragments of days, a quick scene or two here, sometimes stretching a little longer. Familiar faces appeared, indistinct and time- weathered.

⊨⊨ ⊨⊨

I dozed for an hour and woke hungry.

I wiped sweat from my forehead as I trudged to The Outpost, a restaurant alongside the motel. I pulled open the door and stepped into blessed coolness. Right away I noticed immobile musicians in framed eight-by-ten photos hanging on the walls. There were few customers and I gazed at the photos as I leisurely made my way to a shaded window booth, my preferred seating. Many bore inscriptions to Dale and Dakota, sometimes expressed as D & D, whoever they were. The Eurhythmics, Pretenders and The Clash welcomed me as I slid into a booth.

"Did all of these musicians eat here?" I asked the waitress, a cute, shapely redhead with high cheekbones, full lips, and a slight gap between her two front teeth. Her bemused bluish-green eyes looked at me through small wireframe glasses. Spiffy uniform: knee-length black skirt and yellow blouse, school colors for the U of Missouri Tigers. A name tag above her small, left breast identified her as Amber.

She glanced at the photos. "Nah. Dale collected 'em when 'im and the band toured."

"Who's Dale?"

"One of the owners."

"And Dakota?"

"His wife. She's the chef."

"Interesting. What's the name of his band?"

"Well, they was the Hungry Tigers in the sixties. I never seen 'em then 'cause I wasn't old anuff. Come the seventies they sorta switched to disco with a little punk rock throwed in and called themselves The Limestone Rockers, but that didn't go over 'cause the two don't mesh, I guess. Then in the eighties they changed their personnel some and their name to the Spring River Band, playing mostly country and bluegrass with a few soft rock tunes throwed in. They got a plenty solid followin' round here. They only tour every so often 'cause they's gettin' old. Usually, they just play in the bar on weekends." She jerked the pen she held toward the back of the restaurant. "It's right through that there door."

"Wow, thanks."

She grinned. She hadn't skimped on dental visits. Her teeth looked immaculate.

"Well, you was curious. Dale's tendin' bar. Stop in and see 'im. He's a regular gabber once he gets revved."

"Maybe I will."

"So, whadda it be?"

⊨ ⊨

I paused at the door. Dale grew-up in Carthage. He might have known a few of my childhood pals. He might have known me.

No harm in having a short one for old time's sake.

I dipped my hand into my pocket, rubbed my one-year chip.

"Just going in for a pop and conversation," I said.

He won't pay you much heed if you're sipping Pepsi.

"Maybe I'll have one beer. Nurse it."

Good idea.

"Hell's bells," I mumbled to a door, proving that a touch of madness resides in everyone.

I stepped into a well-lit room, quietly cool and much larger than anticipated. A small stage and ample dance floor anchored one end. A scattering of tables and chairs occupied the midsection, and a super-sized TV stared down from the wall facing the bar. There were no autographed photos. Four Latinos sharing a

301

pitcher of beer surrounded a small table. One of them crooned a musical word, and they burst out laughing.

A slender man with a mixed drink and a beer chaser for company perched on a stool at the far end of a long polished mahogany bar. I eased onto a stool down rail, across from where a short, hefty silver-haired guy wearing black small-framed glasses was slicing lemons on a small cutting board and humming a familiar tune. A neatly folded white bar towel draped his left shoulder. He wore a pale blue short-sleeved shirt and his chin displayed a neatly trimmed Vandyke. I couldn't call up the tune he hummed.

He looked up and amicably said, "Whadda it be?"

"You must be Dale."

He raised an eyebrow and frowned.

"I had advance information."

"Ah."

I smiled, and my attention drifted to silver-tipped whiskey bottles lined up like dandies at a promenade. Going hard was out of the question. No way.

Just order a beer.

"Do you carry Guinness?" The words easily slid off my tongue.

He gave me a look, as though he suspected I was an IRA agent infiltrating a devout Protestant establishment.

"What other brands do you favor?" he said.

"I like 'em all."

He grinned. "I got Old Milwaukee and a stout Ozark lager on tap. I think you might side with the Ozark. Think of it as displaced Irish. Pint or ten-ounce teaser?"

"Just a taste." I pulled a twenty from my wallet and dropped it on the bar.

He drew the ten-ounce teaser, slid the glass and a basket of pretzels in front of me, made change.

"Thanks." I looked around, fingering the moist glass, my prop to encourage conversation.

"Slow night?"

"Middle of the week," slicing lemons again, "it'll pick up some later."

"I bet you do pretty well on Sundays during football season." I imagined the TV blaring, a packed house, foot-stomping, boisterous, free-spending fans in various degrees of inebriation.

"Only in my dreams. There's a lot of religion in these parts, and most folks 'round here don't cotton to imbibin' on the Lord's Day." He winked. "At least in public."

"Ah, Blue Laws. I know about them." I pulled my hand away from the tempting glass. "My parents owned a bar Ohio."

"That so."

"Yeah, but," looking around, "it was a lot smaller and not nearly as nice."

He nodded and surveyed the room as though admiring finishing touches beyond my awareness.

"It was a dump, really," I said.

It happened without a thought. I lifted the glass and sipped. The lager had a stout's pleasantly bitter taste and smoky flavor, its alcohol level capable of fueling a fire. I drank.

"I useta to live in Carthage."

"That so."

Yep, Amber was right, I cynically thought, Dale was a real loquacious fellow.

"I hear you play in a band."

"Uh-huh."

Frustrated neither of my conversational forays had gained traction, I took a deep pull, drained the small glass. It went down easy.

"Refill?"

Just one more.

"Yeah."

He slid a fresh teaser in front of me.

"You ever cut any records?"

"A few."

"Any hits?" Too late, I pictured boxes of unsold records in his garage. I drank a third of the beer.

"We had our fifteen minutes of fame. 'Missouri Blues' made it to number twenty on the Billboard chart. It was in the Top Forty twelve weeks. 'Got the blues headin' to a place I usta call home.'" He had a soft melodious voice, reminded me of James Taylor. "Our big hit 'I'll Be Missin' You' climbed to number eleven."

Before he could sing me a sample, the guys at the table pushed out of their chairs. One of them said, "Adios, Amigo," and flipped Dale a friendly wave.

He cleared their table and wiped it clean. Back behind the bar, he tore a strip of Saran Wrap and covered the bowl of sliced lemons.

"You must sell a lot of tequila." I tossed a handful of pretzels into my mouth.

"Lemons are for gin and tonics. Tequila takes limes. So when didcha live here?"

I paused my chewing and tried to sound coherent, not easy with a mouthful of macerated pretzels. "'46 to '54. That's when I finished sixth grade and we moved to Parma, near Cleveland."

"'54's the year the Tiger auditorium burned."

"The Tiger!"

Dale flinched, and then slowly looked down. Moist globs of pretzels had shot out of my mouth and decorated his pale blue shirt.

"Gettin' a mite carried away there, aren't you," he said, calmly brushing the soggy morsels from his shirt and toweling the bar.

"Sorry. I loved that place." I wiped my mouth with the back of my hand and gulped down the rest of my beer, wetting the image of the majestic Tiger burning.

"Lucky for you, I'd covered the lemons. Need a refill?"

"Make it a pint. Why settle for less when you can have more? Friend of mine said that." What happened to Tom after he left Ashland?

He drew the brew and slid the pint glass in front of me. I immediately inhaled a deep pull.

"So where'd you go to school?" he asked. He withdrew the pretzels and unhappily brushed his shirt with the bar towel.

"Eugene Field and Mark Twain."

His eyes opened in surprise. "I'll be damned. I went to Mark Twain."

"Did you know Leon Zubeck?"

He stroked his beard and damp pretzel crumbs tumbled down. "I probably wouldn't've known you or him 'cause I didn't start high school until '58. Way I count years I was 'bout two grades behind you when you went Back East."

I'd steered into a dead end. He carefully ran the bar towel over the plastic wrapped bowl of sliced lemons and stowed them beneath the bar, He wiped the knife and cutting board dry and sent them below.

"So what about the band?"

"My wife, Dakota, and I pulled one together after high school. She's got a husky, sexy voice."

"You've got a smooth voice," I said and drank.

"Thanks. Folks don't hear her much anymore. She got real interested in the food end. Started working at the restaurant. Turned it around when she upgraded the menu—home cookin' you might say. Folks around here took to it as quick as they hurry to church on Sundays."

I drained the glass.

"Another?"

"Yeah." I pinched a cigarette from the pack in my shirt pocket. I felt good.

"Plus the war messed us up," he said, putting down the fat glass as I lit up. "I useta smoke. Them cancer sticks will kill ya. Don't do much good for your sex life either, and they killed Nat King Cole way too soon." He eyed my glass. "And watch out. Tangle too long with the Ozark and tomorra you'll feel like a mule kicked you in the head."

"Advice taken, but I gotta tell you this beer tastes terrific." I lifted the glass and drank deeply, put the glass down, wiped my lips with the back of my hand, and stubbed out my butt. "So, the war messed up the band."

"Uh-huh."

I drank as he launched his woeful tale. Not one to take chances, Alvin, the drummer, an avowed pacifist, sought refuge from the storm in Canada. Vic, the rhythm guitarist, bet on good luck and lost.

"He came home minus a mess of fingers. That put the kibosh on his strumming." Dale regretfully shook his head and wiped the moist circle the bottom of my previous glass had imprinted on the shiny bar. "Wrecked his spirit."

The man at the end of the bar stood on unsteady legs. "I feels pretty good. Guess I'll mosey on home, Dale" He brushed pretzel crumbs from his rumpled shirt and weaved toward the door.

"Ken's a postal carrier," Dale said as he cleared Ken's drained glasses and toweled the bar. "Few months back his wife left a note thanking him for good old times, but she and some guy planned to kick off new good times in Little Rock. Turns out he was one of Ken's best buddies."

He shook his head, flipped the stained towel over his shoulder, and strolled back.

I thought of telling him I was a postal supervisor and squashed the idea. I didn't want to talk about work. I wanted another pint. He drew it and set it in front of me.

"So, you seein' the old sights?"

"Yeah." I blinked at the cold glass. I was feeling a tad lightheaded. "I did a quick cruise around downtown. Looks spiffy and the courthouse as stately as I remembered. I drove down one of the streets we lived on. It was strange. Either I couldn't recognize the house or it was gone."

"Either's possible, especially with a house that old. Everything changes. Did you know Belle Star lived here?"

"I only knew Jesse James robbed the bank."

"Jesse may have passed through, but he never robbed the bank. That plaque came down after old Norman Anderson retired. New bank president didn't like the Wild West image, especially since there was no historical reference. Apparently, it was Norman's pleasure." He stroked his beard. "If you're plannin' on lookin' up your old school friend, you might find he's not with us anymore."

"His parents had a farm on the edge of town. I always figured he'd take it over, but for all I know he may have his name etched on the wall in Washington."

"I didn't mean that. He might've moved away. Lotta people did. If Mom and Dad were still around, they probably could've helped you. After they passed, Dakota and me hung up the wheels, came home, and took over the motel."

"You own that, too?"

"Yep." He cleared his throat. "We remodeled, and I wanted to call it the Rest Your Ass—"

I burst out laughing. "Great name!"

"I thought so." He chuckled. "Dakota nixed it, and she was right. Like I said, there's a lot of religion 'round here, and since the interstate threw us off the beaten path, we had to depend on over-night sightseers not staying in Joplin or folks with visitin' relatives they couldn't squeeze into their houses. Any guesses how many would book a stay at the Rest Your Ass?"

"So whatcha do?"

The door opened. Two thin men sauntered in and flumped down on stools near the door.

"'Scuse me," Dale said.

He seemed to be in front of them before my ears had registered his words. The door swung open again and a ruggedly attractive, deeply tanned woman glided in wearing faded blue short shorts and a low-slung red halter top that displayed a generous helping of her abundant natural assets. Two brawny men dressed in jeans and sweat-stained T-shirts trailed behind. They all looked to be in their early thirties, and they settled at a table in front of the Super-sized TV. The taller man strutted to the bar, and ordered a pitcher of Old Milwaukee and a gin-and-tonic. He had rough whitened hands, as if he worked with concrete or sheet rock.

"How's 'bout clickin' on the game, Dale?"

Dale picked up the remote and beamed in the game from Philadelphia. I caught his eye after he filled their order. He filled a frosty glass and set it in front of me. I sucked off the frothy head, and drank deeply.

"The motel name . . . we settled on the Spring River Inn," he continued as I stared at the delicious brew. "We even book a few conventions. That started after we bought the café, remodeled it, and added the lounge."

"Your entre-pre-neurial skills amaze me." I drank.

"Once you settle down, you gotta make a livin' and consider the future."

"I wish I'd a done a few things dif-ferently. A genetic joke al-always got in the way."

"Sounds like it's time for you to part company with the Ozark."

"Cut off time, huh, you keen-eared devil." I drank. The glass was almost empty. "I do okay, but I've made a lot of mis-takes."

"How so?"

I gathered words. "I don't know when to stop," I said. "I'm an alcoholic."

The door swung open, and a young couple parked at a corner table.

"They want curb service," Dale said.

"I best be goin'."

I drained my glass and put it down. His hand gripped my forearm.

"I like you. There're places you can go."

"I know," I sighed. "I been there."

⇒+ +⇐

Sinister creatures buzzed me. On wobbly legs I swatted squadrons of dive-bombers intent on doing me harm and quickened my pace. I squashed one gorging itself on my forearm, leaving a red smear. Once inside the cool room, I searched walls, spotted six despicable, disease-carrying, needle-nosed bloodsucking manifestation of God's mistake and mashed the varmints with a courtesy copy of the *Press*.

I doused the itchy welt on my forearm with cold water. Ice from the machine in the alcove six doors down inviting, but I'd have to run a gauntlet of winged vampires and my legs were suspect.

Woozy, I shook off my sandals, stripped to my underpants, and lay on the bed. The stale taste of beer lingered. I'd been too long without drink and, like anyone long denied a pleasure, simply overindulged. A foolhardy urge to return to the bar for one of Dale's gin and tonics burst into my addled brain. I knuckled it down. I didn't want to make a complete ass of myself.

I used the remote to click on TV, channel surfed, and drifted. I remembered Tom asking me about the Greenhouse Effect and his belief that overpopulation caused many of our problems. I wondered how many people the planet could comfortably support before it collapsed like a ruptured balloon. Tom always had a keen interest in philosophy. On a farm near Sebastopol he dropped acid, certain his trip would reveal the meaning of life. He waltzed around the corner of a barn and saw Donald Duck.

Tom said he felt lonely. I thought of myself passing empty time with Drink, washing my real and imagined woes. How alone I felt when I blindly stumbled into bed.

The infernal bite itched, and I scratched.

On ESPN, two earnest women were competing in a nine-ball tournament, their high skill demonstrated by their efficient strokes and their near-perfect positioning of the cue ball. I was surprised when they occasionally missed. I yawned, switched off the TV before their best-of-seven match ended, and stared at the dark screen.

I'd never been a joiner. Aside from playing team sports and being a dues-paying token officer in a postal union, I'd never joined anything. No bumper sticker or window decal had ever adorned my cars. I'd always believed in my singularity.

AA surprised me. I liked the people, their sincere openness and honesty. So, I attended meetings and listened, tempered my drinking, found a sponsor with whom I felt reasonably comfortable and worked the steps, content that he and his fellow drunks liked me. Had I been a thief when I secretly only wanted to know how to ameliorate my alcohol cravings? But I had failed again. I wondered what the future held.

I yearned to hear Sally's voice. She'd understand, give me support. The two-hour time difference meant it wasn't too late. I picked up the phone and immediately put it back in its cradle. Slurred words would only upset her.

I lit a cigarette, and stared at my reflection in the mirror above the bureau. Familiar faces came forward, stamped in my mind as they looked so long ago, only time-faded, like photos left too long in bright light, dreamlike.

I yawned, crushed out the cigarette, switched off the light, and left the air on high. I'd rethink in tomorrow's sober light. I lay my head on the pillow and closed my eyes. In the darkness sweet sleep cooled the heated alcohol coursing through my veins.

CHAPTER TWENTY-SIX

Tour buses parked outside The Outback signaled a crowd and noise. I'd hoped ice water and a quiet cup of strong coffee would soothe my dry throat and quiet the clashing cymbals in my head. I squeezed inside, my ears at once assaulted by a horde of babbling, ravenous, young mouths. Kids everywhere. Had I known another topnotch place, I would have fled.

Where to sit?

I spotted Amber toting a tray of plated steaming food, weaving around packed tables with chairs askew, too focused to catch my needy stare. Biceps I hadn't noticed the previous day, told me she was stronger than she first appeared. I spied a small vacant table crammed into a far corner as though it were an afterthought, maneuvered through the mob and staked my claim. I squinted at a photo alongside the table. I knew the face, but couldn't place it. I rummaged through shreds of memory. Ah, yes, young Willie Nelson. A few minutes after my recollection, Amber darted over and I ordered coffee and a glass of ice water.

I fished a chunk of ice from the glass and smothered the welt, which had calmed down but still itched. Ice water soothed my parched throat. I beckoned Amber twice for refills, one request filled by a waitress whose name tag I didn't bother to read. The caffeine slowly muted the raging cymbalist, and I focused on the menu. My angry stomach made the choice. I laid the menu down and pushed it to the other end of the table, indicating I was ready to order. An enormous amount of time passed before Amber appeared and swept up the menu.

"Ready?"

"You work out."

"Uh-huh."

"I stopped in and saw Dale. You were right. He sure is a talker once he gets going."

"Told ya," she shrugged.

"I hear Dakota's quite a cook."

"Sure is." Her foot tapped an impatient beat on the floor. "Look, I don't mean to be rude or nothin', but I got more orders comin' out than there's channels on cable. So, whadda it be?"

I devoured a deep bowl of Dakota's delicious chicken noodle soup and downed two glasses of 7Up. I left a generous tip.

I pushed through a thick wall of humid air to my sun-baked rental car. I fired the engine, cranked up the air, and set off. I thought of Mom's driving lesson in the Plymouth. The light touch of my rented Toyota Corolla's power steering and brakes, the ease of an automatic transmission, the comfort of contoured seats, and the dash ducts that wafted cool air would have delighted her. If only I could ride time backwards . . .

On South Main Street I stopped in front of Mark Twain Elementary. Surprisingly, it looked much the same, though time-worn, like an aged but comfortable jacket. I remembered when the bell announcing the end of our recess malfunctioned and our fifteen minute outside play time stretched into the better part of an hour before the teachers noticed the extraordinary length. I remembered making a maraca out of a light bulb and papier-mâché. I smiled and drove to South Garrison Street. Nothing along the way looked familiar.

My heart picked up a beat when I turned onto Clevenger Street. I'd walked it many times going to and from school, ridden a sled down it a few times. It was shorter than I remembered and not as steep. I braked across the street from what I thought was Larry's house. It looked old, somewhat shabby, its roof in need of repair. Halfway up the driveway and off to the side, where Larry and I fired BBs at cans simulating Henry's pockmarked car, a dusty black Packard, its tires gone, rested on stilt-like blocks. I wondered if Larry's grandparents ever came inside to watch TV. Larry said they always stood outside the living room window in good weather and looked in through the screen.

I hadn't seen or heard from Larry since . . . when? "Sometimes it's not good to stir the past," Julie said. He had probably moved. I lifted my foot off the brake and rolled further downhill, following sled tracks in snow and the skipping beats of carefree kids on bright summer days.

I parked alongside the picket fence bordering our former backyard, got out and strolled down the sidewalk. The fence, a sad memory of its former self, in need of paint, many of its pickets leaning backwards and cockeyed, others spilt, some missing. The house looked fairly well-maintained, though a good sandblasting would reveal tiny specks of light in the stone. Ancient window frames betrayed their age. I looked up at my old bedroom window and remembered the snowy night Cathy and Mom rescued the frozen Plymouth. When the weather turned warm, I peed through the screen instead of going downstairs to the bathroom. Had I been afraid of the dark or lazy?

I stood at the corner and peered down Forest Street. Imagined Mom returning home from work in Bertha's faded car, or Cathy pulling up in the Plymouth to cart me to Little League. I glanced over at Emily's old house. For some reason I pictured her in a pink pant suit at a PTA meeting in Oklahoma City. I had no idea why.

My childhood home was much too small. The image of a doll's house came to mind. I tried to envision the downsized rooms. I wondered if I'd carried a house key. Did we only lock the doors at night?

I remembered lying on the dining room floor in cold weather when Mom vacuumed, the vacuum's warm exhaust bathing my face. Watching *You Bet Your Life* with Mom. We sat on the couch. Or, was there also a chair? Late night Charlie Chan movies, when she sometimes fell sleep, and I had to tell her who did it.

I sighed, and faced Forest Street. A tall streetlight replaced the bulb that hung suspended over the street from wires. I looked up the next block, toward two exhausted houses where three homes had once stood. Connie's boarded up old place invited the next demolition.

Across Clevenger, the two ranch style houses that'd displaced the ball diamond where Larry, Connie and I practiced baseball had not aged well, though the oak saplings planted in the front yards now offered generous shade. A black cat scampered across a yard, stretched its lean torso, and vigorously clawed one of the trees. Wendy said old Cyclops never returned from one of his nightly prowls. A woman kneeling in front of a flowerbed glanced at the cat. I hadn't noticed her bent frame when I parked. I thought she had also spotted me, and I smiled, but she returned to her troweling, and I retreated to the car.

Clevenger Street remained a simple one-block sled run. On the other side of Forest Street, the weedy field and slim dirt path leading to the creek was now blacktopped and christened Wood Avenue. It crossed the skinny creek and ran parallel to the woods.

Leon's farm was not far. Would I have found a listing for Zubeck in the phone book?

I braked at a stop sign, where Wood Avenue formed a T junction with a paved farm road, the western boundary of the pasture and woods. In my day the road had been dirt, trafficked by farm vehicles, their wheels spinning huge dirt storms, and by tanker trucks spewing DDT as they roamed an "insect-infested" countryside. Off to my right, only a memory of a pond remained. A wide-mouthed conduit now channeled the creek under the street.

I thought of knocking on Leon's door and sighed. What if a blind man answered? What if his aged parents, assuming they were still alive, opened the door, stared at me with failing eyes, and said their son had perished in Vietnam?

I turned, drove a short ways, and pulled into a graveled driveway. Right away, I knew something was wrong. The farmhouse looked naked. No orange-spotted chestnut tree. Years ago, I'd read an article in *Smithsonian* about chestnuts and a blight fungus. The splotches hadn't been Leon's trickery after all.

I dodged a scurrying rooster and parked by the barn. On a warm lazy day I'd sprawled high on bales of hay and chewed on a piece of straw. The rest of the day eluded me. I stood for a moment and admired the house's new coat of white paint and shiny aluminum gutters, then walked toward the back door. I stepped up to the small porch where Leon ran in agony and looked down, as if I expected blood stains. I searched for a doorbell. Finding none, I rapped on the screen door and rearranged my thoughts. I knocked again, louder.

Anxious seconds passed before the door slowly swung open. A thin, elderly woman peered at me through clear-framed glasses, her thinning white hair close-cropped. She wore an old style gingham housedress dress with buttons down the front.

"Yes?" she said. Her uneasy eyes squinted into me and past me.

"Mrs. Zubeck?" I hoped she'd turn the pages of her history and find my chapter. She cocked her head, pursed her lips. "Leon and I were friends when we were kids." She held her chary stare, her focus shifting from my eyes to somewhere over my shoulder and back. "There used to be a chestnut tree alongside your house. My mom worked at the Big Smith overall factory."

Her eyes softened. The hint of a smile deepened the wrinkles around her mouth, told me she'd found my chapter if not yet my page. "It gave good shade," she said, then looked at me as if she were appraising livestock. "I expect I recall you. You were one of the taller ones. You don't take drugs, do you?" I shook my head and flashed an innocent grin. "Forgive my rudeness, but we got to be careful. Not like it used to be. Oh, now I feel like a rude old biddy. Please, come in."

She unlocked the sturdy aluminum framed screen door, and I stepped inside. She wore white sneakers, no socks.

"Drugs are turning people dreadful," she said as she locked the screen door, closed the inside door, and turned the deadbolt. She faced me and gestured toward a large bowl of lemons. "Would you like a glass of real lemonade? I always put out four glasses in case company comes."

"Maybe later."

"Something to eat?"

"Thanks, but I just had lunch."

"We're in back." She touched my arm. "Come sit a spell." I followed her down a short hallway. "Joe, Joe, one of Leon's old friends come to visit." She paused, glanced over her shoulder, and her face quizzed me.

"David," I said. "David Crobak."

Screened windows shielded the open three sides of the high porch from DDT survivors. A modest garden out back: lettuce, strawberries, corn, tomatoes. A quiet fan rendered a steady breeze. A pitcher of lemonade, a sweaty stainless steel ice bucket, and two extra glasses anchored a white tea towel on the small table between Joe's rocking chair and a porch glider that reminded me of the one in our breezeway at the stone house.

"It's David, one of the taller ones. His mama made the overalls you wear. 'Member him scatting outta the barn faster than a spark shoots outta a Roman candle when you asked him if he'd seen any snakes inside?"

Age had whittled Joe's muscular physique. Barefoot and un-shaven, he wore a loose fitting pair of faded Big Smith overalls and a baggy white T-shirt. His weathered hands took hold of the chair's arms as if he'd intended to push himself up and lost the energy between thought and action.

Instead, he offered his steady hand. "Howdy. I don't rightly re-call sayin' what Martha says, but I did find black snakes in the barn every now and then. Found a bull snake once. Big sonbitch."

"You watch your language, Joe Zubeck," Martha said, easing onto the glider.

"Ever see a blue racer?" I said.

"Yep. Don't know how they got the handle. Ain't no faster than any other."

"Sit a spell," Martha said, patting the cushioned seat beside her. She smiled, pushed her feet off the floor, and sent us into gentle flight.

"Very cozy, I said.

Joe guzzled iced lemonade from a tall glass and wiggled his toes.

"Jim comes 'round few days a week. Painted the house."

"Jim's our handyman," Martha said. "These days we're down to just a few acres, this side of the tracks. We sold off the land on the other side a few years back—"

"Nobody wants to farm," Joe said.

"Joe's right. We was hoping they would, but just last year they plowed under the downside acres and put in roads for new hous-es." She sipped lemonade. "Jim knew. Said he didn't think they looked like any farmers he'd ever seen. But they was the only ones who paid the asking price." She let out a tired breath.

317

"Ain't nobody wantin' to farm these days." Joe waved a dismissive hand. "Cain't blame 'em. Big corporations run 'em into the ground. Gonna come the day though, you mark my word." He squinted at me and his tongue chased a wandering drop of lemonade from the corner of his mouth. "You know Leon in Vietnam?"

"No."

"He knew Leon when they were children, Joe." She looked at me, her eyes dancing. I wondered how often they had company. "Why I betcha there's a picture in the album."

She halted the glider's rhythmic sway, pushed herself up, and scooted into the hallway.

"We were friends in grade school," I said to Joe. "I was in your barn once, but I don't remember you scaring me by talking about snakes. I do remember you hoisting bales of hay like they were nothing more than oversized pillows. Your wife may have me confused with someone else."

"I see. Martha's mixer does go haywire from time to time. Iced tea turns into lemonade, or vicey versa. Remembers things wrong." He chuckled, put his glass on a coaster on an end table, and rested his head against the back of the rocking chair, closed his eyes.

Then it hit me. Leon served in Vietnam. The armed forces would not have accepted a one-eye man. Had his life traveled beyond Vietnam?

Martha returned lugging an encyclopedic-sized photo album. It must have weighed ten pounds. Before I could rise to assist she plopped onto the glider, laid the tome on her lap, and patted her chest to catch her breath.

"We didn't take many pictures back in the 50's." She opened the album. "These are all black and white, like the world back then. Here's his eighth grade class at Mark Twain." She pointed to Leon, taller and better looking than I remembered, his eyes and brows dark. I imagined girls intrigued by his rock solid chin and angular cheeks. I looked for evidence of a scar. I thought there were faint lines alongside his right eye and on his right cheek.

"I'd moved by then."

I momentarily felt disconcerted as she flipped past a few more years. The way people looked in the photos, their clothes, the shape and size of their parent's cars, the .45's ushering in rock 'n roll had all seemed so *modern*.

"Here's Leon and his 4-H club his senior year in high school. They came out to our place a few times. We hired some of 'em for summer work. That's when Jim hooked up with us." She turned a page. "This is Leon when he played on the basketball team. He was very good. We went to all the home games."

I studied the photo, looking for another familiar face, found none.

"They whooped Joplin his senior year," wide-eyed Joe said.

I imagined skyrockets blazing across the sky after Leon's team defeated Joplin's perennial powerhouse, a train of cars snaking through town, horns blaring, headlights flashing.

"Leon was right smart, too," Joe said.

"He always had his nose in a book. Honor roll all four years. Oh, here's one of him and—shoot, what was her name—his date for the prom. I should've written it down. I can feel it percolating. You just wait, it'll come to me in a bit." She rested her hands on the plastic sheeted page. "We were hoping Leon would settle down and take over the farm, but the good Lord had other plans."

"Jim comes a few times a week."

"Now hush, Joe Zubeck, he knows that already." She looked at me. "How long did you say you're here for?"

Sweaty and ready to scat, I dreaded more pages turning, the hint of past tense in her voice, an album for a life not fully lived.

The muted clamor of hammers and buzz saws hitched a ride on a slim breeze and drifted in through screened windows. I wondered why Martha and Joe sat here listening and watching.

"Just for today," I said. "I had business in Springfield. Since I was so close, I thought I'd pay a visit. I carry a lot of good memories from my time here." I glanced at Joe, his eyes droopy.

"How's your mother?"

"She passed away a few years ago."

"I'm sorry." She paused, her expression pensive, as though viewing her own dwindling years. She retrieved the glass from the table, sipped lemonade, and put the glass back on the towel. "My, it seems like only yesterday you and Leon were kids. I 'magine you been a lotta places."

"Ohio, then California. I live in Oregon now. I'm a postal supervisor."

"That's good, steady work. Delbert brings our mail. Over twenty-five years now, rain, snow or shine. Came on horseback the days they had the road shut down for paving. We gave him a dozen eggs and a bushel basket of corn---"

Joe's musical snores interrupted. She tenderly shook his arm.

"Did I fall out again?" He yawned and rubbed his eyes with the palms of his hands.

Martha watched him until he yawned again and opened his eyes wide, and then she turned to me and said with certainty, "I do recall you playing out back. They say that happens when you get old, things you've long forgotten come rolling back. I do so like the old, slower times when days didn't whiz right by." Her hand patted her chest. "Nowadays it seems like you hardly have time to enjoy the sweet warmth of spring before baking hot summer muscles in."

"John Deere's in the barn. Did I ever give you a ride on it? Jim got it runnin'. Jim's our handyman."

"We already told him that, dear, and Jim fixed the one you bought in . . . I believe it was '51." She looked at me and shook her head. "The old, rusty heap from your days is out behind the barn collecting the weather and anything else that happens by."

Snakes, I reckoned.

Martha refilled Joe's glass. I shook off her offer of a glass, though my throat felt dry. I wanted to soldier on but why. Why linger? Why tear the fabric of their memory? They had deftly avoided further mention of Leon. I'd come to see a ghost.

"So, way I heard it your mother married some man from Ohio," she said.

"Uh-huh."

"Musta been nice for you to have a father again."

"We were never very close."

"I'm sorry to hear that. A boy needs a father. Where was it he was from?"

"Parma, near Cleveland."

"Larry told Leon 'bout him. I didn't know your mom. People said she worked hard and was a good Catholic. We're Lutherans, a' course, like alla Joe's family."

But the story needed telling. "I really need to get something off my chest. It's something that happened back then that's been bothering me off and on for a long time. It keeps coming back like a recurring bad dream and the program I'm in . . . or maybe I was in—or may still be in—encourages you to get it off your chest."

Martha looked me with interest. Joe looked like he was dozing off again.

"Jim had a similar problem 'bout sixteen years ago," Martha said and winked kindly. "Go ahead. I'm all ears."

I sucked in a bracing breath.

"Did Leon have trouble with his eyes?"

"No," she said with a slight catch in her voice. I imagined she thought the question odd. Her eyes narrowed thoughtfully and she bit her lower lip. "Why I bet you're thinking 'bout the accident out back."

"I know he got hit by a snowball with a rock in it and I heard he had to see doctors in Springfield and even St. Louis. When I left he was still wearing a patch over his eye."

"Why, Doc Griffin, God rest his kind soul, took care of him right here in Carthage. He did a right nice job sewing up the gash." She paused and for a few moments her face worked a puzzle. Then a cheery smile erupted and she sent the swing into an easy motion. "That gosh darn patch! I heard 'bout it from . . . I can't think of his name, one of his friends. He only had to wear it a short while. After Doc Griffin took out the stitches, there was no need. When I found out he was still wearing it to school and round town I asked him why and he said he did it 'cause it made him look like a pirate. We thought it a bunch of tomfoolery."

I rubbed my forehead. My topsy-turvy past was giving me a headache. The Tiger had been a vast, red carpeted resplendent theatre when I was a kid. I often wondered how my adult eyes would view it. It burned the year I left. Jesse never robbed the bank. The stone house's warmth resided in remote memories. Leon hadn't painted the chestnut. He was playing pirate.

Martha's fingers traced the edges of the album cover. What held me back? Why not make my amends and depart? What if my confession inflicted pain on others, memories of a lost child? The fateful day was clear in my mind's eye, Leon taunting us from the high limbs of a dying chestnut as Larry and I molded weapons. Wait a minute. We were kneeling side by side, Larry and I. He didn't ladle snow. His hands sank as deeply as mine. Windblown snow cascaded down when we threw and I ducked. What if? I bit my lower lip. Who had aimed, thrown, and struck the bull's-eye? The question without answer, lost in the memory of a memory of a memory. Once again, the useless confessional speech I'd rehearsed a zillion times played in my mind. Luckily, I'd even prepared one for his parents.

I said, "Whew that makes me feel better. That patch had me worried. Of course I should've known it healed all right when Joe asked about Vietnam." I rubbed my clammy palms on my pants, as if to smooth my resolve, swallowed the lump in my dry throat, and pulled in another bracing breath. "I need to tell you something. I was hoping to tell Leon, but—"

"It's too bad you weren't here for Mother's Day," Martha said. "Leon and his wife were visiting and you could have told him then."

"Leon and his wife?"

"Been hitched over twenty years," Joe said. "We got two grand-kids off at college. They's right smart too."

"Leon and Sandra are in Arizona, around Tucson, studying insects."

"Arizona? Insects?"

"Doin' hot bug research," Joe said.

"What?"

"Why course you don't know," Martha said. She reached for the glass and sipped. Put the glass back on the table. "Leon went to the University of Missoura. He was almost done when he got his draft notice. After the war he finished up and then went to Iowa State. That's where he met Sandra, a right nice girl from Des Moines. She likes bugs, just like Leon. Here, look see."

She flipped a few pages. The photos now all in color. Leon and his parents on the University of Missouri campus. In worn jeans and a T-shirt, he sported a goatee and mustache, a friendly grin. Licorice-black hair draped his shoulders. He looked like a typical Berkeley hipster. A deeper page revealed him clean-shaven in reg-ular Army kaki, followed by a few grainy photos of him in Vietnam.

She turned to an eight-by-ten picture: Leon in military dress standing in front of the house.

"I took this right before he was discharged," Martha said.

When I was young, I memorized all of the army insignias. I rec-ognized the First Lieutenant bars on his shoulders and gave a cur-sory look to the colorful rows of service ribbons on his chest. I had no idea what they signified. Two medals held my eyes: a Bronze Star and a Purple Heart.

"He was wounded?"

"Some shrapnel tore up his leg. He's all right now, 'cept his eyes."

"Oh?"

"They were always so playful. Now there are times when they seem to carry the weight of the world." She sighed and turned a page. "Here's Leon and Sandra. Aren't they a lovely couple?"

Sandra's large, luminous eyes stared at me; hair the color of fresh chestnuts cascaded over her shoulders, an enchanting, irresistible smile. Pages of wedding shots: walking down the aisle, at the altar, rings, the kiss, their linked hands as they cut the cake, bride and groom dancing, posing with parents and friends, and running through a rice shower to a Lincoln Continental with Just Married soaped on the rear window.

"What's he call himself?" Joe asked. "I cain't never say it."

"Leon's an en-to-mo-lo-gist," she said, pleased to have correctly pronounced the difficult word. "So's Sandra."

"I call him Bug Man," Joe said.

"I threw the snowball."

"You and others there that day," Martha said her voice strangely devoid of malice. "Oh, even though the hospital's only a mile or so up the road, I said prayers that weren't even invented on the drive. The road was so snow-slicked, I was afraid we'd slide into a ditch. The good Lord answered. We rushed in, Joe carrying Leon. The nurse jumped out of her chair like she'd just sat on a tack. After they told us Leon was gonna be all right, Joe and me fretted while they stitched him up. We figured a careless kid accidentally picked up a rock with the snow. The next day Leon said what cut him came from the house side, when he jerked his head dodging. He said it felt like a knife cut him." Had devious Larry slipped a blade into his snowball? "So Joe got to thinking it must've been a pointed broken branch. Like a lance, you see. To this very day I thank the good Lord my son didn't twist another inch or so and lose an eye."

Joe yawned as he stared out the window. Following his trail, my eyes glided over their simple garden, slender cornfield, and the railroad tracks. In the cul-de-sac, where endless corn once roamed, skinless wooden skeletal frames bearing hopeful dreams were rising.

"That was a long time ago," Joe murmured. "Kids throwin' rocks."

"Sure you wouldn't like some sweet iced tea?" Martha said.

And so I stayed, sipping lemonade as cloud shadows played with the sun. Joe nodded off a few times. Martha said the worker's hard day would yield a healthy appetite and sound sleep. I asked about old friends. Charley Seven was an attorney for The National Congress of American Indians. Larry worked at Leggett and Pratt. Connie up and moved to California after high school and never looked back. They didn't know Wally.

Twice Martha said the name of Leon's prom date was on the tip of her tongue, only to have it slide into the past.

Friendly handshakes followed a tasty pork chop, mashed potatoes and sliced tomato dinner. Martha and I hugged. She said she'd tell Leon when he called on Sunday.

As I drove back to the motel, I crossed the short bridge spanning the creek and, feeling whimsical, pulled onto the shoulder and got out. The light was thinning as I stared down at a slender run of water, usual for this time of the year. I spotted a worn trail. Kids still played here. I wondered what I would say to them if we met, what games engaged their imaginations. I eased down the bank, stepped over the creek, and slipped a few times climbing up. I paused, brushed dirt from my pants, and listened for voices and heard none. I edged into unfamiliar territory, trees I'd known when young now tall and stout, surrounded by an invading army of thistles. I paused by the drystone wall, hidden beneath decades of decaying vegetation. Future archaeologists would uncover it and decipher their own conclusions.

I eyed the trodden path that curved toward deep, unknown woods and wondered what would have happened if Mom had not married Henry. I thought about the junctions of my life, of anyone's life. I listened a while longer and then hiked back to the car.

At the motel I called Sally. The machine answered. Probably out with friends. I told Sally I loved her. I lay on the bed, pillows cradling my neck and back, flicked on the TV, pressed the mute button, and searched for something mindless, settled on the Cardinal game beaming in from Philadelphia. I tore the tab from a can of Sierra Mist I'd bought at the vending machine a few doors down and bit into a Snickers bar. The mosquitoes were either sleeping or buzzing other prey for I returned unbitten.

I quickly lost interest in the game. I didn't care who won. I clicked off the TV, brushed my teeth, turned the air down a notch, and switched off the light. My head sank into deep pillow. One day without drink.

The following morning tour buses packed with parents and rambunctious youngsters departed early. The atmosphere inside the Outback was calm. I ordered fuel for the road: link sausages, scrambled eggs, two pieces of generously buttered and jellied wheat toast, a small stack of silver-dollar-sized buttermilk pancakes, a tall glass of orange juice and two cups of coffee. I didn't see Amber. The air was pleasantly cool as I strolled to the motel. I gathered my belongings and checked out, eased into the rental, turned on the engine, and slowly drove away. I sped up as I entered the freeway onramp, the town receding in the rearview. As I melded into speeding traffic, I beat down my mind's invitation for an enjoyable after-meal smoke. Surely I could wait until I met Kansas City.